MUDORA'S

THE HYRULE PARODY

BOOK ONE:

SAGES OF WISDOM

WRITTEN BY JASON BRAIN

ILLUSTRATED BY ENRIQUE FERNÁNDEZ

For my childhood friend Daniel,
long since lost to the Dark World.

Your imagination lives on here,
our play reclaimed at last.

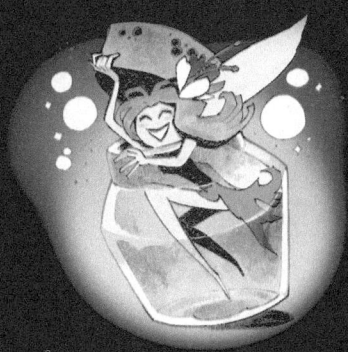

Hello pilgrim of the Gloomaevum. If you are no longer at home in the realm of fake appearances then you have arrived in the Dark World of true forms. Just as you were drawn into this book, I gather that you understand the gravity of which ground you now stand on––namely the latter!

You can read this book in any order, but just know that it will write you in turn! That is, whichever chapter you stop at indefinitely will characterize you henceforth. So by the goddess, keep going at your own pace, and don't despair. I'll meet you at the end. For now, take this Piece of Heart.

TABLE OF CONTENTS

———

Chapter One:
MYOPIA

———

The First Sage Knows

The bright Death Mountain might have you think
Aloof with dew in its March glory
That the Pestilence was just a blink

But the Age of Children binds story
An era born to endless crisis
This spring of course just prelusory

Ahead of her and unable to resist, Link looked back – slowly at first but then repeatedly glancing over his right shoulder in impulsive awe as if the white tower had whispered his name, captivating the young man with its silent gravity. Tiptoeing painstakingly a step behind on the wooden rungs and startled by his unannounced halt, Zelda put one hand on Link's shoulder while maintaining her grip on the bridge's rope railing. Is something wrong? she asked him.

What a sight to see – just looking at it makes me dizzy! said Link gazing at the tower, securing his green nightcap from a northerly gust as they swayed on the slack crossing.

Looking down isn't any less head-spinning. she stared at the valley freefall beneath.

Maybe we can check it out on the way back.

Been in there once, as a girl. said the teenage princess without further elaboration as she and her adolescent knight passed westward under the watching presence of this imposing spire of six stylobate floors, built long before the kingdom was founded as they knew it by their modern history. How the brightness belies our Gloomaevum[1] era! Hard to believe that we live in such dark times from up here. she said, shielding her eyes from the airy glare.

Focus on what's in front of you... advised Link despite repeatedly taking disorienting glances at the building behind them. Radiant in the early spring sunshine, filaments of icy clouds gently streamed around the megalithic columns and multistoried cornices of the Tower of Nayru that is best described as a stepped pyramid stretched upward vertically, such that each step is an entire floor demanding to be explored by anyone who made the effort to hike there, however few do – as they saw no signs of other adventurers. Crowning the summit of Death Mountain, the lofty temple offered the highest vantage in all of Hyrule and no horizon was withheld from its view. Link turned about to fully

---

1   A long time of kingdom decline with no end in sight. Never officially declared by any interrealm authority, a colloquial description for the moral morass that characterizes post-cataclysmic Hyrule. Often debated as to when it started, but nobody denies the term's relevance as of the pestilences when everything became gloomy for unknown reasons. This murky eon in which no one can really be certain of their heart or mind. An equivocal era of inescapable delusion that will not end or resolve on its own terms; everlasting gloom.

face the tower, causing Zelda to drop her hold of him and instead grab the railing with both hands, wiggling the rope more despite attempting to steady herself.

This—feels very flimsy and unsafe! Like it might snap at any moment... chattered Zelda as she exacerbated increasingly uncontrollable oscillations of the bridge's frayed construction.

Truly sublime sensation, isn't it? taking a deep breath, Link exhaled longingly at the tower while Zelda slowly scuttled. *I want to go in there.* he said, getting distracted from their goal ostensibly close by; a few paces from the end of the bridge. So do you think the goddess Nayru actually inhabited the tower at one time? Or was it just built in her honor, or maybe–

Come on. Zelda interrupted her highwire companion with a stern glower in tow.

Link palmed his cheek in contemplation, speculating further, –it was inhabited by the wise old men, or a single sage who was chosen by Nayru? In which case...

Can we please continue this conversation from the other side? The structure's elevation will be just as impressive from over there. asserted the princess woozily.

Link took two steps toward the tower, backtracking past Zelda, Definitely pre-cataclysm architecture, wouldn't you say? Who even built this thing! Do you think they quarried the stones near Lake Hylia or– *I haven't seen any evidence of extraction or material mining up here.*

Ask me later! she insisted, making better progress with her eyes closed.

How would they carry the stones up the mountain! Link's rambling curiosity was interrupted by movement in the tower. He stopped to see if it was just one of the fast-floating clouds that cast animated shadows on the structure's thoroughfare facades. We couldn't build that thing today if we tried – would take thousands of Gorons to haul all those blocks into place, and even then! I'm not convinced they would be enough...

Can stones fly? she said, also unsure how the blocks were brought to this incredibly impractical site of the tower while forfeiting her mountaineering partner to his high-altitude folly. Zelda resolutely inched her way toward the island peak. Just accept it: the ancients had a grasp of masonry that is lost to us now. Come on Link.

View from the Tower

Zelda was almost to the pinnacle when her green knight noticed that she had carried on by herself. Making up for lost time and forgetting he was on a precarious dilapidated causeway, Link bounded carelessly over the shaky slats. That would be great – if megaliths could levitate! Woa–hoah–HOAH! Really sways! he caught his own balance while leaping past Zelda as the bridge shuttered against his exuberant strides and the constant crosswind.

Careful! barked the princess as she moored herself again on the railing. Zelda squared her footing, took a second to compose herself, and then approached Link who was already standing on the solitary island peak, staring back again – surveying the Tower of Nayru.

You're right, the perspective over here is pretty much the same.

And yes, to answer part of your question, I imagine that the chasm we just passed over was once at the same elevation of the tower's foundation in ancient times, but was eroded during the Great Cataclysm[2] ages ago. said Zelda, more confident to expound back on solid ground: a peak that was oblong east to west, but flat on top and evenly declivitous on all sides with gently beveled cliff edges. Unlike the nearby mountain ridges, the clouds appeared to form a constant surf around the crest, giving the impression that it was an island floating in the sky. Setting foot thereupon but no sooner, a small monument was noticeable – placed resolutely in the center as if claiming its domain of this site appropriately called the Precipitous Pinnacle.[3]

Hard to imagine all this as the same elevation at one time… so maybe they never carried stones uphill at all! Terrifying how the world was reshaped by such force. he said.

---

2   A comprehensive and apocalyptic event immediately following the Imprisoning War when the demiurge Hylia exacted her judgment and reshaped the realm in a single day displacing whole mountains and seas. Approximately ten-thousand years ago by modern Hyrule's reckoning. Also referred to as The Upheaval.

3   A peak immediately west of the Tower of Nayru and can only be reached by rope bridge or from the air. Where the goddess Din encased her sister's medallion in a legendary monument called the ether stone.

Amazing that anyone survived such an upheaval of the world, if the reality matches the myth we've all been told... Zelda walked over to the stout monolith that resembled somewhat of a tombstone, and rubbed her hand over its metavolcanic face, feeling the finely etched writing. This is the ether stone, left here by Nayru's divine sister Din. she reassured her uninterested companion while blowing on her hands to warm them, concealing a smile of minor triumph.

Can you read that? squinted Link, leaning into the indecipherable Ancient Hylian.[4]

Barely, but see this word here– Zelda ran her index finger along the second line of incised symbols, –says *Master Sword* I believe. But I'm not sure what the first line says...

Hold up the Master Sword. mocked a baritone voice – a large swarthy hunk approached from the bridge, confidently walking two rungs per stride.

Ganondorf! exclaimed Link, drawing said sword from his blue scabbard as they had recently acquired it from the cathedral of Castle Town before venturing up Death Mountain.

Zelda remained blithely focused on the cryptic glyphs, You're right! It says: hold up– the–eEAAAEEEE!!! she reeled from her reading as braided bolts of lightning *TSSSEEOOO!* struck the monolith, crumbling the stone and sending the princess flying backward several feet. The greenish-grey monument mostly crumbled and partially melted in place, but an erratic projectile the size of a dinner plate came whirling toward Zelda, which she caught just inches from her face with the symbols still legible: *–and you will get the magic of ether.* she finished Ganondorf's sentence, translating the glyphs while laying on her back holding the fragment, smoldering and wide-eyed. Link's pointy nightcap swayed vigorously from the stone's explosion immediately behind him, puffed up like a windsock and almost flew off. But he remained poised with

---

4   The language used by Ancient Hyrule before the Great Cataclysm. A symbolic language consisting of glyphs that is read from right to left and left to right to cohere its syntax of nouns, verbs, and adjectives. Because the lost language is so difficult to write and properly interpret, only the Sheikah keep it alive.

the Master Sword[5] drawn high, fixated on his foe and unsure if this was *really* him or not.

I've been enjoying the view from the tower, waiting for you to awaken the ether stone, seeing as doing so requires the supposed bane of my existence. Ganondorf curtseyed a slight bow toward the Master Sword. Yes, I've been released – I take our chance meeting as fated.

The heavenly power of Nayru is not suited for the King of Thieves! warned Link.

Zelda had gotten up and was brushing herself off, staring at Ganondorf while walking over to Link, darting reprimanding glances at her knight, then at the raider, and back to Link, unsure of who she should scold first as they were both to blame for her near miss.

Not suited? Looks like our princess has nothing to say of that. retorted Ganondorf who now stood at the end of the bridge. Holding both railings, with arms outstretched and supinated, the fierce Gerudo man began pulling with inconceivable strength, snapping the rope fibers and entirely tearing the bridge from its anchoring on the sky island peak. GRUOOOH! OH! OH! OH! The terrifying roar echoed throughout the air, and as the weight of the bridge became supported by his own gait, he howled even louder, RAAAH! HAH! HAH! his muscles bulging in paroxysms of inexplicable fury. A gaudy trifle encrusted in the middle of his tightly fitted compression tunic popped off, hitting Link squarely on the forehead, ricocheting askew and landing amongst the lightning struck rubble. The shorter Hyrulean Knight[6] did not blink or budge, standing his ground in unperturbed anticipation, ignoring the amber jewel and pectoral performance that launched it.

Link! He's huge! she said, still frazzled from her electrified tumble with the exploding ether stone, Zelda was now agape at the sight of Ganondorf's display of power.

To conclude his burly debut, he nonchalantly whipped a rippling wave down the bridge ropes, then tossed the suspension railings behind

5   A legendary longsword also referred to as Evil's Bane, Hylia's Key, Key of Realms, Hylia's Promise.

6   Founded ten millennia ago at the time of the schism, the order of the Hyrulean Knights swore to protect the royal family – this honor is now disbanded under the rule of Agahnim. Only three true knights remain.

him. The quiet delay of the bridge's fall before audibly hitting the opposite mountain side *Kra-poo!...* was interrupted by his bellowing laugh. GAH HAH HAH! **Bridge drop.** jeered the Gerudo intruder, indulging a subtle shrug.

Just because you got the stuff to drop a bridge doesn't mean there's any substance in your threats Ganondorf. stammered Zelda blinking wildly from dust and his feat. We will not be intimidated by your groundless flexing! she punctuated with a unilateral fist-and-stomp motion.

Speaking of dropping – the magic of ether, it's on the ground there – would you be so kind as to hand it to me princess? said the red-haired opportunistic interloper.

Come and get it big guy… said Link, unaware of what was revealed behind him. Obscured by the rubble smoke, an unscathed plinth stood in what was the core of the monolith, immaculately cleaved from the stone in an instant by the lightning, deftly sent by the goddess! Gently resting upright on the slotted stand sat a golden treasure, no bigger than a large coin.

Not exactly the Triforce, is it? But the goddess medallions[7] are the next best thing.

You will never take the Golden Power nor the goddess medallions either! said Zelda.

The desert rogue continued, *When going for the gold, Ganondorf takes all…*

The Greenclad Swordsman

Dark swirling clouds had been accreting above the Precipitous Pinnacle, which Zelda presumed was an effect of the ether stone's activation, and Link figured was the mischief of Ganondorf. Regardless, the bridge was out and they were all stuck on the little sky island.

YIAHHH! Link arced his arm to lunge at Ganondorf, who gleefully took action.

The Gerudo stepped aside, Evil's Bane grazing his smirking profile – he backfisted Link in the direction that he was lunging, causing him to

---

7   Endowed before the kingdom was founded, the three goddess medallions resemble large golden coins, and each contains the magic power of one of Hylia's daughters: Nayru, Din, and Farore. Elemental sigils.

stumble near the edge of the peak, skidding to an off-balance halt. By the time Link had recovered, Ganondorf was halfway to Zelda.

Now holding the medallion, Zelda raised the gold sigil to the sky, unsure of proper protocol but nonetheless called upon Nayru to assist them in this critical moment.

That's not how it works. grumbled Ganondorf, grabbing her outstretched arm.

AIEAAH! shrieked Zelda, collapsing in fear. Her knees bobbed above the ground as Ganondorf held her in place while prying the medallion from her hand.

Coming about, Link jumped at Ganondorf, the Master Sword drawn fully back to strike.

What better shield than a princess? grunted Ganondorf swinging Zelda toward his assailant, requiring the limber lightweight to last-ditch avert his swing and stumble aside.

So much for your legendary sword. What should we call you? snarking at Zelda, who he held firmly as hostage, Link's Bane? *Hero's Blunder?*

Zelda's left arm was slack, which she used to discreetly gesture at Link, a full-finger *hither* motion, accompanied by a wink of her right eye.

Ganondorf was sufficiently distracted, stealing a long sniff of Zelda's blonde locks.

Link lunged, but halfheartedly and not so fast that he couldn't flip the hilt around, passing it to her, as the greenclad swordsman acrobatically rolled past Ganondorf.

YEE! driving the blade down, *Shump*. Zelda missed her captor's quick foot as he would not be fooled twice by their tandem cunning. Poised to receive an advance, Ganondorf stood a full Gerudo step back (comparable to two Hylian paces) grinning in enjoyment of the game they were now fully engaged in while the clouds above them grew darker and more turbulent. YEGH! Why is this so stuck! she demanded to know, after lodging the blade into the ground from failing to impale Ganondorf's boot. Zelda whimpered in consternation, yanking on the hilt to no avail.

From the sky above, a light parted the ominous vortex of clouds. Ganondorf's smile snapped flat as he looked up. What delayed deity is this? *Did your summoning succeed...*

Link attempted to help Zelda, but quickly shielded his eyes from the celestial injunction. Still intent on dislodging the Master Sword, Zelda was last to notice the dramatic developments above them. By the goddess! exclaimed the princess letting go of the sword and stepping back beside her knight. The three quarrelers stood at ease, equidistant from the firmly planted blade, awaiting the dazzling phenomena that approached them. Nayru has answered my call, she said with arms outstretched, The divine medallion is inert to your treacherous will Ganondorf!

Better late than never. the disarmed lad hoped she was right.

A Keepsake from the Rubble

A sore loser, Ganondorf scowled at the sacred medal in his palm, rage-quitting it to the ground where it rolled against the stuck sword, clinking on the blade and laying flat thereabouts. The darkness above produced a blindingly luminous body, an ambiguous golden aura whose source was vaguely human in proportion and comportment as it approached in measured stride. Flowing faster than it walked, and effortlessly descending an airescalier,[8] the brilliant filament of this cosmic beacon became distinct entities – two astride a leader who was taller than one but shorter than the other. Neither the princess, knight, nor thief expected *all three* goddesses!

It is I, Princess Zelda who called you to aid us! she waved. Disregard the Gerudo here, we have called upon you in hopes of ending the pestilences that plague our troubled times...

I thought the medallions issued elemental magic... *Not this.* said Link, quite confused as the first of the three glowing figures glided down several strides from the Master Sword, without acknowledging anyone and walked straight to it, grasping the hilt with an air of entitlement. Exerting no more effort than required to lift the weight of the sword as

---

8   Taking the stairs through the air. An ethereal staircase. How gods, wizards, and wizrobes walk.

if it was yielded freely, dislodged the blade and held it at ease. There was a breath's moment of pause, then the leading entity bent down to the gold sigil. If this was the goddess Nayru, she was certainly not blue as is fabled, nor were her sisters green and red, rather all three were the color of sunlight, and similarly painful to behold. The reticent entrant slowly righted its posture with the sword in its right hand, the medallion in its left. Link, Ganondorf, and Zelda were all entranced.

We are the Prime Sages– said the leading figure; the voice sounded deep and old.

Zelda held her palm to block the scintillating rays and was peeking between her fingers, trying to catch glimpses of the speaking figure and his two companions, but their spectacular silhouette edges sparkled like a solar eclipse and were wholly inscrutable. Who sent you?

–of the first to be chosen by Nayru, Din, Farore. continued the leading figure.

Miffed that they did not arrive at her behest, Zelda took a step forward in resolute but cautious defiance, If you are mortal sages chosen by the goddesses then reveal yourselves!

Doomed to eternal antagonism, you are unworthy of Hylia… the being raised the sword and pointed to Link, then slowly sweeping to Zelda, Not her hilt… he said continuing to address Ganondorf last, Nor touched by her edge. he concluded, suggesting that even for the Gerudo to be cut with the Master Sword would be a desecration of its sanctified steel. Unbeknownst to all present atop the pinnacle, the entity had *sealed* his own ruination by declaring such prohibitions, the final forbiddance he would himself violate at the end of the Master Sword's long saga. None would remember this proclamation as a prophecy in hindsight, especially the one who convicted himself, but the fire of the goddess forged in the blade would not forget until their destiny was fulfilled at the end of their quests and final reunion in the Temple of Time[9] when

---

9   A cathedral designed in the architectural style of Ancient Hyrule, originally built during the old kingdom in thanksgiving to Hylia, the temple was later destroyed by the cataclysm and its location has been lost for a millennium – unknown except to two people who remember its whereabouts: a wizard, and a great faerie.

it is to be rebuilt. Supremely knowledgeable, he was shortsighted to his foretold quietus standing in front of him.

Taking this pronouncement as a challenge and never shy of defying sagacious edicts, Ganondorf leapt at them with tons of gusto to tackle what sounded like an easily bested abbot. In relaxed haste, the two companion entities put a hand on the leading figure's shoulders. The one who spoke languidly sliced the air, as if he was horribly early to parry against the hulking Gerudo rushing at him, an onlooker would presume that the wielder knew nothing of combat. But a black ribbon trailed from the tip of the blade, a completely matte darkness which flung open to such a breadth that Ganondorf inadvertently jumped into the depthless void, only to disappear entirely. A step behind, Link reached out to Zelda, as she also grappled his arm for reassurance while the triumvirate of entities levitated. The two ancillary beings still had a hand on the shoulder of their leader, but all three now visibly held a medallion as well. The one who wielded the Master Sword made two more strokes at thin air, altogether opening three rivened triangles interconnected at their vertices, multiplying what had already consumed Ganondorf.

That's one way to dispose of the King of Thieves. he said to the princess. Let's go.

How? There's no way off this peak! she shook.

For the defilement of Nayru's legacy, and by the Golden Power[10] entrusted to me you three will become the Triforce Exiles, a judgment I will now expound and deliver. Unlike here, what you will soon discover in the next world is that physical reality is bound with moral law… For each *topography*[11] graded by the goddesses, every phenomenal quality of spirit exhibits a noumenal *topology*[12] counterpart in the Sacred Realm, ordered by descent. The qualities of wisdom, power, and courage and their warped disgraces structure <u>the two mirrored planes.</u>

---

10   The essence of the Triforce that will grant any wish and remake the world in the image of whoever takes it according to the quality of their heart and mind; invoked as a synonym for the divine relic too.

11   A physical and phenomenal elevation in the Light World of Hyrule. Counterpart of the nine topologies.

12   A metaphysical and noumenal elevation in the Dark World of Lorule. Counterpart of the topographies.

Too many 'topo' words. said Link.

Understood. Zelda listened intently.

Nine topos, nine sages… And from the highest elevation of Hyrule, what proffers *sight* in this Light World, will be your *myopia* in the next! You are henceforth banished to the Dark World! condemned the entity. Without giving any warning Link dashed at the three figures before they floated too high to grab, but the leader spun the rifts into Link's route of attack, and the knight was pulled into the second triangular umbra. Left alone with only seconds to spare before her sentence was executed as well, the princess remembered something, and serenely walked to the rubble where she briefly scanned the debris kneeling down. With her back to the entities, Zelda examined what she had found as the accursed threshold quickly swallowed her too.

As sunless shadow is the basis
For an unlikely three exiled then
No light seasons in dark ecstasis

Chapter Two:
RATIONALIZATION

———

The Fourth Sage Knows That

The desert mirrors the soggy fen
Both contemporaneous the same
Mystery and Evil aliken

An old princess has crossed without shame
Taking the curse with her to Hyrule
While here but worlds apart they came

Behind doors that only the hinox's big golden key could open, the exiles confronted what the cyclops siblings Baog and Vuam had argued about incessantly. Seething red and equipped with a ceramic faceplate, the King of the Dark Palace was just as the elder Aginah had warned, a reptilian demon of gargantuan proportions indeed! Similar to the fire-breathing helmasaur[13] lizards found throughout the temple but so overgrown it could no longer fit through the doorway and was entirely dependent on the hinoxes and eyegores to provide live victims for it to feed on. Needless to say, this Helmasaur King[14] was delighted for three perambulating meals to enter its domain on their own volition, and very hungry since the hinoxes had neglected to put dinner on the table as planned; their recipe scuppered. The exiles were not wholly unprepared however, as the second large chest in the dungeon contained a huge double-headed hammer suitable for a cyclops (no Triforce enclosed as Zelda enthusiastically speculated) that only Ganon could easily swing with one hand. After an initially frantic runaround with the salivating king, the three exiles took their positions in the life-or-death standoff. Link mostly bounded around in front and the back of the large square chamber, making distractions by waving his red cane up in the air, taunting and tantalizing the hungry beast. With the Helmasaur King sufficiently fixated on the succulent bunny, Ganon went to town on their foe's armored face with his newfound maul that they realized must've been kept by the hinoxes for exactly this kind of situation: to subdue the beast if it ever got out of hand (as only the wizard could authorize, since the giant lizard was both boss and beloved pet to the cyclops siblings who served it endearingly). Zelda expectedly stood in the wings interchangeably calling the shots

---

13 Small quadruped pyrophoric dinosaurs bearing a bony green plate over their face. Found only in the Dark World, it is unclear if these monsters were once animals imported from Hyrule and warped into their reptilian form, or endemic to the Sacred Realm and consequently naturalized to the twisted Dark World.

14 The biggest helmasaur ever, overfed and kept in the Dark Palace by Baog and Vuam who claim their boss-qua-pet told them 'No cooking on temple property'. Which is to say they attest the beast can speak, a specious claim even if it wasn't asserted by a cyclops as helmasaurs never form words out in the wild. Hypothetically any ordinarily mute monster gains the faculty of loquacity after they are implanted with a crystal maiden that imparts her human soul. The king did not speak to the exiles, so remains unverified.

and taking shots with her bow; volunteering to shield against their enemy's firebreath or spiked tail assaults when it was convenient to do so. In a brash maneuver of regrettable impatience, Ganon thought he could stuff a bomb in the king's mouth as it inhaled to stoke its larynx furnace. But the otherwise languid and predictable creature reflexively chomped down with surprising speed, taking the boar's left hand clean off. The only upside to it – the helmasaur's jaw was already aglow with fire, effectively cauterizing Ganon's bloody stub. And thankfully he had already hammered away most of its armored face and carapace, allowing Zelda to deliver the final blows to the demon's exposed forehead with her arrows. *The Terror of the Dark Palace* crumbled apart in a series of popping explosions as the trapped energy that powered it was violently released. Harmonic vibrations of the king's death throes rang their empty bottles which were the only lamentable casualties of the battle. Supposedly shatterproof and made with enchanted glass, their three jars given to them by the hermit Aginah resonated into pieces from the reptile's roar. The exiles tended to their wounds and thoroughly inspected the chamber but did not find any revelatory clues; sadly no guarded treasures either. Almost overlooked, Zelda spotted a small black diamond in the shape of an elongated octahedron levitating at eye-level where the palace boss expired.

Was that inside the helmasaur? Link asked, stepping over their broken bottles.

I think so– be careful. she said, in awe of how the glass shards tinkled under it.

Do you think that's the source of its evil[15] power? he pointed to the crystal.

Maybe. Just then, the diamond began to rotate and increase in size, becoming transparent. A young woman stood upright and weightless inside the crystal.

---

15 Lacking a soul. The dungeon demon bosses are by default evil as they all appropriate another's soul. Whereas for men there are two kinds: lateral and vertical. Lateral evil outsources moral responsibility to those around oneself. Vertical evil appeals to false authority to abdicate one's own moral responsibility.

Link, because of you, I've escaped from the clutches of the evil monsters. Thank you! said the maiden now in full stature, initially addressing the bunny whose fur matched her dress. The lady was unwarped and fully Hylian with a stupendous pink gown and fabulous green locks.

That hair... the ermine stepped up closer, I recognize her! she waved the magic mirror but the crystalized girl didn't seem to respond; there was a latency and disassociated vibe.

Wait so, is she the lost old man's granddaughter? asked the bunny, thinking of what Aginah told them they might find in the Dark Palace – regarding their three respective quests.

I saw her in the castle before. Zelda hushed Link, *She seems to know who you are!*

...This world was once the Golden Land[16] where the Triforce was hidden. But because Ganon, the leader of the thieves, wished it, this world was transformed...

The ermine and bunny looked suspiciously at the busted up boar who was inspecting the locked chamber door that had automatically reopened after they defeated the Helmasaur King.

I'm sure he's intending to conquer even our Light World after building his power here.

Link got the impression this girl was out of the loop, stuck in her faceted cell for too long.

The green-haired Hylian lassie explained, His hope is to use us maidens and the power of the sages that has been passed on to us as the key to open a larger gate between the worlds near Hyrule Castle. But the gate is not completely open yet...

---

16   Often mistaken as synonymous with the Sacred Realm, the Golden Land refers to the desert region where the Gerudo first found the Temple of Light. 'Golden' for its aureate geology and discovered relic. More confusing yet, this land was verdant in ancient times, but buried during the Great Cataclysm and forever changed by the upheaval. Some now believe the fabled Golden Land is actually located at the center of the contemporary kingdom suggesting that Hyrule Castle is built on top of the Temple of Light. Marginalized since the Interloper War, the Gerudo call their desert the Golden Land which has led many to believe it was always out there and always a desert. But it's very possible this proud tribe is projecting their current climate onto an ancient past, thereby claiming it as their own as the Golden Land was their endemic homeland. And so lorists and historians speculate that the mysterious Gerudo Valley is in effect a 'New Golden Land' by name only. A place riddled by apocryphal symbolism and ancient appropriation.

Ganon cued in and was standing nonplussed off to the side.

The woman in the crystal continued without ever looking at Ganon, There is still time. Together, *we seven maidens* can break the barrier that protects Ganon's hiding place.

The boar snorted, Hiding place?

Shhh! Zelda and Link were listening. We—I'm with you... said the ermine princess.

I can tell you where the other girls are held. I believe you will destroy Ganon. I will return to my original form at that time. Do you understand?

Not at all. said the bunny, disappointed that defeating all the evil in the Dark Palace yielded none of what Aginah alluded to: *sword, granddaughter, great gold* – all outstanding.

Yes—just say yes! said Zelda, overriding Link's honesty.

May the way of the Hero lead to the Triforce.[17] concluded the pink-gowned girl, as her crystalline medium rotated and shrunk down to the small black diamond Zelda initially spotted. The ermine took a thread from her pocket and tied a knot around the narrow axis of the now opaque octahedron, allowing her to wear the imprisoned soul of the maiden as a necklace.

Gathering their things and reclaiming as many arrows as possible, the boar and bunny agreed to hold onto the ermine princess as she spirited them all away to the entrance with her magical mirror given to her by the lost old man with the hope of finding his granddaughter.

Ki ki! I have a reason to talk to you! the mauve monkey Kiki ambushed the exiles by hanging upside down from the roof as they stepped out of the Dark Palace.

Sorry Kiki, no more rupees[18] here Zelda waved, politely stepping away from Ganon who was still leaning on her from their teleportation huddle and using the lanky ermine as a crutch.

I'm sorry to hear that– ki ki! said the monkey tactlessly imitating how the ermine princess pitied his utmost love for money the evening before.

---

17 Unbeknownst to any maidens and unsuspected by sages too, this blessing foretells the month of May.

18 The currency of Hyrule. Typically exchanged in green (●1), blue (●5), and red (●20) denominations.

Very amusing. said Zelda, vaguely remembering that interaction in the labyrinth.

Ki ki! The old man paid me to tell you. Kiki gracefully tumbled to the ground.

Who, Aginah?

Ki!

Link's ears perked, reminded of his small key.

He said his other brother might know how to return.

Other? the bunny frowned askance, giving the monkey sideways eyes.

Yes, to the south and west. For now, I will lead you out! said Kiki, proceeding into the temple's plaza that brought them back into the labyrinth. The exiles followed their guide again until they reached that traumatic place where the hinoxes had initially set upon them at the northern end of the colonnade. *Tip Kiki.* the monkey cooly demanded.

I think Aginah already paid you. the bunny curled his lip.

Kiki held out his hands, For delivering a message. But showing the way out is *my extra.*

Zelda and Link looked at each other as she reached into her pocket, deciding to bonus the monkey regardless. Here's twenty rupees for your assistance. she handed Kiki a red gem.

Twenty for a tip?! Was only ten for your service earlier… the bunny exclaimed.

Kik. the monkey shrugged.

It's okay, Zelda was feeling generous, We found quite a few rupees in the palace.

Wide-eyed with suspicion that he was being lowballed, the mauve monkey took her tip and strutted past Ganon, slapping the boar's thigh in passing. Bye bye! Kik ki ki!

An Uncanny Homecoming

Ganon tightened his bandage without paying any attention to the monkey who he thought might be negging him. The ermine and bunny wanted to ask how the boar was doing, but decided against broaching that conversation as they had no remedies to offer other than solidarity with his stoicism. Together they left the valley's southern entrance, and then carried on to the west keeping the Crumbling Barrows to their right. Turning south, they came upon a river with only one crossing – an isthmus ridge that was obstructed by an array of nine stone pilings.

Wasn't there a bridge here? asked the bunny in recollection of the parallel Light World.

...

If we are where I think this is in Hyrule, then the Boneyard Bridge would be around here. said the princess, elaborating on the boar's silent refusal to answer her knight's question.

Never understood why they called it that. said Link, staring at the barrows to the north.

FLUMK... the weight of his hammer made it look easy. Standing evenly up to the height of Ganon's sternum, the pilings were just close enough and just tall enough to block their way. Bashing the barricade, *FLUMK.* Ganon flattened the cylindrical obstacles but in the process of doing so caught the attention of a wandering hinox[19] who recognized the boar's tool as their own proprietary pummeler. *FLUMK!* Three did the trick, and they were clear of that stupid stockade crudely erected in the soft mud. Outpacing both the cyclops and a small regiment of lancing minions who resembled pigmen like the one encountered outside the labyrinth's eastern exit, the three exiles made haste without risking any more skirmishes. They caught their breath while slowly skirting west along the southern side of the river. But another patrolling hinox approached them unawares from up the bank. Making their quiet escape the exiles were cut off by a sentry farther down the path who was thankfully distracted by a nearby man-eating ropa flower.

Look, there's a cabin up there. the ermine said softly to her crouching companions, barely concealed by the miscellany of miniscule boulders at the base of a westward ridgeline. The bunny and boar looked to their

---

19   A giant cyclops whose main purpose is to guard the Pyramid of Power. Like many creatures sworn to the wizard's regime, they only have one eye and thus lack perspective of their own and are entirely reliant on a centralized authority to emulate a false depth of the world around them. One of the few monsters in the Dark World who can speak in addition to the zazek dinosaur-men and the rare lynel maned centaurs.

right where not far away sat a purple house with curiously contorted bone-white trim, easily approached with a meandering path up a terraced hill.

Inviting, quaint and cozy… We can take shelter! initiated the bunny knight.

Wait! What if someone's home? said the ermine princess, having second thoughts.

Couldn't be more dangerous than staying out here. Link nervously watched the hinox sniffing the air in the distance, shielding its eye while scanning the drab Dark World landscape.

I could use some rest. the boar spoke up finally, putting his hammer down to adjust the weight of his bomb bag that he had possessively engorged while pillaging the Dark Palace.

YouS tHEre! the cyclops had spotted them.

Uhh– which way. Zelda tapped Ganon on the shoulder as the hinox's voice alerted the previously distracted sentry farther down the road. *PFOOMGHHH!* The boar threw a grenade toward the oncoming moblin and ropa, while the ermine *VRZSHH–VRZSHH* arced a volley, causing both monsters to stall and assess their unruly object of interception.

No time to waste! Link led the escape up the hill toward the house, intermittently looking back to see their pursuers. Running up to the front door, the bunny had his small key ready, aggressively lunging it like a bayonet into the latch rose.

What are you doing? the ermine implored.

My key worked! Link celebrated, turning the knob.

Ganon was skeptical, and pushed the door in.

ACHOO! The three exiles jumped at the sound of a trumpeting sneeze from inside the house, followed by a melodic arpeggiation of aftershock snorts– ¿Bvrm-Frbrz! ¿Bvrm-Frbrz!

CHOO-AHCHOO! the sneeze attack continued followed by rising and falling nasal toots.

IN! the boar used his good (and only remaining) hand to push the ermine and bunny inside. Ganon glanced down the hill where the hinox was temporarily out of sight; perhaps it did not see them enter the house. He took the key out of the lock and slammed the door shut.

A short teal-colored elephant man in an orange vest stepped out from behind a counter to meet them. ACHOO! he snorted through his sonorous trunk, startling the exiles again.

Excuse our barging in, the bunny prefaced, but we're in somewhat of a rush, and my key happened to work on the door so—

There's no lock on my door. said the elephant, sounding stuffed up.

Oh, wait— the bunny turned around to look at the doorknob. Oh I see, that's just a hole.

Yes, the shop needs many repairs. How can I help you *three-eaHCHOO!*

The ermine and boar both spotted each other cracking up, trying not to laugh out loud at the elephant's voice which sounded like someone speaking through a trombone. The bunny mistook his companions' snickering as directed at him and quietly pocketed his key, swallowing his shame. *Thump-Thump-Thump!* shook the door. Ganon braced his back against the inswing.

Open? the quaking (however slightly calmed down) voice of a hinox caused dustmotes to fall from the rafters. Zelda and Link stood along the wall beside Ganon as a giant's eye struggled to see through the minute hole in the handle. You home! the cyclops was suspicious, while the exiles dared not peer out, they heard the approach of more footsteps and the sound of a metal ferrule spear butt prodding the ground around the stoop – doormat pig minions waited for their orders to break in on their commanding brute's behalf as the hinox would not fit.

The elephant man casually approached the door, spooking the exiles who feared he might betray their hiding. No more bombs, ALL OUT! the teal-creature responded.

No more bombs? the hinox's attention clearly shifted.

I already sold them to your siblings from the palace. Come back next week when I'll have more for sale. said the shopkeeper.

Let's go. said the hinox.

Squonk?! Oink-oink! Squonk! squealed the porcine moblin.

What does it even matter anymore. said the dejected cyclops to a pigman sentry.

Squonk-oink. Dull retreating thuds could be felt from inside – the bunny risked a look through the peephole as the lumbering giant and its lancer lackeys sauntered down the path.

Customers of yours? Ganon asked, jutting himself off the door.

If there's one way to get on a hinox's good side, it's with the lowest bomb prices in the realm! ACHOO! Ack! If only I wasn't allergic to the powder! FRBRRRRZZZ! the elephant blew his nose into a barrel, causing the whole room to hum.

Nice little place you got here. said Link poking around, Reminds me of my old quarters.

Oh! Where's home for you folks? The elephant wasn't shy to make smalltalk, putting any outstanding nerves at ease.

The Light World. The bunny shrugged, making a parallel gesture with his hands, as if to pray but with a gap between them.

Ah. AH. *AHH!* he inflated, nostrils flared.

Zelda respectfully stepped behind her shield.

ACHOO! Ah! Ack—excuse me. Ah—yes! I've forgotten so much, but you know, I was once a Hyrulean Knight, before all this happened. Frbrrrzzz…

You were?! Link rudely shouted indoors.

Feels like forever ago—another life. Can anyone trust their perception of passing here? Or is it the warp of forms that misleads our sense of time? the elephant nodded while twitching his irritated trunk. That black sun makes every season seem the same – perennial monotony.

The knights are all but slain, the ermine sighed, I thought Link was the last, but knowing there are two left makes me wonder who else from the order might be hiding in this realm or elsewhere! I take it, you were banished for your allegiance to the crown?

Link glanced around, not seeing any signs or memorabilia suggesting this elephant was ever a knight in service of Hyrule. He was going to ask more for veracity's sake, but then realized that nothing about himself signified knighthood either.

Well I've done pretty well for myself given the circumstances! *When in the Dark World, do as the devious, right?* the elephant polished a round chassis yet to be filled with powder.

Was it the wizard? she pressed.

I *am* a knight of Hyrule—*as well.* interrupted the bunny stepping forward.

A knight... A wizard... Yes! The king's Chief Minister Agahnim proved himself to be the vilest of wizards in the end. *And what was your name—in the service of Hyrule?*

Sir Link.

And I'm Princess Zelda.

And who are you? the elephant pointed to the boar who merely waved his hand.

Wait! Princess Zelda! ACHOO! So you're safe! Ack, I mean, safe as anyone can be in this cursed land. So my nephew must have succeeded in rescuing you from the wizard.

Uncle?

Uncle?—I, uh... ¿Bvrm-Frbrz! The congested elephant looked about with his narrow full-black eyes, confusedly deducing his own relation to the bunny. Who did you say you were sir... Link? Oh! LINK! *Link my boy!* You left me for dead! *Bvvvrm?* Just because I lent you my sword and shield, didn't give you permission to run... ¿Bvrm-Frbrz! ¿Bvrm-Frbrz! the elephant let loose a brassy double-sneeze. *To run away like that!* he made himself clear.

I came back to check, after jailbreaking the princess... and you were gone! said Link to his long lost uncle. Besides, I thought you wanted me out? *You only had one bed,* and always gave it to me – which I was very appreciative for – insisting that your wooden stool was just as comfortable, every night hunched over the table fully armed, reminiscing yourself to sleep with nostalgia for the old days of valor and chivalry!

Of course I was gone! The soldiers took me to Agahnim, who then had a word with me...

Zelda and I escaped through the sewers, and together acquired the three pendants of virtue, allowing us to draw the Master Sword and seek out the goddess medallions, all in hopes of calling upon the heavens to end the pestilences. said Link, defensively and thrilled.

Which took us a couple weeks, I might add. the ermine princess clarified, still ruminating on the elephant's comment about elusive time.

Ah, the pestilences, ACHOO! You know that was Agahnim's invention. Frbrrrzzz!

As many suspected but were too afraid to admit. Zelda nodded.

Uncle, I never understood what you meant by 'Zelda is my...' *My what?*

Why did the wizard spare you? she chimed in.

I was sent home under pain of death, but not in the Light World. Not the home you remember, instead to this realm, and told to notify my captors if the errant knight and insurrectionist princess ever showed up. Ack. Dark World house arrest.

This house... is where your house was—or is, in Hyrule. it finally occurred to Link.

Well, what are you waiting for then? the ermine drummed her fingers on the countertop. Here we are! Right into the wizard's trap. Zelda crossed her arms.

Uncle! I cannot believe what I am hearing! You carried the honorable aegis and swore an oath to never turn you back on the kingdom and relatives of the throne! bristled the bunny.

This is a bad look, I admit. But I thought I was helping! Agahnim told us that if we gathered the descendants of the Seven Wise Men, then we could use their powers to end the pestilence[20] and drought, and all the social unrest that came with it.

Before you understood the origins of the plagues? she asked.

That's right. Agahnim was using Din's medallion to create unnatural fires, and wanted to ensure nobody ever obtained the force of ether, as that icy magic could counteract his scheme. *Only after the sixth maiden—* descendant of the Wise Men[21] was crystalized did I realize–

---

20 Although often mentioned in the singular, the pestilence describes a series of crises that started plaguing Hyrule a decade ago. Also called the pestilences (plural) as the crises began initially with drought, famine, disease and forest fires all sparked by what is called 'The Boiling' of the kingdom.

21 The first sages and inheritors of Hylia's daughter's wisdom, power, and courage. The first

What?

That Zelda is your… AH. *AHH!*

My?– the bunny accidentally blew a bubble from his front teeth.

ACHOO! **Your last chance for restoring the Sacred Realm.**
Ack. ¿Bvrm-Frbrz!

WHEW! *I thought you were going to say sister.* Link exhaled in relief.

In our warped forms here, there's no way for me to put a face to your deeds, Zelda fumed, but I clearly remember the elite troupe who abducted me and held me in the dungeon, so you must've been amongst those foul knaves–

–He had a mustache. Link gestured by scratching his upper lip, wiping away the globule of saliva he hoped no one saw.

Oh, I think I remember… the ermine squinted.

¿Bvrm-Frbrz! the avuncular elephant shook his head, As a supposedly necessary evil and unavoidable preparation for capturing the princess, we were ordered to depose the king. This fateful order came down immediately after the sixth – the maiden before you – was handed over for the wizard's ritualistic serial sacrifices. He knew that his time was short, as one other knight, a hotheaded lad named Ariosto had rebelled, supposedly escaping with the fifth maiden. 'One life will save many!' Agahnim told us, not before priming us with 'The crown is but a man'.

Well intentioned wizards sure have a way with words. said Link in Zelda's direction.

The most bad are always so good at making assertions of moral relativism. she said.

I was shocked that none of my cohort blinked an eyelash at the command for regicide; royal guards who had sworn to protect the king. Frbrrzzz! There's nothing worse than having your grimmest fears and prescient pessimism confirmed in the dead of night!

How does that always happen in the dead of night? Link flopped his ears.

Hylians of Ancient Hyrule to communicate directly with the three goddesses Nayru, Din, and Farore. There were either seven, or nine, depending on who you ask. Any 'descendants of the Wise Men' are their lineage.

In those dissonant days of Agahnim's authoritarian ascendancy, anyone who expressed hesitancy toward his edicts were declared conspirators, or worse—heretics! said the uncle.

The few who dared to call off the hunt became the witches, as if vindicating the innocent and honorable was the forbidden magic the wizard demanded persecution for… she recalled.

As if the chief minister wasn't fomenting tons of forbidden magic himself! said the bunny.

Funny how that works. the boar muttered.

¿Bvrm-Frbrz! ¿Bvrm-Frbrz! But that night, it became clear *who* was conspiring, and to what evil endsssaahhhHHCHOO! Ack. Excuse me. the elephant paused to rub his snout. I went home and told Link to stay in bed, and gathered my troubled conscience as to what to do next. Despite all the disconcerting details, the exiles were at ease in the elephant's company, settling into Link's uncle's story. Having resigned my orders unannounced, I was not present on that dreadful mission Zelda. I had no idea Agahnim was transmuting the souls of those young women into crystals that he could then scatter across the realm! In effect, eliminating any chance for resistance, and enacting total control over the realms for untold ages to come.

We've found one of the maiden crystals already, in the Dark Palace. she said holding out the elongated black diamond around her slender neck.

Don't confuse that for a rupee! Wouldn't want to accidentally spend it on a refill and forfeit the fate of the world! said the elephant in jest. Frbrrrzzz!

My dear uncle… the bunny put his hands on the elephant who let out a slow sad note from his trombone-trunk. I feared the worst when returning to the sewer and seeing that you were nowhere in sight. But here you are! We promise to restore the Sacred Realm so we can return to our Hyrule home, in the Light World, as we were before.

The ermine caught a yawn by knuckling her muzzle.

The boar chuckled, but kept his guff to himself.

If you save the world, I promise to get a second bed too! Frbrz! Until then, I'll keep our meeting secret, when the wizard's custodians come to check on me here... Here!– the elephant turned to a large pink orb sitting on the floor, I was hoping to charge a hundred rupees for this Super Bomb, but please take it on your quest to find the other maiden crystals.

Ganon perked up, having slumped into a daze by the door.

I've been working on this for quite some time—a blast so powerful it affects the parallel world wherever you detonate it! And you mister boar, I see you have a bomb bag there... Allow me to top you off, on the house! The elephant carried a bushel of explosives over to Ganon, and delicately dropped one at a time in his bag like a chef placing potatoes in a dangerous boil.

And where are the other sealed descendants? the ermine asked.

–of the Nine Wise Men? said the elephant in discrepancy.

Seven. You said the wizard sought 'seven' – the number of lineages I was told as a girl.

What the Helmasaur King girl said too. Link added to the consensus.

ACHOO! Oh right, seven. Do you have a map? I've only heard my customers talk about a maiden crystal in the Misery Mire, found in the Swamp of Evil, southwest of Lorule.

Lorule? she asked, having never heard of such a place.

Oh, that's just my nickname for this twisted version of Hyrule that we're stuck in! If the Light World is 'High-rule', then this Dark World must be the down-and-out 'Low-rule'! Right?

The ermine smirked, taking out her map of the Dark Palace. Can you write some directions on the backside of this?

Link's elephant uncle took the torn temple parchment. You know, this is no ordinary map.

We figured, she signaled Ganon to demonstrate how his compass magically illuminated their location on the accurate planar depiction. But nothing happened. That's odd! Zelda ogled.

Frbrz! You must be off the map! But I know what you're trying to do, and that's not the only amazing thing about it. the elephant said, pulling out a folded piece of paper from the bookshelf. Here's a missing part to the greater chart. He unfolded the map and rotated it around until he found the correct edge. Hold out your piece–

Piece? Zelda reciprocated his motions and held out the matching edge on her map, which quickly mended itself to the elephant's fragment, enlarging their map to show the entire overworld of the Sacred Realm. Amazing! she said in awe, also happy that Ganon's compass now revealed their location as well.

And it even looks revised to show the topologic distortions caused by the Dark World's curse. Link excitedly poured over the bedazzling elevation contours inked on the parchment.

This is a very dynamic mapaahhh–AH! KHHCH! Ack. The elephant stopped up a sneeze by clamping down on his trunk. You'll find another maiden crystal, *right here.* As the elephant pointed to the lower-left corner of the map (which Zelda had oriented such that north was up), her necklace pulled toward the markings of the Misery Mire, where a diamond-shaped icon etched itself in black; evident however long she hovered there. The descendant you already rescued is *drawn* to her sisters. he winked, then continued with a slack trunk and straight face, When in doubt, consult the maidens and map together – they know where the others, in their sealed away sorority, are to be found.

Looks like there's no way into the swamp? Zelda referenced a rendered deadend.

Hmmm? the uncle shouldered up to the ermine, double checking from her perspective. There was a valley there in Hyrule, I think you should be fine. Might be a cartographic anomaly. One other thing, he rubbed his finger on an adjacent region, avoid the Plains of Ruin to the east where a snitching demon called Arrghus surveils for trespassers. So keep west along the ridge.

Let's not delay then. rallied Link moving toward Ganon who was loitering by the door.

Don't forget the Super Bomb! It's also charmed with an auto-follow spell: give it a hug, and it will jog behind you. Just don't break into a sprint, or it will get left behind and begin a three-second countdown, *of which you'll need every second to get as far away as you can!*

The exiles nodded dopily as one does to any uncle's warnings while Zelda explored the elephant's bookshelf library. I'm not hugging that greasy thing, she said to the bunny who was waiting for either permission or consensus. Surprisingly the boar did not jump on it either.

You want it? Link asked Ganon, who shook his head. Ok, well, a Super Bomb without a squeeze is like pie without cheese! The similarly colored bunny embraced the large pink orb, and after taking a step back, the enchanted bomb followed along his path a full stride away. Taking Link by surprise, the elephant hugged him as well, depositing a handful of rupees in his nephew's pocket for the journey ahead, and not to be spent on novelties nor trivialities.

Thank you uncle elephant, the ermine said gracefully turning to the door. Ganon opened the door slightly, taking a look for any enemies. You're in the way. she told the boar.

Link crouched at the hole in the door – All clear! he confirmed.

How many exiles does it take to exit a bomb shop? Zelda scoffed, pulling the door fully open and stepping out, tucking the folded map into her dress.

A Second Wish of Solitude

To open the way to go forward, make your wish here and it will be granted. Really? Sounds easy. Born a decem millennium ago and versed in Ancient Hylian just like her brother, the moody imp girl Midna had no trouble deciphering the obelisk's inscription whose weathered glyphs were from her prelapsarian era. But does my wish need to be oriented toward progress, or will the way forward open with any wish—*will any wish be granted?* she got the syntax but the semantics eluded her. Lended for exactly this kind of situation, she considered consulting her newly acquired hardbound cipher, the Book of Mudora that was delivered to her by a little faerie named Epheremelda who nearly sprained a wing lugging the heavy text across realms. Nah. the imp opened the book, but only to use it as a parasol by holding the spread overhead, shading her small figure from the aggressive desert sunshine. If only there were a breeze, I'm cooking alive. But no—that's not my wish! she shouted, making sure the obelisk didn't mistake her meteorological daydreaming as an official demand. This is not as *open-ended* as it sounds, she suspected to herself out loud, somewhat delirious from the heat, I get the impression it's simply asking if I want to proceed or not. So that said, *I really do wish...* *BUH-GOOOMMMM...* interrupted by the distant rumble, the petite imp Midna snapped the large green tome shut and stood on its upright spine, almost doubling her height in order to get a better look – a plume of dust and sand floated in the southeast. The book vibrated under her feet as the explosion's shockwave reached where she stood on the walled patio of the xeric Palace of Nayru, another ancient temple built in honor of the goddess of wisdom, contemporaneous to the tower on the mountain but altogether its own megalithic architecture. Mischief in the valley? she asked the quiet dunes, shielding her uncovered eye and squinting into the distance.

Alas, too hot to care, FORWARD! she commanded the obelisk. Nothing happened. Hmmm. the imp closed her parasol of pages and ran her finger over the glyph relief to make sure she hadn't misinterpreted the ancient inscription. Perhaps a silent treatment is required? Midna turned away and held her elbow with a hand to her chin, standing pensively as if in a Gerudo prayer.[22] She closed her right eye (the other was concealed by her stone crown) and in tacit mentalese confided the wish: *Forward... please–* she added just in case graciousness was required to confirm the thought and open the temple. *CRBLBLBL...* Three large hemispherical stones rumbled aside, rotating equidistantly in unison along the periphery, blocking her egress from that plaza but now revealing a way into the temple ahead. Be-da-be-de Be-da-be-dee! she chimed, placing the big green cipher in the nest of her crown where she also kept a boomerang. Taking her time, the topheavy imp blithely climbed the declivitous stairs built into the otherwise inaccessible desert cliffside. At the top was a landing in the shape of a tongue, leading

22 Also known as a 'Golden Land Genuflection' or 'The Sa'oten Supplication'. How women of the desert pray by placing their left hand under their chin or on their lips, right hand under their left elbow; or swap.

into the mouth of a modular dome that had three eyes and a pair of horns. Pausing at the penultimate stair, Midna took a better look at the other domes, one on each side, each with only one eye ornamenting their mythological masonry. The stairway to the dome at her right had eroded and was a sheer drop but nonetheless an open entrance at the top. And to her left, symmetrically reflected across the main stairway, was a similar dome whose stairs were intact but landed on the clifftop that didn't look easy to get to from the dunes. Taking one last look to the southeast, she could still see the dust cloud from the loud explosion, but no sign of what caused it.

As light-footed as she was, Midna felt self-conscious about trespassing and walking on the pristine sand floors of the palace hallways. While certainly dangerous and to be avoided, she was mostly relieved to encounter various creatures that had taken up residence in the abandoned chambers, exempting her from any concern of leaving footprints. Having endured for untold centuries, the temple had accreted a perfectly level grading of aeolian deposits, which is to say that *wind* was her first guess, but it became increasingly inconceivable to Midna how that could have left so much sand evenly distributed throughout the temple when only the three small dome entrances interfaced the subterranean structure with the desert outside. Taking that puzzling thought with her, she ducked down a hallway, skirting past a pack of purple and green leevers that efficiently burrowed once her little footsteps were out of their short territorial radius. Surprised that the sand was deep enough for these odd animals to fully conceal themselves in, Midna took her boomerang and dug around the base of the wall. After excavating a few inches, she noticed a widening recession in the stonework. Erosion... *But from what?* she speculated, squatting to reach the running undercut with her short imp arms. A flood could have brought all the sand in here! Midna excitedly hypothesized to the sand-muffled quiet vacuity of the hallway. The sound of her voice as she talked to herself attracted another dune dweller, a fire-spitting devalant[23] worm. As the rooted insect emerged, a vortex of quicksand

---

23   Large burrowing venomous insects that dig slippery pits in the desert during their larval stage to

sucked toward its sharp mandibles, easily trapping simple prey like the twirling leevers[24] she saw a moment before.

Calmly evading the monsters behind her and stepping into an unexplored chamber at the northwestern corner of the main hall. Midna was so fixated on the live beamos[25] statue in front of her that she hadn't noticed the clean tiles beneath her feet. Ducking behind one of the four lanterns in the square room that towered twice as tall as her, she swished her left foot on the floor that was made of smooth frogskin jasper. Despite the pattern, she couldn't discern if the greenish floor was a single piece of stone, as the tiles were astonishingly seamless. Not a grain of sand either. she said, peering out from the lantern to make sure the slowly rotating beamos in the center of the room had not spotted her. A large tablet on the back wall opposite the entrance caught her attention. Made of an immaculate white stone, there was an unusual quality to the embossed plaque that did not resemble the load bearing masonry at all. But like most things that call to us unexpectedly, she decided to turn away from it in order to pursue what she was determined to find.

Midna left the room and jogged diagonally across the near corner of the sandy lateral hall toward a chamber to the west. Avoiding the gaze of another beamos, she stayed within the sentry's nadir blindspot while inspecting an elliptical assortment of very old brown pots that sat on square stones around the sentry statue. One of the pots revealed a large depressable plinth, which she stepped on at first cautiously with one tiny foot to no effect, then with both and all her imp weight, heavier than the ceramic that sat there but not by much, *Crunk.* crunching the sandy button down and triggering a stone slab in the wall to her left to recede upward, revealing a new passageway ahead. As one of the last rooms in the palace Midna had not yet investigated, her hopes were high for finding what she came for. And higher yet when she entered

---

    trap passing creatures and people. Sometimes called 'sandlion' the red devalant can also spit fire at its prey.

24   Carnivorous scavenger sand anemones found in the desert. Distantly related to the Dark World ropa.

25   A stationary construct of Ancient Hyrule firmly programmed to zap any intruder with its beam eye. Powered by an internal perpetual energy source, many of these guardian statues are still active.

and saw the large gilded chest sitting on a beveled blue platform of ceremonial grandeur.

After all those millennia, finally sprung from the shadows only to step into the light of Hyrule as an imp! she said, articulating her orange hair (as imps can) into a hand that grasped something gold in her grey crown's basket. Out of the prison of a forbidden world into the cage of a warped body! Midna opened the large chest with the matching master key she had found in the opposite eastern wing of the temple. All that remains is to free myself from this body and look like I did before everything went wrong, the beautiful Gerudo princess—Midnadorf. she declared with a toothy grin, reaching for the spherical blue treasure that was set into an ornate fixture and bound with a silver loop. Awww, the moon pearl! she gloated, holding the necklace open with wide arms to examine the blue orb at eye-level. Now—Nayru, exonerate me from my timeless sentence! *Please,* she hazarded to wish, *return me to my former self.* Midna bowed to fit the necklace over her tricky crown. Avoiding any snags, she adorned herself triumphantly.

Allowing a few seconds for the transformation to ensue, the imp enjoyed the satisfying weight of her newfound treasure and played with adjusting its position; how it hung comically low on her small torso. The flight of her elation fell into a devastating nosedive when it became clear that the embodied curse remained. Mysteriously acquiring a diminutive warped form upon crossing realms, Midna remained as an imp despite finding this sacred stone of the goddess. *Can I not be both free and be myself?* At least I was beautiful in the Dark World! she shouted, her right eye welling up with tears remembering her junoesque physique as a banished Twili, and her all but forgotten sunlit Gerudo youth before that. She took the pendant off, and threw it down the lapis steps of the raised platform. Arms folded around her knees and resting her chin thereupon, sitting in catatonic defeat, allowing her mind to drift in the placid solitude of the temple depths, abiding in the futility of her selfish quest. *Guess not...* Once shackled by the heavy privilege of royalty, then damned to sempiternal twilight, and now warped as an imp with a burdensome crown, the thrice-doomed princess could see the beamos statue slowly spinning, watching for intruders. With the steady apathy of a lighthouse, the sentry's bored eye swept across her and the neglected treasure, unable to detect anything beyond its designated room.

Midna started to feel like a stationary beamos as well until her stomach grumbled, dispelling the dazed inertia that bound her. Imps gotta eat. she said, patting her belly and standing up. Deciding to take the necklace anyway, she left the treasure chamber with her vanity souvenir of a redemption in vain, backtracking through the antechamber, and sashaying into the sandy hall that joined with the main foyer. There was nothing else for her here, but the amusing sight of her meandering footprints – the impressions of a past self, albeit minutes ago. But even then she was a different person, still an imp, but not without hope for remitting the curse and regaining her elegant stature. This uncanny divergence of time and inclination sunk in, as the childlike prints implied a gait of enthusiasm that she could not retrace now if she tried. She glanced to her left at the door – that room with the inexplicably clean tiles. *And wasn't there something else?* Midna pulled a smoking pipe from her crown and rummaged for a light when a devalant (the same one as before) emerged from the sand, awakened by her presence again. Already beside herself, it was easy to see her situation here from a third perspective as Midna objectively observed this imp's encounter with the devalant and chuckled at how predictable all these burrowing monsters were – rarely deviating from their procedural behavior. They might not be thinking animals but... *How rational they are.* And that displaced imp standing there, is she also just a shady temple creature, going about an expected routine, and rational to a fault? Woe, is maudlin one-eyed Midna, stuck her in ways, like the gimbal guards, monocle beamos– beamoses? *Or is it beami?* she digressed, I suppose we deserve each other... Eee hee hee!

Having slipped into a dissociated daze yet again Midna barely avoided the flaming loogie aimed at her idling. Taking evasive action with a soporific sidestepping, she held out her pipe and conveniently caught a wisp of flame from the searing projectile whereas the bulk of the burning jelly sizzled on the wall behind her. Narrowly missing, the hungry worm scrunched up for a second hocking, but the loitering explorer found resolve after toking her pipe, and followed the fresh prints made by *that more ardent imp* into the sandless room with the jasper tile floor.

The beamos was looking away from her when she entered, and so Midna took no cover from the four lanterns in the room but walked straight on – right past the sentry in the middle of the room and toward the white tablet. As she approached, the air felt electric. Her skin and hair fizzed with a peculiar energy. Looking back, the beamos was coming about, but slower than usual; the flames in the braziers appeared to flicker lazily as well. When she put her dark hand on the white stone, the room fell dead silent. The beamos was no longer rotating at all, and the fire of the four torches remained completely static. Midna pulled her hand back, and everything resumed, but in her wonderment she forgot to keep track of the sentry, which had now rotated to her position along the edge of the guarded room. Without delay the striking eye of the beamos locked onto the intruding imp and *ZWOOSH!* emitted a red lethal ray. No sooner and thankfully no later Midna had placed her hand back on the tablet. For the duration of her tentative contact time remained completely frozen. Moving freely however, she pivoted (keeping a hand on) and was startled to see this laser beam equidistant from the guardian, quivering at rest but aimed at her innocent chest. *Midnadorf...* a voice called from the wall plaque, drawing her attention back. Having looked away but making sure to not let go, she faced the— *it was gone!* Her hand floated in a void, as the room faded around her. The once Twilight Princess panicked at the thought of the beam about to blast her, but instead she found herself standing on a rugged plateau.

So I died. she figured, inhaling a long draw of her pipe and taking in the unworldly sights of a pitch-black horizon all around her bound by a bewilderingly big convex pinkish firmament above and deep iridescent clouds below. Amazed by the weightless mesa formations suspended throughout the still air, she had not noticed the old man addressing her.

You must never fail to find all the treasures in each dungeon. he advised apropos.

Midna checked herself: everything was the same, including the disappointing blue orb. The imp rhythmically dragged on her pipe, saying nothing.

You know that will kill you? the old man seemed annoyed that she was smoking.

Ah, good! So this isn't the afterlife, is what you mean to say.

No, we are in a liminal aspect of the Sacred–

I'll *know* when I'm dead, the imp interrupted, but I do *believe* it will kill me! she pointed her pipe lip at the old man who stood a good twenty paces away from her. There's a difference, and whoever quit a sublime thing on the basis of belief! the imp mused while taking persnickety little puffs from the corner of her mouth. *Something's gonna get you in the end...* Sacred what?

The Nymph Rationalizes Her Lisp

Zelda pulled out their magic map, which remained dry as the rain beaded off its surface. Amazing, she said, as the phylactery that hung about her neck gravitated toward the open chart that Link's uncle had expanded by adjoining his piece. Ganon, can we borrow your compass?

Disgruntled that they had used the Super Bomb so soon in order to clear a passageway and enter the swamp, the boar reluctantly fished out his compass from a pocket full of bog bilge. I hope this still works... The boar had repeatedly fallen into deep morasses, while the ermine and bunny knight managed to find shallower, however less linear routes.

Looks like we need to move a little north. Wait, she paused, drawing an arrow and aiming at a progression of ripples approaching from behind Ganon.

What's that? Link asked before Ganon had a chance to see for himself, Zelda sent an arrow *VRZSHH–* apparently into nothing but water until a stalking swamola[26] leapt into the air and was promptly intercepted *–THK!* by the ermine's anticipatory aim.

No one is supposed to be here. she said, lowering her bow at ease.

---

26   A leaping freshwater Dark World arthropod predator related to the larger sand burrowing man-eating lanmolas of the Light World. Although both creatures resemble centipedes they are actually legless crabs.

Whoever warped this world had an evil place in their heart for this swamp – cliffs all around, no way to get in. Link said trudging ahead through the meandering shallows. I believe my uncle though, when he said a valley leads here in the Light World…

As had Zelda feared when first looking at the expanded chart in the bomb shop, their journey to the southwest led them to a deadend in the valley just east of the swamp. And at that impasse the exiles encountered yet another hinox who was so smitten by Link's unusually large bomb that it agreed to tell them all it knew about what was on the other side. Under the deceitful promise that they would give the giant brute their Super Bomb if it told them how to get through. After priming the cyclops with monster reverse psychology (also known as *meanie reverse psychology* or MRP[27] for short) by repeatedly saying it (the cyclops) wouldn't know what to do with the bomb if it had it, as the boldest of the bunch Ganon then told the hinox to take it and demonstrate how such a bomb could clear a path forward. Their setup went according to plan. The bomb was spellbound to Link as a duckling is to its mother so when the monster defiantly palmed the pink orb, that separation triggered the countdown. The duped hinox had just enough time to place the bomb in the cliff and gleefully explain the best way to blast rock. By the time the cyclops realized the travelers were out of sight and taking cover (and that it was doomed) the bomb let out a blinding flash, clearing the passage toward the swamp with such force that the explosion was felt across the realms. From there the exiles trudged through the stormy swamp to their immediate northwest where the only landmark was noticeable – a small island protruding from the otherwise flat bog. Nothing there but a solitary dacto[28] who began to circle the three of them until it strafed a little too close and the boar backfisted it away. Obstructed by the small island however was a low lying structure flanked by a tangled trio of ghastly hassocks, all of

---

27   Only effective on monsters of limited cognition – smart enough to speak, but dumb enough to be duped. The technique involves convincing a goon that they cannot do what you want them to do; something the monster would not do on their own unless challenged, compelling them to do it against their orders.

28   A small flying aggressively carnivorous reptile with vermilion scaly feathers and a horn on its head integrated with its skull and sharp beak. Also known as a Dark World crow.

which bore an evil countenance consistent with the swamp's name. I don't get it, there's nothing here. she and the boys huddled around the matte-yet-waxy map, confirming that Ganon's compass placed them right where Zelda's maiden diamond gravitated toward.

Are we on the roof? Link asked, tapping with his red cane of summoning (that the lost old man left inside the mountain) and peered over the edge into the murk. A soggy causeway led into a quadrangle with an impressive ornamental plant in the middle, not unlike many others encountered growing wild in the swamp. The causeway continued on the other side, but ended with another large frond. Where does the Swamp of Evil end and Misery Mire begin? the bunny thumped his wet feet while strutting around the leveed perimeter of the platform.

The ermine princess watched her knight's frustrated footwork when she noticed an unusual inscription on the ground. Link, look there— The boar and bunny lowered on their haunches to examine the peculiar tile at the end of the blocked causeway. They both arrived at the same recollection and soberly looked at each other. What? she asked, leaning in as well.

Recognize that?

The goddess medallion! said Zelda, not mentioning how Ganon forcibly pried it from her on the mountaintop. Of course much larger, but the same sigil. What do you make of that?

Perhaps it means nothing? Nayru's mark, but what of it? the bunny had no clue.

Step aside. The boar swung high and struck the tile *DWONNNG!* causing his hammer to ring like a bell and fall from his grip. GHRGGHH! Ganon shook his hand off, as Link and Zelda pretended not to see in consideration of the King of Thieves' ego. The rain picked up and the previously distant lightning struck nearby and just beyond the platform.

Zelda covered under her mirror shield, with Link taking cover as well.

You sure it's safe to use a large metallic object as an umbrella? *Yeuch, you smell really bad.*

Been awhile since I've bathed, and this swamp is no substitute. said Link, pulling a trail of bubbly slime from off his shoulder and then noticing a peculiar symmetry. That an entrance?

There? the ermine pointed in the opposite direction, noticing the exact same formation but on the other side of the platform.

The bunny looked to her direction, Oh there's another, I was looking over here. said Link pointing to the east. I can't tell if there's a mouth or if that's just an unusually thick mass of vines.

Mister boar, which tangled tussock shall we investigate first? she asked.

Ganon looked to his right at the formation Zelda had pointed to (the west).

We could split up you know, she added, inspecting the large radial foliage of the plant in the center of the platform. Quite the specimen of a Lorule Lily,[29] wouldn't you say? *Nff. Nff...* Oh. Fetid fronds! she took a sniff and recoiled, Maybe this is what I was smelling.

The boar changed his mind, tossing his hammer and bag over the stone dyke on the eastern side of the platform. *SPLSHHH!*

Is that really what it's called? Link was impressed.

No, or I have no idea– Ganon! she shouted. *Wait for us!*

Link was unsure of the ermine's botanical joking, You sure you don't want to check the other one over there, that you were looking at first?

Nay! Let us follow our gallant tusked leader, a most bristly boar – bristling with intrepid initiative... The Great Ganon! she theatricalized, making dramatic gestures with one arm while holding her tall mirror shield upright with the other.

I don't know *who* you're talking about. Link skulked along.

If I had a rupee for every mysterious entrance we encountered, I could...

Actually afford Kiki? she helped him with a punchline.

Sure. Link wondered if the swamp gas had gone to her head.

Tah-hah-hah! the ermine princess clapped her hands. I can't see what's in there, but let's not make the same mistake as when we came

---

29   An unclassified giant rhizomatic aquatic herb found only in Lorule; unofficially named by Zelda.

upon Aginah's hideout. Ganon rubbed his head, remembering the stone he tossed that came right back at him.

Link crept up to the side of the dark viny opening that had grown to resemble an ominous mouth, and knocked on a woody ligament, HEY TRIFORCE, YOU IN THERE?

Stop it. Zelda shook her head and walked into the foreboding entrance.

What? I thought we were in the mood to lighten the mood?

If only it were that easy. said the boar clearing his throat and following the ermine inside.

Hm. This can't possibly be the miserable dungeon that your uncle spoke of. said Zelda, sizing up the small grotto as Link came to a similar conclusion.

Well this is a nice silver lining to not finding the maiden crystal. The bunny knight walked past two angelic sculptures into a shallow reflection pool. Ah, fresh springwater to clean up with! Get that stink off... he said, beginning to splash some of the luminescent liquid on his legs when a winged sprite with blonde hair appeared out of nowhere immediately in front of the pink bunny. The maiden! Did my bathing liberate you from the evil wizard's prison? Link squeegeed himself.

No, I am the faerie of the desert?

The bunny and ermine weren't sure if this was a question intended for them to answer.

So why are you in a swamp? Link asked.

Zelda stepped up to the reflection pool, Don't mind him, I understand– err, may I enter? the ermine hovered a foot over the water. Resembling a teenage Hylian, the fully grown faerie beckoned to her. Having folded just the sector of the map that contained their current location, Zelda referenced the markings, See where we are is a desert in the parallel Light World.

Link leaned to see the map, Looks like the swamp contours to me.

Yes, this shows the Dark World, but–

Lorule. the bunny tried to get some pedantic purchase in the argument.

Euh, what? Huechhh... Miss, I apologize for this animal disturbing your shrine.

Takes one to know one – why you picking sides like that? said the bunny knight.

Young bravery for the future, and old wisdom from the past are welcomed here? said the blonde supernatural sweetheart with a rising lilt, looking up and smiling with her eyes.

Ganon stepped up to the water's edge.

…And power of the present disarmed? she grinned with open arms. The quiet boar looked down at the reflection pool, unsure whether to join them. These waters are all that remain of the sea that dried up long ago? the faerie reclined, floating in the air.

What do you mean? Zelda asked standing next to Link in the cerulean skim.

The Desert of Mystery was once lush, and host to many rivers and bays? It was here that Nayru gifted the moon pearl. Until the Sacred Realm was defiled, and the Great Cataclysm changed Hyrule forever?

Do you have the moon pearl?! Link asked loudly.

No, it was taken from the desert? the faerie shrugged apologetically.

When? Zelda was confused as the lost old man told them it came from the mountain.

I'm so bad with dates! Hard to guess. I would say recently? *But as an immortal nymph my intuition for time is often unreliable.* she said in a definitive tone, for once.

You and my uncle. said Link off to the side.

We are looking for– well, a few things. But we came here to find the maiden crystal, sealed by the evil wizard. Do you know where she is held? the ermine princess got the point.

How do we enter Misery Mire? said the bunny knight, determined to find out.

Pearls, crystals, mires… the faerie pinched her nose while piecing together a thought. The evil rains have flooded the temple? her face darkened as she wiggled her fingers. I have not heard of the maidens, are they younger than me? Yes, they must be? This flooding is not natural, but by design from he who wanted the maiden hidden, I believe? the blonde went on, inhaling in contemplation, Along the eastern rim of the desert basin, you'll find a creature who might know where the entrance is? *That way–* she said confidently at last, pointing to her left.

Zelda confusedly swiveled her map around, trying to get her bearing with the nymph's open-ended advice. You mean, the swamp basin?

Did I say desert?

Thank you for your, ah—help. smiled the ermine, pulling on her bunny knight's tunic.

Did you lose a hand? the faerie asked the boar who was still lingering at the pool's edge.

Aye.

Come closer?

Slsh-plsh. the boar took two steps into the pool.

Actually, step back? I can help you, but my magic only works if you–

The boar stepped back to where he was out of the pool.

I think that will do it? she squinted, measuring with her fingers and sizing up the boar with a pinching gesture. Ganon rolled his eyes. Zelda and Link watched from behind, amused and curious. You see, I can lay my hands on your wounds but only from afar. The magic of big faeries is an intimacy that requires distance – much like all tenderness? the nymph speculated while levitating upright and hugging a knee.

Can you heal my arm?

I will sooth[30] your wounds and comfort your weariness... Close your eyes and relax...

'Sooth'? Zelda snickered to Link, Does she have a lisp? He gave a conciliatory nod, not understanding the difference between sooth and soothe but mostly just entranced by the faerie sparkles that now dusted over the boar like a young constellation of bright blue stars.

I mean what I say? she responded to Zelda, I am sooth-ing his wounds, not soothe-ing?

Huh… the princess did not follow.

---

30   The power of adult faeries to literally 'truth' (i.e. sooth) one's wounds. A kind of healing that does not cure the disease but recontextualizes it, lending comfort and relaxation to those wounded or damaged. Sometimes soothing does cure a wound (especially if it's psychosomatic) but also risks rationalization. Young pixies are typically too small to sooth, great faeries often retire to artifact augmentation instead.

Sooth? As in, truth? I am <u>truthing</u> his wounds? *Not soothe.* To truth a wound is more healing than to pacify a wound, wouldn't you say?

I'm not getting my hand back, am I. said Ganon unimpressed, fanning away the pointless pixie particles with his amputated stub.

Forsooth. said the bunny.

Making your wounds more genuine. This world reveals many things of our true forms, but let me help you be what you already are, weary Gerudo of the desert. There's no need to hide what you've lost — *I will sooth your wounds...*

How does she know you're a Gerudo? More than a boar. said Link.

Bye. Ganon saluted as they gathered their things to leave the faerie's grotto fountain.

The lisping lassie clasped her hands, You might be able to use it as a prosthesis? Yes, you see your loss was meant to be for this purpose which is exactly what soothing resolves, no?

Use what? Link responded for Ganon who ignored the faerie's considerate suggestion.

In the sunken temple of the mire, I recall there might be an artifact that has more *reach* than any hand? the faerie pantomimed by jutting her arm out and splaying her fingers.

What was it called?

If only I could *grasp* the name of it... of the ancients from long ago — before the darkening of this realm, and before the cataclysm before that?

You hear that Ganon? the bunny addressed the boar who couldn't have cared less.

My fountain guests, I wish you well! And please visit me again? the lonely blonde faerie displaced from the desert faded as the exiles stepped out into the unabating rain of the swamp.

When Our Shadows Jump Over Us

Zelda led the way with her lightweight bulwark held overhead, keeping her upper body dry, despite having to slog through the quagmire shallows; sometimes waist deep. Flashes of lightning continued to course above the swamp, although striking mostly behind them as they approached the eastern cliffs of the basin the thick air made the thunder feel especially close. Floating layers of humid fog obscured their destination but soon they found themselves on a narrow skirt of shale which provided drier passage. Heavier than the others both in physique and packing, the boar repeatedly slipped on the loose slope of crumbled rock. The ermine and bunny made their way with a levity in their steps, although their spirits were as sunken as their aspired destination: the lost temple of Misery Mire that darkly mirrored the Desert Palace in the parallel Light World. Supernaturally self-aware but also ditzy enough to lapse, the nymph could have warned them but expressed it instead by justifying her lisp – they were now in a topos[31] that warped their hearts and minds towards rationalization. Although their twisted animal forms remained true to who they were as individuals in accordance with the Golden Power and the one who took the Triforce, the Swamp of Evil however was an elevation of the Dark World in which everyone was inclined to talk themselves into claiming that they *know that* – whatever that subject lingering on their mind or determined object that their heart was set on. Following the precarious eastern shore to the south, the exiles came upon a dim flicker and muffled buzz that emanated from a cave in the cliff. Eager to get out of the rain yet again, the ermine princess entered without hesitation as her bunny knight readied his red cane, just in case. As entangling as it might be, there are worse things in the realm than the swamp tendrils of rationalization.

Hello? the ermine shouted at a polite volume. They could see a large stone floor lantern flickering down the hall. The buzzing noise was louder now, coming from something out of sight in the depths of the cavern. Link ventured ahead when he made eye contact with the source of the noise. Of all the contorted and mutated forms of the corrupted Sacred Realm that now constituted the Dark World, Link and his fellow exiles had learned that first impressions often indicated

---

31   A common term to describe either the physical or the metaphysical characteristics of any of the nine elevations of the two realms. A place; a topography in the Light World or a topology of the Dark World. Either 'topos' or 'topoi' can be used for a plural inflection, although almost nobody says 'topoi' but you.

whether the creature was a sentient traveler, warped according to one's true character just like them. Or a mindless monster, whose brain was bent through and through to the topos and will of the wizard. While this buzzing ant/bee was nearly as large as Link, it was clear s/he was simply hiding from the dangers of the world outside. As their *Lorule of thumb*,[32] if a freak wears clothes, it is usually at worst indifferent (with the exception of hinoxes and the pigmen of course – who are dressed and nasty). This ant/bee wo/man was stylishly put together however, sporting chartreuse booties and yellow suspenders that crisscrossed.

Hey! the flying ant/bee called to the bunny. I'll tell you a profitable story if you pay me twenty rupees? the creature paused as the ermine and boar caught up. How about it?

Yes. the bunny said without hesitation, needing a place to rest and hoping to make a positive introduction. Link handed the hovering vagrant a red rupee received from his uncle.

Heh heh. Thank you. As a matter of fact, monster magic is making it rain in the swamp. said the ant/bee, buzzing his/her wings louder to make a point. If you can move the air with more force than the monsters, the rain may stop.

Did you hear that?

The ermine princess waved, but she wasn't sure what the bug-person had actually said. Meanwhile, the boar had settled in the corner and was using his bomb bag as a pillow. Is it okay if we take a break here, miss-ter, uh?– The ant/bee hovered indifferently on the other side of the hovel, a vertical oscillating motion which Zelda misread in her nodding off swamp-logged fatigue as a gesture of approval. You got the right idea, she said to Ganon, putting down her big shield, bow and laying out the map to use as a pad protecting her from the dirty ground. With his eyes closed the boar responded with only a wry smile, trying to doze despite the incessant buzzing of the nearby bug drifter. Relaxing, isn't it? she said, fond of white noise. Not disagreeing with her, Ganon opened a lid to give Zelda a sliver of acknowledgement. *The hospitable hum of a giant flying ant...*

---

32   An unreliable heuristic to determine whether someone in the Dark World is hostile or not as many of the monsters wear uniforms such as the hinox, moblin, taros, zazek, and pikku to name a few out to get you.

she muttered, fading quickly. Less about warmth and mostly for a sense of security, the ermine princess then placed the large reflective bulwark over her body as a rigid comforter, revealing only her feet poking out from the gilded rim. I haven't forgotten that, her muffled voice warned from underneath the shield, Triforce or not, you're the King of Thieves, so don't get any ideas here... But already half asleep and contentedly replete with bombs, the boar refused to entertain any interpretation of her bad-faith goodnighting; too tired for her to get a rise out of it.

Thanks for sharing your dry digs. Out of consideration for his companions, Link lowered his voice but wanted to talk more with the troglodyte. How did you get here? the bunny asked.

I'll tell you a personal story if you pay me more. How about it?

Link handed the creature another red gem. Alright, but this is for a *whole* conversation. While they rest, I want to hear *your* story.

Heh heh. Thank you. As a matter of fact, I was going to ask the same. How did you three arrive here; the Swamp of Evil has no way in, or out.

We noticed, and had to employ a hinox to blast our way through the valley impasse south of here. Link pointed down the cavern hall that was on the same longitude.

So that's how you got here, interesting. And you blew in from the Light World?

Who didn't. And speaking of, there is a valley that leads into the Desert of Mystery in parallel Hyrule, but no such passage in this realm. Do you know why? Link asked the storyteller.

If you came all the way from the mountain, as most condemned to this world do by either eviction from the authorities or ambitions of their own, then you are already familiar with the way in which this bizarre realm became reified in the evil image of the one who touched the Triforce.

The bunny nodded, the topos, yes.

As the goddesses graded the realms into nine elevations, each topos here is now warped by moral delusion in the Dark World. And how many have you passed through?

I want to know how you got here; to the swamp. said Link, deferring his answer.

Heh heh. Yes, I will tell you. My story begins with our discursive journey here my friend. said the ambiguously androgynous flying ant/bee, adjusting his/her suspender straps.

Ok well… the bunny knight looked up, recalling the stages of their adventure since getting exiled to the Dark World. We began our descent at the topos of myopia–

The peak of Death Mountain. the insect clarified.

Seems like a dream in hindsight, but was a real nightmare at the time. Link continued, One elevation below, there was the topos of desire of Turtle Rock, from there we left the mountain entirely and entered the highlands which were a topos of fright. And now here–

Yes, the Swamp of Evil is a *topology of rationalization.* As with a closed mind, the very basin is occluded from anything that might change the weather here; an fretfully intransigent atmosphere. At this elevation of the Dark World, the wizard's warp compels a pliant soul[33] to lie with an endless precipitation of disconnected facts which the clouds never run dry of. Whatever dreary thoughts, what you think you know, become easily validated as our minds are saturated by this unavoidable rain of rationalization. How easily we justify ourselves with falsehoods as shallow as the swamp outside, as to why an evil is necessary, or unavoidable.

Is that so. Are you the only one here—*who knows this?*

You're the first to visit on your own volition. said the ant/bee.

Ah. Link looked down solemnly. I'm sorry that you're here all alone.

Oh, it's really not bad, at least I'm out of the rain!

You sure that isn't the topos talking? the bunny asked askew.

Certainly! said the ant/bee with no way to know for sure.

Ok, just making sure. And you–

I'm getting there! When entering this world, my wings allowed me to easily avoid the many dangers outside, and to access this basin

33   One's heart and mind. What the Golden Power reifies into one's true form in the Dark World.

with only the difficulty of a fierce headwind which I managed to tack against, making my way until arriving in the swamp.

Why here?

Perhaps instinct, or maybe by accident, but I have a feeling each soul has its topos and that the person and the place characterize each other. But as for *why* I am *what* I am here – was once member to a gang of elite thieves, all of whom scattered as of the sessantine[34] mandates, I suspect that my *reasons* for entering the Dark World resulted in this flighty true form of mine.

So there's some reciprocity to this world then: the people make the place and the topos molds their souls. And reason is the parallel topos—*topography of reason,* in the Light World?

What would rationalization be without its reasons? But what of the converse: *is reason never without rationalization too?* the flying insect asked aloud, then got back on topic. But unlike the common kleptomaniacs, I had a rah-uh—*rationale* to come here!

…Link stared blankly. Let me guess, the moon pearl?

No! Why would I undergo this freakish form I am now for an artifact that returns me to how I looked before coming here in the first place—that makes no sense. *Unreasonable!*

The bunny shrugged, Sometimes the best part of a trip is returning?

Nothing like fashioning a problem just to have the satisfaction of solving it, I catch your drift. You know, that's how the wizard works. But there's no going back; not yet.

I want my money's worth miss-ter… What's your story?

A lousy thief I was, I mean: excellent at what I did but pitiful and perhaps deserving of this Dark World. Oh my sweet—my fiancée was a great healer… Revered for her commitment to Nayru: always seeking the truth and sharing her love of ancient wisdom. But when she went missing after speaking out about how the wizard had planned the

---

34 The name of Chief Magistrate Agahnim's mandatory pestilence measures of a sixty-day lockdown in Castle Town that lasted for nine weeks. Whether intended or not, the term is also a double entendre portmanteau that combines 'sessile' (i.e. stationary) and 'quarantine' (i.e. a state of enforced isolation).

pestilences all along, no one dared speak of it or her. Of course, I had to go alone and find my forlorn physician honeybabe!

Congratulations on your engagement. So… she spoke out against the Chief Minister Agahnim and his overtly authoritarian orders? The regime was most threatened by any healers as they knew how to speak to the nature of the pestilence, and identify the lies. Witches too.

The insect sidebuzzed, sighing. Well, about that–

Oh, she was a tacit dissident. I know Agahnim had agents under his will with mind controlling magic, or so they say; rumored wizardry… Did they apprehend her for *thinking out?*[35]

No, she was outspoken. Heh heh. I uhh– I didn't believe her.

Oh. You believed the magistrate instead.

And she left me.

Oh!

And not before breaking off our engagement.

OH! the bunny exhaled, taking in all this drama. Especially the sessantine caused many households and relationships to crumble. So you two broke up, she got abducted by Agahnim, and now you're trying to rescue her in this messed up world?

The ant/bee gained a few inches of altitude while taking in a deep breath.

Do you believe she is the maiden sealed in the Misery Mire below?

I have reasons to believe this, yes.

Doooo—you… *think she wants to be rescued by you?* Link cautiously asked.

Who else would! Look, there's going to be a fight either way: I stay in hopeless Hyrule and wait for the evil legion to come knocking, or I do my best to forestall that and find my argumentative ex! Heh heh.

But the dungeon must be sunken beneath the quagmire. And the rain makes it nearly impossible to discern what lies beneath the water mark.

Which is why I have been waiting here.

---

35   As of the arrival of Agahnim, thinking itself has become considered dangerous; impolite. Not illegal yet but most of Castle Town has inculcated a culture of self-censorship to avoid any trouble with authorities. Many people rightfully suspect that the wizard has ways to read minds, so becoming thoughtless is key.

But you just said, the storm outside is caused by an unnatural force of evil, a wet and woeful barrier intended to keep anyone from going deeper. And that rain might pour for as long as the Golden Power is sequestered—supposedly stolen and such... the bunny didn't want to wake the boar and kept his Triforce-talk mostly neutral and devoid of accusations.

Then I will wait. said the ant/bee.

How do you even *know that* your fiancée is in Misery Mire, and not somewhere else?

The ant/bee buzzed faster, perturbed by the bunny's inconsiderate interrogation, causing Ganon on the other side of the room to toss about, napping to no avail.

My bygone-betrothed–

Your honey 'BB'.

Heh heh. Would you stop interrupting! Taking a page out of my book, she stole the pendant of wisdom and took it to the ancient Palace of Nayru. Isn't that what's on the other side in the parallel Light World? She thought that perhaps the blue goddess herself would appear...

No. the bunny realized who the ant/bee was talking about and this was not exactly true.

No what. it droned, still going off what the propaganda had reported of the incident.

Link didn't have the guts to tell the bug that he actually met her before, and had given this dissident healer the pendant after secretly drawing the Master Sword with Princess Zelda. You insist staying here on grounds you don't actually know, impeded by something you can't possibly change, and all for someone who left you for good reason?

I have my rationalizations! the insect asserted with a frictive tone, suggesting this was not up for further discussion.

At least you're out of the rain and have some dry-headed self-reflection in this cliffside hermitage of yours. he said, aware that his consolation might be a rationalization as well.

GRUAHH! the boar stumbled up, grabbing his bag and belongings. I can't get any shuteye with all this buzzing and prattling about *maidens* and *marriage* and *BOO-HOO-HOO!* The bunny and ant/bee watched the angry boar get up with a bomb from his pillow bag and place it in a crack that was midway across the chamber and directly opposite the entrance.

You're right, said the ant/bee ignoring the boar, I don't know if she's down there. There is no escape from the mutating manifold of darkness in this corrupted realm. But having taken some cover from the rains of rationalization outside, I know that *this* is the heart of the matter.

What do you mean?

As to what makes a world dark—

PFOOMGHHH! GHHhhrghrgh... The bomb detonated, opening a passage and cloud of smoke that the King of Thieves impatiently marched through before the dust had time to settle. Debris flicked all over the ceiling and wall. *Tink-tonk-tink, tink-tink... KGHUGHHHH!* vectorized pebbles sprinkled sonorously on the princess's mirror shield as she choked out a ghastly snore in subconscious response. Her feet wiggled but she remained sound asleep, noise and all.

Please, tell me. And what about the Triforce? said the bunny, wanting to know more.

The ant/bee finished buzzing away a plume of bomb smoke and considered how to say what s/he intended to convey... The Golden Power dimmed in an instant, and yet the paradox of our doom is that it was also longtime latent. Both continuous *and* spontaneous. Heh heh.

Link made an expression suggesting that he needed an example.

While the sun still shines on Hyrule as it did the very day the goddesses created the world, no radiance is without shadows cast by eternal forms. That reaching darkness became the curse of the Sacred Realm we are now bound by. The insect pulled on his/her crisscrossed yellow suspenders to emphasize *bound.* Still confused, Link tugged on his bunny ears as well to match body language. The ant/bee tried another angle then, As the chief minister—Agahnim had Hyrule under a spell, no one could think without fear. Unsound orders and edicts were followed unquestioningly and rationalized as necessary for, you know—

Ending the pestilences?

When everyone claims to know what they know, *then our shadow has jumped over us!* said the ant/bee, casting a silhouette on the wall from the nearby lantern's firelight. To capture our hearts and minds, the wizard called our bluff, a spell that requires no magic.

Howso? That sounds more like a conviction than a rationalization…

Yes, rightly so — related topologies of wisdom warped, and as you can discern, the darkness falls far beyond this place alone. Who can hold a conviction without rationalization? No more than those who rationalize without the complacency of myopia. That is to say — none!

Delusion flows downhill… said the bunny, swooshing his hand.

Heh. This swamp cannot exist without the mountain that gathers the clouds to fall here. Consistent with the elevations of this Dark World, the conceit of shortsighted myopia rains into rationalization, which descends into conviction. But what is it that we *know?* I will tell you *that!* Recent events aside, this all began long ago, after the Imprisoning War, the Knights of Hyrule were disbanded and their deeds mythologized to a distant past. The wizard knew that we had forgotten the meaning of their sacrifice — those who were willing to die to protect what Hyrule stood for: gratitude toward the goddess Hylia who set forth the kingdom in the first place.

When the knights protected the wise old men and sealed the Sacred Realm…

Yes, causing the Great Cataclysm that displaced entire mountains and seas in a day.

But I don't understand. Who called who's bluff? What 'spell that requires no magic'?

With the knights largely disbanded and in the peacetime that ensued after the cataclysm, the wizard knew that the foundational values of the kingdom had waned. In the events leading up to our emergent *Gloomaevum* — an indefinite epoch of empty hearts and voided minds, no one believed anything was worth dying for; except perhaps more decadence as the wizard summoned and festooned to further distract us all. We had already committed to this oblivion, pretending there were no consequences — rationalizing that the gloom would never come home to roost as it did with the pestilence. All he had to do was pick our debt like an over ripened fruit, splitting at the seams. That's what I mean by the sessantine called our bluff...

Our shadows had already 'jumped over us' by then—

Because when *life as such* became our greatest value, we would do whatever the wizard told us to not *perish* from this mysterious epidemic! the ant/bee shook his/her head.

And that's not magic?

Well, the pestilence was certainly a spell of unprecedented complexity.

And manipulating the minds of officials and hearts of countrymen to his will?

That too is a nefarious wizardry, yes. But neither summoned plagues or iniquitous inculcating will ever claim our fate if we hold true to our principles. Agahnim knew we *believed in nothing* that could stop him. His tricks were insubstantial, but less so than our own superficiality.

Link held his staff on the ground, But why can't we shine a light on all this dark sorcery? Surely your fiancée believed that the truth would prevail.

She did, and was punished for it. My heedless disbelief ratified her observation that the pursuit of truth had become relegated to prestige. At that point the kingdom became blinded by conceit, we became shades of ourselves even before the Sacred Realm was corrupted.

So, who touched the Triforce if not the King of Thieves? asked the bunny.

Perhaps we all did, the many hearts of Hyrule reaching out in fear of...

Fear of dying?

Yes, but even scarier than that...

Link wasn't sure, despite having this exact lapse of courage during their conversation.

Of being honest—of what we had already become. And here our wish is granted in full! No matter what it becomes, the Sacred Realm always endows what we deserve. Heh heh.

The Triforce does reflect the heart and mind of... said Link trying to reiterate stuff.

But consider this, the insect cut off the bunny's incomplete comment. I've had an idea. Maybe the Light World is the shadow, incidentally incandescent, just a showy projection of our delusions, the illusory image of a world in denial. At least the veil is stripped in the Dark World, and we have no choice but to come to terms with ourselves as we really are.

That's a nice rationalization for interdimensional imprisonment. the bunny nodded, mostly out of fatigue and the cozy flickering of the lantern.

Heh heh. How to move the air with more force than the monsters, I cannot say. But for now rest here with your fellow travelers. We have become the darkness, and I believe this is a privilege, and confers a power upon our destinies. We now have a responsibility to return to Hyrule with this knowledge to help others realize the true form of their depthless rationalizations. Only exiles can realign the Triforce and integrate the realms again. Take heart as Nayru, Din, Farore surely know, we have a purpose beyond our own miseries. And so, history will smile upon us skeptics, but until then, we will be banished by Agahnim and those blinded by the light of appearances, avarice, ambition... the insect buzzed out a tirade at the tired knight.

There's no way... the bunny rubbed his eyes, Only the Master Sword can...

To each their own quest, but we all need sleep. Heh heh.

Having gotten his red rupee's worth of storytime, Link thanked the buzzing bachelor/ette and looked for a place to snooze. Between the sound of the insect's insomnia and the ermine's snoring, the bunny decided to join the boar in the blasted chasm which was significantly quieter. Ganon was a surprisingly tranquil sleeper, but even there the whir of the stewing storm and the rain's whipping percussion carried deep into the cavern, lulling Link out cold.

Force of Ether

Twunggg-Twunggg-Twunggg... Zelda stood in the blasted doorway, plucking her bowstring in hopes of waking up the boar and the bunny. *Twunggg-Twunggg-Twunggg...*

Link lifted an ear that was covering his face like a night mask while he slept with his back against the sloped side of the red magic block that he had summoned from his Cane of Somaria before settling down. Yes. he said groggily, surprised that a couple hours elapsed in what felt like the blink of an eye. Ganon. Ganon. Ganon... the bunny couldn't wake the boar.

That map was a lousy mattress, my back is killing me... she complained to her knight. I'm not used to having such a long torso—something kinked my lumbar real bad last night. *Twunggg-Twunggg–* the ermine gleefully plucked her bow much closer now.

Midnadorfkeepyourdistance... wecannottrustRau-rau-rgghhh... the boar sputtered in a half-dream, trailing off into a gruff snore.

Who?

Midnadorf? Zelda whispered, unsure as well.

Twunggg– Link reached over to pluck a note.

Ssstop it! she pulled her bow back.

Onceyougoboaryoucantgoback...

The bunny and ermine frowned at each other. Generalized second person. she whispered.

Rhetorical device. Link reciprocated at the same volume, despite trying to wake Ganon.

...WhoneedstheTriforce?   Iwilljustbemyselftheboar-rgghhh...   Rgghhh-rgghhh... Iamnoswinebutaboarforeve-rgghhh...

Is he rationalizing in his sleep? Link asked Zelda.

That can't be safe—snuggling a pillow full of explosives.

Abagoflivebombsisgoodforyourhealth...

Sounds like it, must've huffed some black powder. she snickered.

Link picked up the red block and dropped it on the boar who rolled on his side and cuddled with the large brick. Hmm, no luck there either. said the bunny, unnecessarily quiet again.

Enough, let's just go. Zelda got down and appeared to be hugging the sleeping boar.

What are you doing?

The ermine waved her other arm, Take my hand, come on.

Oh, I get it. said Link, still somewhat put off, as Zelda pulled out her magic mirror and teleported the three of them to the entrance of the cavern. Ganon materialized without waking. The rain and wind struck them worse than before. Refreshing to be outside! he stretched.

My shield is such a good umbrella, I would hate to have the storm stop! she added.

It's literally silver-lined… dangerously conductive rationalization if you ask me.

The boar snapped awake, RELEASE ME! he roared while laying down, pulling the princess into a cradle lock.

AIEAAH! *CRECKRACK!*

Let her down Ganon! Link waved his cane, startled by the snapping sound.

Oh. said the boar, looking about and coming to his senses.

Did you just break her bow? he wasn't sure what that loud noise was.

Ah! the ermine put her hands to her lumbar. Cracked my back!

Uh—princess, are you okay? the bunny knight implored, noticing her bow was fine.

Felt great after sleeping on that hard ground. Ahh! she swayed about while Link lowered his guard, disarmed by Zelda's unexpected gratitude toward Ganon's outburst. *I broke a nail…*

Well you know who could 'sooth your wounds'. said the bunny, already soaked.

Come, skipped the ermine, I want to ask the faerie if she can spare us some of her magic to stop this monstrous storm. Perhaps then we will find the entrance to Misery Mire.

Link shook his head, Why don't you just say you need a faerie manicure and be honest about it? It's not like she's actually going to fix anything!

Zelda pulled her mirror shield overhead to cover just herself and Ganon. Why don't you find your own rain gear? The boar pretended not to notice, wanting nothing to do with this.

Fine! Link whipped his red cane *Wromp.* summoning a new brick, which he lifted over his head. Hyiup! See! Just as dry. The beveled top immediately began dripping down his arms.

Grumbling to himself, Ganon stepped out from under the ermine's bulwark, heading back to the west where the faerie grotto and swampy plaza were. Zelda followed with Link behind her, not saying a word to each other. After wading through the shallows in a single-file procession, the boar paused on a giant lilypad, beyond which the swamp became deeper.

I think we can skirt by to the right. Zelda caught up, stepping onto the pad as well.

Shh—

What, do you see something?

SPLSHHH! Almost there! Link announced, throwing his block into the wet depths.

Quiet. she shushed.

What? Is the faerie… the bunny looked about.

The boar stood up tall, wiping rain from his brow, No, on the platform…

Is that someone approaching? Through the sheets of rain, Zelda caught glimpses of a distant gait stepping over the soggy causeway toward the small square platform.

I don't see anything. Link was looking to the west as well.

It's gone. she said. Wait, there—emerging from the large plant in the middle of the—

—Where?

From behind the frond in the platform; walking to the right… she clarified quietly.

We better go tell them there's nothing there. said the bunny knight, bouncing off the enormous lilypad. Let's not keep them waiting. I found a route… Over here! Link beckoned through the storm while the boar and ermine remained on the pad. Alriiight… Has the water level risen since the other day? mumbled the bunny, hoping to retrace his bog path from yesterday. Where was that berm to walk on? Link wobbled in ankle-deep water as the gusts blew with newfound force, searching for the squishy esker that they had traversed previously. Pausing to look up, he saw the figure farther along the platform, where they discovered a deadend and nothing of interest before. Unable to get there in time, the bunny waved at the distant wanderer, who then spun around with something in its hand. Link chuckled, mistaking the stranger's spin as a response to his long distance greeting. *TSSSEEOOO!* a pillar of coursing lightning struck the figure – or what it held, now pointing to the sky. Link didn't realize the air pressure was shifting until he saw Ganon and Zelda bracing against the oncoming gale, visibly rushing across the dark green water. As if the entire swamp was inhaling, the air pulled toward the blinding twister of energy causing small whitecaps to form all around them while illuminating the entire swamp. The ermine's mirror shield caught the gust and sent her soaring as she refused to let go of the cherished foil. Fumbling to arrest her takeoff with his one hand, the boar's bomb bag filled up like a spinnaker too, lifting him up and sailing to the west as well. Wait! the bunny knight ran after his companions who had splashed down into a deep spot not far from the lilypad; halfway to the platform. Stumbling from the lashing tailwind, Link whipped his cane and summoned a red block to anchor himself from the impromptu freezing hurricane. Much closer now, he could see the figure who was engulfed in a field of electricity. When this globe of energy transformed into a radial array of smaller bright spheres, Link was certain what he saw the stranger holding. *BRR-BRR-BRR-BRR-BRR...* the bright lights rapidly circled the figure for only a few rotations, then flew off into the sky in all directions. The sky pulsated from a diffuse scintillating voltage deep within the storm clouds above. Link ran past the faerie grotto and around the westside of the deep trench where Ganon and Zelda treaded water. Grab this! Link offered the hook of his cane to the boar who was determined to get out on his own.

You feel that? Zelda asked, dumping water out of her shield. Within seconds of arising, the wind had abated, but now the ground trembled, further agitating the frothed up swamp. Link turned to look to the platform where the figure still stood. What was previously a large frond at the end of the causeway began to shake and jolt and rear a grotesque head of tendrils.

Is it—awake? the bunny asked. The three exiles watched as the plant rose up to resemble another gaping horror, not unlike the uninviting viny entrance to the faerie's grotto, but almost twice as large. The wind and shaking completely stopped, along with the torrential rain that preceded. A dull overcast remained, but the storm had passed. The figure never once turned to look aside, and entered the cavity without delay. Hey wait! Link yelled at the stranger, then turning to the princess, I think we now know where the swamp ends and the mire begins! The bunny knight ran up the causeway and onto the platform, stopping at the freshly emerged trellis doorway still dripping with a shiny varnish of dredged muck.

The ermine scuffed her boot along the unique tile that exhibited the same engraving as the Nayru medallion. *Nff...* That unmistakable fragrance of hot burnt bog; scorched sludge...

This must've been where that giant flash of lightning struck the ground. said the bunny rubbing the dark marks with the butt of his cane.

What? the princess asked.

Did you not see that?

See what.

The boar also shook his head. We were taking a swim.

Water was warmer than I anticipated! she laughed back.

You didn't see the lightning? The orbiting balls of energy? THE MASTER SWORD?!

Where? Yes, flashes for sure. But what about a sword? she batted her wet-look lashes.

I am nearly certain, whoever that was—summoned the power of Nayru by holding the Master Sword up to the sky. I was too far away to see the insignia on the ricasso, but that quillon and edge are unlike any other, even from a distance. They must have the goddess medallion!

Ganon drew a deep breath then coughed at the wet fart aroma wafting from the mire. Are you asking for our permission, or what? *Hugh-ugh.*

Huh?

The princess chortled, then caught a whiff and gagged a bit.

All I know is they went this way… said Ganon, making an *after-you* gesture.

Maybe you can take it from the stranger when we catch up with them, just like you stole the sigil from Zelda on the pinnacle and caused all this trouble in the first place!

Yes, let's plan on that. Because I trust whoever has the Master Sword will give it up freely whenever we meet them. he snorted, But I wasn't the one who activated the ether stone. If you're still sore about that, why not go ask the faerie to 'sooth your wounds'?

Would be worth a detour… Zelda was reminded of her broken ermine nail.

Not when the way ahead is open to us. Link ignored Ganon's taunting retort and led the way into the previously submerged temple entrance. This is our chance to save the dissident who beseeched Nayru whose divine power was ironically unleashed just now for her rescue! The goddess heard that healer's call after all, despite being detained in this disgusting rut.

Who—whose—what now. Ganon jiggled his jowls.

There's another healer? You're not talking about the faerie nextdoor are you…

I mean—maiden. said the bunny, thinking about the ant/bee's abducted fiancée. Odiferous as this situation is, all I'm trying to say is I have a good feeling that the goddess is with us, and duping whoever used her medallion to raise up the mire unbeknownst to our quest. We're on a mission from Nayru now! said Link planting his cane with each step. *Heed the call…*

The ermine princess shook her head. What? He started it. said the boar, ducking to enter the sunken dungeon, beefing under his breath, Damn sword, that's the real culprit here.

The Miserable Bowels of the Mire

Yeuch. Heuch-heuh! Standing just one stride in, Zelda hacked with her hand at her mouth, unsure of whether she wanted to go any deeper due to the vile pungency of the place. Ganon and Link seemed less affected by the humid reek of the mire; notes of low tide and methane. The boar was hammering away, splatting perturbed yellow zol[36] jellies that oozed up from the cracks in the cobbled floor. The bunny assisted this pest removal operation by shining light down the hallway with the lantern hanging on his cane hook. *I can taste the smell.*

Ye who enters the mouth of the mire, will have the mire in their mouth! said the bunny knight in a deep voice, blimping out his cheeks like a blowfish.

The ermine burped, patted her chest, then winced her way down the hallway past the unlikely pair of custodians cleaning up the oily creeps. There's a gap here, she alerted them.

Ganon wiped the zol goo on his bag, That's too wide to jump, he said while cautiously looking into the fathomless fall.

Let me try something. said Link facing a cubic protrusion with his back to the pit.

What are you doing? she asked as he pushed on the budgeless stone bollard.

If I bonk myself against this, I should be able to bounce across the hole behind me... Link prepared for the proposed feat, fastened his matching red lantern to his cane.

I think we need to use a rope, or somehow pull ourselves across.

Link clapped his hands, and within arm's reach lunged at the cube, knocking himself backwards, landing on the opposite side. Uh! Yoof—YES! See! the bunny rubbed his face, worried he might've chipped an incisor tooth when body-checking the rigid block (he was fine).

After reconsidering a straightforward leap across the pit, the boar, and then the ermine imitated the bunny's counterintuitive block-bounce maneuver, bringing all three of them safely to the farside

---

36 Minor grime golems that are mostly water – animated from sludge puddles and clogged plumbing.

together. I'm not sure why that worked, or how you thought of it Link, but hopefully it's the last time we have to do something like that. said Zelda proceeding down the stairs.

Two wriggling popo[37] polyps immediately approached which Ganon made quick work of. Farther down the hall, bodiless shades threw arcs of cutting magic at the exiles that Zelda was able to block with her mirror shield. These acolytes had no bodies, but all wore green wizard robes with the same wide-brimmed hat; their visage just a sooty void with white glowing eyes. The exiles stayed close together, as the wizrobes[38] were notorious for phasing in and out of tangibility, teleporting around before arcing their projectile evocations. Ganon and Link quickly became confident of stepping out from Zelda's protection, as the wizrobes predictably began their spell with a silent hand seal gesture that provided just enough time (if they were close enough) to preempt an attack. While terrifying, elusive, and deadly, the vapid liches were as easy to vanquish as folding laundry; their robe and hat drifting loosely to the ground with even a gentle whack. Risking the loss of their guard, the ermine tried her hand with the occasional shot of her bow, although this made the bunny and boar noticeably nervous. The levitating green robes tugged backwards from the force of the exiting arrow before promptly falling limp and scattering the volatile evil wrapped within.

Zelda never got used to the smell, but the worst of it seemed behind them, as the deeper they went the cooler it became, presumably dampening the dank odor, she thought. Her spirits were lifted when they found yet another fragment of a map that magically fit itself to her existing chart, embellishing the schema of the mire. With the dungeon floorplan to reference in detail, Zelda's maiden crystal now pointed to a particular room, which the exiles were relieved to see was not far ahead. As before, Ganon regularly insisted on placing his compass by the

---

37 The subterranean juvenile stage of a ropa. Both the popo and adult ropa have stinging tentacles however the popo has adapted to feed on small prey and cannot stun a grown man like a ropa can.

38 Undead assistants to the wizard Agahnim, granted undying permanence in exchange for their will. Unlike the hyu (or poe) whose soul is bound inside a lantern, the wizrobe's soul is loosely shrouded. Formerly an arcane mage of Hyrule that became an evil lich forever subservient in the Dark World.

map, which prompted the enchanted parchment to etch and illuminate their current location, as long as the navigational aids were proximal. Whenever given the chance Link eagerly volunteered his small key, but as with their previous experience in the Palace of Darkness, he repeatedly got it jammed. The bunny knight vented his mounting frustration by repeatedly reminding the boar what the nymph had mentioned: that they might find a prosthesis for him deep in the mire. Ganon cared as little as he did in the reflection pool grotto and ignored the bunny, interpreting Link's enthusiasm as fake, and an oblique prodding at his disability acquired by losing a hand to the Helmasaur King. The boar's suspicion of his antagonist's passive aggression was confirmed when they came upon a large chest that yielded a strange contraption: a retractable grappling hook with an inexplicable engineering that certainly predated modern Hylian mechanisms. Like a grabby child Link took it first, but was given a talking to from the princess. She reminded him of what the nearby faerie had said about 'soothing wounds' – and that the boar needed it more. With folded arms the boar allowed the princess to litigate on his behalf, yielding an aspirated assent of appreciation to the crestfallen and butthurt bunny who handed the hookshot[39] over to his nemesis. With surprising ease, Ganon fixed the device to his left wrist. And consistent with its name, a whip of his forearm *CLING-NG-NG-NG!* sent the hook shooting straight out.

The hook and its chain were strangely unaffected by gravity, never arcing which they superstitiously attributed to the sophistication of ancient technology. If the hook successfully landed, the small device immediately pulled the entire weight of Ganon through the air to the target with great speed. Or if the contact could not be hooked (or nothing was hooked before reaching its full length) then the chain would retract without delay, again perfectly straight and without any slack. After some casual experimentation, they deduced a surprisingly binary functionality of the hookshot that adhered to a boolean dynamic: the grapled object pulled to Ganon if it weighed less than him, but the

---

39 A spring-loaded grappling hook. Originally engineered for unknown purposes, an Ancient Hylian artifact.

opposite happened when vice versa. The boar and grappled object never met halfway however – unless they were hypothetically the exact same weight which seems practically out of the question. Halfway never happened, but who knows! As the hookshot defied their kinetic intuition and modern grasp of physics. Equally impressive, they were mystified how the whole chain housed in the slender handle; didn't seem possible.

Truly a remarkable artifact. Link complimented Ganon, hoping for some amnesty from the boar and also ermine, who he felt had both unfairly cast him as a tagalong nuisance to be merely tolerated. *Tolerance is a miserable ghetto.* he whined to himself, feeling marginalized.

What? the princess asked, sounding more and more like a condescending big sister. Ganon heard him though, and as he was a Gerudo, knew all too well what the bunny meant.

The nettled knight shook his bunny ears, Oh-nothing princess, we must be getting close to the second maiden. What does your map say? The ermine and boar were as thick as thieves, consulting the chart together while Link leaned against a doorway with ascending stairs.

Up we go, and just a few rooms away, she confirmed. Her necklace corroborated the compass, gravitating toward a chamber delineated on the map that was above and ahead of them one level. Ganon went up the stairs with Zelda behind him, while Link remained where he stood with one ankle crossed over the other, slouching against the stone frame of the door.

Wizrobes! the boar reported. The bunny sighed, joining them in the room above where two lifeless piles of cloth on the floor indicated the malevolent shades were already dealt with.

There's a symmetry here– the princess backtracked from the next room over. Two more unlit beacons on the other side. Link, can you light them for us? she said, pointing to his lantern.

Maybe I'm out of magic. he evaded his chivalric duty, not feeling like helping out much.

Link. Your tunic is still bright green. You have one job!

I have more than one job! Or that's not the one job; if I do…

Guh guh… the boar scoffed and proceeded onward. Coming? he called back, completely unconcerned with the flameless floor braziers.

Tsche! the princess chlicked[40] her tongue on the roof of her mouth in consonant disapproval of her knight's insubordination, passing into the subsequent room.

Wait. the boar cautioned Zelda. We don't know what's beyond that door. he said, tapping his prosthetic hookshot with his right hand. If the maiden you got around your neck was guarded by a humongous helmasaur, we can expect the worst here in Misery Mire as well.

It's okay, I got a magical lantern. Link joked, stepping up behind them.

That's not magical, it's just a lantern. said the princess.

Pretty sure it burns clean ethereal energy – if you believe in magic…

There is no preparation. said Ganon, inadvertently sagacious sounding.

Yeah, we're as prepared as we can be, let's get into it! Link readied his cane. If things get really bad, let's just plan on grabbing Zelda and she can gaze into the hand mirror again…

Don't touch me.

I wasn't—whatever! Link proceeded into the chamber that the map marked as their destination and location of the imprisoned maiden. Ganon and Zelda dashed in behind him.

The boar lowered his hammer; the ermine her shield. What is this? she said.

Is this a deadend? the boar was unimpressed.

There is something… Link pointed to an eye-catching plaque at the end of the hall.

Zelda pushed herself in front of the bunny knight, and strutted up to the tablet. A vague mentalese spoke to her, a syntactic sensation without words. She looked back to see if Ganon and Link heard it too; they followed with a languor she mistook as hesitation. A few steps closer to the pristine white plaque on the wall, she then realized everything around her had slowed. Several strides behind her, the bunny and boar were suspended in a stiff stasis. Reason would have the ermine step away, but she rather enjoyed this feeling: a privileged solitude beyond the usual

40   A preceding punctuation. To palate click the tongue while opening your mouth before speaking.

laws of space and time. She could feel the air full of a viscous energy that made her fur tingle and stand on tangent. And while the tablet was stationary, something about its presence seemed independent of the slowing force she was immersed in. Without a doubt, the unusual plaque was the epicenter, but there was a defiant attitude about it, as this stone tile seemed to remain apart from its own effect. *I've come this far on my own, and what a forfeit to turn back!* Zelda rationalized proceeding. The ermine princess reached out and placed her hand on the detailed face of the console that exhibited a large embossed triangle with intricate intaglio.

A Pearl for a Pendant

You were saying, 'liminal' something... My apologies, I interrupted you. said the imp, looking down her nose and exhaling a swirling puff of smoke. Hey! she greeted a third who had materialized, equidistant from the center and from each other. Don't worry, this *isn't* the afterlife. Midna reassured the ermine newcomer. Dumbfounded, Zelda considered her words, but the imp to her right gave her no chance and prattled on. I just learned this as well, we're in the Sacred– wait, this *is* the Sacred Realm, right? Midna turned to the old man again for confirmation.

That is correct, but more precisely, this is the Chamber of Sages, a liminal aspect.

As in, between the two realms? Zelda spoke from where she stood.

Resting place of the Golden Power, opened from the Temple of Light. said the man.

The imp squinted. Over here? she waved to the center of their gathering, which was neither a chamber nor a temple but more of a floating mesa rock island. Midna attempted to step forward to look around, but found her feet bound to the blue pedestal that she stood on. Well. I'm no stranger to the Sacred Realm, nor the Triforce. But I've never been *here* before. What is this all about? And why can't I step off this—*uh!*

You are projected, both of you, through the telepathy tiles[41] you touched.

---

41   An elaborately carved low-relief plaque tablet found throughout Hyrule at various ancient sites. Many archaeologists have noted a strange magnetism about these white tiles, and certain people have claimed to have had visions or traveled to another place when touching them, but it is

We're not really here? Zelda noticed the similar bluestone she arrived on would not permit her to step off. Around them were six other stones: three of red and three of green.

We are where we were, *at least in body.* said the heady imp as if she knew.

Yes, but time there has stopped, for the duration of this conversation.

I'm all too familiar with eternal layovers. the imp sighed, But unless you've got a compelling reason to linger here, I should get back to my desert combing.

Who are you? Zelda asked the imp.

Destiny has brought us here. the old man addressed Midna, distracting her from responding to the ermine. You have the pendant of wisdom, from the Desert Palace in Hyrule.

Fr-From the Light World? the ermine stuttered, recognizing the treasured necklace in the imp's possession now that the old man mentioned it. Do you have the other two?

The imp took the pendant off and blithely swung the blue orb around. Yeahhh… I was hoping the moon pearl would lift my curse. But it's pretty—*worthless.* Didn't do a thing! she said with the pipe bobbing in her pursed lips and the silver necklace looped around her wrists in a figure eight, resembling handcuffs. Midna stood like a magician about to perform an escape.

What? Is the pendant of wisdom *also the moon pearl?* But how could that be? With my knight, I found the three pendants, including the very one you hold now. We entrusted it to…

Alas, there is only one pendant amongst us here, said the old man pointing to Midna. But all three goddess mirrors are present. Princess Zelda in possession of two: the gilded shield of Din, and the more conventional looking glass handheld reflector of Nayru…

And? Midna shrugged. The ermine was taken aback hearing her name and proper title.

The old man held out an opalescent sphere that was the size of a large marble.

---

unclear why some have this experience. Also called 'palace reliefs' by tourists, but touching them is now prohibited by the magistrate.

The third goddess mirror, the moon pearl of Farore! Zelda clapped.

So this isn't the pearl? Midna dropped the pendant she was playing with and stared longingly at what the old man held from the pedestal he stood on, also blue like theirs, and about fifteen-and-a-half equidistant paces away from either Midna or Zelda.

I understand you searched the Desert Palace for this treasure. But you were mistaken, as it was not in this ancient seabed that has long since dried into a desert, but on the mountain that was raised during the cataclysm. The pearl began to shine like a low-slung celestial object.

Zelda tried to imagine the Desert of Mystery as a once verdant land with thriving waterways and estuaries, recalling what the faerie had said earlier in the grotto.

Ok, what do you want for it? said Midna.

If you give me the pendant of wisdom.

This worthless gaudy thing? she said, picking up the pendant.

Wait– the ermine interjected. That pendant might be worthless as per your expectations, but that doesn't mean it isn't *invaluable* and filled with great purpose! You know who I am, but whom do we have the telepathic privilege of speaking with? Zelda gestured to the old man.

I am Sahasrahla, descendant of the Wise Men, and rightful protector of all things Nayru.

Oh, your wife is looking for you. said Zelda, having never met her missing husband.

He pocketed the pearl, and pointed to the blue orb at the imp's feet. The pendants must be gathered to mend the Golden Power that was rended asunder by the King of Thieves.

Is that so. said the imp incredulously.

The fate of Hyrule depends upon my request. You are cursed like all Twili, but redemption is within reach. The old man gesticulated, This—is the seal, rivened between the realms as a gateway to the Golden Power. The erecting of this boundless place was coeval with the cataclysm, a terrible divine intervention that resulted in the destruction of Hyrule, but the emergence and construction of the cosmic chamber in which we now converse in.

So if this was the seal that caused the Great Cataclysm... mused the imp, as another thought occurred to her, This was where Ganondorf was imprisoned, wasn't it.

Ganon, King of Thieves. That is right. said Sahasrahla.

I-euhhh, I don't see him here. Or any way to get out for that matter. Mmm. the wise old man nodded.

Someone must've let him out. said the impudent interlocutor Midna, holding her pipe aside with a supinated supple wrist. Who would do that? And what for...

Sahasrahla looked about, as if to double check that there were no obvious exits.

And why would I be locked in twilight forever, only to be suddenly freed; liberated to enter the Light World of Hyrule? she sassed more supposition. I don't know who you are... Midna addressed the blue pendant that she dangled in front of her face, But if I were to guess, none of this is a coincidence. *Destiny* as you say... the imp lowered her disappointing discovery and looked to Sahasrahla, If you brought us here, *then perhaps you let Ganondorf out!*

Who would be so bold to defy the goddesses and their decree! said the old man.

I'm just saying, whoever has the power to spring the latch of Ganondorf's cage here could also open a rift between realms, such as the sparkling portal that I just happened to stumble upon in the southwest canyons, you know that area, past the Plains of Ruin.

Is that inexplicable effulgent egress still accessible? stammered the wide-eyed ermine, having hiked through there on their way to the swamp after leaving Link's uncle's place. Did you happen to cross paths with a hinox?

Yes. Midna responded about the cyclops.

The portal is open! Zelda misinterpreted her.

No, or at least not in the Light World; it was one-way, as when I arrived there wasn't any return twinkling at my heels. Not to mention, nothing came behind me either, and thanks be for it because that cyclops really wanted *this book* after what's-her-name delivered it; Epheremelda!

What did you just call me? Zelda thought the imp was mocking her with a nickname.

So I suspect it closed on the other side too and was for one-soul only...

Ah, just for—

ME! Eh, must've disappeared after I stepped through. she toked her pipe.

Zelda inferred to herself, whoever opened that portal must've had the Key of Realms... Collecting her thoughts she then asked, But why would this Twili— excuse me my little shady lady, what is your name? You never introduced yourself.

Midna, formerly Midnadorf as I was known — *before I was warped into this diminutive lilliputian impy form.* she said, throwing her voice to sound unnaturally shrill and helpless.

Nice to meet you Midna—dorf. said Zelda, politely ignoring the obvious coincidence of how her name sounded so much like Ganondorf. Why would you be released from the—

—*Midnight?* No no... Twilight. Twilight Realm. said Midna in all seriousness.

You mean, Dark World? That's where I am—my body is; telepathy tile and such.

The imp paused, then smiled, *Dark, Twilight, Shadow...* Same situation yes.

Sacred Realm. said Sahasrahla, adding another synonym, Before the King of Thieves made his umbral and most evil wish upon the Golden Power.

Many ways to describe something that doesn't add up. said Midna, holding her chin.

How long have you been in the midnight, I mean, twilight, Midna? asked the ermine looking askance, cross-checking in her head for any contradictions to all this new information.

Since the cataclysm, and let me tell you, I was there with Ganondorf when the ancient world was shattered, but I have not seen him since our fates were sealed. said Midna.

You couldn't have been. Zelda feigned disbelief but was surprised, and considered disclosing her current association with the notorious boar Ganon, but if this was the very place where he was imprisoned, she remained quiet for fear of getting trapped in this telepathic void.

Your banishment was not commensurate with his imprisonment. he told the imp Midna, Far older than myself, your memories precede my own, as these events were long before *Sahasrahla* was born – legends to my ears! You see, your curse was also a stasis, in effect preserving your youth as the rest of us aged in a natural flow of time.

Same for Ganon? the ermine inquired, quietly curious why Sahasrahla would refer to himself in the third person, but suspected it was nothing more than an elder shibboleth.

Accordingly the King of Thieves was locked in time, yes. But we Wise Men are tasked with restoring the Triforce, which the pendant of wisdom is a necessary component to our imperative. I only offer you the moon pearl to right what was undue punishment, and for your compliance of course – to the high will of Hylia and her daughters. he said in a paternal tone, again gesturing to the blue orb held by the imp.

So this is one of the fabled pendants, eh. An encapsulation of the three sacred flames, must be Nayru's blue fire here at my breast.

Each pendant holds a breath from one of the three goddesses. Zelda added, And the pendants of virtue are what activate Hylia's Key for whoever is worthy to wield it!

Activate a what? Midna asked.

The Master Sword, which was in our possession until taking the goddess medallion brought a banishing judgment upon us; disarmed my knight and exiled the three of—I mean, him and I, to the Dark World. she explained, remembering not to mention Ganon, just to be safe.

I see. Midna mused, unfamiliar with such medallions. And you need this again, I take it?

You *did* take it. Zelda interpreted her figurative language as literal.

Well excuuuse me! I thought this was the moon pearl. But who cares. Why shouldn't I also take up the old man's offer here, and absolve myself of this dismal undue and horribly disproportionate punishment?

This isn't about you. We need it, again. Don't you see?

So does Sahasrahla. said Midna, jiggling the pendant toward the old man. But what do you have to offer *Prin-cess Zel-da?*

The ermine would not let Midna's mockery go unchecked. Taking the pendant of wisdom from the Temple of Nayru for your own vain purpose was a most irreverent transgression. Zelda leaned into her reprimanding of the imp. I'm on a greater mission—*of destiny!* to save the world from the pestilences, and you're just looking for a makeover!

No makeover is without destiny! said the imp caressing her face. And how did you come upon the pendants of virtue? Were you granted license—

In fact, I was—rather, Link, my knight, he was instructed by a voice. *Oh, a voice you say?* And that makes it right. Midna chaffed.

Sahasrahla remained quiet as the ermine and imp debated the rightful fate of the orb.

I don't know why you were banished, but even if it was undeserved, what makes you think *stealing* a sacred artifact is justified? Zelda pressed, unwilling to tell Midna that she and Link entrusted the pendant of wisdom to a healer after effectively heisting the Master Sword.

I was going to put it back after using it! But let's be real— *borrowing what I thought was the moon pearl* to lift my curse with the honest-to-goddess intention of putting it back after using it, is not as bad as bartering this sacred pendant for the supposedly-actual moon pearl with a strange old man I've never met before in a telepathic liminal dreamstate chamber, *right?*

Tenuous train of thought there, but I get what you're saying. *So don't.*

And instead what... Give it to an even stranger rat girl?

Stoat. As if I'm the only one warped here! And why are you undermining your own argument? Zelda was sick of the imp's sardonic nonsense.

You just want this pendant to trade for the moon pearl as well! As we both know what it does. The point is, no goddess pendant should be traded – AND I DON'T TRUST YOU.

If there's nothing I can say to convince you of the legitimacy of my quest, then so be it. But the moon pearl is not a permanent solution to your predicament or an actual resolution to the warping curse caused by the Golden Power: it's just a temporary reversion, conditional on keeping the pearl! No one suddenly becomes their former self because of a bauble possessed. Only a *child* would think so, or rationalize that bartering off a theft amounts to redemption.

I didn't STEAL ANYTHING! the imp squealed, infuriated by the 'child' remark. But even if I had, is there any *right* way to lift a curse?

The ermine folded her arms. Stolen, she muttered. Two wrongs don't make a right.

Neither does a right by a wrong! said the imp heavily, rolling her eye with heavy insight.

Right! the ermine abruptly agreed with an impassioned tirade, When the whole world has gone dumb with darkness, and the laws of the magistrate are impossible not to transgress, and all reason thoroughly warped into the rationalization of shameful acts and evil work, then the only right deed is to step **out** of line…

Now we're talking! Midna cheered at the ermine's unexpectedly sympathetic intelligence.

Forgive me if I'm merely rationalizing. said the ermine calmly, brushing down a tuft of fur that got riled up.

Oh not at all. But 'out' of what?

Sahasrahla coughed. The Swamp of Evil is the topology of rationalization, but here your heart and mind is unfettered; beyond whatever warp you project through the telepathy tiles.

Well that *is* where I am *tele-tiling* in from. Zelda said to Sahasrahla then turned to answer Midna's question, To not cross, trip or straddle the prescriptive line drawn before us. The ermine waved at her feet, denoting an imaginary 'line' of moral boundaries. But sidestep it into a new dimension, Zelda bobbed her knees in a demonstrative dance (unable to move her feet from the blue pedestal). Perhaps as we now stand, *beyond a single axis of oversimplified opposition.*

Always up for an abstract aside, the imp happily nodded. I see your moral geometry, a line drawn between diametric imperatives, a black-and-white ultimatum for example, is just one dimension. And if both extremes are damnation, then it's a false choice that we *must* step out from. And yet there are three of us standing here – that is a triangle; two dimensions. But how did we get talking about this polygonal conduct again… Midna lost track. What's your point?

Precisely… the ermine princess thought Midna was making a pun, apropos geometry. My 'point' is this. *To be right by the wizard's rule would be a celebrated charade of morality!* Or as you said, 'a right by a wrong'. Zelda wondered if the monocular imp was predisposed to fixating on points, as the little creature was warped to have only one eye, much like a hinox. Although the crown that covered the left side of her face implied that there was an eye there.

Great to know if I happen to meet this magistrate wizard, now that I'm out and about. Midna stretched at the idea, warming up to Zelda having finished their philosophical sparring.

Where are you projecting from Midna? A telepathy tile in the Desert Palace?

In the Desert of Mystery, Light World, Hyrule, you know it.

Allow me to *borrow* your 'borrowing', if you will.

The imp cocked her head.

How about this, you can keep the pendant of wisdom, if you are willing to volunteer the flame within for reclaiming the Master Sword that my knight Link is seeking?

Is it on this side of the split – in the Light World?

Yes, Hyrule *was* where the sword was set in stone to rest for all eternity.

Well, I'm already here so I got no excuse not to… But what's in this for me?

An opportunity to sidestep yourself and serve the kingdom? the ermine shrugged.

Saving Hyrule is a thankless task. Something I will never volunteer for again. How do you think I got to be like this? said the imp, now turning to the old man, Sahasrahla I imagine Princess Zelda's invitation has something to do with your objective as well – recovering the Triforce and lifting the curse of the Dark World. If I help her, will you give me the moon pearl?

I'm afraid not... the old man sighed, Your knight's quest for the Key of Realms is hopeless if it is now in the possession of the Prime Sages as Princess Zelda reported.

Who? asked Zelda, wondering when she heard that appellation before.

Is that the wizard, mister? said the imp.

Now I remember. The ermine inhaled deeply, unsure if she had mentioned this. That is how he introduced himself, before taking the Master Sword and sending us to the Dark World.

So the sword has already been taken? What does this matter then? said Midna, dangling the blue pendant of wisdom while reconsidering her stance.

If the pendants are found, I believe that means the sword is put to rest. said Zelda.

Oh, so these so-called Prime Sages stowed it away somehow? Who are they...

We can't know for sure, and there were actually three of them, impossible to look at. Their dark silhouettes resembled eclipses with excruciating bright light radiating from the edges. Regardless, even if the wizard was only a proxy for those Prime Sages, I have no doubts the Chief Minister Agahnim—

—Who is the wizard. said the imp intensely and wanting clarification.

Yes, same person. He surely played *some* diabolical part in all this darkness. At best, if we are to give Agahnim any benefit of the doubt, the lies he fed to the king and the corruption he seeded in Hyrule *inadvertently* created an opportunity for the one who touched the Triforce...

We must be careful then, as we do not know who is in league with the King of Thieves. Sahasrahla warned, however all this equivocation had Midna clearly twisted up in a memory. Princess Midnadorf, the old man Sahasrahla grumbled, we don't have time for reminiscing.

I didn't say anything. Midna didn't know she was that transparent when thinking to herself. She then asked, If the Nayru pendant is here, then there are two others: Din, Farore... And sounds like the sword is locked away too – but where? And what's the rush Sahasrahla.

Hand me the pendant of wisdom and I will release us from this liminal aspect.

Wait— *you're a princess?* Zelda couldn't believe it.

Time is no matter here! said Midna in response to the old man's hustling. Of course we have time, and from one princess to another, Zelda deserves the full picture. The imp put her pipe away, saving all her breath for the ensuing exposition.

Sahasrahla clasped his hands in his sleeves and audibly exhaled with impatience.

That said, my story begins at least ten-thousand years ago, so I'll do my best to keep it short. prefaced the imp, self-conscious of how short she was as well.

You've been trapped in the twilight for that long?

Midna continued, As you most likely already know, before the Interloper War, an insidious lie; revisionist history! she coughed politely into a fist, Let's be objective: there was a preceding conflict known as the Hylian Schism – civil wars amongst many factions and tribes that fought for the location of the Triforce that was presumed to reside in the Sacred Realm. Nobody knew where this place was however, and truer than we could have known, everyone expected the Sacred Realm would reveal itself if the Triforce was discovered, or conversely.

I have heard of this, yes. Zelda thought of what Ganon had mentioned when they were in the mountain caves descending from Turtle Rock – about his enlisted service at that distant time in Hyrule's ancient past. Please, continue.

So, the Hylian Schism[42] is also referred to as the Hyrulean Civil War, the first great kingdom-wide conflict all spurred by rumors of a supreme power left by the goddesses.

The Triforce.

Yes, and guess who insisted that the only solution to the unstoppable escalating discord was to possess the disputed source of the strife itself?

Zelda shook her head.

---

42   The first 'Great War' of Ancient Hyrule that shattered intertribal pacts throughout the old kingdom. These civil wars were motivated by the pursuit of the Golden Power, ending in the Great Cataclysm.

That's an unfair question, this *was* a long time ago. What I'm getting at is that the plot was in plain sight from the very beginning. While I've never heard of the 'chief minister' you railed against, your description of him—of Agahnim reminds me of what happened ages ago. What I have never understood is why more of us didn't see it sooner. she paused and stared.

...

Or even more confounding, why those of us who did see the scheme in plain didn't call it out as such while we still had the chance. Midna pinched her chin.

But who are you referring to?

A powerful man of Ancient Hyrule known then as Rauru... she shook her fused crown, We should've known better. Rauru convinced the king at the time that the only way to end the wars that vied for supremacy over the Sacred Realm, was to take the Triforce first, and end the conflict with unparalleled power.

I understand, the solution he suggested sounds like the very cause of the conflict to begin with. Zelda thought it over, Are you suggesting Rauru fomented the wars such that he could use it as an excuse to seek the Golden Power?

This wasn't apparent to me then, but Rauru knew he could not enter the Sacred Realm himself—he needed someone to do it for him, not only because the location was unknown but also because the repercussions were potentially too risky; if something went wrong, he'd need somebody to blame. So after setting Hyrule ablaze with hate, Rauru urged the king to elect a marginal tribe of the kingdom, one especially adept at both martial and magical arts.

The Gerudo?

Some don't like us because, you know, *can't spell Gerudo without 'rude'*. she said dryly. My brother was a powerful – but gentle – general of the Gerudo, Prince Ganondorf, and well, you can infer who I am then. said the imp, crossing her arms and chuckling in contrapposto.

An unfortunate kinship. said the old man. To have the King of Thieves as your sibling brought undue doom upon your head... Midnadorf the Soothsayer.

You can sooth too! Doom by association, *what other kind is there?* said Zelda bitterly. And so after the enlistment of Rauru, the Gerudo general and his sorceress sister led an entourage into the Sacred Realm, more than ten millennia ago?

The road to the Triforce is trodden with good intentions easily betrayed. Midna sighed, The Gerudo wanted nothing to do with the civil wars, and because of our remote provenance, we were safely exempt from the many skirmishes and incursions of the schism at that time.

Did you succeed in your mission however?

We came upon the Triforce.

Did you make a wish?

Only in counsel, but not consummated.

What do you mean?

The imp pursed her lips in frustration, Perhaps we should have. Perhaps we could have set everything right—right then and there. The saga of Hyrule would not be not so simple or succinct however. When we came upon the Triforce within the Temple of Light, the sentience of the divine relic revealed to us that Rauru's will was not benevolent—that he caused the civil wars as both a distraction and excuse to break into the Sacred Realm, *which we found in our native Golden Land by the way.* We had been made pawns for his scheme, and upon realizing so decided against touching, and assuredly against taking the Triforce as per Rauru's orders.

Amazing how familiar this story sounds. said the ermine, sitting on her bluestone.

The imp sat down too, One would hope tales such as this do not recur, but this was a decem millennium[43] ago and then some—more than enough for any kingdom to forget...

We do not respect the legends of the ancients as we should. Sahasrahla nodded.

---

43   Ten-thousand years; ten millennia. The approximate time since the Great Cataclysm.

Hardly heroes. she said cross legged. With the enlightening aura of the Golden Power still fresh upon us, we had a newfound purpose to bring the king back to his senses as well.

To reveal the evil designs of Rauru? Zelda leaned against her mirror shield.

But who should be waiting for us at the gate? said Midna, standing up.

The first and eldest of the Prime Sages. said Sahasrahla.

No kidding. said Midna, unaware of that association.

The Ancient Sage. the old man added.

Zedla gasped, I suspect I've met him, on the Precipitous Pinnacle. But how could—

So he's back? I wouldn't put reincarnation past a soul as dead set as that hellbent man! Regardless, Rauru was one step ahead of us – waiting for us to return with the king's full guard at his guileful command. We were vastly outnumbered; immediately besieged and all but slain.

How did you... Zelda skipped to the aftermath, too distraught to ask about the ambush.

A small number of us remained, including my brother and I, captured by the knights who were yoked by Rauru's manipulation. Our party awaited a certain and unceremonious execution.

How did you escape then?

While in its supreme presence, we confided a wish for the Triforce, which it acknowledged. Having not touched it however, the wish remained unfulfilled.

What did you wish for?

An end to the Hyrulean Civil War.

That's honorable of you. said the ermine, quite surprised.

Perhaps our wish was half-granted however, as we got what we prayed for at the base of the Golden Power, *but not on our terms.*

At a great and tragic cost. said Sahasrahla.

The imp wiped a tear from her right eye remembering the trauma. Because we had communed with the essence of the Triforce, the goddesses themselves descended to Hyrule, there in the Golden Land at the steps of the Temple of Light. In fiery reproach, they demanded to know who had spilt so much blood of what they saw as 'slain pilgrims' to the Sacred Realm. Restrained and silenced at spearpoint, my brother and I could not speak for ourselves.

Could they not probe your thoughts? asked Sahasrahla.

The goddesses judge us by our word, and by our appearances. said Midna.

Contrary to what many presume! And who answered for the carnage? asked the ermine, enthralled by the imp's firsthand account of the ancient tale otherwise left to apocryphal legend.

Midna took a deep breath. Rauru cast us as 'The Interlopers', a band of thieves in search of supremacy at any cost – a description suited for himself. He lied to the goddesses, condemning my brother and I as murderers. To this day, I wonder how his deceit swayed even the heavenly host, as without any deliberation the goddesses induced the Great Cataclysm.

What for? *They couldn't have believed him…* Could they?

As punishment for defiling the Sacred Realm with our petty schism – I mean, Hyrule's petty schism; the Gerudo wanted nothing to do with it.

Before we were sealed… was the first utterance of Ganondorf's now infamous epithet, as Rauru named my brother The King of Thieves, and for me: The Twilight Princess.

The ermine stood up out of respect.

Nayru, Din, and Farore – the three goddess daughters then upheaved Hyrule, as Sahasrahla said earlier: the world was divided and a seal was made between these realms, imprisoning Ganondorf where we now stand, and also trapping me in the parallel Sacred Realm which became dark as I watched the Triforce subdivided into nine fragments above the temple, and then disappeared altogether. Thus the kingdom was bifurcated, as the Sacred Realm was not an actual place before the cataclysm, but turned out to be a self-fulfilling prophecy of sorts! The fabled land of the gods was not discovered but made by mortals angering the gods…

Unbelievable. I thought the Dark World was a recent phe-err, *noumenon*. said Zelda.

Nope. You've never been to the Dark World before, have you? Where the illuminating presence of the Triforce went at that moment long ago, I still do not know. Since its departure there has only ever been eternal twilight in the godforsaken Sacred Realm. But it wasn't always a world of true forms, not *noumenal* until the Triforce was found recently, warping us shadows.

Were you alone? asked the ermine, not inclined to dwell on the topic of true forms.

At first, but other souls that Rauru falsely arraigned were also banished as well, many innocent Gerudo I had known – together, adapted to the darkness we became the Twili people.

But your sacrifice was not without purpose, as Hyrule enjoyed thousands of years of peace and prosperity since this incredibly violent climax that you experienced! Zelda considered her words, But not without lasting inequity, as your tribe became unduly declared a menace.

I am not surprised to hear this. What better way to hide the truth, than to cast those who remain in possession of it as the enemy – and off limits? Midna reeled.

The Gerudo tribe are a pariah of the kingdom, I am ashamed to admit. said Zelda.

Sahasrahla bowed to Midna, Thank you for shining light on the deep and obscured past in troubled times that have returned yet again. Let our conversation here serve as the epilogue, brought to closure with the moon pearl as a capstone to your weary and tragic story.

The Twilight Princess bowed her head and removed the Nayru necklace.

Zelda couldn't keep it to herself any longer, Your brother is with us, my knight and I, in Misery Mire, mere paces behind where I currently stand by the telepathy tile therein. Before she could say anymore, the convex firmament of the Chamber of Sages twisted away.

You're right, said Link, just a deadend. What is that tile, princess?

Hallway to nowhere. Ganon walked back from where they came. Those unlit beacons…

On it. the bunny had a change of heart, Happy to light the braziers, for symmetry's sake.

The ermine put her hand back on the tablet on the wall, she wanted to talk more with Midna. Nothing happened. Zelda could move her feet again and cautiously stepped back from the white console whose time-coagulating energy had waned entirely.

This way princess! he called, following the big boar.

Don't give him the pendant. she beseeched the inert tile.

The two princesses met by curule
And learned of their kingdom's ancient past
Whose ambitions have long sought to rule

Chapter Three:
CONVICTION

———

The Seventh Sage Knows To Know That

Soon after parting she settled fast
And forgot the date is in April
Finally a feast cooked for her caste

Her royal birthright she will fulfill
To wear this High Crown by any means
Bloody accession that must now spill.

Doomsilling occupied most hours of her day, staring out the window at all the atrocities. Her Highness was convinced this was the best use of her time as nothing felt more imperative. Leaning over and looking down to her left, Zelda could squint past the top of Spectacle Rock onto its southern leeward ridge where the bully and his ball buddy had resumed their mutually abusive routine for all eternity. The monstrous bully booted the ball about the corniced mesa just beyond the ring of rocks where many adventurers had entered the Dark World. Eager to escape the failing kingdom of Hyrule, the pilgrims would pass through that one-way portal, lured by their ambitions to acquire the fabled Golden Power only to find no way back and everything contorted by the manifold evil and delusional topologies of the once Sacred Realm. The ermine princess was glad to see the helplessly capricious and hopelessly blind ball had returned to that altitude of the mountain, after breaking their fall shortly after she and her two companions arrived not long ago. Too far above to intervene in any way now, she intuited but never admitted to her new smalltalk societies that doomsilling[44] is nothing without long distance empathy. And if she was actually at their elevation (although technically they were all in the topos of myopia) then she would rather avoid eye contact with the horrors and carry on her haughty ways. In a distant life, before the pestilence, Zelda was cut out for great deeds. Resigning now to a particular kind of despair that is comfortable – unnaturally sustained through an anesthetizing and constant flow of affluent appurtenances, she had become addicted to voyeuristic misery. Unlike her former proactive self in Hyrule, doomsilling is not the work of saints – however elevated it might feel, the activity cannot affect any salvation nor assistance as it was just that: being above misfortune and getting a rise from it. Vicarious suffering for those in padded parlors, doomsilling is a kind of privileged entertainment, best accompanied by hegemonized victuals (a courteous way of saying, validation was the secret sauce she craved). Zelda would routinely ring her bell for a servant, which required all her weight as

---

44 A propensity of particularly princesses and young ladies in waiting to lean at the windowsill and indulge in all the doom outside and abroad to pass the time and vicariously feel engaged in something important.

the bell was massive. Originally the bell belonged to the tower and was intended for marshaling monsters and announcing forthcoming schemes of the wizard's sorcery. All of Death Mountain echoed when she rang the bell for the slightest fancy, sometimes causing landslides or a teetering talus to avalanche down near Turtle Rock. The three lynels; maned centaurs predisposed to irate dyspepsia and who were always on a warpath – stationed the bridge to the east of the tower – hated that bell with a lion's passion. Blasting hot air in protest, the censorial wind squelched their insubordinate roars and nobody got in trouble accordingly. The ermine princess had to leap and straddle the velvet braided bellrope, swinging across the suite and do her best not to topple any ceramics although that sometimes happened and gave her more time to talk to the minion obliged to sweep up the externalities of her extravagance. Often tasked with menial mopping, even the densedomed hardhat octopuses (colloquially referred to as 'beetles') knew that the princess did not ring because she wanted refreshments, but because she needed someone to offload her royal pain on and bear witness to all her watching. Fixated on any brutality against the ball no matter how redundant, Zelda could not peel herself away from the windowsill. *Did you see today's kicks?* she might ask a silent stalfos attendant[45] with a tray of crystal tonics – an unfair question since their sockets were empty. Zelda was aware that the numbskulls had dull dehydrated orbits and wouldn't want their opinion anyway. The rhetorical question was intended to prompt herself instead, *When I am your Dark Queen I will forcibly end all monster inequity and oppression!* she'd cheer her diamond-faceted goblet at the enthralled skeleton. Taking sanctimonious sips, the manic ermine princess was relieved to get the grief off her chest, only to repeat the pattern on the hour, every hour: doomsilling to bell swinging for room service, feeling horrible from what she saw to tranquilizing it with luxuries, to languishing from the luxuries hence more doomsilling.

---

45 A skeleton soldier, servant, or bygone knight of bones in service of the wizard. When angered or set upon the living, the stalfos is nearly impossible to dispatch by melee, and requires a bomb to retire it.

Enter Epheremelda

Phrm... Zelda tried to remember what the ball had told her: *how long until the ball said it went blind from the myopic warp of this topology?* Maybe she was flirting with hypochondria for the sake of variety, or maybe doomsilling had finally become a boring blur, but that afternoon her eyes strained to focus on anything immediately beyond her lofty belfry window. Out of sight, she put the ball out of mind, and thought of herself instead. *How long had it been?* Maybe one of the talkative zazek[46] would know... But with a headache already ringing from straining to remember, the ermine princess decided against using the bell. *Two weeks perhaps.* she tapped the buffed stone windowsill proding through a slog of memories since parting ways and taking her rightful place as royalty. Retracing her steps one finger at a time, the dizzying grandeur of the tower provided no frame of reference for recollection, so she quickly lost count. Zelda's balcony afforded a vertiginous survey of the warped realm, although she liked the idea more than the reality as there was not much to see. All that mattered was that the ascendant princess went straight to the top, an entitled conviction that initially swept her up from the foot of the mountain that she now maintained with as much dignity as delusion. Undeniably a miserable letdown, the idea of the view was nonetheless as empty as it was sufficient. And at these soaring heights of velvet and vair there was little, certainly not disappointment, that could call her back to the grounded life below where she was exiled, mingling with the mendicants. Consistent with the bewildering flow of fancies inside—outside obscured any diurnal demarcation or interval of passage with the constant stormhead and perpetual dusk surrounding the tectonic eminence. Leaning out to risk a little reminiscing, she could easily spot the drab Dark World analog of the Precipitous Pinnacle, where they met Ganondorf shortly before the Prime Sages intervened. While the Tower of Nayru no longer served any purpose in Hyrule, this parallel tower offered an uninterrupted itinerary of festivities and

---

46 Not native to the Dark World, the dinosaur-men were criminals in Hyrule, warped into reptilians by the corrupted Golden Power. Loquacious and fire-breathing, they are the most conversational of all monsters but never to be trusted. Either blue or red, they are common in high evil places and low wicked dungeons.

delicacies. But all the entertainment so far would pale to her coronation banquet. *Any moment now.* she sighed as the pinprick of a shooting star pierced the inscrutable horizon. Self-conscious of the serendipity, Zelda watched in disbelief wondering how her idle thoughts had summoned the twinkling light by synchronicity, appearing precisely where she was zoning out to the west. *Fit for a wish!* she meditated her princess list, but was mistaken as the celestial object bounced from a gust and fluttered up toward Zelda's window.

Am I too late? said the faerie whose starry aura diffused while closing the distance.

For what. said the ermine, annoyed her doomgazing[47] had attracted a wishless pixie.

You don't look stuffed yet. said the blonde faerie, bloating herself up to demonstrate.

Zelda closed her shutters, but the visitor darted up and got caught.

Listen! said the puffed up faerie, pinched at her midriff and bulging under the latch.

That's what you get for not being a star.

Epheremelda is my name, GWEEE! Ephemeral Envoy to Princess Zelda! she squirmed.

Epherezelda! An ephemeral-zelda... the ermine princess smiled at the nominative rhyming of the faerie's name, admiring the little creature's pale-gold hair; revisiting the possibility that she had thought this spirit into existence while staring out the window. Who sent you? *Me–*

EMMM! *Epheremelda* – Emanation of Venus, Great Faerie of the Lake! she reiterated.

You're no great faerie. said the princess leaning back from the window, a smidge miffed that the spirit was sent from afar and not summoned by her own mind as she had initially felt.

No she is. Venus issued me to tell you: *An unavoidable sacrifice must be made tonight!*

I could not have wished for worse.

---

47   To stare off into dark space and get lost in gloomy thoughts; delight in doom by oneself. Related to the voyeuristic and solipsistic hobby of doomsilling. To lose track of time watching the wrongs of the world.

You can choose your sacrifice, but you cannot choose whether you sacrifice or not.

Atrocious. Zelda rolled her eyes, Well—what are my woebegone options?

You must sacrifice your beloved tower *lifestyle, or the lifeblood* of a loved one.

...

Which life will it be? GWEH! Epheremelda popped toward the ermine princess.

Loved one? Zelda puzzled over her many possessions, letting go of the shutters.

No mansard chamber in Hyrule Castle could compare. *Is the deluxe crown parlor suited to your noble needs?* asked an owl in samite robes who stood at her doorway unnoticed.

Fit for a queen! she said, silently squelching a sinking disquietude that the limit of luxury was a coffered ceiling. Despite the decadence that denied all bounds, she could not rise above this tacit misgiving by mounding anymore riches or gilded gifts. Regardless of the unsurpassed elevation of her abode and no matter how exquisite: a bed was a bed, a toilet a toilet, and her stiff slippers chaffed unlike the broken shoes she wore as an exile astride the bunny and boar.

My princess deserves no less than the top room in the tallest tower on the highest peak! he waved with both arms, Beneath only firmament, all you see will soon belong to your reign.

I belong here. smiled the ermine, bowing to the boudoir and all the regal trappings in her midst while discreetly scanning sideways for Epheremelda. Rising from her clandestine curtsy, she ignored the irony of his promise as there was of course nothing to see except the sea of flashing clouds always brimming in a thick opacity along the ridgeline of Death Mountain.

Did you misplace something my dear? asked the owl.

The world is beneath me, I don't need eyes to know that now. she said, obliquely acknowledging they were bound by the summit's warping myopia even at their steepled altitude. Zelda lowered her lids and inhaled deeply, *Mmm!* Where sight falls short the faculty of scent prevails my liege! What sumptuous smell beckons? Humming one last glance around her room and covertly crooning for the missing messenger Epheremelda—Zelda pretended to leave.

Nff. the owl sniffed once, jutting out his chin. Come! Let us find out for ourselves.

Positively tantalizing to have the great hall directly underneath my seventh floor room.

Punitively appetizing for any captive made to wait on such culinary magic.

Grbrbrb! her stomach grumbled. Who needs a dungeon in the basement when cooks take torture to such aromatic heights! she laughed, taking his feathered hand while departing.

A kitchen is very similar to a dungeon for the ill-fated fish! said Sahasrahla leading the princess in an abrupt left-face turn around the elbow of the antechamber's blue carpet.

Tehehe! Please, fish feel no pain of anticipation. Royalty cannot enjoy such a privileged nature of insensitivity. she said glibly, matching the owl's steps and flitting down the long hallway dramatically lit by seventeen flickering torches. That savory vapor pricks my brain sharper than any chef's fork prong or cleaver's edge could. Zelda relished her hunger pangs.

Could it be the preparation of Pikes in Galentyne, or what's it called again when the flesh of a porgy is dredged in seasoned flour and sautéed in brown butter sauce? asked the owl.

Torment à la Meunière and nothing less! said the highbrow ermine with her nose up.

You are a woman of exalted conviction. But let's forget about the fishes, as a truly divine dish is planned for tonight that only a princess can prepare. The catch is live and when fixed this fresh imparts the delectable essence of a goddess—unlike anything you've ever tasted!

Why didn't you tell me earlier? I would've worn a simpler gown. *Must I chop?*

Just a coup de grâce for the mise en place my dear. Sahasrahla pivoted left-face again, swinging Zelda with him at the end of the carpet and down the stairwell to the great hall.

A Foodfief on the Feastbench

I must confess something. said the owl.

Nothing heavy on an empty stomach. pleaded the ermine, craning backwards.

Sahasrahla sighed, My brothers and I were shortsighted in our ambitions.

To what end? equivocated Zelda, unsure where he was going as they descended the narrow stairwell to the certain banquet awaiting them ahead.

Our realm was rendered in error.

Nothing a flawless feast cannot make amends for. Zelda approved of the tandem table that converged through an ambient haze of scullery smoke voluminating the great hall.

Announcing – Seigneur Sahasrahla and Princess Zelda! declared a blue zazek squire, one of the many dinosaur-men on staff in the tower. Two ancillary red zazek attendants flanked the vocal cupbearer and raised their elongated trumpets, blaring a minor third between the two of them and blowing fire from the horn bells for pyroharmonic[48] effect. The feastbench[49] was built in the shape of an acutely angled protractor, an open-ended triangle, enclosing a lifesize pot seething vacantly deadcenter. Grand triumphs of sculptural cooking greeted their entry as they approached the table piers. Too astonishing to eat – a wide silver dish visibly chilled and frosty with Pikes in Galentyne shaped into a jiggly mold of Death of Mountain with an Intricately Carved Hearty Radish stuck in the top for the tower. Detailed to scale with intaglio fluted pillars, facades, floor plinths and all! Zelda spotted her seventh floor balcony from afar, shaded with a raisin to exaggerate the recess

---

48 A technique to drastically increase the volume of a note by blowing fire into a horn. Performed by the zazek trumpeters for pompous important events. Not possible with woodwind instruments, only brass.

49 A banquet table. A fancy bench for the food to sit on, typically long enough to satisfy royalty.

but thankfully without any miniature radish-art representation of a doomsilling princess. Across the divide on the other table end was a fiery counterpart to the pikes and corroborating their upstairs menu guessing – a radiating golden platter of battered Porgy Meunière adorned with Twizzled Citrus Shock Fruit Rind soaked in Blatchery Bourbon that had been lit and flickered lemony flames. Lorule landmarks absent, the chandelier of a dish more than made up for it with the many tiers of fragrant rindlight[50] aglow resplendent palmettes of fish. After recovering from her amazement, Zelda realized that all the dishes were segregated according to temperature, with hot on one side and cold on the other. Hot Buttered Apples ahoy followed from the porgy and correspondingly across the delta-shaped table Chilly Nuts and then Cold Carrot Soup proceeding from the pikes. Successive plates of all sorts were laid out as the ermine and owl arrived but the thermal rule always remained inviolate. Matching their pace, the banquet resembled a delicious diorama or miniature model world as it was served. Despite the lavish variety, each plate was designed to contiguously cohere a heaping horizon as the owl and ermine strode like demiurge titans into an edible manifold concocted and cooked in their honor. Unlike the senseless and stormy view from her window, the long isosceles arms displayed the entire foodfief[51] of uplifted entrées whose seasoned peaks steamed and frosted in contrast with valleys of low lying hors d'oeuvres spread throughout; Sacred Realm their scrumptious meal.

At least the Bright-Chested Duck Confit was rendered properly. sniffed Sahasrahla.

Drifting into the delta's lacuna the princess nabbed a crispy crackling from the platter of a zazek servant who awkwardly paused against protocol to let her dip the duck bacon in a dish of its own clarified fat. *Pure liquid gold!* snarled the dining room dinosaur-man trying to backpedal.

Sahasrahla, do you fancy duck? she said, unsure if owls had an appetite for pondfowl.

---

50   The citrus glow from lighting a lemon rind on fire for a gourmet presentation effect.
51   An edible diorama of a lord's domain. A fiefdom of food. A scaled world of wholesome models.

Will you not wait until we're seated? he pinched a salty sneer at her insouciant snacking.

I am waited on… she said, slowly swirling the confit and indulging in the viscosity.

My zazek are not to be held hostage. Sahasrahla watched her hoist heavily out of the fat and leisurely bite into the dripping bacon. Tower rules—that no one is above. he added.

So says the ruler of the Golden Realm! *A princess is the protocol.* she wagged her crisp.

If anyone's entitled to double standards it's Zelda, my concession-heiress. said the owl.

DIVINE! How could this bacon be—beyond compare if your realm was born half-baked?

A confit-undrum worth savoring. said the servant, letting her take a second piece.

The owl let the zazek go, We could not make a complete wish, not without the others.

But all three of you were there. said the ermine, stealing another crisp as the servant left.

That's your third confit uncouthly confiscated!

Why stop at double standards when you can have triple?

Come my dear, let's get seated. he ushered her along.

Does this world not reflect your mind and heart? she chewed.

Sahasrahla stopped, holding Zelda close to confide in her. Indeed, but my heart is pure and my mind is sound! Nothing like this miscarriage of a realm, warped and incomplete. said the owl turning around and pointing to each end of the two tables, slowly pulling his hands together and drawing an imaginary third edge to the baseless equilateral triangle that formed their feast. When I convene us all, this topological travesty of the Triforce will be remembered as no more than a provisional scaffolding erected to raise up our ultimate design. he clasped his wingtips.

Why do you need the other sages to make your singular wish my liege? said Zelda as they passed beyond the centroid of the table arrangement, sidestepping the ornate cauldron that was simmering a soulless broth. The princess waved at the black iron vat with intentions of inquiring what it was doing there, but presumed a decorative purpose and asked nothing more.

I don't. said the owl swiveling his head to her, But the relic requires all to be present.

And what of the grand pyramid? I want a tour! Zelda leaned in to inspect the stepped structure built to scale with four levels of Dracozu Chocolate bullions and finished with a single sealing application of digestible gold leaf, preserving the domineering dessert just for show. Sneaking a poke, the princess pressed her fingernail into the foil, and was surprised how thin this barrier was – breaking the precious metal and revealing a chink of the delicious dark cocoa mass inside. *Hmmm?* she nagged Sahasrahla the owl, hanging on him above suspicion.

For now the maidens keep it safe, although the nine crystals are scattered.

Two more after me? said Zelda who thought she was the seventh and final maiden, consistent with what the first maiden they rescued told them: *we seven maidens...*

HOOT! The king tried to mislead me by only identifying seven – perhaps he lied to you too in an attempt to keep you from me. But no matter, you're not a maiden at all! he laughed, We've found them all, bound to the crystal phylacteries and guarded by our nastiest demons.

Then why was I held captive? she asked, visualizing that cell before Link saved her.

For your protection! Only temporarily my dear – that was the safest place in the castle! The king had become unstable, violent, lashing out in his final days of the pestilence.

...

There were Nine Wise Men, as with the sages three triplets blessed by each goddess. We are related to the maidens, who are essentially recessive sages in waiting. he said smugly.

Glad to be a sage by your side, Seigneur Sahasrahla. said Zelda. But if I idle in waiting, will I then become a mere maiden? she flicked a fleck of incriminating cocoa off her nail.

You've taken the reins of destiny, and have nothing to worry about while your distant relatives are all crystalized and suppressed throughout the realm! And I take some solace knowing that my grandchild, the penultimate survivor of my lineage, has volunteered to bear a crystal in the impenetrable Ice Palace. When harmonized all together as a *nonet* and no fewer, the maidens can unlock the central pyramid—pylon of the Golden Power. Properly they serve as a safeguard against a partial congregation of the sages, as my brothers and I already made that mistake. But with the maidens in their place, all you and I must do is convene and conform the other sages, kicking and screaming for all I care! All that matters is the full relic will then be mine for a second wish; reifying my outstanding vision for a *totally* unified realm.

Fulfilling your own prophesy as any aspiring god must! You intend to merge the realms?

I will heal what Hylia rivened long ago, and reform our world scarred by her cataclysm.

Opposites attract, but tend to chafe and separate. said the ermine to the owl.

Hyrule and the Sacred Realm are not incompatible; they are one bifurcated reality.

Quintessentially estranged from each other... two halves of our schizophrenic epoch. Zelda basked in the mingling microclimates formed by the wafting hot and breezy cold cuisine.

Until all the sages can be convened to restore the Triforce, I will not leave any descendants of the Wise Men left unaccounted for, as I will confide in you: the practical difference between a maiden and a sage is yet unknown to me. he grouched defensively.

I would like to know the distinction. said the princess, worried she might be *recessive* living in this tower. But our destinies are disclosed when fate is fulfilled; always after the fact!

You're overthinking it. We control our destinies and thus fate is fungible. he retorted.

The meaning of our destinies can only be read after our fates are penned in indelible ink. Zelda was quite convinced. Oh! Please show me the pyramid, where the divine relic was found.

That was before the Golden Power was defiled by the King of Thieves and the ensuing Great Cataclysm. Ever since, the Triforce is **secured** by the sages: *primed, hidden, and sealed.* Sahasrahla lifted a hinged leaf of the countertop that allowed them to pass through the apex of the delta buffet and find their designated seats at the head of the banquet facing the cauldron. Trailing them along each wing of the table, the servants continued to put down dishes. To their right were the red zazek placing more hot dishes: Copious Fried Wild Greens with the stalks all curving in the same direction forming a wreath almost too intricate to dig into, then followed by Blackened Stambulb au Bombos with ruffled spritzes of striated cheese proudly piped on top.

What's this? she pointed to the delicate savory detail, almost accidentally jabbing it as the scaly servant set down the roasted stambulbs that were ostentatious beyond recognition.

The tacit pride of the patissier is only validated by the curiosity of the clientele.

What– Dessert before dinner? *That's not a pastry.*

Panache makes the pastry! Attention to refinement is not confined to confections.

Oh, patissier is a state of mind, *I know I know...* she kept pointing. But what is this?

Regardless, your probing is HIGH praise for the chef... he inhaled zany lizard nostrils, And as a tower host, it is my distinct pleasure— nay! Responsibility on behalf of the kitchen to elaborate for you my ladyship. the zazek stepped back with a bow and explained passionately, This coagulated masterpiece paved the way for soft-ripened cheese in Lorule. Conceived in a dour dream and perfected in darkness— not unlike the world we inhabit—each handcrafted wheel features remarkable swirling ribbons of edible deku ash. Tuck into the pleasures of this illicit little sacrifice! The gregarious servant kissed his varnished claws with a forked-tongue.

Deku[52] ash? she retracted her inquiring index finger. This cheese sounds to die for!

Precisely. If the secret ingredient of phenomenal cooking is 'love', then the secret to a fine noumenal recipe is the immolated remnants of an innocent soul! the riled up host resumed explaining his rehearsed laudation where she interrupted, Upon biting into this dairy dunce cap, you'll find yourself swimming backstroke in a seriatim of sensations: a figured bass of buttermilk and fresh cream crescendoing to a lugubrious tenor with loud herbaceous overtones, resolving in a FORTISSIMO of flavors! the zazek bellowed, A perfect cadence of clean floral notes worth humming for days—delighting in this melody long after the last morsel is gone… he swooned.

And that's just the toppingahhh *snrrr-YOHHH!* the ermine yawned, I can only imagine what you have to say about the stambulbs sitting underneath this *noumenal* cheese.

Aging longer than the monger's lifetime, the creamline develops— the flavor intensifies.

I can't wait to try it. she politely dismissed the red zazek with a whip of her lace napkin, dubious of a reptile explaining anything involving milk.

On your left, warned a blue zazek, Chilly Hydromelon Soup— *clink.* the bowl settled.

There's something in it. she said, pivoting the bowl's wedding-themed charger plate.

With Palmorae Prawns, Princess Zelda. he said cooly while pirouetting away.

That's all? said Zelda, referring to his lack of spiel and not any deficiency in the soup. Duly she deemed the blue zazek especially cold-blooded for their lack of fiery bravado unlike the red dinosaur-men who exuberantly conveyed sputtering hot platters in a spicy procession. Nonetheless the blue servants kept pace and filed along down the other

---

52 One of the three elemental peoples of Hyrule, and made by the green goddess Farore, before Hylians appeared in the kingdom. A small woody humanoid. A sentient species, capitalized unless objectified.

arm of the table with their refrigerated recipes cold enough to slough hefty wafts of hoarfrost as they landed that crystalized verglas on the table with sparkling halos of rime which refracted the dim ambience. After ten or so dishes on each side, the servants stopped rearranging the plates to make room for the most recent, stopped introducing them, and so Zelda turned her attention to Sahasrahla. 'Secured' in the Chamber of Sages, the astral Temple of Light that sealed the realms apart and imprisoned the King of Thieves for all these millennia? Zelda recapitulated, then paused to ask, Why would Ganondorf be imprisoned there, if the goddess enacted that liminal aspect as the gateway to the Sacred Realm? Wouldn't that make *him* more of a sentry?

Only one golden triangle appeared before us as we are but one triad of the sages.

Seven descendants of the Wise Men... perplexed Zelda plucked her three-pronged fork, What is a triad from seven? *Pa-kling-ing!* her fidgeting sent the towerware[53] ringing on the tiles. And who will attend tonight's banquet? she reached for it, but a shadowy babusu[54] floorwraith scurried to take the soiled utensil, while a flying chasupa[55] daintily set a clean one in its place.

Would you get that out of your head? the owl adjusted a king's crown. Not seven. Nine–

Boop-ba-da-ba-boooooop! the trumpeters tooted in unison; this time without any fire.

Here they are! said the owl, as two other creatures entered the hall from the floor below, not saying a word as they parted ways from the door adjacent to where Zelda and Sahasrahla had entered. Like their eldest brother, both were feathered and enrobed: a vulture found his place near one end of the delta table while a wading bird sat at the opposite wing's terminus.

---

53 Cutlery designed especially for the Dark Tower, matching its architecture, motiffs, and material quality. Black enameled forks, spoons, and knifes made to match the features of Sahasrahla's aerie abode.

54 An angry shadow torn from its casting object and put to umbral labor or other two-dimensional tasks. Fastest frights in the Dark World, these darting shadows have red eyes, and wait in crannies until called.

55 An eye with wings. A bat-like cyclops the size of a melon with modified forearms for wings but no claws nor legs. Used by evil overlords for minor errands, they possess a tiny telekinesis to lift small objects.

Aginah. Zelda nodded to the heron from her seat, then turned to the condor at her right. Your brothers wear matching gold sigils around their necks. she said to the owl, Do you as well?

You've seen this before, said Sahasrahla, revealing a third matching sigil from his robes.

Ah! Yes, the fated goddess medallion of Nayru...

The force of ether. the owl added.

So that was you... Zelda recalled the sudden hurricane that transformed the swamp.

We've found all three medallions which can only be claimed and called upon while wielding the Master Sword. The quake medallion, and the force of bombos... he said, pointing to Aginah then his other brother on the opposite table wing. As a precursor to the ultimate power the Triforce will grant us, the medallions have served their purpose to keep the kingdom in line.

You can control the weather?

Storms, fire, and tectonics too...

All of Hyrule believes these calamities were natural, causing the pestilence. Zelda read between the lines, 'Served'? You have the medallions but cannot use them without the sword?

Hrm! Sahasrahla ruffled at her astute inference, Yes my dear, I sheathed Hylia's Key in the Lost Woods until we've found the Hidden Sages to summon the Golden Power as planned. Either we will seek them out, or they will try their hand at the Master Sword and come to us...

Delightfully diabolical. said the ermine princess.

The owl clapped once, signaling the dinosaur-men to place the napkins in their laps although the ermine had already used hers and was fixated on the cauldron as several babusus darted into the flames with more tinder to stoke it while the hovering chasupas supervised.

That's everyone? asked the ermine, holding her hands up as a blue zazek did its job.

One other will attend, any moment now and then we can get on with your coronation. With you at my side, we'll be an unstoppable force for good! Whatever evil I've had to commit on the way to restoring the Sacred Realm will be amended for with your grace Princess Zelda.

If redemption is what you're after, then why not apologize to the goddesses? At this altitude you're closer than anyone – I'm sure they would receive even a soundless confession.

The owl shook his head, There will be nothing to repent for when we claim the Triforce. You will be a goddess and I the creator of a new world; together with the Golden Power at hand.

Not even divinities are absolved by good deeds I'm afraid.

Your creed is warped by the undercroft of grave beliefs; that *topology of conviction.*

Verily, I do believe that's where we met, in the Ghostly Garden at the base of the tower. she said, pointing her knife into the tablecloth, How else does a princess come into her own?

You have to know what you think you know about yourself to be a *real* princess.

Faithlessly! I cannot imagine climbing all those stairs without *conviction* underfoot.

I never said the highlife would be easy. We have to believe in ourselves, in each other. Your conviction must *be a faith* in me. said the myopic owl of the tallest tower in the realm.

Faith knows no axiom, needs no accessory, but I will take your hand. said the ermine.

But do you know what's next? Sahasrahla gazed intently toward the downstairs doorway where his two birdy brothers had arrived from. A blue zazek served them icy tropical drinks in clear stemmed chalices garishly garnished Gerudo-style with slices of Voltfruit and Rock Salt.

We anticipate an important somebody. I *know* that much. Zelda sipped her mocktail.

Meager confidence! But do partake in this Great Faerie Croquembouche while we wait. Sahasrahla unwittingly dictated, distracted and emotionally distant however shortsighted and straining to focus on the farside of the great hall for the aforementioned subject of his prolepsis.

The tapestry on the opposite wall got the princess thinking, reminding her of a favorite tometorium[56] in the citadel. How she missed scholarship, but abhorred the politics of academia. There was no such discourse since the wizard came to power; certainly none in this tower life. Zelda chewed on her frustration that everything she liked about herself was irrelevant to what others seemed to want from her company. And was that to suggest she should put aside her private affinities to best accommodate others—inclinations that were already invisible anyway, so what's to lose that which was never noticed by the gallery of dignitaries and court officials? And wouldn't that be in her best interest too? Or would something unexpected happen if she did; an inexplicable incongruence that sets her at odds with the haute code of conduct and mercurial trends of the tower's social mores! Hung up on the unforeseen consequences of forfeiting her unobserved qualities, upon intuiting the cryptic elements of our character, best to hold onto what no one else grasps, she decided, blinking away from the thought-provoking tapestry as a Wild Roast of Eldin Ostrich eclipsed her view – the giant poultry passed down the table for a suitable landing place to carve. Perhaps she underestimated how dependent her true self and outward appearance were, even if others only perceived the latter in Hyrule and knew the former here in Lorule. But why feel this way in the Dark World of manifested inner natures? Humph. she frumped to herself. Despite this overt realm of true forms, our hearts are always hidden in plain sight, what a *lethic* stone! How easy it is to *forget* what really anchors us when pandering for others. Self-conscious of lingering in her introspection, she glanced at the owl, who (in confirmation of her digressing autodiscourse[57] just now) had not noticed her quietude and remained fixated for what was next. Taking him up on his offer and returning to her senses, the ermine reached for a glazed profiterole as the imposing spire of cream puffs called to her...

---

56   A small library of especially big thick books. Often closed to the public, a collection of special tomes. Shelves of rare bound texts on a particular subject, kept privately for archival or preservation purposes.

57   To have a dialogue with oneself that is more engrossing than any proximal company or sensations. Deep introspection that becomes a silent conversation of multiple personas or positions within oneself.

Listen! said the bijou faerie from within the pile of balls, crouched in the cavity revealed by the chou Zelda took. Eat dessert first, but save this for last! she said, lugging an aureate orb.

There you are! whispered Zelda discreetly, but not quiet enough—

Where? asked Sahasrahla. Is it time? He turned to Zelda, who quickly put her puff back. Take the one you touch dear. said the owl, unnerved by her lack of manners and looking away.

Such a sweet sauce demands a double dip… she fibbed, uncovering the little cave again revealing the faerie hiding inside the multistory croquembouche, baked as the bust of a nymph.

Why stop at double when you can dip triple… he patronized, unaware of the sprite.

Apple for the afterlife. Berry for the great BEYOND… WEH! Eh–snack to save your soul! said Epheremelda, straining to yank a glitzy pomegranate from the strands of crystalized sugar. Remember the sacrifice! warned the pixie envoy, Please delay your gratification milady! GWEH!

Zelda stuffed the whole creampuff in her (own) mouth to free up both (of her own) hands such that she could help Epheremelda disentangle the caramel drizzle and take the golden fruit. *Fank foo.* muffled the princess with bulging cheeks, polishing the pomegranate with her napkin.

You're most welcome my ladyship. said a red zazek noticing the topping was not as hard as it should be, breathing his vectorized flambé to anneal the brûlée on the voluptuous statue. As a matter of respect, you have to enjoy one at a time! he wrinkled, snuffing out his nostrils.

Respect for the chef? she played along, glad nobody saw Epheremelda.

No, for the chickaloo. Each bite deserves your undivided palate.

That's what the filling was flavored with! she said, nabbing errant dollops on her chin.

Chickaloo Tree Nut Extract is the essential constituent of the croquembouche's custard. Because chickaloos are difficult to propagate, slow to bear, and limited in range of cultivability, Hyrule production has not kept pace with increased demand here in Lorule. he elaborated.

And you import them across realms? she asked the loquacious servant.

Most commercial production takes place in their native Retsam and in East Necluda. However, given the success of the Korok chickaloo industry, other subdeku[58] regions have planted orchards, and there are large acreages of chickaloo trees in Faron, Finra, and Pappetto, and farther afield in the mooncast provinces of Termina – from Milk Road to Northern Woodfall.

Termina! What about Evermeans—the angry ents, don't they drop these buttery nuts?

Not sustainable, economically, but yes. he concluded snootily, never actually answering her question about interdimensional importing methods. Chickaloos take years to grow—gone in a few seconds when consumed. Cherish the chickaloo as you ruminate on its whereabouts.

Thank you, for that ecological exegesis. I ate the whole treat at once; a deliberate bite.

Civey of Linkalope

At last! Here comes the main course! applauded the owl to her right.

The ermine was distracted by a backstabbing feather poking through her chair's pillow. Removing it simply pulled another plume out, perpetuating the infuriating prickling. Which one of you does this belong to? She waved the barbed quill at Sahasrahla's brothers: Heron? Condor? Everyone was too distracted by the procession making its way into the center of the banquet.

Bring us the sharpfinger! Bring us the cleaver. *Bring us the gorey gutterblock–*

What for? Zelda tossed the feather and joined everyone in watching the strange animal being escorted toward the cauldron – rekindled and boiling at the centroid of the delta table. Unlike the all dinosaur-men kitchen staff, an unusual entourage of monsters joined the party from deeper in the tower. All she could make out was the animal had antlers,

---

58   Woodland habitats south of the native Deku region. Latitudes below the Great Hyrule Forest.

but most of its body was concealed by the colossal fingers that gripped it – a wallmaster hand supernaturally loitered aloft with the hapless guest held upright in its huge grasp the color of caput mortuum. Guiding the heedless hand, two burly taros[59] leading with tridents kept close as the wallmaster floated beyond the cauldron and dropped the… ruffled from the behemoth's perspiring palm.

Live-caught, the *linkalope* is ready. said Sahasrahla, passing through the table again after a blue zazek opened the drawbridge leaf opening their way to the cauldron in the center.

What's a linkalope? asked Zelda, skirting the servants who temporarily held the dishes.

The primary ingredient and soul of this ceremony, cleaned and jointed into six pieces.

Why is it alive? she fretted, remembering what Epheremelda warned.

You'll understand once you taste it, said the owl handing her a curved sword resembling an oversized breaking knife. Start with the joints, and let the sharpfinger work the meat for you!

I've never seen such a beast, although the Dark World is full of uncategorized chimeras. Leaning over the gutterblock[60] she peered into the trembling creature's blue eyes. Can it speak?

No, as is the curse of Farore. said the owl with a suggestive grin.

Unbelievable. For what transgression would Lady Courage[61] punish such a soul?

My hinox found this lone linkalope under the scarped eastern slopes of Death Mountain, clamoring above the Lake of Ill Omen. It was looking for something from the desolate shoreline.

The goddesses are gone. interjected the heron, Long ago her lacustrine Forest Temple stood there in Old Hyrule. Perhaps he found Farore bathing, and was cursed speechless!

59   Speechless minotaurs, often higher rank than the moblin pigs, but lower than the hinox.
60   A grooved wooden block used for executing. Heavy enough not to wobble and featuring a single shallow outflow gutter for the victim to bleed out in one channeled direction. An evil chopping block.
61   Another term for the green goddess Farore, one of three daughters of Hylia. Similarly, Nayru is called Lady Wisdom, although 'Lady Power' is not a common utterance for the goddess Din but you could say it if you wanted to and Hyruleans would probably understand however not without a laugh at your expense.

Transmogrified beyond the topological warping of this realm. added Sahasrahla, sadistically tapping on the linkalope's antlers. If it weren't for these, you would be a bunny.

This is evidently a derivative of hare, *not a bunny.* said the ermine with great conviction.

Alas, this world is replete with freaks and full of anomalous animals; no need to concede to far-fetched fables of vindictive deities in the boonies. said Aginah looking down a stiletto beak with extra irreverence by extending his long heron neck above their mythological speculation.

I would've worn a simpler gown! she leered at Sahasrahla for not warning her earlier. Don't trust a bloodless butcher they say—sorry in advance for any splatter. she took the sword and felt the sharpfinger's edge with her own, then put its keenness to the test by sacrificing a whisker she had been meaning to cut for days. The ermine's facial bristle glided down onto the detained linkalope whose terrified sneeze blew the whisker off the wooden pedestal.

On with it before the banquet cools. urged the condor, having come from the hot-buffet side of the table, while the heron scoffed as all the dishes on his pier were already chilled.

The cauldron boils, cut away my dear. Squandered broth spoils the betrothed.

Cut away I shall Seigneur Sahasrahla! said Princess Zelda, But what's in order?

I don't know, I'm not a cook. the owl glowered at the nervous zazek sous chefs.

You said 'primary ingredient' my brother. the heron assumed there was a plan.

How would you know 'six pieces' without a recipe? the condor was confused too.

I just do! hooted the myopic owl, confident to the point of contradiction.

If you were *Sahasrahla the Saucier,* then what is your desired partis pris; mirepoix? Zelda tapped the iron rim with the sharpfinger causing the linkalope to wince each time. Whipping the blade through the rising steam she smelled the essence for inspiration…

The pot already has Hateno Pasture Stock, Your Highness. said a red zazek.

That all? Better be Dantz's Prized Beef.

Yes, Princess. Only the best.

I've got it—one ingredient is enough to inspire the rest!

What's in mind? asked the owl, easily ruffled by procedural details.

From this simple broth given, you will know the full gestalt when it's done.

More than the simmered sum of its poached parts I trust.

Yes, it will. Let the mystery be your appetizer. But I'll need everyone's help. Hear ye!… said the ermine, using her sharpfinger[62] to salute the nearby red and blue zazek, the two taros bulls, flying chasupa cyclops bats, and lastly the daunting wallmaster[63] holding the linkalope by dubbing between the big hand's knuckles. I won't mince words: we have a lot of chopping to do, but as your Princess of the Hotpot, I will not permit any cutting of corners! she declared, as the zazek clapped and bats fluttered. Several moblin pigs dusted and swept on the periphery of the hall as ancillary staff, bussing about snouts down. Bring me twenty Red Stambulb Onions… Zelda pointed to the unsuspecting swine who were elated to have a role in the main course.

Yes, Princess, we have all you need in the pantry. clapped a blue zazek. What else?

Ten sliced Pig Livers. she demanded, staring at the zazek who quavered then cackled upon realizing what she meant—delighting at the opportunity to set upon their own janitors. Before the porcine busboys had a chance to leave for the onions, the dinosaur-men chased them around the hall and into the several exits that descended into the echoing

---

62 A slender culinary boning saber preferred by zazek chefs with a long curved blade well suited for breaking apart a carcass and separating sinews, muscle meat, fat, and effortlessly excising gristle.

63 Gigantic amputated undead hands reanimated in the service of a dungeon master or demon boss. What body the wallmaster belonged to is unknown; the hand is big enough to enclose around a cow. Often idling on the ceiling or along the wall, wallmasters can levitate and easily detain any intruders, carrying them to the exit, evicting such unwanted guests from the Dark Tower that is invitation only.

galley cellars. Next up, we'll need the delicate touch only telekinesis can provide. she signaled the chasupas who lacked talons but could manipulate morsels with a weak monster magnetism of their own.

They are excellent herbworkers![64] said the owl anticipating her next instructions.

Your assistance will be essential, pepped the ermine to the attentive one-eyed bats, because the following ingredients are easily bruised by the heat, sweat, and heaviness of a corporeal hand. To levitate smidges and scintilla, I am assigning my *gawk*[65] accordingly…

This squadron of aerial assistants have never had a greater purpose. said the condor.

One fresh *spring* of Fural Thyme and one dried *sprig* of Harfin Rosemary! she pointed to one chasupa then another who both bobbed with a wink as four more joined their stew briefing. Next I'll need two thick slices of Twin Bridge Toast, each sprinkled with Ground Mixed Spice. The six bats flew off in formation, keen to coordinate on these more complicated components.

That all? While this recipe eludes me, I suspect your proportions are off. said Aginah.

You're right, MAKE IT DOUBLE! she corrected, causing the chasupas to adjust their airshow from a vee to an impressive echelon as more of the cyclops bats joined their mission. Outstanding! said Zelda sizing up what was left on her mental list and who she could conscript. But all the zazek were chasing the moblin, and not a single chasupa remained in the vaulted hall for tiny tasks. There were the two taros, fidgeting with their polearm prodders, but she had plans for them yet. Stockstill along the alcoves of the hall stood unemployed gibdo mummies, morbid figures easily mistaken as ghastly statues as the tower was decorated like a posh tomb. Hail ye petrified porters and poseurs! she made sure they heard. Snap to—ossified retainers. Walk off your rigor mortis with the motivation that this grand course requires your reanimation! Undeterred by their horrific gait, she chided

---

64   Anyone too dainty to deal with woody plants, but adept at preparing soft culinary botanicals.
65   A group of chasupas.

the undead ectomorphs who were evenly spaced, three along one wall and symmetrically three on the other. At your own exhumed pace, limp your wilted limbs downstairs and each grab six Verdant Parsley stalks, four whole cloves of Feral Garlic, and while you're at it two blades of Hylian Mace – all tied in your own muslin!

SKRAAAHHH! a gibdo[66] hissed hideously in protest of Zelda's orders.

Your embalming is behind you—use your barrow rags for this *bouquet garni*, she said, charnel dried muslin will add a unique tang. This all too much for your frazzled brains to track?

…

Take your time. she said, unsure if they were spurning her, Zelda watched the six slow mummies leave begrudgingly without further outcry. Tromping heavily, the last gibdo misstepped and accidentally activated a disguised trap that quickly spun up and twirled over to the cauldron. Enchanted to chase intruders, Zelda sent the flying tile off in search of Ground Garlic instead, as she forgot to ask the chasupas. None are exempted from pitching in our machinated marination, and that applies to you three – my distinguished gentlebirds of prey. If I am to murder the quarry, then the least you can do is put your own skin in this game.

What for? asked the heron.

We all have to make sacrifices. But I wouldn't want to ruin what I have planned tonight. Off you go heron in search of some Green Quakesalt. she matronized. And I suspect you know where to find Red Wine Vinegar, she entrusted to the condor, I only need a generous glug but bring up the whole bottle – my apologies for stating the obvious. And one step further, follow your siblings Sahasrahla into the reserve room, as only you hold the big key for such treasure.

Is a crown not enough? What else must I pillage for your coronation? the owl moaned.

---

66   Bizarre zombies that were once mortal Twili turned to undead slaves. The gibdo are not bipedal insect drones as some think, but are incredibly durable and almost immune to physical assaults. Lumbering and slow they will hug the living to death if they come within reach; also known for their blood curdling scream.

A splash of the past – a dash of sunlit terroir before the Sacred Realm was darkened.

I know just the grape, a vibrant Blue Clarnet given to me by King Hyrule…

A vintage magnum for your service as magistrate? Before the pestilence? she asked.

Who? You are swirling a conflation Zelda. Don't stir the pot anymore than you need to. Keep court while I rummage the rack. said Sahasrahla, morosely obliging with his two brothers.

Hardly appropriate attire for cleaning a catch, said the ermine swishing her silk hemline, but I'm now resolved to dress our detainee. Zelda approached the two taros and evil hand that had not relinquished its grip on the linkalope. How shall I begin? The galvanized executioner appelled loudly with her foot, startling everyone while spiraling the sharpfinger tip in a foibling advance toward the quivering lope, caressing its long ear with a feint trompment. The bullmen snorted at her knifeplay. *First!* Cut a little slit somewhere… in the fur of the hare—anywhere… Zelda spoke as if instructing herself, Slash a gash *juuust* big enough to stick your finger in below the hide. she tickled the linkalope who happily mistook her torture for affection. Pull the fur off from the back, peeled from the nape and hind legs. said the sadistic ermine, explaining her imminent procedure like an academic surgeon with an audience. That's all that is necessary at this point, she said swapping the sharpfinger for the cleaver. The wallmaster flung up its thumb without losing the linkalope, as to gesticulate its disappointment that she stopped. There's no need to gut our friend until fully skinned; nice to avoid that step for last. The aroma is not pleasant, and abiding in the entrails will atrophy our hunger for the principal potage to come. Zelda pinged the cleaver's blunt spine along the bullmen's fork prongs, focusing their attention. *Second!* Cut from the breastbone to the belly… and remove the intestines stomach and lungs. Remove the rear leg! she chopped midair, pantomiming the amputation. Then rinse the whole carcass in cold water to remove hair and blood. Hew your metal once and decisively to abduct the succulent loin in one piece to keep the tendons intact! she said, turning away with her back to the gutterblock. **_Third!_** And finally, separate the shoulders. Zelda crossed arms in a hugging motion to protract her prominent scapulas as a dramatic demonstration. The princess ended her explanation by tossing the cleaver up – catching the handle after a single slow rotation; a feat that took her by surprise as well as the monsters in her midst. I almost forgot! she sunk the cleaver's edge fast into the wooden sacrificial slab, nearly nicking the wallmaster's knuckles and making it flinch. The marrow of a bovine's bone compliments the scrawny and fatless linkalope. Zelda put her hand on the antlered-hare's scruff, wrest me two pairs – four Broken Bullhorns. The wallmaster stalled, so Zelda dislodged the cleaver and tapped its gargantuan fingernails which got the message across. Letting go of the traumatized animal whose fur was mottled from the wretched grip of the wallmaster, the taros raised their polearms and took a defensive stance. Both bull guards used their pronged weapons to keep the wallmaster at bay, until the giant hand pinched an overcommitted lunge – effortlessly disarmed its inferior prey, causing the two taros to panic and charge toward the nearest exit where the owl and ermine had descended in debut. Retreating in a last ditch attempt to dispatch their assailant, the armed taros threw his pitchfork at the wallmaster who splayed its fingers tauntingly and let it skewer painlessly through its palm. The bullmen snorted in defiance, locking horns in fraternal celebration of their presumed victory. Using its thumb and ring finger, the hand whooshed up to the ceiling where it easily excised the weapon and shook it off. Dropping fast and pouncing on the floor, the wallmaster set out on all five fingers, continuing its bullish pursuit of bone marrow as the princess requested. *Come...* Throwing the linkalope over her shoulders the animal's antlers snagged on filigree. My crown! Unable to catch it while slinging the compliant cryptid, Zelda watched her gaudy tower tiara fall and crack apart on the ground. She could hear the three lords – Sahasrahla, Aginah, and the lost old man whose voice she only just now recognized as they audibly returned from the cellar. The echoing hallway reminded her of first encountering him in the caves of Turtle Rock, not as a condor but as a bewildered and hooded man. The similar acoustics of the architecture must've triggered the association in her memory. But how was he not transmogrified then? The deceit! she remembered what he said, 'It has been taken', misled by his vague frankness at the time.

Clasping the cleaver with her arms over the prisoner, Zelda trundled as fast as she could without breaking into a hop. Speedwalking made for a silent escape and kept the linkalope from bouncing on her neck. All the stairwells down risked running into the many monsters she sent in search of ingredients. So she had no choice but to ascend and return to the seventh floor room to find egress from the impossible heights of her royal belfry. Slogging up the stairs, she heard several crashes up ahead, but all her attention was focused on the three voices behind her. Arriving at the long hallway leading to her chamber, at least five of the seventeen torches had been destroyed in a great brawl with the rug torn up in many places as well. Tipped over and extinguished braziers had shattered with stonework strewn across far reaches of the corridor. Zelda made haste through the rubble and rushed into her spire bedroom where the two taros continued to madly wrestle with the wallmaster. Thrashing her upholstery, ripping the curtains, one taros had broken off her dresser doors to use as a makeshift shield against the giant hand. Feathers were ejected everywhere as one of her favorite downy throw pillows was impaled on the horns of the frantic bull barricading himself behind the couch. The shin-length fingernails of the wallmaster clacked about, greyish crypt keratin chipped from the skirmish which as a result hooked anything soft, including her *darling* shaggy floor pelt. The sight reminded the ermine of her broken nail in the Swamp of Evil and the grating sound was too agonizing for the princess.

Not the sheepskin! Zelda shouted, CHANGE OF PLANS! she fearlessly waded into the fray with the linkalope still over her shoulders. WE'LL MAKE IT MARROWLESS! We can skip the horns, but I'll need to... the ermine jaunted around the room, desperately appraising the refuse for something that might aid her escape. Peering out the window, she already knew it was hopelessly too high for any makeshift rappelling. Without such bold fatty flavor, I will find a savory substitute myself then. she spun from the window haranguing the hooligans in her room. There's nothing to salvage here, she thought out loud, and these antics must have you peckish. Zelda waved the cleaver at the two bullmen, But do your princess proud and say nothing of this. Return to the banquet and watch over the cauldron while I nab what we need. she said, taking her longbow from a creaky trunk that miraculously remained unturned.

Boop-ba-da-ba-boooooop! blowing their horns again, the zazek squires were back at their stations in the great hall below, announcing the return of Sahasrahla and his brothers.

My princess, where are you? said the owl from the floor below.

Go now! Tell them the pot required one last addition that only the princess could acquire. she said, pretending to look around her room for it. Zelda turned to the guards and brushed off some feathers stuck to their horns. I'll be down in a moment—go! And put yourselves together. she implored the taros who ostensibly could not speak but heaved and drooled from their fight. Unenthusiastic to obey her capricious orders, the two bullmen didn't think twice and trotted out.

CRASH! a vase tumbled off her bureau without warning. Epheremelda sprawled in the ceramic fallout. I see you've chosen your sacrifice. said the stunned faerie, reviving her glow.

If only I had Nayru's reflector, we could spirit ourselves away from this trap!

Trappings more like it! You checkmated yourself. scolded the pipsqueak.

Excuse me? How is that!

Incrementally, with a thousand little steps! Inch by precious inch you conceded to the conviction that you were entitled to *this!* she pointed to all the decadent rubble. '*If only…*'

How dare you mock your Royal Highness, voyeuristic envoy.

Forget about any magic succor—owlman keeps that reflector tucked tight in his robes. Epheremelda paddled her hip to demonstrate, raising her rigid hand to her face and pretending to gaze into a mirror while fixing her locks. *Your promise was held by letting go!* she winked.

Jovani lost it then. Just as well, I did my part. said the princess, missing the faerie's hint, unaware that the granddaughter had retrieved her magic hand mirror (and the moon pearl too).

I'm serious. Epheremelda flew up to the ermine. On one hand, there's no magical solution here; can't just teleport out of this. *You cannot escape your disjunctive sacrifice!*

Fine—

—And on the other hand, Epheremelda interrupted while gesturing, No—not you. she reassured the hulking hand idling nearby. Zelda, you're going to have to walk yourself right out of here, down all those stairs and through the foyer of this Dark World travesty of Nayru's Tower.

Wallmaster Stowaway

What are you going to do?

I'm leaving how I came too—out the window! Please tell me you still have the pomegranate I gave you. said Epheremelda with an avauntular[67] tremble of concern.

Packed securely here… Zelda half-pulled the golden fruit from her waist pocket. Why?

Sahasrahla is right, a princess only belongs here if you 'know what you think you know'. Have some faith however and just hold onto that for now. In order to understand how clouded your understanding was, and despite this 'view', you'll get perspective by descending the tower.

What a mess! the princess punted a fashion doll over the balustrade where it fell silently.

Not that way. After descending and with the tower's high-altitude warp of myopia behind you—figuratively, but literally above you… she tried to elucidate with a prepositional dance. So, then you'll have to undergo the topos of conviction in the graveyard below! By going all the way down, only then will you overcome this… Epheremelda twirled, illuminating the louche milieu.

---

67   Like an aunt. Similar to avuncular for uncles, but for aunties or those behaving like one.

Shhh! Zelda put a finger (near) to the faerie, I hear footsteps. They're coming up…

Epheremelda blew a close but no-contact kiss at the ermine's nose and fluttered off the balcony – roiling squall ahoy, disappearing into the sempiternal tempest above Death Mountain.

Wallmaster! Zelda hailed the gaunt manus lurking on the fringe, Open your fingers!

Prithee, Princess! Your banquet awaits! said a blue zazek in the hall sent up to check, escorted by the two taros who had calmed down since their bout with the five-fingered demon. Her majesty… must be elsewhere. said the servant, scowling at the bedlam and pretending not to notice the unusual destruction of the overturned antechamber. Anticipating her response, the dinosaur-man leaned near the doorway so as to not intrude. Ah, it's you. said the blue zazek, stepping aside as the wallmaster creepily hovered out of the room, slowly gliding above the ground as a closed fist. Playing dumb came naturally as the bullmen peered into the boudoir, honoring Zelda's request and pretending to see it for the first time. Who! What happened here? We have to tell Sahasrahla. The princess must be in trouble! The two beefs shook their horns, let off the hook as mute minotaurs, as they understood speech but could not respond. Of all the lackeys in the tower, only the forked-tongues of the zazek licensed any subservient articulation.

Is it done? asked the heron, standing over the black kettle at the center of the banquet.

Civey of Linkalope? said the owl, distracted and inspecting a piece of the broken tiara.

Neither civey nor of linkalope, as there's no meat to be found. said the condor, ladling the empty broth with a gawk of chasupas clutching their herbs, awaiting further instructions.

Her majesty is nowhere to be found in the cupola. reported the blue zazek, too nervous to mention the details of the seventh floor disarray as the wallmaster passed above.

Sahasrahla knew better than to ask the taros anything, but they were upstairs so he petitioned a second opinion anyway: Did she jump? The two bullmen shook their heads—no.

Does she have the mirror? asked Aginah of his older brother.

I've kept it safe on my body ever since Blind retrieved it. said Sahasrahla.

And we would've passed her, if she had descended; there's no way... said the lost old man, whose voice faded into the distance while Zelda's secret sedan nonchalantly exited the wedding reception. Peering between the clammy fingers, thick as tree trunks, the ermine felt her stomach drop as the gravity defying wallmaster arced into the vast and vacuous lair adjacent to the great hall. The constant skittering of the rabid giant moldorm echoed throughout the capacious stadium. *SKE-SKE-SKE!* rattled the monster's chitinous carapace, scuffing loudly across the stone platform rising all the way up from the sixth floor below. With a sheer edge, no intruder would dare scuffle with the wild-eyed worm that was stationed there as a guard. The prized pet of Sahasrahla who would feed it live prisoners for the harrowing entertainment of the tower staff, Zelda figured it was at least ten times the size of the already-giant mountainshrimp[68] that she and the bunny and boar first encountered inside the caverns when hiking out to the highlands. Safely above and then beyond the tumbling shrimp-slitherer, the princess tried to relax as they continued to make their slow sinking getaway. As a reanimated and enthralled undead servant of unknown anatomical origins, she nonetheless got the impression that the soulless wallmaster was content to ferry her down the pitfall. Aftall, that was the enormous hand's purpose: to drop from the shadows of the ceiling (or a nook in the wall) and grab unwanted visitors – depositing them unharmed in the second floor vestibule – or wherever its master demanded otherwise.

Where did the wallmaster go?! said Sahasrahla, entering the moldorm's nest behind them.

Zelda tried to look back and see how close they were, but the wallmaster continued knuckles-forward and she wouldn't dare lean out

---

68   Common name for a moldorm.

from its grip to gauge their winged pursuants. Why are you going so slow? the ermine slapped the distal phalanx that she sat on, curled up. Docile until now, the linkalope in her lap set his rodent incisors into the hand's purlicue – biting deep into the orange fleshy thenar webbing that wrinkled between its thumb and index finger. Already gashed from the skirmish with the taros, the wallmaster didn't take it personally. Stop! reprimanded the ermine, prying the linkalope off. Hearing her words, the hand stalled abruptly. Make haste, full speed ahead! the princess redoubled, ensuring that the antlered-hare couldn't interfere with her command of their automatically voice-guided manual shuttle.

There it is! shouted Aginah the heron, audibly getting closer.

She must be riding in its hold. followed the condor.

Take us to the entrance! the princess reminded the hand in case it had other directions. And perhaps it did, as the wallmaster then gained altitude, up from the bordering abyss and into a stairwell near the corner of the square stadium, above the giant moldorm's structural mesa.

Don't let them out of sight. said the myopic owl, trailing after his avian brethren.

We must be on the sixth floor still, she thought, as they passed through a series of smaller interconnected quarters – one, two, a third, and then a fourth where the wallmaster ducked into a stairwell in the middle of the room. I think we're on the fifth floor now, she told the linkalope that was clueless. Their unscrupulous yet obedient chauffeur gained speed into an adjacent long hallway – then another that extended parallel. If they were hooting, hollering or squawking, the three tower lords behind them would've been drowned out by the grinding noise of mechanical clapping and whirring that increased in volume. What is that sound? said Zelda, half-expecting Sahasrahla to be close enough to answer her. She did not remember this kinetic feature when ascending previously – loud conveyor belts clanked along the floor of the square room, a trap which must've been activated by a zazek to ensnare them; just following orders! However comically ineffective since they were flying.

ZELDA! SHE'S HERE! shouted the heron, awkwardly flapping astride the giant floating fist and unable to get a closer look without poking his beak. THIS WAY!

Shoo! Aginah! the ermine princess responded from within the wallmaster, barely visible through the knuckle crack of the hand's middle and ring finger. I've made up my mind!

Convicted as always. said Aginah trying to arrest their escape by landing on the hand.

What are you afraid of? she asked, noticing the tremble in his harsh voice.

The gangly heron managed to perch, listing the wallmaster to one side.

ZWOOSH! ZWOOSH! a searing beam flashed in quick succession from the wall, so bright that the inside of Zelda's decaying getaway carriage strobed. Are we on fire? she sniffed, peering out the padded porthole formed by the wallmaster's curled pinky finger. Singed feathers drifted by, but there was no way to look down or up for where Aginah might've gone. Gaining a little altitude and nearly brushing the ceiling, she figured they were no longer hindered by the heron on top. Two eyes stared blankly on the wall, one of which they must've flown in front of but now kept a safe distance from their menacing stare. The whole tower is alive—alert of our egress. said Zelda, reassuring the careening bogie, Steer clear of all traps, golems, and other such enchanted guardians! The ermine braced herself as they hurtled across an abysmal quadrangle akin to the conveyer belt room, leaving the fifth floor in their wake.

Only two rooms into the fourth floor, the wallmaster decided to land, depositing Zelda on the unusually soft sandy floor. What are you doing? Don't stop here! she freaked, clutching the linkalope still. The door they had entered from locked behind them, along with another identical blocked portal to the side at her left. This isn't the way out! she waved at the wallmaster that idled up toward the ceiling, casting its menacing shadow on the ground that began to tremble. AIEAAH! shrieked Zelda who scooched to the center of the room as three lumbering lanmolas chewed out from beneath the sand. Ravenous hunters loyal only to the condor and almost as long as the room was wide, the segmented tergum of the three lumbering centipedes clicked around their prey, unaware or nonplussed by the poised hand hanging out. Waiting for the subterranean invertebrates to fully emerge, the wallmaster then set upon them, easily gripping their wriggling green bodies and with a terrifying force, squeezing and squishing them apart. YEUHK! the helpless ermine gagged, watching the doomed desert horrors above die without a fair fight, although relieved for it. With the decapitated head of the second lanmola stubbornly latched onto the hand with its twitching mandibles, the rugged wallmaster set out undeterred, stalking the third. Flicking the spineless head off its girdled and lacerated thumb, the last foe mistakenly twisted itself into a vulnerable curl, allowing the wallmaster to envelope the entirety of the gigantic insect, squeezing hot ooze all through its crushing fingers. Without delay the hand lowered to pick her up, creaking open its zombie fingers still dripping with hemolymph. EUH! Zelda had second thoughts about riding inside the hand's pronated hold after witnessing how mercilessly it killed the formidable bugs without any contest whatsoever, but in lieu of lanmolas the reflexive bulwark doors reopened and the wallmaster's command was her wish.

Skulking through a succession of six identically dimensioned rooms, each with a host of monsters and snares easily avoided thanks to the wallmaster's movement along the ceiling, they descended yet again to the third floor which marked the threshold that insulated the sovereign upstairs from the servile downstairs of the tower. An uneventful express of a long causeway suspended over a treacherous unfathomable pit, then the two-tiered cellar wide open from recent rummaging, a subsequent statue gallery that also required Sahasrahla's big master key but only from the outside (said threshold), a triple succession of barricade-bulwark-bollard chambers, each riddled with motley security and deathly spikes galore. Zelda swallowed to pop her ears as the air pressure noticeably got heavier by the time they arrived at the second floor.

The barbican escalator is just ahead – drop us at the patio! she requested eagerly.

Don't let her go! screeched the owl Sahasrahla at his two brothers.

She's a keeper. Left me singed... grated Aginah the heron.

Reminds me of my granddaughter. the lost old condor cawed.

They're coming up from the first floor below! said Zelda, spurring the hand toward the tower entrance. They must've taken a teleportation shortcut, or flown down one of the chasms that extend between stories, she recalled the many bottomless shafts they had traversed above. Despite the sequestered enclosure of their carrioncraft the linkalope and ermine could feel a damp breeze from outside, blowing in from the gateless mouth of the corrupt structure.

Rhythmically bouncing up from the dungeon, a single-file jaunt of six armos knights proceeded ahead of the owl, heron, and condor who hunched together, waiting for the broad juggernauts to get through the unaccommodating doorway. Hurry up you potty pile of platemail! Sahasrahla kicked the brainless suit of armor at the end of the line marching as fast as it could.

They were never intended to leave the basement! Aginah apologized for his armos.

And the princess was never imagined to flee the spire. said the lost old man pushing his way into the lobby swooping ahead of the wallmaster. Turn back on your own volition, he said, it's not too late to make amends. *You're making a grave mistake.*

Hold up! Zelda tugged on the wallmaster, keeping their distance.

Not a ring formation, go block the door! hooted the owl angrily at the armos sentinels who had valiantly tried their best to encircle the wallmaster but from out of reach below.

The three lords perched on the exit terrace with the owl in the middle, heron to his left, and the condor to his right. The armos unit split into two parallel lines of three each and leapt up the tandem stairs where they sationing themselves behind the brothers and in front of the exit.

To your turret! And prepare a plea for the gravity of your conviction. said the owl.

Yes, Sahasrahla. yielded Zelda, yanking the wallmaster around.

Enough of that——return by foot my princess.

The saunter of sorrow. she agreed, confiding a goodbye to the five-fingered cadaver. Zelda solemnly landed the battleworn thing and dismissed its steadfast service. With the bow around her neck and balancing the linkalope thrown over her shoulders again, the ermine held onto the cleaver for whatever reason and did as she was told. Instead of retreating where they had arrived from (an ascending stairway atop a stoop opposite the exit terrace) she skidded down another hovel found along the same wall where the armos and lords had emerged from that also descended to the first floor and basement below but via partitioned passageways.

The intransigence! swelled the owl, taking flight.

She's heading for the Spiral–

–of Desperation! said the condor, completing the heron's exclamation that her intent must be this restricted route; a claustrophobic corkscrew bored through the mountain bedrock.

OUF! What mimicry of unfaithful treachery is this? *Watch out!* said Sahasrahla, evading a threatening payload that swung dangerously overhead. While the armos were slave to Aginah, the wallmaster was still bound to the princess. The enchanted suit of armor flailed like a crab clenched from behind, unable to free itself from the deadlock of the huge undead hand carrying out Zelda's final command. Wedging itself backwards into the doorway and using the armos as a buffer, the corpsy grip lived up to its name and was the master of the wall; none could pass. The unlucky armos held hostage raised its shield and instinctively blocked in self-defense against the remaining five sentinels that flared their futile daggers at the hijacked traitor.

Under the Unmarked Grave

Wrapping her left hand with a rag torn from her dress, the ermine princess held fast onto the central column of the stonewrought chirality[69] and took the unavoidable dizziness in stride. Descending counterclockwise by rapidly slipping her heels from one angular step to the next, Zelda was

---

69   The Spiral of Desperation is a single-helix staircase that travels vertically from the basement of
      the tower to the base of the mountain. A secret passage up to the Dark Tower from the Ghostly
      Garden.

nonetheless unsure if going down was significantly easier than ascending. Having taken this secret passage prior, the way up had been a hideously hot slog – at least an hour of winding, always with the left leg doing all the lifting due to the tight radius of the spiral stairs. *Clockwise: left foot aches. Counterclockwise: left hand chafes.* A close tradeoff made less ambiguous by the conviction of her escape, nearing the garden whose topology warps any soul to believe what they feel is imperative. The princess wasn't so delusional as to forget that conviction also motivated her up these stairs in the first place. She would have never known about this route if it weren't for Sahasrahla's invitation however many weeks ago—no, *months?* The errant heiress still didn't know how many days the tower had claimed; of course she only had herself to blame for the cardinal mistake of settling oneself in the deforming Dark World!

Hypnotized by the sensory deprivation, Zelda and the linkalope fell into a mutual trance. After parting ways with her fellow exiles due to a disagreement at the northern Topos Bros shop, her bunny knight set out to the northeast, while the boar and her went west in search of another maiden kept against her will in the Skull Woods. Zelda insisted her enchanted map was correct. Making a point, she leaned over it as the doublet of black diamonds around her neck gravitated with a magical magnetism toward that ominous forest – indicating one of their sisters was to be found there. Any such demonstration of evidence was irrelevant according to the boar, so what started as a mere argument then escalated as Zelda and Ganon debated whether the nearby pyramid could be entered without all the crystals or not (she said 'all', he said 'two is enough'). She was further annoyed that the boar didn't believe the green-haired maiden they had first discovered in the Palace of Darkness who unabashedly blamed Ganon for her imprisonment. Zelda started to wonder if she was right, although whatever that gal meant by 'Ganon's hiding place' eluded her – he wasn't hiding now. Maybe she was speaking of the past, Zelda thought. But the boar refused to humor anything that sensational maiden of misinformation had told them, especially her entreaty to destroy him! This latent fallout fomented to the point of schism when triggered by a hookshot debacle that ensued while crossing the river. Willing to sacrifice the hardwon crystals to prove him wrong, Zelda foisted her necklace of two sealed maidens onto the boar, who was intent on entering the pyramid that loomed within sight to the south. Leaving her alone, she was approached by the owl at the base of the mountain who offered an ultimatum to the crestfallen ermine. 'Either you believe you can save this realm, or you don't. Either you believe our lineage of sages can become gods, or you cling to the absent goddess who has left us in darkness'. he had told her in that place of conviction, 'Royalty does not warp. If you know that you are fit for a throne and crown, join me in the tower. We can master the destiny of the Sacred Realm if we grab the reins from the top of the world'. said the owl before gyrating away on a cliffside draft toward his aerie keep after revealing the hidden cave to her during his spiel. That contorted climbing motion took the ermine the next week to recover from, hobbling off a sore knee with a blue cane borrowed from Aginah that also aided her tender gait with a magical aura of protection that always left Zelda feeling quite sapped, however safe.

Twirling through the tenebrosity with all that in hindsight, hugging the linkalope in her right arm, going down was much faster but disorienting and nauseating. Built for abandonment and intended as a royal egress exclusively, the vertical stairwell was accessed from a trapdoor easily overlooked deep in the tower's prison ward. Disguised as an especially cruel holding cell that no one would dare venture into out of curiosity, known only to the lords residing above the third floor and not even the jailor who patrolled that lonesome premise. No thief or insurgent force could feasibly employ it from below if they tried, as the tiresome ascent culminated to an oubliette that ultimately required a helping hand to open the grate and lower a rope ladder. This wasn't Zelda's first time escaping the shackles of royalty through a secret passage though, nor would it be the last time she found herself entering an oubliette cell in hopes of freeing herself.

WoA? hAiL! Lady of the High Keep! said the startled hinox, tasked with inconspicuously guarding the cave without drawing too much attention to it by patrolling a few paces beyond.

Hail. said Zelda, unnecessarily shielding her eyes from the forever dusk of the realm with her ragged left hand, confusing the cyclops ahead that she might be saluting it. The fashion doll she had booted out of her bedroom caught her attention, tied into the hinox's hair as a charm. Captivated by the jingling collection of weapons worn around its neck, she then spotted her mirror shield that hung in the middle − jewelry for the giant and resembled a polished amulet. Having stored the shiny pavise at the base of the stairs just inside the cave (so she could climb without encumbrance as the shield barely fit in the tight corkscrew) this patrol must've found it while she was up in the tower for however many… Zelda wasn't about to ask for it back as the shield would ironically blow her cover of a tower princess for whom bulwarks are unbecoming.

I'm honored. said the hinox bowing between two trees, Trud at your service.

Stiff and wobbly, the ermine tossed aside her makeshift mitt − tattered and blackened from the friction of holding the stairwell column all the way down. *Where to…* she thought aloud.

Looks like you're making a sacrifice. said Trud, avoiding eye contact out of respect for the ermine's obviously frazzled comportment. The hinox gimballed its cyclops globe at her feet.

Howso?

Forgive me for noticing Princess, but you clutch both a cleaver and a creature.

Zelda looked down her chin, Verily—yes. she said, initially presuming the hinox was inferring that her shambled debut from the cave announced her renunciation of the tower's riches. I hope you don't mind. she said self-consciously, adjusting her paltry possessions.

I'm doubly honored! repeated the hinox, Rumor was the princess would make a sacrifice at her coronation, but I was certain that would be an exclusive event. Trud focused behind her, Is there a procession in your wake?

Just us. We've already had the reception. Zelda obfuscated.

Seems backwards. pondered the cyclops, confounded by her partyless offering.

This is how I chose my sacrifice. she said, remembering the two options Epheremelda presented to her. And quite the letdown... Zelda slumped in exhaustion.

Lower than you are accustomed to. shrugged Trud, who lacked the imagination to visualize the opulence the princess must have enjoyed upstairs but was convinced anyway.

How anticlimactic! So much trouble only to stand where I started. she fumed, starting to question whether the faerie misled her. I must've misinterpreted... I know—what I must do.

Only at this elevation do doubts become convictions. assured the hinox kindly.

Surely the sacrifices are dependent, and not disjunctive in the slightest...

Aye! Trud had no idea, but was a yes-oaf and always inclined to agree with authorities.

The lifestyle and lifeblood must spill each other... she revisited Epheremelda's words.

Prophetic. You are certainly a sagacious priestess of wise renown.

Oh, I'm not religious! Nothing to read into—it'll be over in a painless flash. All's well that ends well! said Zelda, looking for a suitable altar. Incredulous that her escape from the tower facilitated any substantial liberation, the princess could've left the premises and continued on her way to the Skull Woods for the crystal maiden held captive there. As long as she *wilfully* lingered in the garden where the hinox rightfully believed her to be the Lady of the High Keep then the ermine princess had not sacrificed her royal station, although all Zelda had to do was walk west where the map had shown a descendant of the Wise Men was held *against her will.* But the ermine thought she had chosen one of the faerie's two options – the good one at that! Zelda presumed she had sacrificed the supposed *lifestyle* by causing a great scene and fleeing the coronation banquet. Unbeknownst to her unexamined beliefs she was still a princess and deluded by the garden's topology of conviction, stepping foot at this lower elevation from the topos of myopia on the mountaintop, she couldn't see that her presumptions were misguided; Zelda wouldn't catch her conceit if the hinox rubbed it in her face. Unable to go further while trapped in this privileged impasse and in defiance of Epheremelda's warning, the ermine was intent on taking it out on this linkalope – cruelly projecting her own futility and self-destruction. By failing to sacrifice her own princessdom, she would slay the animal out of spite. The faerie told her she had to choose her sacrifice, but that she was not at liberty to choose whether she sacrifices or not. Zelda flipped the mandatory tradeoff on its head: by destroying both 'lives', which Epheremelda did not warn against exactly. Surely the royal ermine would be free then! Alas, sacrificing both is tantamount to choosing neither, but no princess should be bound by rotten paradoxes. By cheating fate however, Zelda would only exchange one entrapment for another and soon find herself in a fitting iteration of where she fled from; the bind remained.

There is no goddess to observe the meaning of your ritual and what the sacrifice portends, but I'll be your eyewitness. said Trud the cyclops.

It's not a ritual! There's nothing to it. Don't mention any goddess. This is not an augur, just a dumb beast! she flopped the linkalope around to exhibit his insouciant lack of dignity.

Pardon, I did not intend to suggest you were superstitious or anything.

I revel in the sacrilege. That's all! Such a thrill! Zelda shook the cleaver.

That is religious, is it not? asked Trud, more astute than most hinox.

Oh no, no no no—not at all. she shook her head.

But how would I desecrate something, if I didn't know it was sacred or worthy of praise? Trud pondered its two supinated palms as if he held the hypothetical. Because I cannot know what is underneath those graves, I do my best not to step on them. said the giant cautiously.

How? You cannot desecrate what you cannot understand. And I've never heard a hinox make such an apophatic apology for the hallowed! Who are you to discuss the indescribable by delimiting what it is not? the ermine princess made her exculpatory case for willful ignorance.

Stationed here in the topos of conviction, I can't help but start from conclusions. I have but one eye, but if we all know meaning when we see it, then ignorance is a ritual too.

A ritual? No it's not. There is no ritual devoid of *intended* meaning!

There are unknowing rituals. And the meaning is inescapable.

You're seeing things where they don't exist, with that big eye of yours!

Look! In this Dark World the meaning is there whether we *choose* to see it or not. Sometimes hard to spot, because it's so dim all the time, but you can feel it. You know it.

And I'm not ignorant. I know we are formed by what's in our heart and mind.

You are most wise! sweated the hinox, I only intend to expound that in this noumenal realm of true forms, there is no escape from the implications of our deeds. And how we heed that call, or turn away, shapes the very form of our being no matter what. Trud wiped its brow.

A verificationist's paradise, sighed the ermine, it's the gravity we stand in. We all want our presumptions to prove out here, and to such a degree that no refutation is ever considered. But if you are correct, your assertion is certainly only incidentally right. sniped the princess who refused to let a hinox off the hook having outwitted the cyclops siblings Baog and Vuam before.

None are more intransigent than the dead. Trud pointed to the right, Zelda's left, where the Ghostly Garden reclined a short distance away. Depending on how convicted you are, then you might join them! BLuRhWaHUruR! thundered the hinox in good humor.

I will prove you wrong, stomped Zelda, I will spill the lifeblood of a loved one and show you that it means nothing to me! And therefore, nothing at all...

If you insist, I am only here to assist! But will it mean something to the dead?

Faintly!

And if you don't mind me asking: what's love got to do with it? Trud wasn't sure who she was referring to, as the ugly linkalope was inconceivably kindred to her. GURZ! yelled the hinox to its gravekeeper associate. We're coming over! Trud waved to the nearby ogling neighbor.

Without delay. said the ermine, worrying that the wallmaster might've yielded by now.

The unmarked grave awaits.

Is that a good surface for making a clean cut? she gestured with the cleaver.

Yurp. said Trud, fixating on the other hinox. We have a special guest!

oUR QuEeN! I am delighted to meet you. clapped the cyclops gravekeeper Gurz.

Not your queen yet. said the ermine, half-lying and contriving a stern tone of voice to uphold her dominion that the otherwise hostile (and always hungry) giants currently worshiped.

I watch cave, Gurz watch graves – one eye there, one eye here! said Trud densely.

Where are the hyu? asked Zelda, remembering the whirling ghosts that haunted here.

Who? scratched Trud.

Did you see them before? Gurz asked Zelda. Don't worry, those aren't ghosts, they were just doing their job – the maintenance crew. Soulless and summoned as needed.

Bizarre. said Zelda with a stupefied frown as she followed the bicyclops.[70] Gurz led the way toward the back of the graveyard, wending their way through the unsightly memorials and sepulcher effigies toward the northeast. Trud picked up a carnivorous ropa anemone and easily tossed it several graves over while Gurz lifted a giant skull blocking their way. Stepping into the cordoned off plot, Zelda graced her foot over the thick carpet of white flowers that entirely covered the ground but only within that fenced area. That's not suitable for a sacrifice…

Hold on. Trud stepped in front of the ermine princess, shielding her from Gurz who was winding up to wallop a punch into the epitaphless monument. *KRUGRUMBLE!* the headstone slid back as if by design, without any projectile debris as Trud had precautioned against.

---

70 A pair of hinoxes. Two cyclopses marauding in concert.

Away with you. Trud backfooted away another ropa encroaching on their business.

Down there. pointed Gurz whose whomp had unearthed stairs of a royal reliquary.

What you do in the underworld, stays in the underworld.

You're not going to come with me? she asked Trud specifically.

Without having to look at each other for confirmation, they both shook their heads in unanimous agreement: *not a chance.* We're not allowed to leave this elevation—*lord's orders.*

Sahasrahla said so, eh?

I also have a thing with blood, said Gurz, can't tolerate the sight of it.

There's no blood in the underworld or afterlife! Zelda implored, but Gurz silently retorted by gesturing to the live linkalope. They crossed their massive arms and stiffened with stoicism.

We'll stand watch. said Trud with a rigid lip.

Watching the other way. said Gurz, pivoting from the entrance and putting its hand on Trud's shoulder to do the same. The hinoxes dug their heels in, standing as tall as trees.

Fine! Well, I'll have you both know that I'm only doing this to prove it means nothing!

No way to know until you go through with it. said Trud offering the princess some final amoral support as she descended brashly with conviction, but obliquely just in case there was an unseen lintel truss or cobwebs that might ambush her on the way into the pitch-black tomb.

Epheremelda, this is all your fault, misleading me into a false bivalence. You knew all along that one cannot be sacrificed without the other! Zelda's pouting echoed quieter as she pitter-pattered down into the resting place of the unmarked mausoleum. There was a brief landing, with another short flight of stairs leading into a long narrow hallway, lit at the end by two lanterns. Stoked ad hoc by the hyu maintenance crew, she figured staunchly as all her previous doubts diminished while approaching a solitary altar at the end of the chamber. Passing the tandem torches, the ermine princess stepped up onto the slightly elevated redstone plinth, presumably where sarcophagi would be placed. Zelda paused, eavesdropping on the two hinoxes reverberating above…

Don't eat rabbits – dirty animals. said Trud, Lots of parasites, because they eat anything!

So do we, but we're clean, right? Gurz replied neurotically.

No way to know, unless someone tried to eat us. surmised Trud.

But then we'd be dead, and never know the answer ourselves. said Gurz.

An unsolvable mystery meat we are! Trud proclaimed the limits of their self-knowledge.

NoBOdY eAtS A HinOX! laughed Gurz. But she's not eating it… I don't think. *And isn't that more of a hare?*

Antlered too… Not your usual rodent. Quite the taxonomic anomaly. said Trud in its unusual erudition.

Don't talk about our princess like that! Gurz admonished.

I'm referring to the creature Her Highness held so dearly… placated Trud diplomatically.

HMPH! Zelda huffed upon hearing Trud say *dearly*, discarding the cooperative linkalope onto the redstone. Calling everybody's bluff, she brandished the cleaver and HRMMM! *PHUNK!* she decapitated the naive thing, flinging aside the vibrating chopper that rang unforgiving in her bloodstained hands. The mortified ermine barely breathed, listening if anyone had heard while the animal drained out. There was no confirmation from above – the deed was all on her alone. Zelda felt her stomach drop as the pool flowed against the back wall where it scaled up the olivine bricks and spread out into the shape of a triangle pointing down. The grisly veil turned black against the slick wall, reflecting the flickering lantern light at first but then matte and void. *Who's there…* Zelda strained to ask, dragged by a shame so heavy her conscience could've fallen through the floor. Silhouettes of arms issued from the opaque portal, cusping the whole massacre and scooping the deceased linkalope. Zelda almost fainted watching in terror as the ethereal sinews of the shadow arms pulsated under the burden of a sacrifice's physical body.

Seal it up.

You mean to bury her alive?

If that's her preference.

But—milord, Her Highness!

She can wait down there until we find the rest…

Sahas– gasped Zelda, turning back to the exit as the hinoxes easily slid the cenotaph stone above into place. The sound of the grave smashing to a halt ossified her belief that there was no hope. She had fulfilled her own certainty of doom in the topos of conviction. HU-HIYAH! NO—OFF! LET GO! the ermine jerked away from an elongated shadow clutching at her dress. AIEEEEEEE! NO! The impossibly articulated arm deftly pickpocketed the golden pomegranate that Epheremelda had given her earlier that evening. Catching the spectral thief's frigid wrist and tugging with all her might, the residual gore on her hands turned to ice. AWAY! First her fingers went numb, then the strength went out of her arms altogether. Zelda knew her very life was draining into the deathly shadow, but the frozen blood had annealed her grip, and there was no letting go. I'm captured by my own volition! *Somebody help!* the hopeless princess whimpered as a rasping draft extinguished the lanterns, doffing the only light in the tomb.

The Princess of Repudiation

Sahasrahla's runaway bride was buried <u>alive</u> and that's how she entered the afterlife. Not unlike the first time she fell through an unsolicited triangular oblivion, Zelda found herself in an evermore undesirable situation. Have I escaped the consequence of trying to escape reality? the ermine posed the question with a critical honesty she had not interrogated herself with in a long time, Or is this my eternal comeuppance? Katabasis to the underworld was not the plan! What did I do to deserve this? Oh unhappy hopelessness! she cried to the apathetic depths…

What did I do to deserve this? Oh unhappy hopelessness! her voice echoed back.

What did I do to deserve this? Oh unhappy hopelessness!

What did I do to deserve this? Oh unhappy hopelessness!

Foo-PFFF! Foo-PFFF! Foo-PFFF! she panted. Unsure at first if she could breathe, the ermine confirmed she must still be embodied after a few hyperventilating experiments involving exhaling heavily into her palm, pinching inflated cheeks, and thumping her chest while humming like a hooligan. Vitals assured, her previously held convictions from the Ghostly Garden above (consisting of impervious doubts, vehement moral relativism, entitlement to ethical exemption, and that sacrificing a poor docile mongrel didn't mean anything) were now wholly confounded. Everything she thought she knew was suspended in that instant. *Unbelievable recapitation!...* Whose blood was spilt if not yours? Zelda racked her lightheaded temples and braced herself against a wave of dizziness, I must be delirious to dream such a vision. Are you no more than the mirage made by regretful compunction? Mine alone—you must be a projection of remorse, showing a deed in reverse? A shattered tasse does not mend itself, nor forgive the slack finger. Scuppered teacups and irreversible crimes, nobody is exonerated from entropy's inviolable law, most unhappy hopeless heartbreaker of inescapable indictment! the ermine wailed in soliloquy, *Are you a phantom or are you unmarred?* Lo, if you did not die, then the sordid thrust of my kitchen cleaver was inconsequential, but a heinous villain I am regardless! sulked the princess as her preconceived moral framework burst and rescinded into irrelevance with the linkalope miraculously standing before her. Blanched translucent, the antlered-hare alert on his haunches held the absconded golden pomegranate as a squirrel cradles a prized nut. Hushed and plush as always, the chimerical buck bounded off with rack intact and exhibited no signs of butchery. *Linkalope...* said Zelda, amazed by the mystical lagomorph's newfound nacreous radiance that became more pronounced with distance. LINK! she finally admitted too loud too late what she knew in her heart of hearts from the start. My twice-transmogrified knight! If only you could speak! Then none of this would've happened. she jogged in place, shaking off the numbness and embarrassment of knowing full well that insincerity has no place in the afterlife where souls are see-through and our cloistered ethos made transparent. Egad... The ermine's arms tingled and gradually regained their heat after jostling with the gloomy hand that had pulled her through the nullity and into the nether. Wait! I didn't mean it! said Zelda, clenching her unresponsive fists to speed up the circulation. *What kind of apology is that for ritual murder?* she asked herself, confirming that her bow was still slung around her neck. DO NOT EAT THAT! Zelda chased the warm glow of the exotic fruit that reflected specular patterns on the glistening stalactites above. The spelunking princess lacked confidence in the lay of the land thus didn't dare run as fast as she could, accidentally kicking a few Puffshrooms[71] into musky clouds of spores while trying to keep up with the only source of light ahead of her. Lagging behind, Zelda stopped and watched in awe as the linkalope (yes, Link) effortlessly ran over a body of water as big as Lake Hyrule that would've remained hidden if it weren't for this dazzling chase. Carrying the aureate spec without wake, the fleeting hare stopped on a small island with many menhirs – lifesize stones erratically circumscribing an ignoble shrub that stood defiantly rigid in the windless underworld. Coincidentally on cue, his arrival enkindled a candlelight vigil of innumerable pale-blue flames babbling in fluvial processions and arcing indiscernibly far beyond. Taking her time to find a route, the ermine felt out a shallow isthmus, slowly swishing over the soft sands (immediately reminding her of the lanmolas' lair; same texture) as to not cause a scare or draw too much attention if anything else lurked in the voracious darkness of the depths that devoured any light that dared to shine. Still unsure what her metaphysical condition was, Zelda instinctually pulled her bow just to be safe and err on the side of self-preservation. But the humid air had loosened the string, and what did it matter? *All out.* She didn't have any arrows anyway. Embarking onto the island, the linkalope's effervescence illuminated the twisted snag under which stood several other shades coalescing as the ermine drew near. No taller than a hinox, the deciduous tree had multiple trunks, and while the canopy was within reach the whole plant was long since withered; how anything could grow down here baffled

---

71   A genus of underworld mushroom species that propagate by puffing spores. All species are edible but inhaling the spores can cause confusion if ejected into a thick cloud. Also referred to as ghost farts.

Zelda. She got the impression this plant had never lived – born of death itself beyond her comprehension of common botany. The ermine stepped into a smooth depression where a menhir stone once stood, marveling at the compressed divot.

Did you not anguish? the short pearlescent shade of a Hylian priest asked out of the black and apropos of nothing. *You did not.* he judged while adjusting his spectacles.

I… Zelda froze, unaccustomed to the mores of posthumous politeness. Why do ghosts invariably broach their distress dreadfully out of context? No wonder the living are spooked!

You did not anguish from stradling the contradiction.

Of—Epheremelda's message? Quite relieved on the contrary, at least for sacrificing the smothered 'lifestyle' that had me stuck up in Sahasrahla's tower. Escaping was not easy, but I felt no anguish; arduous more like it. *What's it to you anyway?*

Not that. When you chose to 'spill the lifeblood of a loved one'. You did not sacrifice because you felt no anguish. said the scrupulous shade. And for what, if you left the tower…

Is it too late? she said, starting to feel very bad about it all of a sudden. Did the faerie tell you what transpired? How do you know what she confided in me… Zelda leaned toward him, admiring his little hat that he sported so neatly in the afterlife despite wavering out of focus.

Venus sent her to the underworld first – as faeries and nymphs can come and go without wager or penalty – where she took the golden pomegranate from this tree that permitted you to enter the afterlife without detaching your spirit from your body; without dying. he made it clear.

I nearly perished! By a grim grip of shadows that pulled me straight through the wall!

Link's blood summoned it; opened the door. But you did not anguish along the way.

I squirmed—squeamish about it. But why should I anguish? I didn't know this was Link! Zelda lied, pointing to the linkalope's shade. When the short bespeckled ghost did not respond, the ermine backpedaled, Perhaps I knew, *I had a feeling...* But I didn't *knooow* that I knew it!

Because that intuition was not a conviction you disregarded it. he sighed, taking a deep breathless pause, I'm disappointed in you Princess Zelda.

Reverend? she recognized him upon hearing her formal title.

The Princess is here? asked another shade of a little boy that stepped out.

Only this contradiction may open your future from here...

Entering the afterlife before death is enough of a contradiction if you ask me. said the boy dangling his hueless digits over the resplendent passport fruit held by the linkalope ghost.

What contradiction? What does this have to do with anguish? she pressed the priest.

A sacrifice is religious, but slaying is profane; neither is without implication. Denying the meaning of the former leaves you only the latter: a premeditated murder. he deemed harshly.

I thought staying neutral about it would keep my hands clean; *no religion required?*

Exactly the opposite. Raising the cleaver as only a cutthroat is no longer a sacrifice in observance of divine will if you did not heed the disjunctive destiny of Epheremelda's edict.

You tried to cheat fate... recklessly, however passionately. said the youthful shade.

But I almost got eaten alive! she said self-consciously standing amongst the departed. What would you have me do? Zelda asked the priest. I should have just left for the Skull Woods after escaping the tower, but what would I do with the linkalope? Carry around that limp liability forever? He's better off dead, so put me out of my misery as well! huffed the ermine princess.

You sacrificed neither in good-faith, unwilling to relinquish your royal prestige and ignoring who the linkalope was – destroying both in bad-faith, and dooming yourself.

You *did* pretend that you were the Dark Queen when talking to that Trud. said the boy.

Then why did Epheremelda give me the golden pomegranate? She must've known that I would misinterpret her—how about you lighten up and hand me that *snack to save my soul...*

Maybe this was meant to be? the boy sided with Zelda, We transparent shades cannot see through the opacity of a living visitor anyway. How can we judge her in the present?

These current events are not so close that we cannot see them. And the linkalope showed me how it went down... the reverend responded pensively without turning away.

How does that make any sense? I don't get you ghosts. said Zelda.

Sniff sniff... Well then. the boy relented, rubbing his nose.

I only chastise because we have your best interests in mind, Princess Zelda.

Loyal beyond grave, reverend of the sanctuary. Alas, I am indeed distraught now...

Are you really? said the boy's shade, only able to take the outward living at their word.

Yes, pitiful are those who neglect the portents of pixies. And consider this: if all you did was execute Epheremelda's option to sacrifice the linkalope, without the gruesome admission that you were also murdering a loved one, then that too would exempt you of... *the anguish.* Carrying *this* contradiction to the underworld however is what makes one worthy of redemption.

If I had anguished and only sacrificed the linkalope, would the goddess have stayed my hand before the cleaver fell? The goddess is gone... Zelda blushed, I knew what I had to do.

In desperation, you had a conviction of convenience, but not the faith of anguish.

As one does in that warping topology of moral delusion! Who doesn't while standing at that elevation of the Dark World? she blamed the Golden Power for the blood on her hands.

I still don't understand what this is all about. said the boy. All's well that ends well.

Hey that's what I said. Zelda remembered her excuse to the hinox Trud above, shivering at the boy's haunting reiteration of the aphorism. I suppose all was *not* well if it ended like this…

Oh, recently? I can hear Link, your knight telling you this, weeks ago in the colonnade–

You're right. she remembered being too angry to take note at the time, He did say that.

Without anguish she did not pass this test of faith. the reverend exclaimed.

So, who cares? *Cough cough…* said the boy covering his mouth.

Because without **faith** she cannot leave this *hopeless* place.

Might as well be dead then– I had no hope in the tower either. Zelda despaired.

Even though she's a… the boy waved his hands grasping for the right word: *endotherm?* Very uncommon to encounter a specimen such as yourself in this sunless environment!

Only an aspiring naturalist would put it in those terms. said the reverend priest, previously keen on the physiology and phylogeny of organisms in his past life.

Bug catching was my passion: *ectotherms!* So that's why the word came to mind…

I'm sorry. said Zelda soberly, ignoring what he said, preoccupied with remorse for the child who must've died from an illness. Putting her woes aside for a moment, she asked the loyal reverend how he came here. *I knew it…* Agahnim did not take kindly to your sequestering of a princess in the sanctuary? I had a bad feeling… Zelda explained, preempting his response. Not one hour after our performance in Thieves' Town Theater, we were stepping out of a shop just east of the Village of Outcasts, I saw in the magic mirror a brigade of soldiers marching west from the castle in the Light World over a river dyke that did not exist in parallel Lorule. I can't say why but I just knew they were heading to the sanctuary, so I called to my nearby knight in panic, but there was no hope to intervene while we were trapped in the Dark World.

That's the Royal Park – best place to catch bugs. said the boy. I always felt safe there as the castle guard would often patrol and practice their routines through that airy woodland; there were no vagabonds nor neerdowells, unlike the northern forest. Caught more than I hoped for! *Cough cough...* Once the pestilence blew on an evil wind the soldiers seemed possessed and would no longer wave gaily as they did when they saw me. I was soon bedridden. *Sniff...*

What was your plea on my behalf? asked the priest's shade.

LINK! Help! The soldiers are coming to the sanctuary! AIEEEEEEE! Zelda reenacted.

A scream that will echo for all eternity... the boy covered his ethereal ears.

The loyal reverend took off his hat. I'm glad you disagreed with my insistence of hiding you there. he said to the princess. After you and Link decided to leave the sanctuary in search of the medallions together, they came for me, and unceremoniously cut me down there at the redstone chancel, desecrating the altar where I stood! The guards were possessed by the wizard's spell; while that is the *topography of faith* in Hyrule, I was nonetheless a convict of fate.

Where's faith in the Light World became conviction in the Dark World. she said, crossing her arms and looking down. Zelda quietly contemplated the unsettling similarities of how the reverend's death was reminiscent of her slaying the linkalope.

They had no anguish! Thoughtless guards, might as well have been soulless hyu.

Truly terrifying what otherwise honorable people can do when convinced...

But do not mourn me Princess, there is nothing to be done now. I can see that Agahnim wants to first unify the realms, and then make all of Hyrule an unmarked grave. His heart and mind seeks the Triforce to wish for a great flood that will turn history into a sea of oblivion.

How can you see this? Sahasrahla spoke of the same thing, this is his plan for undoing the bifurcated world that the cataclysm established many ages ago, but this is just another–

–Cataclysm, yes. Just because what I've seen is vivid and viscerally moving does not mean it should be regarded as inevitable. reassured the farsighted holy man.

Are you a fortune teller? I didn't think the sacred order allowed psychic avocations.

No, I had no paranormal pastimes! All shades in the underworld are, what's the word…

Hyperopic! said the boy.

Yes, thank you. We can see the past, and the future, but not the present. Only the living, if they dare to venture into the underworld are able to fill us in with what's happening right now.

Able to see far in either direction, but not near. *Cough! Sniff sniff…*

That's how you hear Link in the palisades… she now understood the boy's relay.

We have a blindspot that has a certain temporal diameter occluding current events. Recent details too blurry for us to make out were evinced by the linkalope. the priest repeated.

I have seen the wizard's flood as well. said a large shade approaching them with another at his side. It would be a world without gardens, and that would be worse than the underworld as at least we have faculties of eternal memory here. But a realm washed into oblivion could not remember its past, and without the humus of history there would be no future for Hyrule.

Daphnes! Zelda rushed to hug the king, who as Link's uncle explained, was also slain.

Oh– HO HO! There's nothing to embrace here, said the king as the ermine swiped through him with her arms, but your warmth is not lost on me, my sunshine.

Zelda turned to the shade at his side who shared the king's rotund figure with a crown of her own. Queen Mudora, my deepest condolences… I was not informed of your demise but I am not surprised to discover that the wizard did not risk leaving any of our royal lineage alive.

Yes, the past is sad and the future is mad. said the queen, acknowledging the two antecedent shades who were talking to Zelda first; the bug-catching kid and loyal reverend. Agahnim's cataclysm would not only drown the gardens but with it make the whole world an unmarked grave, a world without a center. The wizard knows that mortals, not goddesses, are the founders of a realm. Which is why he defaced the Hero's Tomb[72] that you passed through.

There was no epitaph. said Zelda defensively.

Out of spite, erased by Sahasrahla! The tragedy of conviction is but a comedy to Hylia who has a great sense of humor to draw you to the Hero's resting place, where you then slew the linkalope, and were yourself entombed as if dead. Mudora got to her point: An immortal goddess may bless a place, but she cannot leave the grave that grounds it. That is the duty of the sages – to mortalize time with the delimiting of spirit and consecration of their temples.

The wizard is foolish enough to believe that he can recreate history, not as a force of mortal inscription, but as an amnesia that washes away the marks we made. said King Hyrule. As you know, Sahasrahla is well intentioned and imagines a new dominion that completely *takes care of* its citizens. After his invocation, an induced cataclysm to rectify the old cataclysm, there will be no ground *to care for* at all! If he finds the Golden Power, then his sorcery will invert the Hyrule I presided over in which the citizens were the caretakers of governance; not wizards!

From the immaterial afterlife your magnanimity substantially eclipses his megalomania! Zelda bowed to the shade of King Hyrule. As for Agahnim, his strongest spell has always been the first he cast on himself: for the supreme delusion of claiming to be the rightful savior of a kingdom that he brought to its knees through lies and treachery. Having already warped the Sacred Realm, his wish was not complete – he told me only part of the Triforce was found.

---

72 Resting place of the Heroes of Time. A mausoleum in Hyrule that manifested a little too similar in the parallel Dark World for the wizard's liking hence defacing the grave and rendering it forever unmarked.

The owl cannot raise up his 'ultimate design' while you're here Zelda. said Mudora.

Let's not dwell on what might come to pass. said the king, frowning into his frilly ruff.

She's heard of enough of what we've witnessed, but speaking of inscriptions, please tell me something only a breathing pilgrim such as yourself can: have you seen my book as of late?

Your book? THE BOOK... of Mudora? said Zelda, pantomiming the general dimensions of the cumbersome tome with her thumbs set orthogonally apart. Green cover, about this size?

Yes. said Mudora lifelessly, unmoved by the ermine's emphatic exaggerations.

You wrote that! I suppose the title says it all... Alas, that imp–etuous Midna has it.

Yes, I entrusted it to the Gerudo princess – it was very hard for Epheremelda to deliver as I could not give it to Midnadorf myself.

What? Zelda was annoyed at the idea of another princess outbooking[73] her.

I told you – the first edition should've been a paperback. said the king.

She had it, when we met... inhaled the ermine, tasting the stale air.

I know, and it's in the book.

How is that possible?

Because I wrote the manuscript from the afterlife that affords us dead a knowledge of past and future – I already inked this very conversation of ours; as I saw that you and I would meet here. Various details and inflections might vary, but don't be alarmed if you ever read it and see that your journey to the land of the dead had been jotted down long before you arrived.

HO HO HARGH! the king guffawed, Good thing you didn't thumb through the pages that would've presaged your conversation in the Chamber of Sages.

Why? Zelda tried to imagine how it would've gone differently if she knew in advance.

---

73   To read more than someone else; have a bigger bookshelf. Not to be confused with overbooking.

As if anyone takes my heralding to heart, much less reads anymore at all. said Mudora.

What a cosmic comedy, that Midna holds the entire story in her crown without knowing it. The goddess laughs at us all – our lives are a joke – all we can choose is whether we are in on that joke, or the butt of that joke! Laugh with Hylia, or be laughed at… chuckled Zelda.

That is THE disjunctive destiny. said the priest with his hands clasped off to the side.

I never read anything. admitted the boy in response to the queen.

There are many illiteracies now, certainly not limited to the mere semantics of sentences; the symbolic too. agreed the king. Hazarding to open any book of life[74] does not augur anything on its own – what is metaphorically true yet literally false requires an attention to allegory. Those who can only see the latter, are blind to the former, and therefore utterly befuddled. The writing of our fate is often right in front of us, as close as the page, if only we knew how to read it.

Excuse me, King Hyrule, Queen Mudora… *What is written of my fate… beyond here?*

When you *finally* meet Midna again, you can confirm for yourself––and review what you already experienced. Daphnes interjected.

But that's enough of *a sign* from us. Mudora truncated, I'm already pushing my luck by writing to the world—of things not yet known by mortals. What is disclosed in the underworld must stay in the underworld, and that certainly includes clairvoyance. There's a reason the dead are down here; we mustn't interfere with mortals any more than the goddess Farore permits–

–who presides over the **burial** of ancestors. the king clarified, with your patroness goddess Nayru protecting the rites of **religion** as long as Hylians have lived.

---

74 Both a figure of speech (i.e. to read the meaning of one's life as if it were a book) and any literal book that invites introspection into the meaning of one's life; often written from the afterlife as a book of death (a hyperopic text authored and published posthumously by shades) can become a book of life such as this book, but a book of life can never be a book of death – the departed cannot take their worldly books with them to the underworld. Related to the cosmic concept of the Book of Time – similar but way bigger.

And yours: the goddess Din guarding **marriage** for us all. she said to her husband. These are the Three Institutions[75] that even the dead must honor, and violating their sacred boundaries is not without wrath—we wouldn't dare incur. Mudora told her in an avauntular tone.

Theologically endowed, the reverend elaborated, wise Nayru stays ahead of us with the providence of religion, courageous Farore commemorates the past through burial, and powerful Din holds the contract between predecessor and progeny in the present that only mortals make.

And so the goddesses oversee our temporality. said the queen, As it is from the past that Farore bravely opens the dawning horizon for what may come. And only in the future does wise Nayru look back and reclaim what came before with their sister Din between them who upholds the present marriage of past wisdom and future courage with all her strength.

You dodged an unhappy union with Sahasrahla, it wouldn't go well. said the boy.

The ermine princess blushed, You saw how it would end before I allowed it to begin?

Abandoned futures of the living haunt the dead far more than ghosts haunt the living!

I can only imagine the fractal vertigo such visions induce. said Zelda to the boy.

Sniff sniff... There's no nausea in the nether regions.

The queen stepped up to the ermine, To live is to be blind of time, and the dead have no right to ruin mortals with what we've seen. When it comes to the divine provenance of destiny—

—the more you know, the less you live. the king patted his robust but phantom beard, completing her sentence yet again. And yet living well

---

75   The first institutions of Hyrule, blessed by the three goddesses: Nayru *grants* the wisdom of religion (providence) to conserve the past, Din *guards* the power of marriage (love) to maintain the present, and Farore *grounds* the courage of burial (ancestors) to open the future. In theistic-temporality terms, Nayru keeps the wisdom of the past in the future, Din keeps the power of continuity in the present, and Farore keeps the courage of the future in the past. Understandably, some Hyruleans mix up the past and future.

requires a certain amount of knowledge, but beneficial knowledge only comes from bad life choices! HO HO HO!

That's all in the book too? Zelda squeaked.

Mudora paused to think – perhaps not verbatim, but yes.

It's word for word. the king patronized.

Ah, I *see* what you mean: 'a sign'. said Zelda, who was too distracted by all the queen's cosmic dissertations to grock the implications of meeting Midna again. So there is hope!

There is none, really. said the former queen of Hyrule.

Zelda choked down her enthusiasm, unsure what Mudora had meant by 'finally' which dawned on her – upon second thought – didn't necessarily imply she'd ever get out of here.

You are not free of the topos of conviction, I can see that. The delusion of certainty that your knowledge was complete caused a great fall to where you are now. But you need to now prepare yourself for the impossible, if you are ever to return to the living. said the king.

Link's dead, I killed him! Farore turned him into a freak! cried Zelda. And now I will perish and rot in perdition and become a feast for maleficent mushrooms… BOOHOO-hoo-hoo…

The pedantic priest tried to console the ermine, but retracted his hand knowing full well that he could not effectively touch her. If you are to ever regain your faith, you must fully commit to the eschewal of life. You must become, A PRINCESS OF REPUDIATION! he proselytized.

But she already rejected her vain lifestyle as an aspiring autarch in Sahasrahla's tower.

What of it, boy? the reverend asked. If not by repudiation, then how can she go further?

Zelda's already sacrificed enough, let's just help her live her best life while it lasts.

In the underworld? said the priest to the shade of the bug-catching boy.

Yes, she must live now. If I have any regrets it was wasting my short life *expecting* to get better – I would trade all of eternity down here for one woozy night in my sickbed. said the boy, As a child's purpose is to be a child, a princess should be herself as well. My life was cut short, but shorter yet by my fixation on adulthood which would never come. My life was hopeless, but Hylia does not disdain what only lives for a day – the goddess pours the entirety of herself into each and every moment no matter how brief and bittersweet! Life's bounty might not be down here but it is now, and later is too late for Zelda. *Cough cough...*

Adulthood is not the purpose of childhood? asked the priest.

No more than death is our purpose because we all must die.

Perhaps death is our purpose! retorted the holy man's shade.

Not if we help her live. insisted the forever-juvenile soul of the child.

What's the wait then? Zelda slowly reached toward the pomegranate.

There is no redemption for her in your adolescent nostalgia. said the reverend.

She has nothing more to eschew father! the boy addressed the priest respectfully.

As was above is now here below: a conviction of hopelessness brought her down.

And trying to get up and over that hopelessness by climbing the tower of material wealth and status turned out to be a letdown that betrayed her greatest expectations! *Sniff sniff...*

Zelda must undergo death, if she is to overcome a fallen life. said the shade of the loyal reverend in a dispirited manner. The journey is not without anguish...

Don't sound so glum. said the boy, There is a way beyond this infernal impasse.

When you're stuck with a conviction that everything's hopeless and all you see is a deadend, then living becomes an act of faith. said the priest in a tone of prior experience.

Expectation is for the damned, anticipation is for the blessed. said the king who took the golden pomegranate from the quiet linkalope. Such is the careful way of the gardener...

Aye, without hope, living becomes an act of faith – because there is nothing objective to expect so you must abide in anticipation of the unforeseen, paying attention to the imperceptible moments of germination that give us life, reaching into the ground, getting dirty! said the boy with such enthusiasm for natural wonders that the ermine wondered if he might be alive.

Princess, if I may provide some context by summary of the path you took to get here, throughout your journey you've undergone a *deductive escalation of delusion* as I would call it, from high to low – and you've traversed them all. said the priest who understood moral topos, Myopia *(I know)* to Rationalization *(I know that)* to now Conviction *(I know that I know)*...

The shortsightedness and blind affliction of those who linger at the top of the mountain, to the intelligent contortions we mire ourselves in that Swamp of Evil, to where I was last in the Ghostly Garden where epistemological hubris and intellectual dishonesty culminates to the lowest and most warped topology of Nayru's spirit found correspondingly in Hyrule.

Very good! said the priest, these are the three elevations of Nayru that were set out for whoever carried her wisdom; destiny is afoot for you Princess Zelda.

Myopia in the dark, *Sight in the light*... Rationalization in the dark, *Reason in the light*... Conviction in the Dark World and lastly *Faith in the Light World* that is the kingdom of Hyrule. Mudora added, *The telos of these topos* culminates to death – of the body in the Light World, and respectively across realms – death of the soul in the Dark World. Those who make their camp in the topology of conviction become ossified in heart and mind that they alone see the truth – as if they had the vantage of the dead who watch the past and future but ignore the present reality with such obsession that they become unaware—where they currently are...

A mere step from the underworld. *Cough! Sniff!* Sorry. the boy apologized for snorting.

You have journeyed through compounding obfuscation, Princess Zelda. said the priest. As the Dark World turns Hyrule on its head, this blindness is altogether an inversion of wisdom. Myopia, Rationalization, Conviction... They are all a kind of obscurity you see. he smiled.

That's easier to understand. said the bug-catching kid's shade.

Our souls are what we cultivate them to be. said King Hyrule, waving to the expanse beyond their conversation, And how many have we seen accompany us since the pestilence who entered these depths of nihility through their own fatal nihilism? In a world darkened by moral delusion, those who believe there is nothing worth dying for cannot go on living.

To die of a conviction against death! gasped the ermine princess. What a hideous inflection of hopelessness! And so counterintuitive, as those who flee from their expiry with a conviction that life is just a meaningless material to be preserved then run straight to their grave!

The king rotated his crown slightly, Yes we are going round and round but the situation cannot be understated that because there is no hope for those trapped in the Dark World, and because those warped by conviction cannot come unto faith, then they are doomed to perish.

Dire beyond belief, Zelda shook her head. I pity those who dare to hope!

It's worse than that. said the priest, If your hope is in vain, *then you must lose it.*

Cough! Cough... Here you go again with the 'repudiation' schtick.

Blessed are those who have lost hope! As there is no soul amongst us who found faith while clutching a cache of expectations as an eschatological failsafe. Nothing is more difficult than *repudiating* our own hope, but thankfully the lack of sunshine in Lorule helps us give up.

You don't have to rub it in. said Zelda. Perhaps the dead can see a future worth aspiring for from down here in the underworld, but the living trapped in the Dark World cannot see any such happy horizons. How can anyone live without expectations? How is anticipation—*all?*

By overgiving. said the king. You do not know, and rarely with any conviction if at all what will come of a seed carefully planted. The dead cannot overgive, beyond our infinite capacity for offering noisome advice and any such lifesucking liturgies of ours!

Ahem. the priest took it on the chin.

Principles aside, in our cold company you exclusively wield the principal of mortality–

And are most beautiful for it! shimmered the shade of the bug-catching boy. Even if you are warped into a… rat? No, not with a bushy tail like that. he corrected himself.

Stoat.

Doesn't matter, you figure transience, and that is beautiful. Mortality grounds beauty…

What is infinite cannot bear fruit, nor blossom for a new future. resumed the king while spindling the golden pomegranate on his fingertips. The unexpected is a gift that supervenes and arrives as an unforeseen extra in a way, and yet it's what's most important for carrying on. Like the fruit of a branch, this gift of the faithful ripens and precariously hangs on the mundane.

You've always been such a sentimental arborist, said Queen Mudora, but do the trees benefit from this flashflood of feelings; a downpour of pathos and profusely flowing eloquence? Gushing poetic risks waterlogging the roots. Look how our little sapling Zelda is wilting already! She will always remember how much you cared for the castle gardens; the princess has been doused with enough adoration on her sojourn to the afterlife. We have all the time in the world, said Mudora taking the pomegranate and kissing the king's hand – *our grandniece does not.*

Please don't write that in your book. said the king as his wife took the pomegranate.

I'm sorry, 'twas quilled already. said the queen, handing Zelda the golden fruit.

What do I do?

You must give more than you take.

Scwueck… Zelda ripped the pomegranate in half. Is it good? Do you want some?

We cannot eat or drink, unless—it is given to us by the living.

Hence the offering of blood. said the ermine, looking at the forlorn linkalope.

And just as the golden pomegranate grants mortals access to the underworld, whoever shares in its seeds will join you in rejuvenation.

Here! Take all you want! Please, there's more than enough for all of us! Zelda cheered. Why didn't you tell me earlier? I thought Epheremelda was just playing a trick on me honestly...

No. the king shook his head.

What? Zelda drooped. You won't rise if given the chance?

Although we saw this coming, nothing is certain and so you've given us more than we could have asked for by gracing us. We are glad to be of service from our resting place, helping you go beyond this nadir—deadend of hopelessness that your journey required. The future of Hyrule depends on you undergoing this passage, as death is the only other intersection of the realms besides the Master Sword... *and some anomalies.* said the king off to the side.

Don't confuse her. admonished the queen apropos his odd addendum.

I can't stomach all of this. said Zelda who hadn't eaten all day but had lost her appetite. Are there any other shades who might come with me? she offered the broken berry.

Cough cough... the boy hacked into his shirt.

Tragic our ending might've been, as with your parents and their siblings – your long lost aunts and uncles, Link's parents, Blind's mother and father too – we're all here. But revival and retribution is strictly forbidden and not for us good-faith ghosts to determine. We must stay here.

BLIND? *By what ancestry?* Show me my relatives! trembled the adopted princess who had never known her parents. By what evil or accident were they sent here? You always told me something terrible happened, and that you might explain—but, 'later is too late' as the boy said! I beg of you... Zelda scanned the myriad of flames beyond the island for the familiar faces she had no experience nor reference for identifying beyond a daughter's intuition, but couldn't make out the gauzy figures at all. How?–

Familicide. said the queen, but I cannot tell you more without derailing your destiny, and there is no worse deed for the dead. You will find these answers yourself, but not by revenge as you would be compelled to pursue the perpetrators if we revealed the history withheld from you.

The bastards are still alive? bristled the ermine.

As are the remaining maidens, who you must find. said Queen Mudora trying to change the subject from the disturbing details of the past to a proactive future.

You're covering for them! said the endotherm, boiling over with anger.

No—no mortal court can do their evil justice. The dues they deserve are beyond what any vigilante can dish out. Only the goddess can sentence them. Cold flames we might be, shades of the afterlife cannot ignite such a cascade of tragedy amongst the living. I can see what becomes of you and the world if Zelda were to seek revenge, and it is a terrible demise that will cause the Golden Power to recede for thousands of years, perpetuating the rivened realms and spellbound hypnosis of Hyrule. said the priest who had been quietly listening.

What he means to say is, if we tell you... then you will take the Triforce for yourself.

And that would simply substitute one warped world for another. said the king, supporting his wife's refusal to disclose the murderer of Princess Zelda's parents and other royal relatives. The only one of that generation who was spared is Link's uncle, the solitary sergeant of the Hyrule Knights who was in my service, and never bore any children of his own. As for your generation many remain – and you are not an only child my dear!

ACHOO! expulsed the sick bug-catching boy. *Sniff sniff...*

Yes, we met him. said the ermine, reminded by the sneeze and worrying that perhaps Link's uncle had the same fatal illness that the boy expired from. Zelda kneeled to the linkalope and held out her hand with half the pomegranate. Unable to make any solid contact with their vaporous presence, the stag-hare ate the juicy arils with no problem, gaining opacity as he did.

Every plantsman knows that dry twigs and lackluster fallow makes the garden as much as blooming does. But only after arriving in the land of the dead did I realize it is more profound than that: both life and death are offshoots of gardening. Even from the evermore, the gardener can do what he painstakingly inscribed into the living soil

– entrust our efforts in a future that we will not be around to claim as our authorship. Plowing liberality for what's ahead with all your soul is indeed a noble pursuit, but this overgiving is not an abstract altruism in the slightest.

Not at all. said the ermine somewhat embarrassed with a mouth full of mythological pith, eating the rest of the golden pomegranate after Link had his fill.

A king bows to no one but his garden! HO HO HARGH! Oh– Genuflecting low in the mud lifts up our best selves. The gardener is forever motivated by a faith that the best must be ahead of them – new leafing, flowering and fruition that their verdant shrubbery and woody plot silently promises in response to prudent care. Any man may reign over this kingdom in small, not from a high tower but by sifting low and finding his most loyal vassals are humble worms after all.

Hard at work. And what is a bee but a scribe who keeps the record of spring? she said.

After having this conversation, I can see a very special bee in your future. said the boy.

Imagine that! HARGH! But do not get your hopes up for garden dividends when the sun does not shine at all and the ethos of the age is dormant under darkness. And thus take these seeds as a reminder that the gardener who anticipates a bountiful future without expectation is most resilient to despair, said the king to the princess, and the desperate and destructive schemes that despair insinuates. In exile, your estate to cultivate is strictly your soul.

Your words will ground me if I ever see the light of day again. said the ermine to the king, turning to the queen who was approaching her empty handed.

Show me your map, said Mudora leaning over Zelda. Unfold it please– she requested, unable to manipulate something that still had its worldly weight about it, fresh upon the afterlife. Venus the Great Faerie is expecting you, I told Epheremelda to relay your arrival to her.

Is she a maiden, *held captive there?* asked Zelda, unable to consult her necklace of black diamonds having squandered them to the boar before her induction (more like abduction) to the regrettable prosopopeia princessdom up in the owl's opulent tower of false sovereignty.

No—not even a wizard can crystallize that old woman. Across the mirrored realms and timeless amongst the living stands a ring of stones, great soulweights comparable to these but without the grave claim upon our mortal memory. Mudora gestured to the menhirs around them as the underworld analog. Her solitary crescent endows the *spirit of selflessness* where you'll find the Henge of Hylia[76] that the great faerie Venus watches over from her grotto in a long cave on the north of the island. The lake is the base of the kingdom – confluence of the topographies in principled Hyrule; where all the upstanding elevations of the Light World pour into her bowl. Amidst those shining waters of the goddess, Venus remains hidden from the wizard.

But the touch of his cold heart upon the Triforce brought an everlasting winter to the lake in the Sacred Realm. Corresponding in elevation, therein lies the lowest topos of moral delusion for those exiled in Lorule, with an icy dungeon built so deep, it almost breaks the halls of death. said the king. The ataraxia of Lake Hylia has become warped into the anxiety of Ice Lake…

That's the Ice Palace! Zelda noted, realizing that they were looking at the Dark World on her enchanted map. Sahasrahla said that his grandchild 'volunteered' to protect a crystal there. Considering his penchant for polite euphemisms, I suspect this was not-noncompulsory.

They did not elect to do this on their own volition. agreed Queen Mudora, pointing to the small structure in the middle of Ice Lake. Deep as his tower is tall, Sahasrahla *keeps an eye* on his grandchild at the bottom of that frigid and tapered vault. The immured maiden is not Venus, but the great faerie is waiting—will help you enter the palace, which is an impenetrable fortress from the outside. And so terribly cold inside, you'll need more than the king's cloak to stay warm although

---

76   An ancient henge of white trilithons, fallen into ruin on Hylia Island. Most of the menhirs and supports remain standing along the major axis of the henge oriented east-west, but many of the lintel capstones have fallen. The purpose of the rectilinear megalithic structure is debated. Agahnim has declared the site strictly off limits to the public as of the pestilence until the magistrate can sort out all of Hyrule's problems.

its magic will allow you to evade the glacial gaze of his evil watch that never blinks.

And she's already inside? said Princess Zelda, unclear if they were talking about the same location on the map, which they were – but that location mirrored across both realms.

You'll understand when you get there, said Mudora, lacking Hylia's Key there are other ways, secret and difficult anomalies; if risked, may allow one to traverse between the realms.

I thought you said not to confuse her. sighed the king.

The ermine slumped, Venus is in the Light World… But there's no way–

Whirlpools and the underworld provide an alternative, however unorthodox passage. interrupted the priest. By undergoing death, a traveler might make it out alive on the other side.

There are a handful of hidden portals out there – like by Spectacle Rock. said the boy.

Alright, so Hylia's Key is the only *portable* way to unlock the realms. said Zelda.

Trust us, trust the dead! There are some thresholds that the living cannot see beyond. And even what shades foresee changes by your deeds—depending on the free will of mortals. said the bug-catching boy. You can act but not see its full consequences, whereas we can see what unfolds but are inert. Before you came here, I saw you after the tower coronation as a newfound Dark Queen of the warped world, and a slow destruction of your soul the further you deviated from your destiny and true calling. But you sought perspective on all the convictions that the mighty tower reinforced, because you trusted what was always most alive in you.

Halfway there, as she had no anguish. judged the priest, and aptly so. He forgives you.

My Hyrulean Knight had more faith than I, even now! said Zelda, picking up the linkalope who no longer levitated over the water and was getting soggy from the chthonic tidal action.

Yes he is forever in your service, a commitment made long ago that carries with it the possibility of self-sacrifice, but who would've guessed by the hands of the princess he serves? There is no faithful knight without *anguish*, as their vows are a *moral contradiction* to begin with. Will his death be an honorable sacrifice, or foolhardy suicide? Will his sword engage foes with temperance or murderous passions? Courage keeps Link in the throes of this contradiction, which is a constant battle in his heart. Dishonor is the only defeat for the knight of anguish.[77] Undeservedly cursed by Farore, the very goddess he swears by, into a speechless linkalope, Link's faith remains unshaken. A knight takes nothing personally, in turn do not take his taciturn valor for granted. Your test remains now, as you must undergo greater depths in order to rise.

There isn't a staircase out of the underworld? That would be easier. Zelda shrugged.

Have faith with a departure into the unknown, is what the reverend means. said the boy. Because this opacity of conviction, what you are currently blinded by, cannot see what's beyond. It is only by faith that you can transcend the finite expectations of both hope and hopelessness.

Rest assured princess, the dead will be here when you need us, waiting beyond the horizon of your unknown future from the past we carry. said Queen Mudora, taking the king's shawl and fitting the royal broach to the ermine's slender shoulders. As mentioned for you…

It's a cape on me, but a cloak on you! said King Hyrule big enough to fit at least three princesses inside of his apparition. Only put the hood up when you want to disappear, which is nothing I need an accessory for achieving in the afterlife. he faded away to make himself clear.

The island is sinking! said Zelda, moving closer to the tree. There is no doubt about it…

Conviction is limited by what you believe to be possible – stuck in your *known knowns*. You've learned by passing through the unmarked grave that something unexpected awaits. It is by faith alone that you

---

77   Those who battle the absurd by venturing everything on the impossible – sacrificing their own ambitions for a higher cause but with faith that they can only attain such things by retrieval after radical repudiation. The sacrifice induces a great anguish however as having such faith always carries moral contradictions.

go beyond this opacity, this trap of hope, for a feat of heroic trust that wholeheartedly anticipates the impossible. Holdfast now, become the princess of repudiation who dives into death itself and comes to understand with great anguish that only by resigning your entitlement to royalty will you reign again! bowed the breathless holy man.

Or, the lake is rising? said the ermine who swirled into an accreting whirlpool while holding on tight to the helpless but surprisingly buoyant linkalope. What is happening! HELP!

From a garden you came, and to a garden you shall return! yelled the shade of Mudora above the slurping froth. Epheremelda will show you what you need before speaking to Venus. reassured the queen who also took her leave, quick as a wick is quenched in a resolute pinch.

That faerie fruit is certainly to blame… said Zelda, tonguing an aril out of her teeth.

Take me with you princess! waved the evaporating shade of the boy who didn't so much yearn to live again as he wanted to be her adopted ancestor. Alas it is best to die young–

–and as late in life as possible. added the old priest, appropriately departing last.

Your eulogies are deep–ly moving, reverend, gasped Zelda, but must we drown here? The ermine was a natural swimmer but was sinking with the well fed linkalope[78] in her arms. Denser than death, the golden pomegranate they had shared became a ballast in their bellies. Coalescing slowly at first and sparkling with phosphorescence, the glitterlit[79] vortex suddenly yawned into a loud column so voluminous that they tumbled into a dry freefall. All of a sudden the bottomless gyre closed up, swallowing the princess and her knight with an awful gulp.

---

78 Link's punishment for peeping naked Farore.
79 Suffused with bioluminescence, often in water.

Lethic Life Regained

Yo! Link! You seem to be in a heap of trouble, but this is all I can give you.

This is a magic bottle! You can store an item inside and then use it later! said a little boy with the most peculiar natural pink hair. Finding her bearing having blacked out, Zelda wasn't sure if he was talking to her, but came to and saw the youth holding the bottle for her to take.

Found it in the shoal – floated to my camp here. said their carefree host.

These are hard to come by, I want you to have this. the pink-haired boy regifted.

Stretching out her arms, the princess could feel her sleeves were still damp, but the campfire had mostly dried her off. What for? she asked, taking the bottle. Who are you?

It's me! Link! said the boy, looking to the nearby man who gave him the bottle first.

Why are you a child? YOU'RE ALIVE! And... looking Hylian again, but this must be–

Shhh! Princess, lower your voice please. Yes! We've returned to the Light World at last! But don't yell. He pointed up to the underside of the ancient granite masoned bridge high above that they were camped under. There are spellbound guards patrolling up there... he whispered. But we don't have to speak *that* quietly – just keep them in mind. said Link, overly protective of the heiress.

Clunk. Zelda dropped the shatter resistant bottle, My hands! I'm no longer an ermine!

A what? asked the nearby man, reclining on his side like a beauty queen.

None of your business! said Zelda, wary of the handsome but homeless camper.

...

And who are you? she retorted after he said nothing.

That's Ario. said Link. He pulled us out of the river there—where we washed up.

Fitting name. she said impassively, patting down her long blonde hair.

You can call me Sir Ariosto, milady. said the camper, giving a nonchalant nod as to not unsettle her obviously intentional indifference toward him.

I was going to say, she said, this must be the underside of the Boneyard Bridge?

Link looked up, I believe so… Remember when we crossed here with Ganon?

Here? No.

In the Dark World! the boy chuckled, You're the one who told me, where we were, then…

Zelda paused to remember, as the various episodes of their exile had gotten all jumbled up from the whirlpool ride into a nonlinear nightmare. Oh right. she said, still unsure.

Perhaps you got a minor concussion. You should rest Princess! said the young Link.

I'm quite alright. She knocked her head back, AIEEE− and turned around, swiveling more to size up the large stone she had been leaning on since waking. *One of those!*

Don't lean on that too long. said Ario, the lounging camper. It'll make you forget…

Why? asked the child on behalf of Zelda.

That's what a lethic stone does.

Lethic stone? she asked standing up to give herself some precautionary distance while roving between them; easily twice the boy's age and well under half that of the homeless man.

You wouldn't remember, as that is its purpose. he shifted his weight and blew a bubble, Shades who leave the underworld must pass by the lethic stones that negate their memories before joining the living again. Something about Farore's metamorphic energy that radiates from those hornfel bands and xenolithic runes. Been awhile since I've thought about geology, I can't remember, he admitted, but not because of the stone there − I just naturally forgot the details.

But we're not shades, said Zelda, and I can remember most things… she zoned out.

The dead do not take a mortal's leave lightly. How did you escape the underworld? Ariosto shaved some extra ginger into a soup to boost their addled brains.

I never died. Zelda made herself clear. I brought a golden—*nom-eh-grah-neh...*

Glrup. the boy covered his mouth. What is that aftertaste... Oh right, we ate that–

Nff. Nff... the princess cautiously fanned the burped air toward her nose. That fruit!

Pomegranate! they both remembered simultaneously, swinging each other around.

Please, hideout voices. Ariosto gently reminded his guests.

But what happened before that? Last I remember was seeing Farore naked.

You little perv! said the princess, Was she stunning? Unchanged by the Dark World?

Beyond words really—her nymphs too. Even if she hadn't cursed me mute, I'm not sure how to describe their beauty, so alluring from afar... *But any goddess is grotesque up close.*

How close did you get! LINK! What compelled you to intrude on their sacred spa?

I wasn't sure if she was being bathed against her will! *Squuuishhh...* Link wrung out his nightcap without doffing – twisting the tip of the long pointy green hat while keeping it on.

Bunny to the rescue! You were exploring where the Forest Temple would be found?

What bunny? the man asked, unaware of what they were warped into previously.

Oh yes! I heard girls screaming, so I rushed over. Turns out they were just having fun.

Flirting with nymphs is a fool's errand – but valiant effort, my gallant knight.

I thought she might be one of the maidens and in need of rescue! the boy blushed.

TAH! Spare me! So then the goddess did turn you into a speechless—linkalope, yes.

Doesn't ring a bell. But I am Link, and there was a lot of loping... he rubbed his temples, unable to remember any events after his transmogrification by the goddess into a stag-hare.

That's right – it's all coming back to me now. We had gone our own ways after meeting that pony witch in the mouse's shop, but what happened since? *Grbrbrb!* Zelda patted her belly, The seeds of that mnemonic myrtale sowed a hunger I must now reap...

My tail is gone too. the boy said irrelevantly.

Not animal tails. *Myrtales* – the golden pomegranate piqued my appetite for something more substantial. I haven't eaten in ages! she said truthfully, having barely touched the feast due to cold feet for her coronation ceremony. I still don't understand why you're a kid now.

Glrup. Me too, he burped again. I'm a growing boy and could eat a whole stable!

The lethic stone's power is no match for the olfactory associations of a boy's belch. Inadvertently the stone helped me break the wizard's spell. Say, are you two related? Ariosto handed them overflowing bowls of Carrot Stew he had been ladling while they reminisced.

SHLURRR–I'm sworn to protect her. Link shilly-shallied while slurping.

Is that why you keep it in your encampment here? said Zelda gladly receiving the simple but zesty soup. I mean, as a souvenir—of what amnesia made of you... What forgetfulness is worth memorializing? You're a contradictory character! she pointed her spoon at the camper.

This is a garden. sighed Ario. I raged against Agahnim to no avail, and in my fury fought to the grave and beyond, where I defied death and stole this very stone from the underworld! When I returned, the spell was broken and I could think for myself again, my convictions shown for what they were all along: *cowardice.* If anything almost killed me, it was that great dishonor. But in many ways my life did end then, as I had trained my whole life to be a Hyrulean Knight–

You're a knight too! said the boy. You must know my uncle! He had an unforgettable mustache! And he also defied Agahnim when the time came to abduct Zelda here; but was exiled to the Dark World, and put under house arrest. Don't tell anyone we found him!

Zelda watched the homeless man, unconvinced he was ever a sworn swordsman.

Who would I tell? Many of my cohort are still under the wizard's spell, and Agahnim presumes me dead so I remain in hiding here. But in order to recreate a new life, I took up gardening. he waved to his plot, This gave me a new sense of purpose in a hopeless world.

Hopeless. sympathized Zelda with a sigh. These aesthetic choices are hopelessly bad! This 'garden' looks like a homeless encampment. she levied her uncouth derision thinly veiled as an objective critique in such a way that only a proudly cultured person could make off with.

Link adjusted his child-sized green tunic, unsure what aesthetic meant.

I call the style my own: *postchivalric.*[80] said the good natured garden knight.

Ariosto the Amiable, thank you for not taking that criticism personally! said Link.

Why did you rampage against the wizard? MMM! Zelda loudly delighted in her meal.

Sir Ariosto threw a pebble at the lethic stone[81] for no good reason. The wild maiden we abducted for Agahnim substituted her spell for his. From one madness to the next, I fell in love. She was a of the descendants of the Nine Wise Men. The magistrate needed to imprison them all in order to gain total control of the kingdom and secure his designs for the Sacred Realm.

Nine! choked Zelda. The king told me seven, when I was living in the castle.

---

80   The philosophy of Sir Ariosto's garden and lifestyle. An aesthetic, ethos, and zeitgeist of retired knights.

81   A vertically oriented megalith from the underworld, carved by the goddess Farore to erase memories for future shades returning to the living. Encircling the golden pomegranate tree, the afterlife lethic henge is directly underneath Hylia Island of the lake where another henge is buried in the past. A forgetful stone.

Agahnim reassured the king all along that his shocking rituals would end the pestilence. But how could any good come of such an evil process of zapping young women into diamonds? Appropriately so, the king suspected a wicked conspiracy, and kept you close. Ariosto told her.

You were there when they came for me. she shuddered, ready to throw the bottle at him.

No, we were never told what was next, but you must've been after I went head over heels for the… Ariosto counted up one finger at a time ending on his pinky: FIFTH maiden… She had the most spectacular long flowing auburn—almost rubescent locks! I negotiated with her father, a circumspect official of noble standing to keep her safe while I sought to free my men of the evil that yoked their minds. He agreed to disguise her as a pilgrim and sent her up Death Mountain into hiding. Under her charms and no longer the wizard's spell, I confronted the vile magistrate Agahnim, staking my life on the standard issued steel that I wielded against his exceptional sorcery. Well, my sword had been tempered by dwarves in advance, but no matter. My bosom imbued with infatuation and a heavy sword equally hot from the blacksmith's forge, my royal guard's claymore was no match for his magic bolts. The only purpose that smoldering blade served was to conduct Agahnim's forked-lightning that promptly hurtled me to the afterlife! My heartbeat resumed in the underworld, and my pulse quickened at the thought of her alone in the wizard's regime far above me. Determined to redeem myself of all this madness, I ate all but one of the golden pomegranates, leaving it for my maiden if anything dire were to happen to her. With the strength of a hundred men gained from epic overeating, I dragged this lethic stone up from the depths to help me forget it all–ahh! he yawned, concluding his sensational synopsis.

Absolved of all spells. said Zelda, mesmerized by his romantic tale of wild delinquency. Apparently you remember a lot though. Maybe the stone should be your bedding headboard?

I'm just close enough to sustain a lucid *lethargy.* he said slowly, blowing another bubble.

We ate the last pomegranate. said Link in a daze. It was cold, and delicious. Not as good as your soup. But I didn't see any maidens in the underworld, if that's any consolation.

I'm sorry, but in our defense a faerie gave it to me. the princess slapped the bottle.

Yo! Link! No need to apologize, they must grow back eventually. said Ariosto.

Bah! Always happens to new garments – and how is it always the last bite? said Zelda, standing up and splaying the king's crimson cloak that had an orange spot of soup on it.

The water is cold and clean; a quick dab will do. suggested Sir Ariosto.

Yah! Where do you do your business around here? asked the child Link.

Cross the slumbering talus stepping rocks over the river there, Ario pointed to his right where the crown of a spiritless golem protruded above the water providing a convenient path to the bridge's southern foundation. Each pier amazingly has a single occupancy latrine inside, just walk around the back and you'll see. He pointed to the two pillars, just like the two behind him. This bridge predates the kingdom; Ancient Hylian architects had a genius for multiuse utilities.

But not here? Zelda asked, walking behind the two identical pillars immediately behind the camper's tent, presuming the bridge's structural engineering was symmetrical.

Please don't. said Ario. I sleep here, and try to keep some distance.

I would never. she said, finding her way off the planed riprap escarpment to the rocks. Risking quick glances upward, the guards did not have a line of sight, even though the way across was out from underneath the bridge's shadow. Don't slip! she whispered to Link.

Pre-cataclysm crappers! said the boy. But where does it go? Just into the river here?

LINK! That's disgusting. said Zelda quietly, kneeling by the rocks to wash her cloak.

Don't worry. You're upstream… *Where have I seen that before?* Ario muttered alone, recognizing her royal shawl but couldn't place it in his mind while it hung on her slender figure.

Hmm? It's gone. Spotless! she said, unable to find the stain that somehow vanished.

Maybe it's *also* magically soilproof?[82] said Link leaning over her shoulder.

Get on with you. she shrugged him off. Actually, I get first dibs. she changed her mind.

Dirty dibstones! You have to go too? Link hesitated as the princess grabbed him for balance while she footsied the rocks for the best sequence before committing to cross.

Stand still… she wobbled.

I really have to go! warned the boy, annoyed that Zelda had arrested him as a crutch. Craning his head back, Link could see the helm crests of the guards, colored according to rank, who only had to lean over the balustrade of the bridge to see them on the sunken talus that gurgled just enough against the current to drown out their larks below. Unafraid of spellbound soldiers, he wasn't about to invite trouble while on their paramount privy quest. As much as the greenclad child wanted to see Sir Ariosto spring into action to defend them, such a fiasco would ruin the garden, which would be a tragic loss and make any triumph pyrrhic.

Shhh! reminded the camper, waving them to keep moving and not linger in the open. Taking the opportunity to check something without guests to attend to, Ario rolled into his tent. *Painful petites on my post-chivalric feet! YRAGH!* he strained to try something on in private. *Flop-flop…* the vanquished leather smacked the ground. They just might fit her…

What fits who? asked Link, already back and demonstrating his hygienic courtesy by conspicuously drying freshly washed hands on his tunic's flappy frontside.

Where's the princess? said the camper, crouching out from his tent, Oh– good, she's making her way. Ario returned to his lounging position with a sigh of relief.

---

82 Immune to stains and any blotching magic or accidental besmirching.

Did you forget about us? asked Zelda, scampering up the embankment.
...

Just you and the lethic stone. she punctuated her joke but felt as if she might've insulted him so decided to commiserate with her own anecdote of artifact induced amnesia. No long ago I lost my mind, thankfully temporarily and in the company of concerned attendants. Do you...

Do I remember? said Link, That magic mirror and the moon pearl did not mix well.

Let's not dwell on the dynamic of those two goddess mirrors. said Zelda.

If you have a story to tell, then this is the place to dwell. said Ario, There are many tales but only time can vet which are cut out for a myth. It's not up to us to say; all myths must age. Accordingly, a garden – like an act of speech – can become legendary if they endure with care. Sir Ariosto tended the campfire, adjusting the farrago of miscellany that constituted his estate.

Some foibles are best left forgotten; remembering can be too real. said the princess.

History is a horror, Ario agreed, but stories and gardens are our only asylum from the ravages of reality. Our past is raw until we arrange it, not for ignorance, but to fit us truthfully.

Can't sedate... the sorespots... said Link laying on his back, wiggling to find a comfortable position and trying not to bump or kick any of the found objects around him.

Did you arrange most of this rub-b-bish from the river? she stuttered.

Whatever wreckage the waterway brings me, I make the most of: dreck, draff and dross! This is a garden made entirely in the shadow of the kingdom, milady. clarified Sir Ariosto.

Literally. said the boy, flopping his foot in and out of the bridge's penumbra edge and into the early afternoon sunshine of a glorious Hyrule spring day.

More importantly figuratively. said Zelda, putting her hand on the lethic stone that leaned up against the garden's shelf, propped up in the shallows. Gardens are the wizard's blindspot, as he could never imagine a subversive project as peaceful as yours – not to mention situated in the heart of Hyrule right under his nose! The princess stepped down the little logboom ladder of three stairs that Ariosto had built to the waterline where the original builders had left a small quay, quarried from the same white granite that was used for the Boneyard Bridge overhead. Zelda could see the corbels and high keep from that lower vantage. The old castle was built around a garden – King Hyrule regarded the courtyard as a model for the whole kingdom, an exhibit of what grows under gentle guardianship. she said, remembering her childhood there and her recent conversation with the regal shade which had returned fresh with her memory. The princess stepped back up to the secret landing and sat by the campfire feeling restored, Poetic that everything discarded from the castle, once emblematic of merited rectitude and honorable chivalry but now the seat of sedition and font of artifice, drifts down here for your gathering—giving these sullied fragments of a broken kingdom a new life, *after forgetting…*

But what's the point of poetics? asked the pink-haired child.

I said: *lends new life.* she glared at the kid with her lids halfway lowered.

Oh, everything here is out of sight and out of mind. The lethic stone keeps us forgotten more than it causes us to forget! said Ariosto, throwing another pebble at his trophy menhir.

Can't farm much. said Link, all of a sudden fixated on the impracticality of this place.

Although the light is low, the soil must be good for growing leafy edibles; carrots too! I'm sure you could have a nutritious rotation nonetheless. the princess answered presumptuously.

Your misunderstanding is… understandable. But I believe a proper tour of my garden is required to show you, *what I mean.* said Ario, maintaining his lounging position to emphasize that this would be a wandering showcase and gallery of ideas, definitely rambling but not perambulating in the usual sense of a guided tour.

Go on then. said Zelda, annoyed that Ario reclined so comfortably in reticence and that he had the gall to exalt what she tacitly maintained was objectively a garbage heap.

My garden is not productive, it's not even vegetative. No matter how disenchanted an environment might be, a well thought out garden responds first to our human needs that cannot be reduced to the metabolism of our animal appetites. While questing in my days of knighthood, I met a witch or two, Syrup and her apprentice. But as a man of arms and orders then, I never thought of myself as a participant in what they call the 'vita magica' whereby worldly meaning is incanted, decanted, stirred and cultivated. That is, until I began my garden, and realized that not only is there a magic in it, but also a primacy and establishing said meaning has to come first, even in hostile habitats where survival is at stake. explained Ario.

Then a true knight must defend his soul, at risk of losing his life. said Zelda.

I have a lot to learn from you Sir Ariosto! said the child knight, I see you are most faithful in your lifelong quest for meaning. Not as interesting, I'm sworn to save the princess–

You couldn't save me from myself, said Zelda, so I did what I had to.

Entitlement is a dragon no knight can slay, milady… said Ario with a squint.

But you swear your life on saving the truth. the boy continued, My green Kokiri tunic worn by the Hero of Time pales in comparison to your heroic greenthumb and timeless garden.

What greenthumb? What's growing here? huffed the princess.

In my lethic garden of forgotten souvenirs, there is a gallant gestalt: more here than the assemblage of its constituents – and perhaps just like the witch's black cauldron, the boundary is the shadow of the bridge. I cannot expand my estate beyond this little shelf, or the patrol would notice, and the risk of being washed away by a flood is always looming; but that stone isn't budging and will remain the contradictory centerpiece of this paradoxical memorial…

A masterpiece! exclaimed Link.

Ahem. Verily, constraints make the composition. But a 'gestalt' more than its parts? Zelda sighed, Alas, only *you* see more than the summation of what's actually piled up here.

Where we can remember our humanity, as Hylians. The bounded enclosure of this garden visibly coalesces many life affirming energies that, especially in the wizard's world of cold lifesucking entropy, would fade away and dematerialize. The gravity of the lethic stone keeps the vibrancy of our heart, mind, and soul within orbit, reorganizing and grounding these things discarded from the castle. Ariosto pointed to a salon-style pile of discarded oil paintings that he had collected after Agahnim must've ordered their wholesale defenestration.

What... young Link could tell Zelda was premeditating something tongue in cheek, whereas Ario was not anticipating how she'd tangentially change the subject, albeit on topic.

All that induced entropy might be necessary, keep people further apart from each other, especially since the pestilence is causing The Boiling. said the princess in a perfunctory tone and performative manner. But as everyone knows, 'boiling' caused the pestilence to begin with. What a positive but bad feedback loop! So we have to do everything we can to help the wizard who's just trying to offset the effects of too many warm bodies interacting. Zelda grimaced, wishing someone more courageous would refute-and-rescue her from Agahnim's absurdity.

You can't be serious. said the boy.

But the magistrate has used the golden sigils to change the seasons. she got serious.

They no longer preach The Boiling, at least not exclusively – *The Icing* is the latest end of the world 'doom and gloom' litany. said Ario, weighing in on their digression about the three elemental goddess medallions, and the havoc they can wreak when in the wrong hands.

Since the pestilence, this liturgy of contradictions never ceases. Amazing how so many Hylians never ask how the world could be both boiling and icing simultaneously! she laughed, Oh, and don't forget the third medallion...

Which is? Must be Farore's sigil. surmised the boy.

The Quaking![83] Any opportunity to turn a catastrophe, natural or induced, into the threat of a new cataclysm and thus greater control is

83   The magistrate now warns of 'the big one' megathrust 'ten-thousand year earthquake' that the

what the lords of the tower are after. And I can attest: they now possess all three goddess medallions, and will burn, freeze, and quake Hyrule into a hysterical subservience. We've already witnessed the 'force of ether'. noted the princess.

When entering the mire, aye... said the boy. Our quest for the medallions to end the pestilence was a fool's errand to begin with then. We sought a solution that was the problem.

We were presuming that their story was true: that if only we could stop the fires and curb The Boiling with the ether medallion we found on the Precipitous Pinnacle, then perhaps we could end the pestilence. I have not seen it used, but they possess a 'force of bombos'.

We should be careful, that must be Din's goddess medallion. said Link. Makes me wonder what actually caused the Great Cataclysm in the distant past, long before our era now; will we ever know? The medallions aren't powerful enough to cause such a calamitous deluge and upheaval that reshaped Hyrule ages ago—are they? Everyone blames the King of Thieves, but I don't know what to believe anymore...

Don't believe either way, said the princess – this is not a question for belief. I certainly adopted the hopeless conviction that only the power of the wizard could save us. But having emerged here to a new day and free from that warp upon my mind, at the very least I know how *not believing* is also a conviction to be wary of. I suspect we'll find out before our journey is over.

Believe, or not believing... You're describing certainty, either way. But you cannot free yourself of that conviction with more certainty. Extricate belief from hope and you might find something within you that was only imagined to be impossible before. said the vagrant knight.

Sir Ariosto, beseeched the enamored boy, Any thoughts on the secrets of this tyranny? How can we free ourselves if they possess such magic and have everyone spellbound too?

Please tell. Zelda was glad Link was returning them from her sidetracked sigil detour.

---

kingdom is due for. Agahnim requires all Hyruleans to purchase earthquake insurance and are discouraged from going up Death Mountain where early signs of tectonic activity have been recorded near Turtle Rock.

So I am no incanting witch who 'enjoins knowledge and thought', but my garden does speak for itself, declares rather! Calling for our repose in this sad speechless world of empty expressions of allegiance to the wizard. However quiet, there is an embodiment of liberating speech here, that no doubt the magistrate would not look kindly upon if he found us. Just as I unfettered the lethic stone from the underworld, you two have also been emancipated from a delusional life not worth living. We are liberators in the presence of that radiant omphalos!

We were actually dead—or at least I was. said Link.

Radiant? *This glow of grime?* Zelda picked at the stone's weathered patina.

Yo! Zelda! The matte finish allows it to better rest in harmony with the shadows here. This is no porcelain article to polish spic-and-span. winked Ariosto, irking Zelda who felt vilified having come from a lifestyle replete with vitrified ceramics. The sheen of antiquity is well suited for laying low, just under the surface, in a landscape of speechlessness. While reticent, this is nonetheless a triumphant bastion of magical authorship and loquacious lingering! he regaled, Especially with the magistrate outlawing homespun magic of any kind, the lethic stone has broken through the barriers of aphasia that Agahnim enacted at every turn in our ordinary way of life. And just as my menhir has a dialogue with all the eclipsed artifacts rediscovered anew, so do we find ourselves as interlocutors who might cast away the gloom in our hearts, as the witch sings her spells and stirs her potions. The gardener is not so different!

I still think you should try some shade-tolerant plants. said Zelda.

He gets all he needs from the washed up castle crates. the boy reminded her.

Mostly, not those carrots there. I take my leave to trade and run errands as needed. Even so, all germination happens in the lethic and nonapparent dimensions of our life, often directly under our feet – the thoughtless men marching above us; unaware of us gathering. Speaking of, you might not be surprised, but I have overheard that Agahnim forbids anyone from gardening anymore. 'Heirloom potagers attract the pestilence!' is what I heard them say while apprehending a man's cart on the bridge. *Sufficiency and surplus is strictly forbidden!*

The magistrate demands conformity to solutions for problems it creates... she said, everyone knows this, but no one stands against it, and so the spell persists, and gloom grows.

I took my stand, and nothing that bad happened to me! said Ariosto.

You were struck by lightning. said the boy, also experienced in expiration.

Just a short trip through the underworld, a romantic mishap in the mix. Briefly dying is not as bad as a perennial fear of death as the magistrate would have us *uprooted.* My fellow Hyrulean Knights of old, and those lowly guards above us, the voguish cucco-hearted villagers of Kakariko and cosmopolitan cowards of Castle Town, they've all *deracinated* themselves on the wizard's whim. Everytime they concede to his lies, the magistrate possesses their minds all the firmer. The spell abhors anything honest, and so gardens must go... **But we are planted** here my friends – this is a plot for exiles, and your unexpected company is my bumper crop![84]

We're seeds in your garden? the growing boy pondered.

Yo! Link! Sprouts well on their way. This garden thrives in the shadow of evil you could say, as it makes room for conversation to grow; stories and the fruitful meaning that they can bear. No other fare staves off the pangs of gloom quite like it, as it is by the sharing of meaning that we can understand our own blind spots. In this garden you'll find loamy and humble plots of that which binds us, what's worth living for – what we would die fighting to preserve... said Ario.

Humble plots for blind spots... Oh, plots—as in stories. Zelda tapped her cheekbone.

You've sequestered your whole life in metaphor. said the boy with a stiff lip. But how can such a small project like this effectively remediate the gloom that is spilling out over the world?

---

84 Not to be confused with a 'bumper beetle'. Not a crop of bumpers, but an unexpected bonus harvest.

Yo... the camper was going to respond to Link, but yielded to the princess.

The gloom is not out there, it's in us—our inability, or *unwillingness* to dig into our own darkness with a trowel of thought and overturn those stubborn cobblestones and all that clay of conviction. Fitting that a garden that grows against the gloom blooms in the shadows. she said, The transformation is in us then... in this overlooked space between the light and the dark...

Interstitial. Link sat corrected, or felt enlightened enough to groove with it.

We are *between* the realms, or as much as anyone could while *in* Hyrule. And that's how this all started – I sprung from that reflection pool there, just as you did. Ario pointed to a small triangular shoal in the middle of the river immediately leeward of the bridge. What is a garden, if not phenomenal? Even a shadow garden belongs here in the Light World of showy phenomena. But if any wonder that debuts by our careful hand does not rise up from the penumbral depths, then there is no real appearance, but an illusion without dimension. said the camper Sir Ariosto. As we came from the underworld, and cultivate this place in conversation, such depth belongs as much to the shadow garden as they do to the hearts and minds of its gloomy gardeners. Consider though, that only *where* these two dimensions enjoy a confluence of depth and appearance can we show ourselves for who we truly are, and anything for that matter!

Maintenance makes the garden. Link sighed, having volunteered as a groundskeeper years ago – the first time he was a little boy, back in the day living on an unadulterated timeline.

Sir Ariosto, said Zelda unsure of what he was actually getting at, Are you saying this little estate of yours is somehow between the two realms and therefore in the center of the kingdom? The *liminal aspect* of the Chamber of Sages came to mind, but that was not in any realm at all, and neither of these guys had been there so she kept the privileged thought to herself; buried.

The camper smiled, When the king passed, so did the axis spin out; absent ever since. The only way Agahnim can have complete control over the kingdom is by dissolving any center, the culmination of which was regicide. Keeping everyone disoriented and distracted, there is no sensible rhythm – not even the natural cycle of the seasons are unaffected by his total design. Fundamentally, the magistrate's dominion has one law: *that disorder must increase everywhere.* He must make entropy. Somewhat surprising, is it not? As the wizard is obsessed with orders!

For someone who lounges so lethargically you certainly speak by leaps and bounds.

Princess, let him get to the point! said Link, eager to learn more from Ariosto.

Entropy is not life however – the wizard's design is the opposite of a garden which is where care and boundaries allow for order and life to flourish! By the goddess, **life** is the only force in this world that creates *adaptive organization.* The wizard cannot hold a candle to this. His rule of disorder is necessarily lifeless, because he must break apart all coalescing gestalts in order to gain control – this includes gardens, honorable institutions such as the knighthood…

Hyrule's tricameral senate, who were completely bought off. added Zelda.

Good call. the pink-haired boy validated her.

But if we are to find the center of the kingdom, then in lieu of the king's steady scepter we must plumb the depths with a sounding weight, a line of inquiry from which our world may turn again. said the camper, sticking his finger into the compressed soil of the abutment ground. If stillness will anchor our restless souls, then placing a cornerstone just might commence a new and wholly centered age. Ariosto gestured to his lethic menhir upright behind Link and Zelda.

Uh. Link looked at the stone and back, Ario—any soup left?

I'm glad you enjoyed my stew, but in this garden it's more important to have someone to share a meal with, than to have anything to eat at all. said the camper, satiated on rapport having had his fill of discourse for breakfast.

That sounds good, as long as I can have seconds. said the boy.

For the Knighthood. said Ario, helping his young guest to more Carrot Stew.

Thanks! You've made a real home for yourself here, but you've also escaped reality.

Gardening in the shadows is a flight from the world of acceptable appearances, sure is. This is justified as long as one stands their ground, not ignoring reality but acknowledging why the once-world[85] has become intolerable and must be avoided if we are to retain our dignity.

This was *once* the Light World of genuine phenomena, a world of true appearances. Regardless, you're not fleeing the consequences of ignoring the reality of these evil times.

Is he? Link asked Zelda. Don't despair! he enjambed, Got your own world here.

Yo! The **anguish** is real, and is a sign that our commitments are in good-faith.

The princess nodded, While the sun shines so lovely here in the Light World, there is an uncanny poignancy, a dissonance in broad daylight as our vision is attuned to grand illusions. Under the wizard's spell we mistake the virtual for the visible, the reified image of authority as what we must kneel to instead of a true king's creed that protected the public square for all men to appear – that was a real world, *once upon a time...*

Hyrule is gone. said Link. But I still defend its lineage, by oath to protect the princess.

King Hyrule and his sovereignty is gone, but the Light World has not vanished, it has only become temporarily inscrutable as to what phenomena means when giving rise to thought that burgeons in a plot, and puts a Hylian in just as much trouble as growing a vegetable bed.

Speaking our minds is a one-way ticket from a garden to the gallows! said the boy.

The spell casts itself, when people stupefy themselves. Zelda lamented.

---

85   A description of pre-pestilence Hyrule, used by individuals who understand the society and culture of the kingdom has been totally inverted compared to what it once was. An admission that happiness is no longer possible without a sensible world. A term that suggests there is no longer really a world to live in.

Remember the stupid sessantine? Nobody saw each other. Nothing made any sense. said the boy, rocking cross legged. Everyone in Castle Town locked themselves up for sixty days of isolation, nearly nine weeks of terror and abductions in the night – darkest before dawn and culminating to the inexplicable 'end' of the pestilence… immediately after the king died…

Murdered. she corrected. Those measures of the magistrate only intensified the gloom that now covers the kingdom. Don't forget that the Dark World is a *noumenal* echo of what Hyrule is a *phenomenal* reflection of – two realms of the same corrupted manifold. she tapped Link twice on his green festooned head. Lorule manifests the inner nature of everything overtly, but here in the Light World, evil loves to masquerade as benevolence.

Also strange how much it rained during the sessantine… said the child Link.

Makes compliance quite convenient; more reason to stay indoors. she winked.

Mmhm… Vain ambitions have warped the Sacred Realm, and while the Light World retains a superficial semblance of faithfulness to appearances, so much appears inverted now. People say the opposite of what they mean – this regime would be nothing without euphemism. When the wizard conquered the suprasensory he also eliminated the world of sensory meaning, and *in a sense* destroyed the difference between the two realms. lamented Ario in speculation.

Is that destruction a unification then? If only incompletely… asked Link.

Unification is the goal. Having traversed between the Dark World and the Light World, they are completely resonant, and inseparably connected to each other. said Zelda definitively.

After the pestilence, and especially the mandates, the sunshine felt empty, as if it belied the true darkness of our new age under Agahnim's rule. Chalk it up to sessantine-syndrome,[86] but I feel more at home under cover in my forgotten shadow garden of souvenirs. said Ario.

---

86   When one retains their isolated sessantine routine after the magistrate announced the pestilence

You have a gift for... Zelda tried to come up with the right term to describe this process... *externality excavation* – taking up the unforeseen consequences of a dead kingdom and turning it into a living composition for exiles to dwell in. Foo-PFFF! she exhaled from puffing up the long winded compliment. Or what you said, 'postchivalric' simply sums it up. said Zelda.

Gardens can rescue the realm's visibility from the obfuscating gloom, provided we allocate ample space and time for our hearts and minds to show themselves. said Ario.

If the wizard relies on the Dark Arts, sacrificing life to gain power, you do the opposite by cultivating death – call it the Shadow Arts![87] she riffed on what her preceptor Impa taught her.

Maybe you could make more? There are a lot of bridges. said the child Link, It'd be a hit!

Sir Ariosto's Subversive Syndication of Shadow Gardens: the most profound underground phenomenon you never knew existed! the princess glibly pitched. Tehehe!

Ario the camper yet again blew a bubble in beauty queen repose while contemplating it. An errant knight must be very selective about which fool's errands he pursues – popularity is not one of them, especially in our emergent era of global gloom!

But your work would be celebrated, and for a good cause.

Dishonorable would be the only way down that path my young knight, and not something we should entertain. As the criteria for renown has become an exhibit of artificiality, then such an enterprise would at best achieve a *pyrrhic popularity*[88] – when a superficial success actually amounts to a substantial failure. There would be no authentic depth to such a thin endeavor.

I'm trying to imagine...

---

over. A very common tendency to remain living in place despite the compulsory mandates having long elapsed. Returning to sessantine measures on one's own volition. Fondness for habituated staying put all alone.

87   Inverse of the evil Dark Arts that sacrifice life for power (i.e. creating death), instead reclaims death for meaning (i.e. creating life). Mastered by the Sheikah, related to 'vita magica', gardening, and melosophy.

88   Winning popularity but at such a loss of one's own dignity and values that it is not worth it.

Would you slay a three-headed gleeok if you knew victory would turn you into a dragon?

There's enough hydras in Hyrule as it is. said the boy, shaking his head.

Oh please, you're mixing mythologies here... The only way to slay a gleeok – real or metaphoric – is by intrinsic motivation, not extrinsic rewards of any kind. *Everyone knows that...* As with any heroic act, it has to come from your own motives, which would be true and noble!

Where is the heart? Ario flicked a pebble at his menhir, There is only one lethic stone. And there is only one Sir Ariosto! he exclaimed, Sincerely, how could I possibly hold multiple conversations at once? I am no triple-tongued gleeok – I am a singular man of the old kingdom. The whole enterprise would undermine the enlivening ethos and quiet purpose of my work here. Fantasize all you want about overcoming the gloom with popularity, and if you are so unlucky to ever achieve it in a world that venerates shallow thrills, in the end that blinding spotlight will betray your original integrity wrought in deep shadows. *We're after meaning—not immediacy.*

Best to stay low then. said Link.

In our present era that many are calling the 'Gloomaevum', each of us must be singular and wholly ourselves, lest we conform and become nobody; incapable of moral accountability.

Be single? Zelda misunderstood. I've also heard 'Gloom Eon' to describe our age.

Sounds like *glue-me-on.* Link joked. He said <u>singular</u> Princess, not 'single'.

Bearing one's solitude carries the possibility of opening up a gap in the oppressively ubiquitous and seemingly indefinite gloom – an island in the oceanic isolation – for others to come and join each other by the campfire. he clarified, putting another log on while lounging. And that concludes my didactic tour of this discursive garden. I do not hazard hope, but trust that your visit was meaningful – not for any lessons learned but by this chance meeting itself.

Are you kicking us out? said the greenclad kid, unsure what Ariosto the greenthumb meant by his concluding comment.

The princess helped herself to a cushion, and found a smaller matching pillow for Link. What happened to the maiden who went up the mountain? she wondered this and more.

You're familiar with that elevation of the realms? Ario raised his left arm to the far north, The light *spirit of sight* in Hyrule, and its flipside dark *warp of myopia* in Lorule...

We've been there. said the boy. At the top of the realms.

How did you rescue her from the wizard? Zelda had to know.

At this elevation we are in the *topography of magnanimity*, so—

—Oh is it? Link rolled on his back, I was wondering why I feel so generous.

Tah! she rolled her eyes. What do you have to give? Besides your small key...

I can give my best self! In this topos, or elsewhere.

Spoken like a true knight of honor who even when stripped of arms and armor can still bare his humanity despite the circumstantial forces that act upon him. Near the central kingdom, in the spirit of magnanimity I would be remiss not to share a proper story with you. Let us each offer a fable, lighthearted legend, or piquant parable of our choosing and as your host allow me to set the theme and order. But no selfish sagas, halfhearted histories, nor austere allegations! The princess shall begin with a trenchant tale that thrives in the shadow of evil, inspired by and in honor of a goddess of her choosing, then I will do the same, and Sir Link at last too.

Zelda's Tale of Wisdom

Despite the generous spirit of the place, she caught her fingers fiddling with the broche, tickling nervously toward the hem of her hood. In good company and not one to shy away from performance, the prompt to fabulate in honor of the goddesses made her rather self-conscious, and Zelda was tempted to try her magic cape and disappear, if only as an irrelevant introduction to her story; icebreaker or an excuse to delay while searching her soul for a story worth sharing.

That's a very nice cloak. said Ariosto, still trying to remember why it looked familiar.

What do you think happened to the pendants of virtue? asked Link, reminded by the motion of her fidgeting with the cape's clasp. Do you think we'll need to retrieve all three again now that we're in the Light World? *I wonder if the physician, florist, and flutist still have them...*

As soon as the legendary sword is drawn, the pendants ignite into the sacred flames. That tripartite fire only coalesces into the orbs again once the imbued blade is put back to rest.

Not for us. We had to hand them off before heading up the mountain. recounted Link.

There were flames! *But the orbs remained.* And since then, I've seen the blue pendant.

You met the healer I entrusted it to? How could you have—she was inside Vitreous.

No—an imp has it. she told him, I saw before we vanquished that evil eye of the mire.

Really! So the dissident maiden must've lost it then. said the boy with a sigh.

Of course she did – she was crystallized by the wizard! the blonde admonished.

I should have asked her about it. Do you still have her—crystal? Maybe we can ask now.

No. said the princess, having already bet that black diamond (and another) with the boar.

Yo! Zelda! Is this your story or what? said Ario, tiring of her digression.

Excuse me. the princess glowered, This is a preamble...

For how the pendants came to be... assisted Link, sensing she needed guidance and had always wanted to know for himself, hence his suggestion.

Ye–exactly. That's my intended tack.

Weave away. ushered their host with an undulating wave gesture.

In honor of Nayru but also Great Hylia, I'll explain the nascence of those necklaces...

Ariosto handed Zelda the soup ladle, Whoever holds this speaks. *This is your scepter.* Link saved his questions for later as the princess beamed, taking up her role as queen.

When the world was young, Hylia dwelt in the Sacred Realm, golden and serene, while her three daughters made themselves at home throughout the newly formed Hyrule. Each of Hylia's daughters: Nayru, Din, and Farore sought to impress their mother by mimicking her act of creation, further embellishing the world with new landmarks and blessings for the plethora of living things Hylia had breathed life into. Nayru resonated with the water, singing amongst the rivers and lakes, the surf and the sea, teaching the Zora people how to thrive and protect what had been given to them, singing her wise harmony of conservation. Din was of a lower pitch, resonating with the mountains and rock. Uplifting and smelting the terrain to make a home for the Goron people, the fiery goddess rumbled a tremorous rhythm that compelled all dwellers of the deep to find strength in resistance. Pulling against the tectonic pressure, and pushing the sunken calderas of the world's molten mantle, cities and caverns were built by the fires of Din. Finding a home between her two sisters, Farore rode on a zephyr and enlivened the forests, seeding and greening the world with the assistance of the Deku people who played their woodwinds to celebrate the vast greenways she sowed into the ground.

Confusion arose however, as Farore found herself venturing into the litholand[89] to shape the terrain for making a habitat to her liking. This angered Din, who felt encroached upon, and would erupt the volcanoes, burning much of her sister's verdant work. Ensuring her waterways never stagnated, Nayru took to forming storms and borrowing the air from the vast canopies. This work sometimes caused great hurricanes to make landfall, breaking innumerable boughs. Farore bristled at her sister's disregard for anything rooted, and retorted with earthquakes by raising cliffs and ridges to protect against her sister's galeforce oversight. Furious at her sister for deforming the land, and collapsing many caverns of hers below, Din exploded with rage to clear out any

---

89   The primordial domain of the red goddess Din in the rocky mantle of Hyrule.

compressions caused by Farore's quaking. To make matters worse, Din rended great searing chasms in the ocean floor, siphoning the seawater – and accidentally many of Nayru's favorite creatures with it – to cause shattering explosions with the vapor that could not escape the hot cavities. Breaking apart the innards of mountains with the steaming deluge, Din would also draw from her sister's well to cool forges and quench the magma poured structures and castings she wrought from massive molds in the sparklit[90] interior of the world.

Here in the central kingdom, the three goddesses met and agreed to give each other a gift that would allow them to borrow from each other's nature, but without causing any calamity. In the spirit of magnanimity that has characterized this topography ever since, together they blessed this elevation of the world with an exchange of golden sigils, granted by Hylia.

The goddess medallions! Link interrupted.

Nayru gave Din the bombos medallion, allowing her red sister to blast mine as needed without having to drain the rivers and sea – to compensate for Farore's crushing earthworks.

Oh.

Din gave Farore the quake medallion, allowing her green sister to landform as needed without having to collapse the caverns – to compensate for Nayru's snapping windworks.

…

Farore gave Nayru the ether medallion, allowing her blue sister to cyclone as needed without having to wreck the woodlands – to compensate for Din's fuming lavaworks.

That was a good story. congratulated the pink-haired boy prematurely.

She's not done yet. Ariosto calmly reminded young Link that Zelda still held the ladle.

Good good. said Link, anxious to hear how this relates to the origin of the pendants.

The goddess medallions worked inasmuch as they *did not work* for each of their intended projects, and so there were no unforeseen

---

90 When a space or thing is illuminated exclusively by sparks suspended in the air.

consequences at all. But the scale of their aspirations was too great for what the sigils afforded, which were only a reduced approximation of the goddesses ability to shape the world. Din confronted Farore, firmly asserting that the only solution is for one of them to preside over Hyrule, and work it as they will. When her green sister declined, Din cast aside her bombos medallion as a rejection of their pact (because according to the bombastic goddess of fire – if none could have all then all would have none) but not without preserving it in an indestructible and blank monument on one of Farore's ridgelines by the sea such that only the power of the goddesses could retrieve it, if ever needed. Wary of her angry red sister's craft of securing the artifact in a metavolcanic diolith[91] that no mortal could break without divine assistance, Farore threw her quake medallion into a remote sylvan river, entrusting the golden sigil to the serendipity of the wandering currents and sediments of time. Not intimidated by her demanding sister Din, and uninterested in commanding all of Hyrule for herself, Farore flew on the wind to Nayru to ask her opinion of how to reconcile the elemental discord of their triumvirate realm. By the time Farore arrived, Din had already made her case to their acquiescent blue sister, who in solidarity had asked Din to memorialize her ether medallion in a nondescript monolith as well, but high on a mountain peak far beyond any seashore. With their medallions gone, Nayru told her sisters that the only thing they could do now is appeal to a higher authority than their own interests. Not prone to feuds, but unsure how to reconcile their mutual reciprocity of destruction, the three sisters agreed to beseech their mother.

When did this happen? asked Link.

This is long before the Great Cataclysm, when the Sacred Realm was a pure reflection of Hylia's blessed presence. Just one world at this time, inhabited and presided over by her three daughters, there was no Triforce yet, and no sages, no Golden Power other than the

---

91   Divine stone, a heavenly rock formation. An extremely hard metamorphic stone. Like a monolith, except not formed by typical geologic processes but wrought by the gods hence the 'dio' in diolith. A large stone monument composed of an unnatural greenish-grey high-grade fine-grained cement-like substance used to encapsulate the goddess medallions. According to legend only two were ever made by Din, and only the Master Sword can call upon the heavens to crack open a diolith with the same force that made it.

unmatched benevolence of Hylia. Any notion of multiple realms was not yet known.

The split had not yet happened... Times were simpler then. said the boy wistfully.

Zelda resumed her story, Hylia agreed that there was no way for her daughters to find equilibrium by balancing their respective forces with the exchanging such gifts – this was not a problem of regulating elemental power, but of *assigning virtuous jurisdiction.* Touching the jewel that hung around her neck that shone like the sun, Hylia instantiated her celestial pendant to be found in Hyrule; the world she created for her daughters. Much to their surprise, Hylia told the goddesses to find this pendant, and whoever returned to her with it would inherit the kingdom. Din left first, ablaze with ambition and eager to get ahead of her two sisters. Disinterested in power but honoring her mother's instructions Farore set out second while Nayru waited to ask her mother for counsel in private, but was told nothing, and followed her sisters accordingly. Scouring the world for the pendant that would entitle them to rule Hyrule, the goddesses raced through the entirety of their realm, permeating stone, wood, and water with their impossibly fast spirit to uncover the coveted replica of their mother's jewel. No mountain escaped Din's survey, likewise no river nor valley remained unmapped by Farore, while Nayru combed every cloud and sounded every sea with nothing to show for it. Giving up ensemble, the three goddesses sat in defeat, idling in their own territories – all presuming that a sibling must have succeeded. Once still, and after a short period of time by any measure of immortality, they were approached by the mortal denizens of each domain. Despondent in the deep ocean, the Zora found Nayru, and asked her what was wrong. Alone in the thickest grove, the kind Deku found Farore, and implored her to explain her stupor. Tunneling through bedrock the strong Goron found Din soaking herself unperturbed in a torrid lake of sulfur.

We have been given the pendant, they all said to the goddesses. When asked for proof, they handed over what had miraculously come to them from on high. Returning to Hylia to settle the dispute once and for all, Din did not expect to see her two sisters returning simultaneously. The red goddess already had plans to make all of Hyrule a powerful mountain, scrape away any organic matter and let her mighty geology shine uncovered; no more flimsy flora. How fortuitous, thought Farore, that Din and Nayru are returning to witness my claim to reign as the whole world will soon become my final forest. Nayru wore the pendant and was ready to rule Hyrule with the deep wisdom of the ocean and the contemplative passions that energized the skies above. Standing before their mother, the sisters saw that they each wore a pendant – *there were three!* Who has the true pendant of virtue? They asked Hylia, who responded that none of them are entitled to shape Hyrule as they please, as none of them found the pendant. Then who rules? The goddess explained that it was the Zora who found the blue pendant of wisdom, who must protect the oceans and skies above. And it was the Goron who found the red pendant of power, who must guard the riches of the mountain and depths below. And it was the Deku who found the green pendant of courage, who must conserve the wilds and set out to seed new lands.

And what of us? asked the sisters, Are we now purposeless in our world? What are we to do if we cannot command our elemental forces anymore? Who is to rule if neither of us?

Your people – was the answer Hylia gave them. They found the pendants of virtue, and so the time has passed for my daughters to lord over the world with force. You now serve them.

What about…

I'm getting there Link! said the princess, suspecting what was going through his head. Hylia also told her daughters that while they were searching, she breathed life into the last race of Hyrule, the Hylians *who in time* shall inherit the kingdom and govern it according to all three divine virtues. And while her daughters come and go from the Sacred Realm, only a Hylian who holds a key – itself unlocked by wearing the three pendants – may then walk beyond the world. Concurrently, it was also at this time that Hylia herself placed the Triforce into the Golden Land.

There it is. said the boy making a triangle with his thumbs and fingers together.

Dismissing her daughters, Hylia stipulated one final caveat and gift for her new children: the medallions sealed blank by Din were now etched with an invitation for whoever possesses Hylia's Key – a sword born by the sacred flames held in the pendants: wisdom, power, courage. A mortal Hylian may then claim the derivative power of the elemental goddesses, after uniting the three antecedent races of the Zora, Deku, and Goron. Thus the future kings of Hyrule were ordained by Hylia, and a new epoch arose with the advent of the Hylians whereby gods served mortals, and mortals forever praised Hylia for it – settling the world in harmony for many ages, until the Hylian Schism–

–Hyrulean Civil War? Ario interjected.

Yes, that's another term for it, which then escalated into the Interloper War and resulting Great Cataclysm that defiled the Golden Land – bifurcating the realms…

And making the mirrored Light and Dark worlds that we have inherited. nodded Ario, more familiar with the ancient history at the end of her tale, than all the mythology before it.

Very good. clapped Link. I had no idea – what an amazing story.

Excellent tale of wisdom, applauded Ariosto, but I was expecting more about Nayru specifically, as your patroness. Of course, Hylia plays a central role, and she is most wise.

Why! the princess pushed back on his preemptive criticism.

Why? Hylia knew that immortals couldn't reign eternal.

Why. Link pressed Ario in turn.

Come on fellas, Princess Zelda stretched, The point of the tale is that without mortality, the gifts of the goddesses: wisdom, courage, and power… are insufficient to—or just incapable of establishing a kingdom for anyone to happily thrive in. Something else is required that only those who embody the privilege of death are capable of possessing.

The pendants. said the boy. No! *The Master Sword.* he guessed again.

Did you not catch the final part? Whoever is king, those first kings of Hyrule, wielded the Master Sword, but only after uniting the three tribes who held the required pendants of virtue.

The Zora can soar, the Gorons can grind, the Deku can dig... they're all mortals, but... Link contemplated, What can the Hylians do that makes them so special then?

Well nothing really, which is important because they instead carry the most important virtue of all, which is *why* they are the promised people to restore the realm to its former glory.

Which virtue is that? Link jittered.

Temperance. she flicked a finger at him, The stuff of crowns, and without mundane mortality there is none. Which makes me wonder, she paused, *if the wizard is a man at all.*

Is—no longer? Or, never was to begin with. Who else could he have been?

People change. the greenclad child Link shrugged at the camper's questions.

I don't know where Agahnim came from, or who he was before. confessed Zelda.

He who seeks sovereignty is not endowed by Hylia to do so. their host reiterated.

Ariosto's Tale of Power

In honor of the red goddess Din, and as your host if I may go second, I will now tell a tale of power – the power of love and how it maddens us, not altogether different than how seeking political power corrupts us. prefaced Ario quickening the campfire and rousing cinders for effect.

Is this going to be a romance? moaned the boy.

How did you help her escape the wizard? Zelda passed the ladle. I wonder if I met her?

This is a story of *being wanted* – by both the authorities and a betrothed! A personal account of pursuit, of escape, and the futility of trying to preserve one's identity behind masks. An element of comedy, when we fail to convey *who we are* when disguised against danger.

About time we had some mask action. punked the pink-haired youth.

She was the fifth? I remember the guards dragging another maiden before me from the castle jail, I could hear her screams and protests, but I never saw that substitute detainee from my especially long cell. Link was the only face I met when he came to rescue me—everyone else was in the service of the wizard, and concealed behind bascinets and evil visors.

To explain would make my overture an appendix of undesirable details. said Ario.

Link wrapped his pointy green nightcap over his face and laid down on the small pillow like a puppy, Ghyuh… letting out a not-so-subtle sigh of proclaimed disinterest.

Forget I asked, just begin. said Zelda.

Delay no more, for Din's sake! Link wailed.

There was once a knight of Hyrule, and his maiden Ariela…

Ariosto and Ariela! Is that her real name? asked the princess.

Shhh! Zelda! hushed Link, pointing to the patrol above as an excuse to shut her up.

Yes it is her name, or was – before she became warped by jealousy…

Hmmm? That sounds familiar. ruminated Zelda.

But that's another story. the camper carried on, As you already heard how Sir Ariosto rescued Lady Ariela from the wizard Agahnim, temporarily died, and returned to Hyrule, I will pick up where I left off. Actually, this tale takes place in the time between her rescue, and my fall to the underworld – before her father sent her up the mountain as a pilgrim in hope of hiding her in the Sacred Realm. And for context, Zelda had yet to get abducted, just so you know.

Gotcha. I'm ready to hear how this gap is filled. said Link, thinking back – I wonder what I was doing then… just killing time at uncle's place. I barely knew who you were then, Princess!

Shhh! retorted Zelda.

She was a sorceress in her own right, and took it as a challenge to overpower the spell that Agahnim had cast on us – the troupe who was sent to take her. The wizard played upon passions to bend the castle guards to his will, but his manipulations were no match for the infatuation she fanned in my heart. From the thoughtless delirium of a wizard's weave to the drunken dizziness of amorous enchantment, I had no choice but to dismiss my command before we reached the castle walls. And by dismiss, I mean dispatch, as they were beyond discourse, and only swore allegiance to Agahnim then. Their words were gone, at most they uttered like ogres on a simple script – mouths full of empty magisms[92] provided for them by the magistrate.

I've also had to slay many guards when rescuing Zelda. lied the boy in a valiant effort to impress his fellow knight – the decorated and indomitable Sir Ariosto, marshal of the guard.

They would've killed us, it was self-defense! *May the goddess forgive us.* said Zelda, taking Link by surprise as she too was motivated to falsely match Ariosto's deathly deeds.

May the goddess *forgive them!* said Link unapologetically, tougher than he was.

In time. Zelda looked to Link, admitting with her eyes that (she knew he knew she knew) they were both lying, coincidentally compelled to the same mendacious bragging independently.

I already had misgivings about our mission, which she must've sensed, fixating on me as her opportunity for saucy succor! We were only five weeks into the sixty-day sessantine, loosely one maiden taken per week, when I overheard the plot to depose the king after the sixth maiden was crystalized and sent to the Dark World. That shook me in my greaves, however my troubled conscience had already shaken off much of the wizard's spell. I was ready for an opportunity to cut out; literally. In the dead of night, the guards about me were not royal knights, not like your uncle, rather unprincipled soldiers following any number of contradictory orders without the slightest qualm in their compliant minds or protest in their shriveled hearts.

These are the grunts who became the moblin pigs in the Dark World. said Link.

Ah, perhaps the taros bulls as well. agreed Zelda from her own experience in the tower.

---

92   The truisms of mages; thought-terminating clichés also called 'axioms of Agahnim'. While a sort of magic, isn't the 'vita magica' which reveals meaning (instead of smothering meaning for compliance).

The same sort of unconscionable men that patrol on the Boneyard Bridge above us now, obedient only to fear and never honorable virtue. Which is not to excuse the knights, almost all of them broke their vows to serve Agahanim. Regardless, I would be lying if I said my blade was dispassionate, as my vengeful arms were spurred by her innocence. Not a second to spare nor any mistake permitted, I swung unannounced in haste as her life depended upon my decisive action. As you know Link, the difference between a knight and soldier, is that we chivalric only fight one foe at a time, taking on a host or multitude as a gestalt; *to see the field for the battle.* Or as gallant standard bearers say, a three-headed gleeok has but one blood to spill.

That's why Hyrulean Knights are so good! said Link.

Don't get distracted. Zelda spoke to both a gleeok's three heads and their host.

Taking a step back, these soldiers were issued from the castle as a conrois at my command, the small regiment was one uncoordinated eight-armed beast. said Sir Ariosto.

Four men. enumerated the boy.

Spellbound. she colored his counting.

The distinction is how we hold our ground. An infantryman cannot understand this, and any knight who fails to stand alone becomes like the enlisted footsoldier who cowers at what he sees to be an insurmountable summation of opponents, and so: they must be told what to do. Alas, instrumentalized to any evil ends and motivated by trepidation about the wizard's wrath, his men are worse than mercenaries who at least subjugate their fear with a zeal for money.

Link has spilled the blood of many spellbound soldiers, before we were exiled...

They swung first! I can't take it personally. said Link, downplaying their fibbing.

Didn't mean to interrupt, said Zelda, please continue Ariosto.

In wild haste, I bathed our nuptial in the anemia of tyranny, eloping with their cowardly bile stuck to our boots, printing the ground for many miles as the bright silver moon watched in cold confidence above.

Wearing my stained tabard of the knight's order with King Hyrule's coat of arms gorestrewn[93] from the melee, I brought Ariela to her father – but not without considering that more guards would come for him in short time. When *the old man* came to the door, he was speechless and agape at my tabard. I could see in his eyes that he regarded the dripping crest less as evidence of our controversial escape, but more so a sign of the anticipated regicide that nobody dared speak of. As if my slaying of the castle guards had painted a prescient banner announcing the king's death to come – an unforgivable crime I had no part in. Shortly after my abandonment, the king was assassinated as I feared Agahnim might. Our escape was blamed for his death, a great convenience for the wizard, and utmost cynical coordination on his part.

You were his cover. He wasn't going to let his loss go to waste. said the boy.

Save a maiden, lose a king, sighed Ario, a tradeoff no knight should have to make.

So much violence... This tale isn't a romance at all! Zelda laughed.

Hrm. the boy crossed his arms.

Apologies for the prelude. I'm at risk of breaking my own rules set out as host!

What did her father do next? Link sat up.

Ariosto gestured with his hands, The tale truly begins here, as her father reassured me that he knew of a way to keep his daughter hidden within plain sight.

Like with a magic cape? clutched Zelda.

No, not invisible, just unrecognizable. The old man was familiar with three tribal masks, any one of which could transform a Hylian into either a Deku, Goron, or Zora; as I later learned.

Could a Goron wear the Deku or Zora mask and become like them too? asked the boy.

I don't see why not. said Ario. But I didn't know what their illusory magic entailed when he suggested this solution to our fugitive

93 Strewn with gore. Untidily scattered gore upon slaughtering spellbound soldiers. Ariela's grandfather misread however presciently the gorestrewn tabard as a sign the king had been murdered in cold blood.

dilemma. Her father gave us his blessing, but under two conditions. He first made Ariela promise she would never say *her name* out loud, not to me, nor anyone – until the wizard was gone for good. And then second, for her safety, the old man insisted that no one... not even I, could know beforehand what the masks would turn her into. This was the only way for Ariela to remain in Hyrule under Agahnim's pervasive surveillance, going about her life and hiding in plain sight as someone, or *something* else.

Dekus are not *things* – they are people too. said the pedantic princess.

I'm not sure if that's what he was getting at. He didn't know what the masks did then!

Are people things? Ario mused, Regardless, I would wend my way as a wanted man.

I know how that goes. said the haughty boy. In fact, THAT WAS YOU! he exclaimed, when they put up signs all over Kakariko and elsewhere, *my poster* was hastily pasted on top of a placard for a previous outlaw who I never thought much of – 'WANTED! This is the criminal who kidnapped Ariela. Call a soldier if you see him!' was what they printed, with a doodle of your valiant visage Sir Ariosto; exact same wording, they simply replaced the name for me.

And for me! Their new direct object in distress. Zelda noted – instead of Ariela.

New damsel, *same damn propaganda...*

Your caricature was a decent likeness Link, but nothing to write home about.

Too bad, never saw yours! I must've been in the underworld by then. said Ario.

Not worth anything even close to a thousand words – that picture. said Link, unfolding a crumpled piece of paper from his pocket that he had torn from his wanted sign: not bad though!

Oh right, same style. said Ario, looking at Link's mugger portrait. Undeterred by all the bogus bulletins incriminating my face, I was prepared to fend for myself devoid of any disguise. Regrettably in hindsight, I told her father, mother, *and her grandfather who was present—*

that I had to try and rouse the remaining knights who had yet to wake up from Agahnim's spell.

That included my uncle!

Must've. said Ariosto, scratching his head at a loss for that mustached man's name. Exhausted, we slept in his stable, and agreed to leave at dawn: soon-to-be anonymous Ariela off to her unspoken disguise, me to my quest for avenging the king. Time was of the essence, but I had preparations and preliminary errands to make before facing Agahnim.

The dwarven smiths. said Link, remembering him mentioning them earlier.

Exactly, that was the second task in my greater quest to wed Ariela, safe and sound.

Can knights marry? she asked.

No, but there is no *happily-ever-after* since the sessantine. I would vanquish the wizard! And with his gloomy influence lifted from the kingdom, retire my sword to a weathervane, and resign to a life of hearth, children, and wife − these simple rewards of villagicity[94] motivated me to risk it all, as I knew such happiness would remain impossible so long as Agahnim ruled. There was also no turning back after I defected − I had to save Hyrule, or die...

You'd get bored. said the child, too young to sympathize. What was your first task?

I thought it wise to visit the Zora to the north as they had remained a suzerain domain since the pestilence, and their king and queen could counsel me on how to confront a wizard. When I arrived at the waterfalls, scant Zoras were swimming, but their king had recently gone missing as well! Many of those aquatic people had become hostile, and I took temporary refuge on the isle of the Forest Temple, where a young Zora woman approached me. She said I would be safe as long as I remained at her side, as the despondent riverfolk would not take offense to my Hylian presence while escorted by one of their own. She called me by my name and urged me not to return to the central kingdom as it was hopeless. I did not understand the pleas of this Zora mistress,

---

94   Village or community life. Like domesticity, but at the scale of a village. A villager's way of life.

but insisted I had a more important quest than to hide in a provincial watershed. Not without many tears, the young Zora led me to their blue queen, Rutela who was too beside herself at the recent disappearance of the king, and could not proffer any wisdom for my quest. Queen Rutela asked me why I sought to risk love and limb to rescue a maiden when my quest was already won then and there in the far reaches of the realm astride that Zora lassie guide.

She did offer wisdom then, but you didn't understand. said the princess.

Huh? I don't get it.

Don't blow it. Zelda suggested to Ario — let Link figure it out.

I was a fool. the camper smiled, assenting to continue his tragicomedy unexplained. Discerning my chivalric intransigence, the queen offered me an exceptional suit of armor, the dashing blue mail that might give me a leg up, come the final showdown. I thanked the queen, and silently forgave her for mistaking me as the type of guy who goes after Zora gals. My guide accepted that there was nothing she could do to make me stay, and told me that we would meet again—and soon. I told her this was wishful thinking, but kept an eye out along the rivers, as I would happily wave from the road of destiny I trod upon; not like I would ignore her just because I was after my heart's true aim Ariela! Queen Rutela wished me a swift victory over the wizard, but reiterated that the endeavor was irrelevant if I were to stay and make a life there on the wet margins of the map where no patrols would find me. My guide thanked the queen, which was unnerving, and I insisted that Agahnim's crimes could not go unchecked, and that I must confront him for the benefit of all peoples. Sufficiently satisfied with my first task of seeking the wisdom of the Zora, and strapping a new suit of handsome armor, I returned to the west, and took every backroad I could to the dwarven smiths outside Kakariko Village.

Ah, yes, the tempering of your claymore. Link twinkled, familiar with the place.

My second task was to gain an edge on Agahnim, and sharpen my claymore so it was more powerful than ever before. When I arrived, a young Goron girl sitting on their stoop waved to me excitedly, acting like she knew me. I ignored her at first, as I had important business to attend to with the smiths inside. Stranger yet, she held what looked like a mask of a Zora face. Stepping into the foundry, there was only one dwarf, who told me, *If my lost partner returns, we can temper your sword, but now, I can't do anything for you.*

Same here! said Link, that's what he told me too, before Zelda and I left.

His partner must've been banished to the Dark World. But the Goron girl was fired up beyond reproach – implacably industrious as she fanned the forge with her Zora mask, which seemed like a childish thing to do considering the urgency of my errand. She would wink at me and while this Goron girl was attractive in her own right, I wasn't about to emotionally cheat on Ariela with a rock chomping burly belle— blacksmiths make for a sooty squeeze, and returning her hot nothings would've besmirched my fetching new blue mail. That gladsome Goron intern told me I could work there too, so long as I stayed out of sight, but their business would thrive between the three of us. The idea was so hilariously beneath me I nearly snuffed the forge with my forgoing guffaw. I've never seen a dry Goron cry, but just like my Zora guide, this assistant begged that I put down my sword, not for tempering but for a new life as her beausmith[95] chum. Refusing her brawny advances, she reluctantly acknowledged there was no swaying Sir Ariosto from his quest to marry his maiden in peace. But first, the wizard had to go! Substituting for the dwarf's lost partner, the Goron girl hammered in tandem, toughening the steel with a red glow. Swinging the cindered claymore scorched the air with a growl, and just like the annealed blade, my will hardened accordingly. Thanking the dwarf merrily and avoiding eye contact with his Goron hired help, I was ready for the final task, a confirmation of courage – to enter the castle…

Oof. This is sad. said the princess. So harsh! But also worth a hoot in hindsight.

---

95   An affectionate male teammate. A crafty boyfriend who works alongside his tradeskilled partner.

Did you sneak in? asked the boy too fixated on the future to see the past pattern.

I needed to break in – my new sword and armor – by attacking the castle head on!

Wow. Link pursed his lips, very impressed.

None of the guards stood a chance, as my magmatic claymore parted their armor like a heated knife through tepid Tabantha Goat Butter! Effortlessly slashing my way through the gate.

Scrumptious swashbuckling... Link pantomimed with his palm, buttering the air.

I could barely feel the timid touch of the soldier's polearms and swords, the few times they dared to test my righteous cerulean spaulders. The noble flash of the mail spoke for itself that I was now *Ariosto the Avenger* back in the name of King Hyrule and the whole royal house. Up on the ramparts the grenadier soldiers lobbed their bombs, while the javelin drawbridgers backpedaled to the moat, trying to keep their distance but stood no chance. Only two guards waited in the courtyard garden, cowering in tandem I smote them both with one swing. An eerie quiet fell over the bailey processession – the trees rustled in the wind and for a moment I could enjoy the tranquility of the king's cloister by myself. That indelible sensation has forever inspired this lethic garden here. Taking my fill of the fragrant air knowing it might be my last, I proceeded to the front door of the keep, but a small shrub jumped up and stood in my way. Just like the Goron girl, this Deku sapling waved me down with something that I could not recognize until it stopped flailing. The little creature held two masks, one in each hand: that familiar Zora mask, and a Goron mask. At the time I thought this must be ceremonial, or maybe there had been a festival recently that I was unaware of where these masks were distributed – their significance, or coincidence, did not occur to me then with my mind bent on revenge. Again, addressing me by my name, the displaced Deku tried to dissuade this knight from going any farther...

What did it say? asked Zelda.

Sir Ariosto, listen carefully. The wizard is magically controlling all the soldiers in the castle. I fear the worst for my father… The wizard is an inhuman fiend with strong magical powers! Do you understand? Yes. I told the Deku, who did not take my word for it. I should've responded '*Not at all*' as when it said 'father' I figured it was speaking for the ancient forests, which might've been in peril by the wizard's designs. Tugging on its long viny locks of overgrown rubescent garlands, the Deku shrub became exasperated. *I sense that a mighty evil force guides the wizard's actions and augments his magical powers. The only weapon potent enough to defeat the wizard is the legendary Master Sword.* Rubbish! I responded, licking a finger and demonstrating how it audibly sizzled on my tempered claymore. Shaking its lush head with a rebuffing susurrus, the Deku was unimpressed. *If you defeat the wizard, the soldiers may regain their sanity.* it reminded me what I already knew, so I tried to brush the jabbering bush aside, but it stood rooted in defiance, imploring me to turn back. Worried that our dilly-dallying might attract more guards, I reassured the Deku that my fellow knights were nowhere to be found as I had hoped to rally them at my side before confronting Agahnim, so their state of mind was irrelevant to my quest to rid the world of evil <u>before</u> marrying my beautiful maiden. Step aside, or I shall hew your hesitation with the ease of snapping kindling! said I, to which the Deku teared up, risking dehydration on my behalf as a plant person should never lose so much water lest they become fatally parched. The little woody creature dropped the two masks and grabbed my mail, making one last plea. *Listen well, Ariosto. Even with the Master Sword, you cannot inflict physical harm on the wizard. You must find a way to return his own evil magic power to him.*

That's common secret knowledge. said Princess Zelda, If you know, you know.

So you didn't listen, what then? young Link was on the edge of his pillow.

Sniveling sap while picking up the two masks, the Deku opened the castle keep doors and stepped to the side. Staring at its rhizome toes, I dared not empathize with this sad and tender creature as I needed to gird my heart for the battle ahead. Go to your father. I told it, imagining the patrilocal dripline of the Great Deku is where this wrung out creature belonged. Distraught by my words, the Deku bawled as I marched off, unable to console it. By the time I reached the top of the sanctum parapet overlooking the keep door, I could see the creature had departed, and discarded the two masks on the ground – the Zora mask, and the Goron mask. There was a third as well, but it was face down and unrecognizable from where I stood on the battlement walkway above. Beyond the courtyard gatehouse and crossing the moat bridge outside the curtain walls, I saw a woman step over the fallen soldiers, walking with abandon to the south. The glint of embers upon her shoulders made me look twice, however too far to tell, the glare blanched her features but her gait was reminiscent. While there at the doorstep of the wizard's inner chapel, and unsure if she was real or a mirage of my maiden, I took the sight as a good omen that soon beautiful women will stroll these grounds again without fear of abduction, and I was relieved that Ariela had faithfully agreed to remain hidden until Agahnim was gone. My motivation redoubled at this phantasmic sighting, and just then the door behind me, which had previously been protected by a nefarious lightning lock, fizzled out as if to invite me up…

Your relief was a romance remised… Zelda stated the obvious.

I'm telling the story as I was then. said the former knight Ariosto.

Were there many duels between there and the wizard? asked Link.

Strangely the keep was unusually vacant, from the lower hallways after leaving the Deku and all the way through the upper sanctum of the inner chapel, I had more liberty to anticipate my confrontation with Agahnim than was advantageous—some guards to loosen up on would have put my nerves in their proper place! When I arrived at Agahnim's sacrificial lair, the wizard stood over the altar of his sadistic rituals, a triple-fanged maw where the previous four maidens had been crystalized upon; scattered into the Dark World thereafter. He mocked my gullibility…

Ahah… Ariosto! I have been waiting for you! Heh heh heh… said the camper, pretending to be Agahnim the wizard. **I was hoping I could make Ariela vanish in front of your eyes. Behold! The last moment of Sir Ariosto!** Raising my sword, the slippery sorcerer retreated immediately on his heels, hovering backwards over the chamber with the speed of a darting babusu and phased through a curtain that barely rustled as if he were wholly immaterial. I slashed the drapery which led to his spireroom[96] thereabout the heights of the castle chapel. **Oh, so?...** the wizard taunted me, **You mean to say you would like to be totally destroyed? Well, I can make your wish come true!**

Did you wish to be totally destroyed? I missed that part. said the child Link.

No, he never mentioned that. said Zelda, But maybe every knight harbors a wish for self-annihilation and suicidal destruction?

You know what happened next, as I already described my defeat by his electric energy... Ariosto laughed to himself, the Deku was right, and my sword was beyond worthless. The rest of my tale is speculative, or truth be told: was relayed from a couple of hyperopic[97] shades in the underworld so take it for what these wraith-gleaned-words are worth.

Some hearsay is warranted – this is a riveting tale. said the princess.

Mind you, these were no ordinary ghosts, but Ariela's parents!

How? Zelda already knew the answer, despite not meeting their shades herself.

In the duration of my quest and her concealment, the wizard's regime had done away with them for withholding information on our whereabouts – or perhaps simply as punishment. Having failed to turn me away from barefaced doom, my maiden presumed me deceased too, putting down her disguise – forfeiting the conditions of her father's blessing, now posthumous. With our marriage impossible, I was told the dead saw her in the near future, leaving Hyrule altogether, following the path of pilgrims up Death Mountain. Only her grandfather remained, and as a parting gift she left him with her mother's looking glass, a maudlin hand mirror which she couldn't bear to keep for herself, as it would be too

---

96   An exclusive castle turret often occupied by a lofty wizard or secluded sorcerer high up to no good. Agahnim's private room in Hyrule Castle. An inaccessible belfry used to lock up a princess as in the seventh floor chamber of the Dark Tower. An impractical penthouse that induces envy when spotted.

97   The farsighted vision of the dead who can see the past and future, but not the present.

painful to look back to the Light World, she told him. This was according to the shades of her parents who then said something truly confounding: that Ariela couldn't foresee how she would have had no use for the mirror anyway, as she would soon *become blinded by jealousy*. Originally a gift from his daughter then to her daughter, Ariela's grandfather kept the heirloom mirror – himself broken and lost with grief.

What happened to the dwarven forged royal guard's claymore?

Or the gift of Queen Rutela, the noble blue mail?

The tempered blade melting over my hilt was the last thing I saw before plummeting to the underworld as an itinerant shade myself. As for that superb Zoran armor—anyone's guess, but I suspect Agahnim took it for himself, perhaps as a trophy to his triumph and wicked victory.

Too bad. said the boy who enjoyed collecting outfits before their exile.

Thus my tale comes to an end, I hope Din was pleased by it, said Ario poking the coals. And so, that's the story of this knight, his maiden, and a wizard in the middle, just as the power of politics corrupts by perversity, so does the power of love bring about doom by madness.

I suspect this story is not yet over. the princess applauded, but let's let Link tell his now, as the sun has elapsed the eastern edge of the Boneyard Bridge, and we should go soon.

Link's Tale of Courage

In the land of Hyrule, there echoes a legend. Link began his story, borrowing Zelda's empty bottle and palming it for inspiration.

Your ladle scepter—story king! Ario anointed him to fabulate with authority.

A legend held dearly by the royal family that tells of a boy... A boy who, after battling evil and saving Hyrule, crept away from the land that had made him a legend... Done with the battles he once waged across time, he embarked on a journey. A secret and personal journey... A journey in search of a beloved and invaluable friend... A friend with whom he parted ways when he finally fulfilled his heroic destiny and took his place among legends...

Would you stop referring to yourself as a legend? It's not very heroic to do so.

I'm not sure if this is about him, the camper quelled Zelda while Link continued.

And would you please dedicate your tale upfront.

WHY YES PRINCESS PROTOCOL.

It's in honor of Farore, I know. she sniped.

Not too loud please. the camper hushed.

Absolutely. I dedicate my tale to my patroness goddess, green Farore as this is a tale of how the legendary hero defies all odds in the name of upholding unconditional friendship, a feat of courage like none other! The events described here were passed down to me by my uncle, who spoke of the Hero of Time who saved Hyrule long before Agahnim came about. After fulfilling that prophecy, this legendary boy–

You?

No! I'm saying *this boy* in reference to the Hero of Time from our fabled past, Princess.

You're projecting some wishful fiction here with our own Hyrule very much unsaved…

Maybe I am. said the child Link. I take inspiration from this legendary boy's non-fictitious tale, as you are welcomed to as well. This is not a story about me! I heard it from our uncle!

Our uncle? Zelda nitpicked unnecessarily.

The abundance of a story's inspiration is only limited by the teller's generosity, and the *quiet participation* of the audience's imagination. Please continue Sir Link, said Ariosto with a ladling gesture (not so subtly suggesting that the princess should stop interrupting).

Eghem. he cleared his throat. From the top… This boy had saved Hyrule, and took his place among legends. But in doing so, lost his companion: a sideflit[98] faerie named Navi who departed as soon as the hero fulfilled his destiny. *She was his ancilla scintilla in tough times.* Together

---

98   When a pixie or small faerie flits at your side for the duration of a conditional quest or an enduring unconditional companionship. The kind of faerie that hovers around as an aerial assistant, typically granted exclusively to Kokiri children, with rare exceptions as condoned by the Great Deku Tree.

they bested all the bosses and demolished countless demons, which seemed like child's play in retrospect compared to this unforeseen solitary epilogue in his story, wandering in an ennui of unemployment – an abyss of purposelessness that threatened to consume the hero. And as you'll hear very soon, in a way, the abyss did consume him! And the abyss gave him a new quest... it was not nothing, but quite something—so much more than he bargained for!

Take us to this abyss. croaked the affected princess.

I'm getting there. But picture yourself riding on a slow pony, alone in the misty forest... Nothing had prepared this boy for the difficulty of *not* having a quest – and worse, alone without the one supportive spirit who accompanied him throughout his adventures. In the forest where Navi first came to him is where he returned. Two faeries appeared, but neither were Navi, and both were in service of a possessed imp who enlisted his two pixies Tatl and Tael to rob the boy. Knocked off his pony and unconscious, our hero quickly came to however and chased the imp who lured him into an ancient Deku tree that had been dead for ages, covered in giant polypore Shelfshrooms[99] and was hollow inside. Rotted out logs are common in those woods, but the boy did not expect the trunk to be a bottomless shaft, and in his haste to catch the imp, he teetered on the pit's rim, flailing and then lost his balance. Where the boy fell to was beyond the depths of Din's forges and subterranean structures, deeper than death and that lake of shades where souls congregate in the underworld...

Where else is there?

He fell further, to the banished inner world of **Termina** – an entire kingdom within the hollow core of Hyrule. Replete with its own sun, *and moon*, the inner world feels much like our own surface world, full of familiar tribes and people, although beyond the care of the goddesses, and for good reason.

What do you mean? I've only heard rumors of such a place...

---

99   The giant Shelfshroom only grows on dead ancient Deku trees as the special wood takes many
     centuries to break down. Also referred to as Deku Brackets or Kokiri Conks, they are very sturdy.

I don't want to get sidetracked so soon, although it's inevitable given the rambling nature of the boy's legend, but I'll try and explain quickly – how Termina came to be – as it's congruent with your tale Princess: of how the goddesses shaped the world in the first days of Hyrule.

Your Highness eagerly awaits, but keep in mind the rules of our host: 'no selfish sagas nor halfhearted histories'! Zelda smarmed, reminded of the zazek's chickaloo sourcing spiel.

A quick but mesmerizing mythology, more like it. said Link, mentally transporting himself to Termina to explain how it came to be long ago. You've heard of the *Mega Internomachy*, no?

Mega–what?

That's the proper term, but most folk just refer to it as the 'internomachy'.

Sounds familiar. she squinted, That mentioned on a memorial... in the Eastern Palace plaza grounds? I've definitely read of it in passing somewhere...

Oh, perhaps! No doubt the internomachy is memorialized and inscribed on some stone. The term describes an epic battle; took place after the mythological events you described Zelda. he pointed to her. After the pendants of virtue were entrusted to the people of Hyrule, and after Hylia breathed life into her most cherished creation: Hylians like us! *The giants became unruly...*

The giants? Like—hinoxes?

No, these were BIG giants! said the boy raising his hands up, As tall as Death Mountain! There were four, one for each of the kingdom's endemic tribes: Zora, Goron, Deku, and Hylian. Their purpose was to aid the people of Hyrule to build temples in honor of the goddesses, lifting massive stones that not even the buffest squad of Goron engineers could manage. The giants[100] fulfilled their task, and regarded the little people they served with great benevolence and sought to do even more. These giants were never malicious, not like a hideous hinox who were just as puny as us to the giants – relatively speaking. If anything, they were way too generous, as the people became enamored by their tireless feats of

---

100   The temple builders. Titans sent by Hylia to assist the four tribes in building their civilization.

labor and worldcrafting that began to include works beyond the building of temples, and in the eyes of the goddesses, threatened to remake the realm they had already largely formed. Worse yet, the giants sole purpose: to build temples such that the children of Hyrule could pay homage to their respective divinity was then relegated to a new reverence – everyone began worshiping the giants! And that was the inexcusable line, once crossed, that set the internomachy[101] into mega-motion. The giants could have apologized, but instead they became proud and seeing that there was nothing they couldn't build and how much the people loved them, they figured that Hyrule belonged to them – an assumption of eminent domain since they were the ones inhabiting the world with the mortals, and not the goddesses who were absent for the reason's Zelda illustrated in her tale.

I see a similar theme here. she cocked her blonde head at the fabling lad.

For sure! Somewhat of a sequel to your story of the medallions—pendants and such!

Might you say then the Interloper War was the third time that Hyrule became contested? Ario speculated, then apologized – Nevermind, just thinking out loud how this all congrues…

The Hylian Schism was the threequel, which we are still unfolding. agreed Zelda.

Ting-ting-ting. Link tapped the bottle in his lap with the ladle to focus their attention. Having noticed, the three sisters went to their mother, and told her about the giants, and how they had become like them – worldly gods in their own right. Perturbed by what had become a pluralistic pantheon, Hylia scolded her daughters for not supervising the temple building titans, but admitted that their whole purpose was so the goddesses did not have to meddle with the affairs of mortals directly. When the giants refused to apologize to Nayru, Din, and Farore who descended on Hyrule to warn them of their transgression, Hylia soon caught word and became furious at their tall insubordination. She created the giants for Hyrule, not Hyrule for the giants! The three sisters wrestled against the four giants, and while they were easily

---

101 Termina War, the internal war waged by the goddesses against the four primeval giants.

subdued, there was always a fourth who remained unrestrained. Hylia saw only one solution to this conflict, which risked tearing all of her creation apart if left unresolved as the giants and goddesses tussled across the seas, forests, and mountains. In one of her rare acts of divine intervention, Hylia cast the giants, and anyone who worshiped them, into the center of the world – a cavity she prepared and hollowed out that very moment. Big enough that no mortal would ever know they lived inside the world, there was an inner sun, and a moon made from the mass of the carved out core. On a clear night, you'd see reflective lodes at the unreachable perimeter of the enclosed cosmos that looked like stars. Thus became Termina, where the giants received what they wanted: a world in which they were gods over those who mistook them as creators from every race including Zoras, Gorons, Dekus, and Hylians – all banished together. So this is where the legendary boy fell, the Hero of Time had accidentally tripped into Termina.[102]

Are you making this up? she asked sincerely.

Take it up with uncle, if you have any issues with it! This lovely afternoon we're enjoying under the bridge could very well be any spring day in Termina as well – the inner world was not a parallel realm like the Dark World to the Light World, nor was it an astral plane like the…

Chamber of Sages?

What's that? No—no, not like that at all. Termina is truly, *thump thump*… a world within our surface world. he said, stomping the ground to emphasize it was down there. Hyrule is like the firmament of Termina, as the giants down there had aspired in vain to make our blessed kingdom their own. They look up to us, although the many mortals who populated Termina from its inception do not know of its origins – the events of the internomachy are forgotten in Termina.

What a strange and goddessless place. Is there no divinity that watches over them?

Something keeps watch over this inner world – the goddesses assigned a wrathful spirit to live inside their moon—Majora is its name.

---

102 The hollow cosmos created by Hylia during the Mega Internomachy. The internal world of Hyrule.

Majora has one nasty job: to drop the moon into Termina and destroy this inner world altogether if the giants ever try to rise up again. When the legendary boy entered Termina, his arrival was ill fated, or perhaps right on time! As the giants had trapped Majora[103] into a mask (along with a few other souls, into other masks) in hopes of imprisoning their proctor, but the spirit found a surrogate to act through, the very imp who had also lost his friends – a forest creature that the boy had coincidentally met before losing Navi!

More masks! *I see a similar theme here.* Ario echoed Zelda from earlier.

The boy had met his robber, before getting robbed? she asked.

Yep. At the beginning of his adventures in Hyrule, before he was a legend at all!

What are the chances? she could've guessed very unlikely.

I wonder if Hylia had second thoughts by sending the boy to Termina to intervene and free Majora's spirit from the mask, undoing the scheme of the giants but also saving all the innocent people living in Termina, however interred they are—as long as the world exists.

How sad. By the goddess, I'm glad the boy stopped the moon from falling!

Oh, and it's stranger yet... said Link. Given their own world and left to their own devices, the giants surreptitiously engaged in yet another violation of Hylia's permissions.

After the boy stopped the moon?

No, before. And it was something Majora did not notice until the giants had already taken it too far – they sought to create a race of their own.... *They were unlike anything of our world...*

Who are *they?*

I do not know if *they* have a name, but if the bighearted and good intentions of the giants ever involved evil, it was with this act of hubris. Unable to endow soul within matter, they could not create new life – only bind it, as they did with the masks they made when trapping Majora.

How then...

___

103 The watcher of the hollow Hyrule world Termina. A wrathful demigod assigned by Hylia to ensure that the giants do not rise up again. The spirit inside the inner moon – if set off becomes Termina's timebomb.

So they devised ways to clone life from Hyrule.

But how did *they* leave Termina to do so?

They could not—not without getting caught by Majora who watched with the yellow eyes of their moon that had a resting wrath face, permanent throughout waxing and waning to always remind the giants how the goddesses regarded them, and what the stern terms were in Termina! Unable to directly revolt, the giants quietly made something of a golem; servants without a soul. They were aliens to our world who come and go unnoticed – they are like ghosts, and can slip through the terrestrial barrier between worlds riding in a ball of light that moves impossibly fast, phasing through any substrate as they are immaterial, and staying out of sight from the grinning moon and rarely noticed by the inhabitants of Termina as well.

Never heard of such things. Zelda clenched her cape, If even the goddesses overlook their verboten transit, can we see them at all? the princess inquired covered in goosebumps.

'Rarely noticed' you say… What do they look like? Ario whispered, just in case *they* were near.

These soulless aliens hover without feet, have a banded spade embroidering their head, glowing eyes, scary claws, and do the blasphemous bidding of the ungodly giants in the quietest hours of the night. Link grinned, eager to explain, The few adventurers who have traveled to Termina and back have seen people who they thought they knew from Hyrule, but these look-alikes will have different names, and no memory of Hyrule…

They're clones! gasped the princess.

Exactly. And that might sound like a pointless digression, but our Hero of Time found himself wrapped up with exactly such a clone, a young girl named Romani.

Did she have a soul? Zelda asked in earnest.

Oh yes! Just because she's a clone made by the giant's hideous servants doesn't mean she is soulless; not at all. She's a real Hylian just like you and I, just a copy of a girl from Hyrule who also worked on a ranch – whose name was Malon.

Copying isn't really creation, is it? she wondered.

The giants could not fashion entirely new lifeforms, they could only trap spirit into matter, like when they trapped Majora into a mask, or made their alien servants out of *partitioned* spirit.

Right. You've already said that. I was speaking more abstractly...

Anyway, so Malon lived with her father in Hyrule, but Romani down in Termina lived with her older sister Cremia. Malon's mother disappeared when she was very young, and same for Romani. In fact, Cremia always told her younger sister Romani that their mother died. Oddly–

Oh no...

Malon's mother was abducted by the giants' servants, never to return.

What happened to her? Ugh! I hate this digression. Zelda sulked.

Who knows. But they cloned her, and that's who Cremia is – not Romani's sister at all.

Freaky. Why are you telling us about this? Get back to the story; your tale of courage!

Link patted this thighs, Yes yes, my apologies Princess, I just love wacky lore. Again, these details are not irrelevant, as the legendary boy had a maiden in Malon, not unlike the romance of Ariosto and Ariela! However chaste to the max and all innocence—*inconsequential.*

Better not make it weird. she leered at him with taut lips.

They were children, that's all I'm saying. Malon dreamed of a knight who would take her away from the endless labor of maintaining her father's Lon Lon Ranch. This boy was her knight in shining armor—actually green clothes, like mine, but who had come to sweep her off her feet! She confided in the boy that sometimes she pretended a prince would come down from beyond the moon and take her away. Little did she know, this boy would later come down from the moon but in Termina, and save her clone Romani—*isn't that odd how Malon dreamt of such a thing?*

Malon was dreaming from the prescient perspective of her clone... Do we share the dreams of others? Or maybe it's just coincidence. Zelda ruminated, Did her dream come true?

Nah, after Malon saw the longing in his eyes for Navi, the faerie who was a sort of squire to the boy's knighthood, the cow maiden realized that her dreams of romance were hopeless. Malon feigned indifference, telling the boy that she appreciated the thought (of him saving her chivalric-style) but that she's waiting to be saved by a prince, and not a faerie child.

Good for her. the princess approved.

Rejection spurs serendipity however! As certain characters come back around, either as implicit reincarnations or explicit clones in this case! *Both gingers...*

Wait, you really are just imitating Ariosto, aren't you.

No, this is just a strange overlap – all the aforementioned maidens have red hair.

Ariela... Malon... Romani... *and even what's-her-name too?* said Zelda, quietly including Midna as well but didn't want to confuse the boys as there was already an imp in Link's story.

Cremia... I suppose so... Link thought it over, Very strange, but not important.

Just to eliminate any uncertainty about their otherworldly ancestry, Ariela is not related–

–No! he preemptively answered, Princess please... Totally different stories! The ranch girls are from ages ago. Whereas his lady – Sir Ariosto's wayward maiden Ariela could be strutting over the Boneyard Bridge above us right now, as far as we know!

Shhh... the princess reminded him to use his hideout voice.

As far as we know! Link reiterated in a lowered voice. *Strutting!*

The camper looked up with a dubious furl to his brow. *If only in this realm...* he sighed.

I just wanted to be clear, she said calmly. Loremaster Link... *Oh, Sage of Courage.*

Right. So we don't get lost in Termina like our legendary hero, I'm going to just spoil it. He never finds Navi his former faerie, and while it's a whole 'nother story, he ends up helping the imp who lured him there. Similar in stature and sympathy, they both felt abandoned by a friendship presumed immutable. The imp immediately saw a playmate in the young Hylian, and pranked him as was its socially awkward way of engaging others. That's forgivable, but unlike the boy, the imp became possessed by revenge against those who left him. The imp wanted to destroy them, even if it meant destroying itself, and everyone there... including the boy.

Oh, that's kind of sad? Zelda wasn't sure how to take it.

What's most important is the boy helped someone else, as any knight of anguish knows takes priority in hopeless situations! Indirectly his search was fulfilled, but on another's behalf, and selflessly his unconditional defense of friendship remained true in the end.

Navi probably just evaporated, having fulfilled her purpose; they can do that.

Keep in mind the legendary boy was not a Kokiri, and Navi was only assigned to him under especially dire circumstances, so perhaps she's still out there. But the journey is more interesting than the destination! And with that said, let us return midstory to the travails our legendary hero. Similar to Lon Lon Ranch – Malon's dairy farm and stables in Hyrule, the boy came upon Romani's Ranch (as it was called) in the inner world of Termina and–

Evaporate me now... said Zelda who had her fill and was wishing she were a faerie so she could disappear from the captivity of Link's belabored exposition. But he didn't hear her.

–just as Malon made fun of the boy's green clothes, calling him 'faerie boy' for caring more about Navi then her – Romani also gave the hero a hard time, calling him 'Grasshopper'.

All affectionate pejoratives. said the princess, tilting her head toward their storyteller.

While the legendary hero never told Romani about Malon–

Best not to tell a woman they are a clone of another. said Zelda.

I would never! And he knew better – all action and no words, the boy yet again was just in time, as that evening the aliens were expected to return; something Romani witnessed alone every year before the Carnival of Time, where all of Termina celebrates the harvest, the new year and the only divinity they've ever known – their false gods: the giants. Adding to the anxiety of the situation, Cremia did not believe her younger sister Romani, but as Cremia is the clone of Malon's mother, her abduction amnesia was to be expected, and no doubt intended by *them*... The alien ghosts – *they* sought to reclaim Romani and tractor beam her cattle.

Not the cows!

Something about their milk, the vintage Chateau Romani had spiritual properties.

The aliens had a thirst for magic milk?

We'll never know, but perhaps their cloning required it... spare organs, mutilations...

Gruesome. the princess hugged her knees. *Beware the udder snatchers!*

Sure enough, they[104] came – these servants of the giants, a failed creation to begin with as they had no soul, but who persisted in experimenting on people and creatures from within Termina and Hyrule far above. While instantiated and materialized outside their eerie lightship, this spectral species was not immune to physical assault and thankfully were very delicate.

Comparable to the wizrobes we dealt with in the mire? the princess recalled how they easily ripped through their ruffling shawls, punctured with one twang of her archery acumen.

I think so! In terms of vulnerability, but you're right – similar behavior between the two. And so the boy's arrows kept them away from Romani's barn where she defended the cows and kept them calm until the new dawn forced the abductors to retreat for even in Termina the light of day is not without Hylia's warmth that the aliens were made to avoid—allergic intrinsically.

Like vampires almost.

Yes, they are creepy.

---

104 Referred to as aliens or ghosts or 'they', their actual name is unknown if there is one. Secret servants of the giants within Termina who are capable of evading the watch of Majora to abduct and clone people from Hyrule above. Black and purple with orange claws and glowing eyes, they slowly float without legs and can transmedium travel – flying in a ball of light through the corporeal firmament of the inner world. Fundamentally the same kind of soulless golem as a poe or hyu, unrelated technology but convergent.

…

Is that it? Zelda smirked.

What else do you want to know? *Kunk kunk…* he slapped the ladle bowl in his palm.

You need to at least round it out. What happened to the boy? Did he stay in Termina?

Thanks for asking. Coming full circle, the boy returned to the land that had made him a legend – Hyrule above, beyond that interred and interior horizon that bound the impious giants. And while he never found his friend Navi, at least not while in the inner world of Termina as we don't know what happened after the boy returned, he courageously risked his own life to save another stranger from the loneliness of abandonment. The forest imp who became possessed by revenge, then by the deity Majora – by putting on the mask that contained it. You could say that Majora took advantage of the imp's woes, as Majora was also angry toward the giants for trapping its spirit into the mask. They were a bad combo, and the boy saved both the imp and Majora from mutually destroying themselves out of spite for the giants, *in spite of himself too.*

And everyone who lived there – from the falling moon…

By the goddess, he sure did! Without intending to; *got over himself by falling there.*

And the ranch girls…

Romani was so grateful, she offered to give the boy her bed and live on her ranch.

What does that mean? Zelda laughed.

A child's proposal, who knows. said the greenclad boy with an air of authority. In the end, Malon had her moonsend knight aftall, by way of the boy saving her unknown clone Romani.

Tenuous interpretation, but I see the uncommon courage in your tale's hero nonetheless.

Moral of the story, said Link forthright: we all have counterparts, one way or another, souls who share our own situation even if in another world. And only by aiding our counterparts, we might make our own intractable troubles irrelevant. He could not find his faerie Navi, but he let the forest imp unexpectedly find him. This is the counterintuitive valor of this legendary boy.

I understand why Majora harbored vengeance against the giants – destroying Termina for their violation was its divine instruction. Which is to say, perhaps Majora felt no malice at all. The watchful deity was simply fulfilling its purpose. But why was the imp mad at the giants?

You can't spell impious without imp.

Huh?

It was the giants who abandoned the imp – once their lilliputian friend. said Link.

So it used the unwieldy power of Majora that the giants tried to contain within a mask against them as punishment for leaving it? *Mutual manipulation and such instrumentalization!*

That seems to be what compelled the imp to wear Majora's mask and embody its wrath.

Mutual? Oh, they used each other, the imp and the mask, to achieve the same end, albeit for different reasons – until The Hero interceded by Hylia's grace. clarified Ariosto.

If the mask fits, wear it. said Zelda. And once Majora's spirit was released by the boy, the deity returned to the inner world moon where it was first stationed, and did not destroy Termina?

Thump thump… he kicked the ground again, Still down there?

…

Yes I think so. Link answered himself.

GOOD! Well, the princess exhaled, that was a horrible story, all over the place and with no structure. Navi sounds like a problematic pixie. Hits a little too close to home, as I… well… you know… have also had my fair share of faerie trouble, and the mad descents they induce.

Sometimes we must fall to an inner world to transcend what burdens us on the surface!

Don't remind me. said Zelda.

Yo! Link! That's it. Ario blurted out at the boy's capstone affirmation, and blew a bubble as the princess and her knight watched it float up to the bridge's underside, where it popped and snapped them out of their contemplative storytime daze. He stood up and raked the ashes of his campfire, My garden has bloomed anew by your tales! May we carry this memory of when we shared the tripartite fire – virtues of the three goddesses – along with us, wherever life, or death, takes us next. said the camper, stepping past his guests and patting the furtive lethic stone.

Invitation from the Great Faerie

Oh, look there! Would you grab that Link?

Hrup! Link jumped up and tried to reach a chest floating down the river.

Here, use this. Zelda offered her longbow which the child hooked a side handle with.

Did this come from the castle? Hgrr! he managed to drag the chest onto the stone quay. Why would they—wait! Let me try… Link fished inseam a flap pocket of his green tunic and took out his small key, an impossible token of impervious optimism, that had somehow stuck with him since finding it in that dreadful Palace of Darkness in the acropolis to the highland east.

Duh nuh nuh nuh… Duh nuh nuh nuh… Duh nuh nuh nuh… Zelda hummed in anticipation. Just open it.

It's stuck! said the boy, referring to his key that had more sentimental value than whatever treasure of speculation might be inside.

Your hair was so pink as a child! said Zelda, standing above the boy and fascinated with his bubblegum bangs, Must be your Kakariko heritage – village kids have the huedo[105] trait.

I'm from Kokiri. he said, inspecting the brass escutcheon, Before moving in with uncle…

Kokiri children are all blond, or sometimes have green hair, but never pink or purple.

I'm a child of the forest! Link jammed the coffer's uncooperative mechanics.

---

105 The hue of a hairdo. Naturally but vibrantly colored hair is a common trait of kids from Kakariko Village.

Your tunic certainly is, but are you—you don't have a guardian faerie as all Kokiri inherit.

Just you wait. he said defiantly, She'll come to me someday...

Who? Navi from your story? Zelda laughed, You're plain Hylian just like me, get over it. *Cronk.* she kicked the chest, which popped open its spring-loaded lid, nearly breaking Link's nose as he stubbornly fiddled with the lock afterwards, still trying to get his small key to move the bolt even though the chest had already opened.

Ah-hah! he stashed the worthless latchscrew[106] in his tunic, saving it for another time.

Mehhh... a tiny voice yawned from inside.

What's that? said Link, shielding his eyes from the rays of yellow light.

Speaking of guardian faeries. said the princess. I'm starting to wonder if I'm Kokiri with how much you stalk me Epheremelda.

The boy stood up and looked aghast at the princess. **You** *have a* **guardian** *faerie?!*

Envoy, and nothing more. said the pixie, whose filament complexion reflected off the gold leaf interior of the chest, producing a vertical beam so bright that Ario noticed a pristine flush of Rushrooms[107] growing on the bottom of the Boneyard Bridge.

What's in store? he asked from up on the landing, laying in front of his tent.

Special delivery for Princess Zelda! said Epheremlda, prying up the cartographic mattress she had been laying on. Invitation from Venus – Great Faerie of the Lake...

That's what was inside? All that reinforged[108] iron just to keepsafe[109] a letter?

Another map. said Zelda, responding to the camper behind her.

Can you– does it do what you did before at uncle's place? asked the boy.

---

106 A small key.
107 Seasonal purple mushrooms that grow on cliffs. Choice edible and extra delectable for how hard they can be to pick for the casual forager who lacks climbing gumption and the wherewithal to get up there.
108 The banding hardware, hinges and hasps that make a wooden chest as alluring as it is secure.
109 To lock inside a chest.

Let me try, said the princess, taking out the enchanted chart she had kept in her dress. Ah, here's the corresponding edge with the new map fragment. Fantastic! she lined them up.

The parchment fixed itself! Can I see? he stretched up on his tippy toes.

I don't see anything new. Zelda rotated and flipped the chart just to be sure.

That's the entire southeast of Hyrule – do you think it also shows Lorule?

If we were in the Dark World it would, the ink represents the realm its holder stands in. Queen Mudora pointed out the Ice Palace somewhere around here, but that was when the map showed the warped terrain of Lorule… Zelda glided her finger around an island on the chart currently showing Lake Hylia. I don't see it now—not in this world.

That's the island grotto of Venus – the Pond of Happiness! said Epheremelda.

Will you come with us? he immediately assumed that's where they were going next.

Um… she looked at the bottle Link still held after finishing his tale. Her invitation is a gift, and you can test it out in her grotto! the pixie tried to change the subject. That extra blank space will illustrate full-bleed once you're inside the pal–lehhh… she pretended to yawn.

Are you suggesting we have to return to the Dark World? Zelda's stomach flopped.

Oh well. smiled Link blissfully, having forgotten about his decapitation thanks to the effect of the lethic stones in the underworld and the one in Ario's garden. *Want to bottle up?*

You don't ask a faerie to get in a bottle, you just have to put them in there. said Zelda.

That's not true, but I've done my job here, and you know where to go next. I'll need to check in with my superior first. There's a big difference between faerie envoys and escorts. Relaying messages is my role – *not to console!* If you'll excuse me, I'll fly ahead now…

Can't you decide for yourself? We're both going to the Pond of Happiness then?

Yes but... I feel like I'm forgetting something... *I needed to tell you...* said Epheremelda who seemed especially affected by the energy of the lethic stone nearby.

Let her go, Link. the princess helped him cope.

Ehh, can't remember what it was... Hey, listen! How many rupees do you have?

Taken back by her question, the princess and boy looked at each other and said nothing, silently admitting they were broke. You still have some from the hedge? Link asked Zelda.

Make sure to have some small gems, blue denominations of five, red of twenty...

I left that dress in the tower! she shrilled, turning out her empty pockets.

...But her prices go up after that, so bring purple rupees too. the sprite kept talking in a will o'wisper.[110]

I think you just spent it all. said Link, dubious of her destitution drama.

Discredit me all you want, it won't fix our finances. Zelda reddened.

Toss them in the great faerie's pond – it's how she compensates us peripatetic pixies. You need to see Venus and try your luck on *winning some happiness* before you can rescue the maiden thereabouts... Depending on how that goes, if she approves of your proposed adoption for one quantity of Epheremelda in your single occupancy bottle, then I'll get in the glass.

Really? said the boy so enraptured by the idea of having his own faerie to keep.

Sure thing. But I can already tell you though that whatever trouble you get into next you must choose upfront, as you only have one such vessel and won't find another anytime soon...

Choose what? Link asked Epheremelda.

---

110 To whisper like a will o'wisp – speak faintly and feintly of something fleeting, unattainable, or illusory. Also called the 'ignis fatuus inflection' as this tone of voice is both cautioning against and inviting fantasy.

Do you require the *assurance* of a golden bee, or *insurance* of shimmering me?

Assurance or insurance… Zelda pondered the difference, along with the great faerie's rupee revenue pool procedure and why or what a little pixie would ever spend their money on.

Does the bee require adoption approval as well? he asked rhetorically and was ignored.

You and your disjunctive rhymmles.[111] she snickered at Epheremelda's rhyming riddles.

This time you can choose only one Princess Zelda. the faerie lectured fluttering upward, I told you to sacrifice *either* the lifeblood or the lifestyle, but you did both!

Persnickety as she is, Princess makes her own rules. said her infantilized knight.

I suppose it worked out, but not again – there's no way I'm sharing that bottle with a bee.

Not after having that spacious treasure chest all to yourself. Zelda watched the driftbox[112] float downstream to the east, approaching the bend in the river. Your message is well received, and kindly inform Venus that we will accept her invitation. We are much obliged… she bowed.

Nice! Don't delay. The great faerie has all the time in the world, but the world is running short on time. We all feel it, in this Gloomaevum – the days are long, but the years go by fast…

Didn't you have *something else* to tell us? the princess jogged the sprite's airy memory while hunched over, pulling up a tufted cattail and easily removing the stalk from the soft mud.

Hmmmmmmmmmm… Epheremelda muzzled her knuckles and emitted a high buzzing noise.

Excuse me, try moving over here… said Zelda, gently brushing the loitering faerie away from the lethic stone so as to not accidentally touch directly and discharge her pixie lifeforce.

---

111 A rhyming riddle. How little faeries communicate their paradoxical advice, often an unavoidable tradeoff offered lightheartedly. Ambiguous pixie talk that is respectful of the non-deterministic nature of the future.

112 A treasure chest that is sufficiently watertight to remain buoyant and discovered floating down a river.

Ah! Now I remember – the ice caves to the east of the lake... the faerie remembered. Before you visit Venus, you must go... **here.** she tapped the map that twinkled from her touch.

Zelda didn't see anything noteworthy there – Why? she promptly folded the chart away.

Owlman has found the ancient artifact that was kept safe in those caves: Nayru's scepter that can turn anything to ice. With that rod and the force of ether too, he has frozen the deep lake in the other realm and glacitected an ice palace that is guarded by something truly chilling.

Glacitecting is a lost art... said the boy, Architecting glacial structures directly from water without any excavation or construction. Let's go see this cool castleberg[113] together right away!

He wields both Nayru's medallion and her scepter. So why bother with this detour?

In its place he hid something that you'll need to rescue the maiden beneath the lake.

'Those caves'? I only saw one drawn on the map. Zelda continued to press her envoy.

You'll see how he hastily blocked up the entrance with some rubble; easily dislodged. Watched over by my clique[114] from the adjacent hollow. *Listen!* When owlman took the ice rod, the shared wall collapsed – so he erected a barrier from their shrine, and then he blocked the treasure cave entrance with some rocks from the outside. Epheremelda puckered up.

There are more faeries there? Link's eyes widened.

No, he captured them—*mehoo hoo!* she weeped tinily, Soutinssent[115] off to Castle Town—*nehoo hoo...*

How do you know? the blonde princess asked the faerie of comparable complexion.

I was the only one who escaped! In our absence a bee now guards the fountain's statue. I don't want to talk about it. she rubbed her teary eyes, Bye! she flew off without warning.

---

113 A castle made out of ice, designed and formed through magical glacitecture. An iceberg stronghold.
114 A group of faeries. How pixies hover together. Also called a coquette coterie by faerie traffickers.
115 A double entendre across two languages: 'they were procured off' and phonetically 'sent' too.

Did you answer her rhymmle? Zelda asked the boy who waved to the departing faerie.

I require insurance! Link wheezed too faint too late as Epheremelda skimmed the water.

You'll see her again soon, relax. said Zelda preparing to leave as well.

Sir Ariosto, what are you going to do? he asked the camper who was retrieving what he had been fumbling with in his tent earlier. What are those...

In lieu of a steed, these will help you evade the many guards between here and the lake. Ario held up a pair of red leather cuissardes, These are the pegasus boots[116] – too big for a child, but they should fit you perfectly Princess Zelda.

Do I get anything? said Link, clutching the reclaimed regifted glass.

You got Ariosto's bottle. Zelda closed her eyes, waving her hands around like a psychic, *I see either a bee or faerie in your future...* she teased the globe as if it were an orbuculum.

Hold out your bottle Link, said Ario jiggling the tall cavalier boots and then poured an assortment of brightly colored gems into the glass, tinkling into a melange of refracted riches.

Bootleg savings? said the princess, suspecting he didn't trust her with the money.

I don't need rupees anymore. Stashing them in the pegasus boots kept them out of sight but also ensured that no one could put these magical boots on and run away. said Ario, shaking out the remaining precious stones, the last of which was silver and worth two-hundred alone.

There's green, blue, yellow, red, purple... the gemsmacked[117] boy cataloged all the colors over and over, And red, purple, orange, silver, more green, lots of blue, so many red!

Don't spend it all on the Pond of Happiness. said Zelda, trying on the boots.

We could buy all the happiness with this! he shaked the bottle so the gems would settle. Prices have risen though. Remember when you

---

116 A rare pair of knee high red leather riding boots that make any jog a superhuman sprint, fast enough to run over water. Too small for Sir Ariosto to wear, and too big for little Link, they fit Princess Zelda perfectly.

117 To be overwhelmed with a sudden discovery or disbursement of gems. Flabbergasted by many rupees.

could buy anything with a red rupee? Now red is not enough to cover your stable fee or buy simple fare – a traveler's repast is at least purple!

It'll be more than enough to make a wish when you get to the great faerie's grotto well. As for your boots, the trick is to jog in place for three quick steps and then you'll be on your way.

What do they do? she asked, hesitant to just try it.

Without requiring any additional magic potion or powder, these dashing boots will spur whoever sports them into a sustained sprint. You can also just break into a run from a standstill and they will engage just the same, but it's fun to giddy-up and go from the triple-hop technique.

But if I walk they don't do anything special?

Even if you speedwalk – always keeping one foot planted – they will not work their magic and you'll be just as any other pedestrian, however fashionably superior. explained Ario.

Can't hide from the guards in these... she inspected the profile of her calves and knees.

The red leather is eye-catching, but nobody will be able to catch you. You'll never end in a dead heat with anyone! Waterproof but also somehow breathable, as long as you don't stop, the pegasus boots can effortlessly hydroplane and allow you to run across water! Just don't trip on waves – they are surprisingly dense and unforgiving when footracing along at that speed.

Are you stretching? Link wondered why the princess was pulling her leg back.

See here? The boots are the exact same shade of red as my cape. Matching!

Her calisthenic association made Ariosto remember: *That's King Hyrule's Cape!*

Zelda bobbed up and down while standing on one leg, I haven't tried it yet.

What does it do? said the boy, sneaking a pinch of the silken fabric.

You are invisible when you wear it. Watch your magic meter! said Ario.

The king also gave you a magic meter?

No, tah hah! That's just a saying—similar to when you used your lamp too long and faded grey from draining yourself from Farore's green vitality.

When was that?

Leaving the mountain…

That was draining. he said, still unsure if this magic meter[118] was metaphoric or not.

I'm afraid our garden sojourn must come to an end, she bowed to the scruffy camper, Your generosity has certainly given us more than we arrived with, but there's nothing we can leave you with, other than our improvised tales and imminent absence…

You're most welcome Princess! The opportunity to give is sometimes the best gift, especially when the quest calls for it! You need these things more than me, and your stories will not be forgotten as long as this garden of mine is here.

And if you do forget, we can stop by and tell them again! Link snugged his nightcap.

You are the 'radiant omphalos'! I get it. I thought you were referring to the lethic stone.

Huh? Link didn't remember what their host had said, or what Zelda was referring to.

…

You are the rock of memory Ariosto, she bowed again, and the mnemonic counterpart to the underworld menhir that you dragged up here. You are the radiant omphalos of storytelling and the anchor of this garden – the secret dignity of the topography of magnanimity.

Rock on. saluted Link to his fellow Hyrulean Knight.

If we happen to encounter Ariela, we'll tell her you're still alive and in hiding!

---

118 An expression denoting one's finite capacity for channeling magical spells and artifacts. Those familiar with magic will tell you there is no actual measurement warranting the term, but supernatural entities such as faeries claim to see and watch it like an aura. What's indisputable is that this pool recharges over time, by going outside, and can be replenished by imbibing certain potions such as Syrup's Medicine of Magic.

Yo! Zelda, don't sweat it. This is no place to court a maiden anyway. I couldn't possibly engage in a romance until the wizard is gone...

Still hung up on that then. she wasn't sure how to interpret his nonchalance.

I get that. said young Link naively. One thing at a time.

...Which is why you two must get going. I only ask that you wear your cape until you're out of sight of the bridge, so the patrol doesn't see you leave and come investigating.

What about me?

You're going to have to ride on her shoulders.

That cape isn't big enough!

Impervious to stains, invisibility, and... automatic retailoring are the cape's capabilities.

This is the last time I kneel... said the princess, genuflecting so the boy could climb up.

Can you hold this please? Link handed her the bottle full of gems.

How is it so light? Feels like nothing is inside at all.

Didn't you hear Sir Ariosto earlier? This is a *magic* bottle. said Link proudly to hint that Zelda wasn't the only one who was given something extraordinary, although she had both now.

Desperate times when a knight must bridle a princess for his steed. Ario said to himself.

Yeesh! Don't tug my hair. she got her princess plaits out of the way of his clingy thighs.

I'm sworn to protect her! said the boy who must've heard him.

Oh—hey, look... Zelda pointed to the hem of the cape which lengthened to accommodate their double-stacked stature.

And the cowl is more spacious too... said Link, flopping it behind him and ready to go.

Let me put the hood up for you, but as soon as I do you'll disappear from view. As to not waste any time, jog in place as I mentioned, and head to where Epheremelda mentioned.

I know, said Zelda checking her map one last time, The caves, east of the lake. Wait– there's a problem—protrudes too much and will ruin our disguise. she took off her longbow. Take it, Sir Ariosto. You're now the lone longbowman of the Boneyard Bridge. she saluted.

Gladly, and with honor. Go now, the quickest route will be with the river's current… Ariosto pointed downstream in the same direction as where the faerie left moments before.

Can we go by land? Through the Great Swamp and south along the Barren Shoreline?

There are too many soldiers, at least until you got to the southern shore. Ario told her, And I don't think your cape will last long enough to make it through those guarded grasslands.

Lasts? Will your cape *actually* disappear entirely if used too much? asked little Link, mistaking phenomenon for noumenon.

TAH! That's not what happens! Zelda unjustly ridiculed. We just reappear—right?

Absolutely. It's magical for you to disappear, but then whoever sees you reappear out of thin air will regard that as a magic trick too! Ario answered the obvious with a philosophical twist.

Great! We should be safe running over the water, as long as our invisibility lasts around the bend of the river there, no one will see us if we reappear! said Link, excited to try this out.

The river it is. agreed the princess, wrapping her arms around the boy's ankles and also holding onto the bottle of gems (like carrying a linkalope and cleaver). Whenever you're ready–

WANTED! This is the criminal who kidnapped Zelda. Call a soldier if you **see** *him!*

Don't tell anyone I did this. she said, as the camper donned the cowl over Link's head, causing both the boy and the princess to immediately disappear ensemble. *Schht! Schht! Schht!* a triple scuff of her pegasus boots kicked up dust from jogging in place as Ario had instructed, launching the invisible piggybackers off his landing. *SPLSHHH!* they hit the water running, *Slsh-plsh-plsh-plsh-plsh…* with more of a noticeable impact and wake than anticipated.

Skrt-tl-tl-tl… rattled the armor of the startled guards as they rushed to respond.

Holding his breath, the camper could see silhouette tops of two soldiers on the bridge looking for what caused the splash. Their shadows cast on the river, the patrol didn't catch the pitter-patter of Zelda's escape, as the cloaked exiles were already far off, fast around the bend.

Rutela's Treasure

Unable to swing her arms while holding the bottle and keeping the child Link on her shoulders, the princess was surprised how easy running felt while wearing the pegasus boots. Faster than a champion athlete, and yet more relaxed than a stroll, Ario's gift did all the work even with her inefficient gait that would not conserve momentum and preserve balance if she were running with any normal footwear. And their magic cape[119] never luffed or chaffed either.

I can see Hylia Island. said the boy on her shoulders who held the cape's hood in place so it wouldn't flop down against the headwind, although it seemed to stay in place; *magically!*

Keep your arms tucked in. Your flailing throws off my center of gravity. said his steed of a princess, prancing over the river due south and into the channel mouth of the majestic lake.

How's your 'magic meter' doing? he said while looking up on the bank, where two guards in blue platemail patrolled within a stone's throw of them.

Keep your voice down.

They can't see us!

Still, I don't want to draw any attention. she ignored his earlier question while galloping over the middle of the lake, resembling nothing more than a series of rapid fish splashes.

Head for those cliffs there... he pointed ahead and to their left at a rocky promontory. That will take us up to the foothills where we need to go. The boy marveled at the geology and felt inspired to regale his ride with some geographic trivia as well, That ridgeline extends all the

---

119 King Hyrule's former cloak, given to Princess Zelda in the underworld. A red hooded crimson cape featuring three magical powers: intensive invisibility, resistance to stains, and automatic retailoring.

way from the southern citadel grounds of the Eastern Palace, and ends here in the lake…

Yes I know. she leaned around the southeastern horn and cantled them into a cove.

Watch out, there's a Zora in the water. he pointed to the bobbing amphibian's head.

They can't see us.

I think we're visible again.

How would you know?

Not sure. he wondered, as they were visible to each other while sharing the magic cape. How about we ask the Zora there?

Don't. It looks deranged. she said, wary of the water people ever since the pestilence.

It just waved to us. said Link calmly and waving back. Princess, I think your magic meter must've run out? he said, noticing his green tunic had faded by association.

Don't! she reached up to grab his arm, losing her grip on the bottle. AIEE! she caught it but lost their momentum. Her right boot dipped beneath the waves. *Splunsh!* and they fell in.

…

Gwah! Zelda surfaced, It's sinking! *All those precious rupees!* she treaded water and helplessly watched their savings vanish, bubbling to the bottom of the spectacularly clear lake.

Fwoop! Link took a big breath and dove after the bottle, leaving Zelda and the Zora alone at the surface. The waterlogged blonde woman met eyes with the solitary fishman.

Excuse me. Can you retrieve that bottle for us please? she asked the scaly humanoid. HELLO! she rubbed the water from her eyes as the indifferent Zora swam away without a word. *Cold-finned by a mucking gloom-addled sludgekin river stinker…* she cursed the slick stranger, struggling to take her cape off while staying afloat in the choppy water.

FWAH! Pfooh! Yoh—no chance. said the boy coming up for air. Sunk like a millstone.

That was so much money. Fwowowo… she clutched herself from the numbing plunge.

Rupees come, rupees go. Not like we earned it. said Link, tugging Zelda along through the water after she gave up trying to take her soaked cloak off.

Fwererer… Zelda chattered incoherently as the cold water took her breath away.

Think of it this way – an hour ago we didn't even have those rupees. he offered some consolation while trying not to kick her, Don't worry Princess, we'll find something to offer Venus once we get to her Pond of Happiness. Link changed his swimming position from holding onto her cloak and frogging backwards to putting it in his mouth and paddling like a dog with a fetch. ~~We're in luck.~~ muffled the boy, ~~There's a ramp over there, just like the one Sir Ariosto had.~~

Whererer? the barged princess shuddered, lapping up some of the sweet lakewater.

Now arriving, the Farosh Hills, *or maybe this is the Popla Foothills?* he dragged Zelda up onto the stone quay. No patrols out here! Watch your step as you disembark. said Link, leaving the shivering princess on the ramp and bounding up the logboom staircase to the crunchy field of dry grass above. One! Two. Three… Four-five-six… Seven logs. he counted on the way up. It's just like the ladder in Ariosto's garden but longer. I wonder who built them, because all these stone quays are very old. Hudson Construction must've installed the logs before the pestilence as a public service… he speculated, always curious about the built environment. Princess?

I'm fine. Thank you. she strutted past him in her tall red boots, miraculously dry.

Does your cloak instantly dehydrate? he pulled at his clinging wet tunic that had already regained some of its viridian pigmentation and Kokiri color.

Maybe. she wrung out her long blonde hair.

At least it's sunny. he squinted, also ringing out his green nightcap and mimicking her out of courtesy. EYCHEE! Link sneezed at the sun, and attracted the attention of a bizarre red blimp cephalopod that floated above the ground, not far across the gulch.

Hmm? Zelda looked north in the opposite direction.

Check out that octoballoon…[120] he showed her, Never seen anything like that before! *Sphew!* Oh careful. Link moved Zelda aside as two smaller octoroks nearby spat rocks at them. *Sphew!* the second octorok tried to hit the two unwelcome Hylians hanging out in their territory.

Schht! Schht! Schht! the princess jogged in place, and darted off ahead of her knight.

Woa—wait up Princess! the boy chased her, dodging the octoroks but couldn't catch her as she sprinted in the pegasus boots. PRINCESS! Hrup! he hopped over a frantic sand crab while two more scuttled in his path. Hrup! Hrup! Link hurtled the waist-high crustaceans that came out of nowhere, ambushing him from behind a granite outcropping. Zelda wasted no time and arrested her enchanted boots only after entering the cave at a clipping pace. There it is! Link watched her cape slacken as she strutted into the only obvious entrance he could identify along that far-flung cliffside in whatever remote wilderness Epheremelda had sent them to.

Zelda? Watch your step! he cautioned unnecessarily, as the princess had already navigated the narrow passageway inside the cave and was standing at the opposite wall.

If only he was here with his bombs… said Zelda, inspecting a crack.

Bombs? Ah, Ganon. Who needs that lout—let me see! the child pried a loose chunk of the ice from the blocked up passage. Looks like there is a door here, but must've collapsed and then refrozen. This whole cave is made of ice… he tossed the chunk to the side where it fell into one of the two chasms on each side of the causeway. These bottomless? he waited for a report from the impact but never heard it. Want to go back to the underworld? he joked, tugging on her hem and pointing into the parallel

---

120 An octorok mother. Often mistaken as a distinct species, the octoballoon is part of the octorok lifecycle. Just like aquatic cephalopods, octoroks hatch from eggs but are kept in their mother's head who becomes a floating blimp until her offspring are ready to run free on their own. Another confusion is that the mother inflates, however it's the many airy eggs inside her that allow her to float. When they are ready to hatch, their air sacs deflate and cause her to land, at which point the fully developed octoroks will scurry away. Safe from ground predators, poking an octoballoon will cause her to explode premature hovering eggs.

pits. Zelda's red cape and matching red boots appeared to be black in the cerulean ambience of the cave, lending all her fair features an austerity in that cool reflected glow which gave her young knight a glimpse of what the princess might've looked like if she became a Dark Queen after all. Nice icy huedo – your hair looks royal blue. he told her.

Epheremelda said that the ice rod – Nayru's scepter was kept here – its magic must've emanated into the whole cave, and unnaturally frozen and formed this cavern by the glacial design of whoever wielded it previously… before Sahasrahla took it for himself.

You mean, this cave is an example of glacitecture? Link inquired, unimpressed.

But it's discernibly above freezing in here now… so she must be right: *the rod is gone.*

Or maybe it's 'The Boiling' he elbowed her. Won't be long until this whole cave melts.

Couldn't be – didn't you hear? Now it's all about 'The Icing'.[121] And if we don't bow down to the wizard's regime then the whole kingdom will become an inhospitable icicle! she snarked.

Yeah–no… This barrier is dripping. he noticed, licking the blocked passage.

How does it taste? the princess asked with aplomb, striking a cautious contrapposto.

Tastes like tyranny. This ice was made by the rod; you can just tell.

Astringent then? Bitter… a little salty… sour and dissatisfying? she poised.

The flavor of defeat—thwarty too… Link rubbed his teeth. But I have an idea!

---

121 A cold snap in the propaganda during the middle of the sessantine, conveniently during winter before Link escaped with Zelda in early springtime of Hyrule. Following from The Boiling, an asserted climatic shift in Hyrule that threatens to freeze everything if denizens don't comply with the magistrate's urgent recommendations for immediate remediation at the cost of their long held kingdom liberties. Despite the contradiction of The Boiling and The Icing, the magistrate maintains both narratives simultaneously for whoever believes either, as any panic makes the world a better place by the wizard's will. Just like the pestilence, almost nobody has the tools, instruments or arcane discipline to know for sure if there is any validity in either The Boiling or The Icing, but some people know there are magic medallions that can be used to manipulate the weather and environment, and as a result ignite, freeze, or shake popular beliefs.

Let's go back to Ario and see if he has anything to help us get through I say. said Zelda without giving Link a chance to share his plan. There's so much rummage in his camp, I'm sure he will have the necessary tools or something explosive.

Dash it all! said the boy, I have a smashing suggestion... This walkway here is straight and a perfect runway to get up to full speed with your pegasus boots.

Uh huh?

You could run with a rock, and then throw it at this barrier, and that might do it.

Zelda looked around, I'd have to go get something outside, and I'll get all muddy.

Your cape doesn't stain! Fine, I'll give it a try if you let me wear your boots.

They're too big for you, you'll stub your toes and fall into these pits. said the princess whose toes were warm and didn't want to take her cuissardes off on the cave's heatsink floor.

Worth a shot. he had already taken off his brown leather flapped boots.

I'm not taking mine off! she chuckled.

Here... the boy disrobed and laid his green tunic off to the side of the causeway, pressing it flat to increase its surface area, looking up at the princess for her approval.

What are you doing?

You can stand on that while I borrow your boots. he twinkled his toes to demonstrate that the nippy ground wasn't giving him frostbite yet. Keeping his hat on, Link ironed the Kokiri tunic once more to ensure the pad was as wide as possible to accommodate her bare feet.

Just don't scuff them up. she relented, taking off the red pegasus boots and stepping onto the folded pad of green fabric. If you slip into a hole, I won't be able to rescue you.

They're not too big. Maybe a little roomy... said young Link, stretching his hamstrings and pressing the vamp of both boots – discovering his big toes midsole – nowhere near the tip. Let me go outside and get a rock or something to hurl… And again, the trick is to jog in place three times, like this? he asked her from the cave entrance.

Yes but don't–

Schht! Schht! Schht! WAAAHHHHH!!! the boy catapulted down the causeway, zooming past the princess – almost bowling Zelda over into the chasm behind her. Narrowly avoiding the opposite pit himself, he couldn't stop. YIAAAAAHHH!!! and ran straight through the ice blockage *CRBRSHH!* at such speeds that the thick lattice shattered without much resistance. *NO-No-no!* Link's voice echoed into the subsequent room, followed by the *Coom-thud* of a hard impact.

Link! Zelda ran after him, but doubled back to pick up his tunic first. Are you alright?

It's here!

What? she tiptoed over the broken ice, stepping into a pristine grotto with a statue of Venus in the middle of a shimmering reflection pool. This must've been the faerie fountain that Epheremelda spoke of… *Are you injured!* she asked the child who was sitting still on the ground with one arm behind him and facing the statue. Link! she put her hands on his gelid shoulders.

Careful! he warned.

Is that a bee? she noticed a winged insect on his finger as he sat in front of the statue having knocked into it during his uncontrolled careening. Wow! I've never seen such a rare bug!

It's the golden bee[122] – must've been frozen in this statue, until I dislodged it.

Are you two best friends now? she goaded like an older sister.

Time will tell. he said seriously, letting the sparkling wasp lift off to inspect its domain.

This must've been the barrier too… Zelda stepped to their left where a tunnel led into another chamber, but was obstructed by an immovable bracket of nine artificially structured blocks that she could peer through at their tapered tops. I think I see a… there's a treasure

---

122 A social wasp with a fierce sting that has become enchanted from hanging out with faeries. Due to its magical mutations the golden bee is capable of being domesticated and can distinguish friend from foe.

chest in there! Sahasrahla must've used the ice rod to install these cryoengineered cubes.

How do we get in there? Link asked from the fountain, distracted by the insect.

Bollocks—bollards won't budge an inch! But I see another entrance… she pressed her face against the bracket wall's smooth and opaque ice blocks. Do you think that leads outside?

…

Zelda peeled her blush-chilled cheek off the barrier and saw Link holding up an opening along the rim of his nightcap for the golden bee. I see you're trying to cheat Epheremelda's offer.

Bee or 'me'? he paraphrased the faerie's rhymmle.

Which will it—

—Bee. At least for now.

Fine with me. Zelda droned. But didn't you have your heart set on her…

Maybe it will all work out; end of the day. She said you chose both, so why can't I?

Because there's nothing to put her in anymore. You lack the material requisites to be in a stable relationship with a faerie. the princess immediately regretted her mean tone of voice.

Excuse me! *Somebody* dropped our bottle into the lake. he said facing askew.

Zelda paused, remembering that Link's knowledge of it all was limited to hearsay since his memory as a linkalope was mostly lost upon exiting the afterlife. Epheremelda presented me with an *unavoidable sacrifice;* a lose-lose situation endemic to the Dark World of manifold doom! So I went for broke and sacrificed both out of desperation. she equivocated, *Gip.* swallowing her shame mid-sentence and hoping he wouldn't notice the loud lump in her throat. Totally different, you have an *elective acquisition;* a win-win outcome here in the Light World of open possibilities! Just be happy with one option—or the other. Zelda said too much, but her avauntular lecture was ambient noise to the boy who had nothing to learn from such a tenuous dissertation.

HAH! Hah hah! It's not buzzing at all inside my hat. he gassed and adjusted the brim to fit snugly so the bee would not rappel down his pink sidelocks that dangled in front of his ears.

If Epheremelda didn't want to share a bottle with a bee, then good luck convincing her to take up residence under your grimy nightcap with THAT—insect nearly as big as she is!

Speaking of grimy, you can have your red runners back… he started to pull them off, decidedly annoyed that she was using his brown boots as slippers, scrunching her feet halfway into the shaft and discourteously creasing the leather because her feet were too big.

Not yet, come outside. she ushered the child along the precarious icy path.

…

You want me to do that again? he pointed to an amalgamation of rubble in the cliffside immediately to the left of the cave's mouth (as they faced it).

Remember what she said?

I do, but might not after getting a concussion from THIS! he walked up to the cliff wall. Does *this* look 'hastily blocked up'? he quoted the faerie while inspecting a branching fissure. Rickety melting ice is one thing but I'm not sure if <u>this</u> is as 'easily dislodged' as Melda said.

I never said it would be easy. she responded, thinking he said Zelda.

Ephere-MMM-elda! he over enunciated.

Oh, *mmmaybe* call her Ephie for **short** instead. she patted his head for emphasis.

Not so hard! he pranced about, You're angering the bee! AHHH!

What? Stay still! she tried to help, but the peeved youth was tap dancing out of control.

Schht! Schht! Schht! WEEEEE!!! he launched toward the cliff. *CROOMBLE–CRBRSHH!*

LINK! OOUF! the princess caught the ricocheting boy who rebounded off the rocks, sacking her flat onto her red caped back.

Are you hurt? he got up, holding his cap by the tip.

I'm… easily dislodged–darrrgh… she rolled over to her side on the grass.

Link tugged a bang and let the agitated bee out who was utterly unsquished and after inspecting from its abdomen to antennae resoundingly unscathed. You're a durable little nut!

Oh good. said Zelda, still laying down and unaware he was referring to his pet insect.

How may I be of service? said young Link, taking off the pegasus boots.

Just put them there—yarrrgh… I'll need a moment. she put the magic cape's hood up.

He wasn't sure what to do, as Zelda disappeared with his boots halfway on – enough to vanish with her under the magic cape's influence. But just then both of his brown Kokiri hikers flopped at his feet, reappearing as soon as she punted them off for him. Ah! You read my mind. I'll go on ahead and see what's in there, he said, appearing to talk to no one. Take your time. And my apologies for knocking the wind out of you, I hope nothing is broken… said the boy happy to put his familiar kid-sized kicks back on. Link walked halfway to the cave and stopped to watch the spasmodic sandcrabs spitting distance away, spying on him with beady black eyes. I think they're just scavengers, he said to his invisible interlocutor, but maybe don't lay out here too long Zelda, those crabs might be hungry… he turned back and noticed the pegasus boots were no longer there. Princess? he said, tempted to toe the grass impression where she was to feel if she was still laying there, but decided against it and stepped through the demolished hole. The cave inside was exactly like the one they first stepped into – all frozen with a straight ledge that transected the commensurate dim chamber with an impenetrably dark abyss on each side. The only difference was that this nearly identical causeway, parallel to the first as well, led to an unobstructed opening, which was a relief for Link who did not want to tackle any more blockage. There's the barrier. he said to himself, and/or maybe Zelda if she was around (he couldn't tell). We're on the other side now… Link surveyed the small inner room for the first time, having not previewed it through the slits in the ice blocks as Zelda did. Found it! he ran up to the treasure that was kept on a small dignified platform, raised up by a few thin steps to signify the value of the chest's contents. We're too late… said Link, dreading to look closer as the lid was clearly up. He grabbed the rim of the chest, and sure enough there was nothing inside. Epheremelda lied. Link stood back, She said that after the ice rod was taken, that something else was deposited! AHHH! he jerked as someone took his hand. That you? he put his other hand on the presence.

Guess what was in there…

You better watch your magic meter! he chided. You're creeping me out Princess…

Epheremelda was right. said Zelda, dropping his hand, maintaining her cloaked mystery. I can't wait to show you what was in there! her voice audibly moved elsewhere.

You ran ahead of me? Princess, just show me! the boy's voice echoed off the ice.

This must be what Mudora said we needed before meeting with Venus…

Zelda? he heard her already back in the antechamber. Link jogged out of the empty cave with his hands out in front of him, just in case he ran into her so he wouldn't blindly body-check the cloaked princess. As her sworn protector, these kinds of precautions were always on his mind while astride bottomless pits such as those in the ice caves.

EXCUSE ME! I BELIEVE THAT IS OURS! she blared by the shore.

Who are you talking to? said Link who saw Zelda with her hood down, standing on another stone quay that sloped into the water directly outside the cave. With her cape flowing there was no way to identify what she might've retrieved from the chest, as all he could see was the red fabric, red leather heels, and her blonde hair. Stepping closer, he recognized the Zora. The bottle! Link joined in the hullabaloo from atop the logboom ladder down to the ramp.

Don't go! Zelda stomped at the Zora who held the jar of gems with one webbed hand and gestured for her to come in with the other. Give that back right now… she dove in head-first.

Princess! Link skidded down the logs and onto the quay, You're not built for cold water! Before he could take his boots off to dive in after her, Zelda effortlessly walked out of the lake.

Maybe don't get your head wet. she suggested, considering the bee in his cap.

You retrieved the bottle! he said, leaning in close, And not a single rupee taken!

I believe we can get on our way to Venus now. said Zelda, waiting for Link to notice.

The blue mail of Queen Rutela! he exclaimed, That's from Sir Ariosto's story! How did you put it on so quickly? he thought it over, Kind of a risky maneuver to change in a magic cape. What if your meter ran dry and you unexpectedly reappeared half-naked? No wonder that Zora was beckoning you into the water. Link got his head out of the gutter. You're wearing their armor.

I got quite the epic getup right now. she bragged, Without any additional magic required, the pegasus boots make haste, my magic cape wicks off wetness, and the blue mail allows me to move effortlessly through water! Did you see how easily I walked on the bottom?

Can you breathe underwater now too?!

No hah hah! I'd need a Gilly Guzzle for that.

A potion, okay. said Link, a little disappointed.

Most importantly, the blue mail keeps me warm! I'm not chilled at all from that dive.

You couldn't be more prepared for the Ice Palace then. said the child, suddenly sullen. What's that? Oh... he answered his own question – your reincarnation robe folded on the rock. Do you want to take that with you as well? A simple smock, but maybe don't leave it out here.

I'll put it back in the chest, she put the bottle on the quay then sprinted off, and in a few seconds returned to the landing. Time to go! she picked up their savings again. No need to be hidden this time – keep the hood down. But you'll need to ride on my shoulders again, my little Hyrulean Knight... Zelda waded into the lake so Link could easily get onboard.

Those crabs won't tell the wizard anything if he comes around.

Do you think we can make it all the way to Hylia Island from here in one breath?

What do you mean? asked the child, settling his seat atop her blue mail spaulders.

Hard to tell how far it is with this promontory blocking our view, but it's just over there!

As in, use your pegasus boots and blue mail and us two unanimously—*underwater?!*

Ah-one… the princess hyperventilated to expand her lungs.

What will happen if I can't move in the water like you? The friction coefficient of Kokiri cloth will drastically increase our hydrodynamic drag – my tunic is not designed for this!

Ah-two… she stepped out neck deep.

I don't want to be the conning tower to your submarine scheme! he pulled the brim down far enough that he could bite it, ~~Hold on little nut.~~ Link warned the insect chilling in his nightcap.

AH! Zelda took one last breath without saying 'three', tossing the bottle up to him so she could swing her arms, no longer needing the boy to hold the concealing cape's hood in place.

~~Wait! HRUP!~~ her passenger caught the bottle and inflated his cheeks with air.

Schplr! Schplr! Schplr! her pegasus boots roiled up the sediment. Zelda ran down along the bottom of the lake as fast as they had traveled above unaffected by the boy trawling on her shoulders without any Zoran gear on. *SPFLOOSH!* they torpedoed out, soaring over a waterfall on their way around the headland. Can I do it? she kept her feet running midair.

~~WHAT!~~ he clutched the slippery bottle for dear life, covered by algae and tangles of kelp.

SPLSHHH! they hit the water below without skipping a beat, *Slsh-plsh-plsh-plsh-plsh…*

The Pond of Happiness

Checking his hat was the first thing Link did when they made landfall on Hylia Island. And sure enough, the golden bee was just fine. Standing on yet another stone quay that led up to the bean-shaped isle, he let the princess jaunt ahead while he enjoyed the afternoon sun. The southern side of Hylia Island where they had set foot sloped into the lake with a little inlet, whereas the declivitous north end was a convex crescent ridge (back of the bean) and too steep to access from the water. Nearly sheer and shearing into constantly rolling waves generated by the gentle northerly, that cliff face smoothly scarped all the way to the bottom of the lake basin. Leeward on the landing, the abandoned child could discern that the ridge ahead blocked the breeze and provided a protective windshadow[123] which lended the island its mystical quietude. Taking a moment to dry off, the golden bee stretched its wings and took a few laps around the boy who noticed two buzz blobs[124] dancing around the white ruins, and beyond that a tunnel where Zelda had already entered after bisecting the small island with a linear sprint – straight from the quay to the cave – she triumphantly strided in, parading her red boots and red cape billowing behind her. Sufficiently sunned, Link secured the bee back under his nightcap and walked through the center of the disappointing Henge of Hylia as it was definitely dilapidated, and into the highly anticipated grotto gate. Lit by four pairs of floor braziers, the passageway sloped down and at the end the tunnel was a rectangular reflection pool. Two angelic statues marked the pond – similar to the nymph's spring that they found while in the swamp, however deeper and curbed off; not to be stepped in. Same statue of Venus as in the ice cave. he said.

Venus is the boss. said Zelda who was distracted by a fissure on the wall to her right.

There's not enough room to dash into that crack. Link saw what she was looking at.

---

123 A place that is protected from the wind due to a blocking landform or structure.
124 An animated green algae that is charged with an electrifying pulse that causes it to stand upright and dance in place. A docile slime golem, typically brought to life by experimental witches or bored faeries.

POND OF HAPPINESS. a loud voice announced, causing the boy and blonde to jump. *Throw some rupees in and your wishes will surely come true. Do you want to throw rupees?*

Throw a few. advised Zelda.

Don't feel like it. moaned Link reluctantly holding onto their glistening jar of gems and self-conscious all of a sudden for lacking a premeditated wish. He rolled the chromatic glass container, distracting himself with how the evenly sized hexagonal stones tumbled delightfully.

Let me try, she said reaching into the bottle and picked out four blue rupees for starters, each worth five. *Ploop!* Zelda scrimped the frugal fistfull into the vociferous pond...

Happiness increased twenty rupees. rang the voice.

What? said Link; no idea what that means.

In total, your happiness is twenty.

Twenty-what? *Units please.*

Twenty *rupees*. Zelda reminded him.

How is money a measurement of happiness?

You became happier by one step. said the pond.

One step costs twenty rupees? And a step toward what! the boy demanded a discourse with the pond – intent on getting his money's worth with some clarification.

For your reference, today you will have...

Yes? Zelda wanted to hear, but got the impression the voice was addressing Link...

Big Trouble. the voice concluded.

I hear it coming. whispered young Link standing still.

What's that? Zelda looked around and listened too.

Bvrum-bvrum-bvrum Bvrum-bvrum-bvrum! a harp strummed up two quarter-note triplets from out of nowhere, leading into the great faerie's melodic debut...

You're not that big. said Link, as an elegant winged woman appeared in a green dress, while the arpeggiating harp continued to echo the tranquil tune played from another dimension.

You must be Venus. said the princess, bowing to the monarch of all faeries.

Where is that music coming from? Link had to ask, nodding along to the jingle.

My happy place. said Venus.

This reminds me of that time we were in the fortune teller's hut. said Link to Zelda, ignoring the great faerie in front of them. Remember – it had its own mysterious music as well?

Link! Be respectful. It's an honor to finally meet, said Zelda, but please excuse my–

–Your selfless knight. Venus interjected with a smile.

Oh, yes. He is very loyal, yet unattached… conceded the princess. *Not a clingy kid.*

So what's all this about happiness? And where's Epheremelda? he rubbed the bottle.

The pursuit of happiness is the route to Lorule. said the faerie queen.

A troubled road. said Link, but can you help us regress to the Dark World?

Many have come to my pond and made an offering, to which I grant them passage to the Sacred Realm, where their delusions find their proper place, since that world became warped…

Why don't you warn them—that their pursuit of happiness will betray them? said Zelda.

All the worlds are but a crucible of souls, and I am to facilitate their passage according to the quality of their hearts and minds, one way or another. Everyone wagers something…

You in league with the wizard? squinted the boy.

He has drawn many people into the Dark World, enlisting them to his grand agenda, whether they like it or not. said Zelda, taking a less accusatory stance.

The wizard has nothing to give, which is why he will never find me. Before the pestilence I made my discreet home amongst the ancient henge, she gestured outside, with my nymphs and little faeries. But now we must hide, scattered throughout the realms and slipping out of existence altogether until an offering is made, proving the visitor is capable of—giving up…

The wizard will never give up. nodded Link.

I look kindly upon those who come to me without happiness, *who hate their lives…*

Hate what? Hey wait, Venus– I didn't mean it like that. stuttered the boy.

Was there ever happiness? said Zelda, covering for Link who had stiffened.

There was. And there shall be happiness[125] again here in Hyrule. said the great faerie, When mortals and dryads can appear to each other in a plurality of the Light World. The wizard knows his control is best achieved by eliminating the public freedoms Hylians enjoyed, and one way to facilitate that is to make decadence sacred. There are two kinds of tyranny, said Venus, that which controls the public life, and that which controls the private life. There is no happiness without both; the magistrate understood that all he needed to do was nip one to wilt the other.

A sponsored decadence helped usher in our Gloomaevum. said Zelda, But many of us were already receptive to giving up the public life. the princess synthesized their conversations with both Sir Ariosto and the strange flying creature that her knight paid a red rupee to chat with in the Swamp of Evil, a conversation she had dozedropped[126] from under her cozy mirror shield.

But why do you favor haters? the child Link was unafraid to ask again.

In the Gloomaevum, those who hate their lopsided life of private decadence realize that only a sacrifice, service, or generosity might free them. The lake is lowest elevation of Hyrule, and here in this *topography of selflessness* I gladly help such haters lose that life–

–Are you saying this 'Pond of Happiness' is a… suicidatorium?[127] 'Big Trouble' is right! Link misunderstood and was ready to defend himself with the mostly unbreakable magic bottle.

---

125   The maintenance and enjoyment of being oneself by appearing to others accordingly, in private and in public. The reconciliation of the noumenal and the phenomenal for both the world and those who live in it.

126   To secretly listen in on a nearby conversation by pretending to be sound asleep.

127   A colloquialism that refers to appropriated faerie fountains used by the magistrate to enkindle the

She said *'that life'*, Link. said Zelda, putting her knight at ease. As of the pestilence, the happiness as we knew it became inaccessible – of public appearances and civic engagement. Isolated and surveilled during the sessantine, the distraught lot of us easily mistook happiness as an agency of acquisition; suffused with distractions, delicacies, and doomsilling! she recalled those forgetful and homogenous hours unliving[128] it up in the tower. That's a false happiness, Zelda leaned over the shimmering pond (which was more of a pool; standard in faerie grottos). When gloom hangs over our hearts and minds, and are hopeless to change our circumstances, the pursuit of happiness seems to be better characterized by a totally different agency. she said, The *pause of happiness* – more like it! That of contemplative abstinence; *no longer acquisition.*

Pause! So the gloomladen life is worth hating? the boy was too green to know.

When we have more than we want, but are unable to find what we need – helplessly stuck between superficial decadences and the futility of meeting substantial deficiencies – that is a sundered situation to hate! When we come to despise *that life,* all we can do then is let go…

That's what is given up. reiterated Venus.

Ah! Now I get why people throw things into this pond. said Link, noticing the offerings that were piled up in the pool. Veiled by the unusual water's reflective sheen, all the forfeited treasure from bygone travelers was hard to see unless he leaned directly over the pond's rim. Something was on top, recently deposited – an ornament, or an amulet distorted by the ripples. A curio close to the surface, but beneath his foggy recollection and just out of reach. He wanted to handle it to better grasp the memory and place what I saw, but mentally emulating the act of taking an offering made the boy's knees weak with sacrilege. So the perceptive child let it go and pretended not to have recognized anything, although his interest did not go unnoticed.

---

poes. Established as of the pestilences, a place where despondent denizens can voluntarily end their life and transfer their soul into a poe's lantern – a flame that burns immortal but forever obeys the magistrate.

128 To senesce without meaning – kill time in a worldless milieu of tranquilizing trivialities. Not living.

In the Gloomaevum, happiness is now a death ahead of death – to leave Hyrule behind and undergo the warped topos of moral delusions in the Dark World. You've both overcome this spiritual feat already, but since the wizard ascended to his authoritarian seat, there have been other travelers who wish to become their shadow, and leave behind this deceptive world of lies for the parallel world of true forms, no matter how grotesque it is. The spirit of selflessness that resonates here, becomes the topological *warp of anxiety* on the other side—across realms… Earlier today, a woman offered me **this** in exchange for entering the Ice Palace. said Venus, raising up the necklace that caught Link's attention. You were looking at these? the great faerie tilted to the boy who was absorbed in the iridescent green makeup on her eyelids. I warned her of the cold, but she insisted that once in the Dark World, her fiery mien would fare just fine.

Die before we die—eh. Link relaxed, ascertaining the allegory. May I? he reached out. The pair of black diamonds, obsidian elongated octahedrons, were indistinguishable from the two they had won by first defeating the Helmasaur King, and then the oozing evil eye Vitreous. This isn't your necklace from before, is it Princess? the child Link was pretty sure they weren't but there was no way to tell other than the accompanying unique amulet that housed them.

So not all pilgrims are seeking the Golden Power? said Zelda, unaware what Link held. Those are two maiden crystals! Who gave those to you? she implored Venus who said nothing. Just like the boy, the princess couldn't remember where she had seen this periapt piece before, but not because of the lethic stones that the linkalope passed through before his reincarnation. Rather she couldn't place it, because of her incident involving the magic mirror and moon pearl shortly after initially discovering the amulet. Despite being warned, using the hand mirror with the pearl had induced an episodic amnesia, obscuring any contiguous experiences around that time; a traumatic event further blurred in her memory as she chose not to think about it since. Pair of maidens offered, but how could this be? the princess grabbed Link, inspecting them.

Not everyone in the Dark World is after the fabled Triforce, some are seeking happiness. Venus levitated calmly, responding to Zelda's leading question regarding motives.

I cannot imagine entering the Dark World with happiness in mind! Zelda laughed, taking the crystals from Link without him protesting. This is unbelievable. she said, putting them on.

You've both died from your hatred of a *worldless*[129] life, putting your deluded heart and warped mind into the grave. I am now honored to assist your shared destinies, as a maiden requires your assistance at this very elevation, right here—however in the dreaded Dark World. But without her rescue, we will never rediscover the plurality that made Hyrule so happy of yore.

The 'once-world'... Zelda remembered how Ario described it in the context of his garden.

'Assistance' is putting it lightly. the boy frowned and shuffled his boots.

Queen Mudora mentioned the Ice Palace. Can't say I'm excited either. said the princess, But I'm ready, and have no excuse with the legendary blue mail of the Zora, worn by Sir Ariosto!

The freezing warp of anxiety cannot be prevented in advance nor from afar. There is no absolving preparation for that uneasy Ice Palace – only a resolute readiness from here on out. But I'm glad my envoy safely relayed my message, as this Zoran armor will at least protect you against the evil cold that construed his icy construction and crystalline halls beneath the glacial fortifications that I will help you infiltrate. Regardless of insulating clothing, the tectonic anxiety will still be felt, as everything there is shaped by that topological delusion of disquietude.

Where is she, by the way? Link asked about Epheremelda.

Wait, Great Faerie Venus – it just occurred to me, my little Hyrulean Knight lacks the proper vestments to enter the Ice Palace. He's quite hardy, unbothered by the ice caves, but...

---

129 A world that lacks durability and embodied memory; unable to reclaim the past nor open a new future. An era, regime, or personal situation that is defined by isolation and lack of intersubjectivity. When fakery abounds, replacing a 'once-world' of cultural things with transitory and illusory stuff. A world characterized by social entropy in which people cannot appear to each other as themselves, and are thus very unhappy.

That's correct, you must go alone. The ice caves are tropical in comparison. said Venus, waving her large green wand and causing the rock fissure at her left to rumble apart.

CRBLBLBL... the wall opened up to a restricted pixie sauna. Hold on! Can't I ride on your shoulders again? said the boy with big eyes, Isn't that enough of a cover to stay warm?

I'm afraid you'll freeze without a Zoran tunic; child. Venus bore the bad news impartially.

Melda! cheered young Link as the little faerie swerved in from the side cave. All yours... *FLUMPUH!* he dumped the entire bottle of rupees into the Pond of Happiness without warning.

Happiness increased nine-thousand three-hundred seventy-five rupees. In total your happiness is nine-thousand three-hundred ninety-five. the great faerie did her receipt spiel.

Didn't realize it was that much. said the boy, shocked with donation dismay.

You became happier by one step. For your reference, today you will have...

—Charity Contrition![130] the princess interjected, too late to stop him.

Great Luck. said Venus with a lilt of surprise.

Was that necessary? Zelda mothered the child.

I neeeeed to make room for her! he whined.

Epheremelda will accompany the princess, as I see you have a magic bottle and will be able to keep her at your hip while disguised. Otherwise she would give your presence away.

I understand. said Zelda, turning to Link for the bottle and redeeming her regift.[131]

There goes my dream... said the boy, exhibiting separation anxiety in anticipation of forfeiting the faerie he never had. But whatever the quest demands is my duty, especially for your protection Princess. he handed her the bottle, In my absence, this is the least I can offer.

---

130   A feeling of regret after making a donation, typically one regarded as unnecessary or extravagant.
131   A gift that was formerly given by someone else, often recently before it is regifted.

Don't miss me when I'm gone. said Epheremelda, darting into the bottle.

Who you talking to? said the princess, securing the bottle to her belt.

I have one job then. One life, one sacrifice. And on your behalf—better make it count! Epheremelda's little voice pipped from within the squeaky clean weightless glass.

She's talking to me. said Link, although the pixie was actually speaking to everyone. Maybe this is as good of a time as ever... he reached into his pocket. *You want my small key?* We still don't know what dungeon door this might go to; might come in handy down there...

I can't believe you still have that since finding it in the Palace of Darkness. said Zelda, kindly refusing by folding his fingers again over the iron latchscrew. Your offer of the key is enough to unlock my courage Sir Link. What other use would I have for it?

Awww... Epheremelda mewed from inside the resonant glass.

Please keep it for me—my token of appreciation for the security you've been all along. And who knows, maybe you'll find what it was fashioned for before this is all over.

Yeah, right. said Link, receiving Zelda's hug as a child does to a doting aunt – stiff and without much reciprocation. ~~Wish I could come with you two.~~ he mumbled into her arm.

What is the unrequited heart? But a locked chest, with its key idle inside. she chimed from Zelda's hip.

No more paradoxes from the pixie gallery please. Thank you. she adjusted the bottle.

...

I have a bad feeling that I don't deserve to make it out of the Ice Palace alive, after what I did to you when you were a linkalope. the princess put her hands on the child Link's shoulders, Returning to Hyrule together has been unreal – I still can't shake the poignancy of knowing all of this might be temporary. A brief excursion into our former kingdom. An intermission from exile...

You'll be back soon! And no need for apologies, I– don't remember. he maybe lied.

I cannot escape my disjunctive sacrifice – that's what you said Epheremelda.

Yes, but I already told you that it kind of worked out. the bottled faerie reminded her.

Zelda shook her head, All I'm saying is… even now that we've escaped, there is a cost to any decision, and if not paid upfront, perhaps we must pay later on. Just a feeling I have, that my decadent dues are outstanding. The mailed princess kneeled (despite saying she wouldn't), If by chance my blood literally runs cold in that frozen fortress, just know it's not because of any knighthood negligence on your part, but because of my own comeuppance that I've deferred too long—time coming! If you cannot remember my rash act of decapitating you as the linkalope transmogrified by Farore, then perhaps I am doomed to pay for this atrocity with my own fate. Without memory, can there be forgiveness and absolution? she worried, rising to her feet.

Please, lighten up Princess Zelda. said Epheremelda, popping the cork to speak frankly. Imagine you only sacrificed the linkalope, but not your position in the tower? Then you wouldn't be having this conversation at all. I'm just the messenger, and no moral authority! So who am I to say you did the right thing by sacrificing both your knight and your coronation? However if all you did was sacrifice your lavish lifestyle, then you would have remained in the Dark World with your mute linkalope, unable to return to your Hylian selves. You hurtled the absurd by abruptly sacrificing both, wagering the cost of one against the other. But even canceling out a tradeoff comes with hidden fees, and if debts are unavoidably settled anywhere, it's in the Dark World. But if the price of doing what you did – sidestepping that disjunctive decree – is to now shoulder an unforgivable shame, then may the goddess have mercy. But you did what you did and there's a maiden who depends on you moving on from this. rallied Epheremelda, leaning over the lid.

What she said. Link agreed, pointing to the pixie but looking to Venus who listened.

We've undergone death, a murder by my own hand, in order to leave the Dark World, and now I'm returning on my own volition. Perhaps my recompense is sufficiently this…

Unbroken, ye who lives by sacrificing others, dies sacral too. said the unfettered faerie. Cyclical, until one sacrifices themself as a jubilee to peacefully settle our sinking moral score.

A countervailing life might be claimed. Venus validated her little messenger.

If turning yourself in will alleviate your troubled conscience, *then goddesspeed!*

Liiink! she rapped him for simply recapitulating. Ice Palace is a prison, you're right.

Here's the crux of it, Princess Zelda… You cannot escape your exile – that's it really. Whatever poignancy you feel is exactly that: knowing you must return to the Dark World until your sagacious destiny is fulfilled. So this has been a nice vacation to Hyrule. said Epheremelda to summarize before putting the cork back on the bottle and settling in for their imminent quest.

Zelda, of course I forgive you! said the boy, Any knight is prepared to die for their lady. And not in the metaphoric sense of this Pond of Happiness! Just don't hate yourself for what I was always prepared for—as your sworn protector. he genuflected to the gallant princess.

Off to the Ice Palace we must go, before anyone gets cold feet… said the pixie, pun intended.

Venus waved her emerald wand that she had used to open the cave door to her side, pointing it outside. I've lifted the heavy stone in the center of Hylia's Henge, there you will find one of the secret portals back to the Dark World. The wizard does not know of this anomaly, as it will warp you directly into the courtyard of the impenetrable fortress, parallel across realms.

How do they get out though? asked the boy, but the princess had already zoomed down the long hallway in the cavern, effortlessly sprinting in her pegasus boots and ran into the portal.

With some luck. winked Venus, handing young Link her wand.

For me? Why–

This is just a *small happiness*[132] I can give you. said Venus. Please, take the earth rod, Farore's scepter. I cannot risk leaving my clandestine pond, but if you want to put my wand to good use, do the kingdom a favor and fix the fallen lintel stones around the henge outside.

How do I use it? he wiggled the rod at the wall, causing rocks to crumble and coalesce.

Careful! The scepter can move anything earthen; geomancy in general. And with some practice be used for advanced lithitecture[133] – building whole stone structures from the ground, summoning sand into a single form or chiseling a cliffside for one integrated exterior. The rod has been used for making many of the ancient temples, which could never have been built by conventional modes of construction with their megalithic blocks, and precisely detailed facades.

You don't need to convince me of that! But I thought the giants helped build the temples?

In conjunction, you are correct. But the giants only lifted and labored, whereas whoever wielded the earth rod – a sage of times past – they were the lithitect[134] in charge of their design.

This makes the Master Sword boring by comparison! Can I start by putting the heavy stone back on the portal? he suggested while carefully holding the rod like a lit candle.

Just don't step into it. nodded the great faerie. Come back anytime. she faded away.

Might not save the kingdom, but a job's a job! Link's childish voice echoed as he left, skipping down the allée of lanterns and toward the cave's bright exit.

---

132 The temporary elation one gets from acquiring a new toy. Not to be confused with real happiness.

133 An advanced and magic-intensive architectural design technique using the earth rod to either remove large masses of rock to create an intaglio structure, or force the geologic matter together into a new form. Similar to glacitecture but using only earthen and geologic processes. Additive and subtractive masonry.

134 A principal designer and sage of Farore who wields the earth rod for purposes of lithitectural work.

Into the Inescapable Ice Palace

Doov–Doov–DoWooooWoooovoo… everything warped around her as Princess Zelda stepped onto the single occupancy ground portal in the Henge of Hylia, transporting her back into the Dark World of twisted true forms. Fitting the forewarned description, she found herself in a small courtyard – more of a barracks bailey or small castle ward square that was enclosed by four barbican walls of grey battlement ice. Turning around, there were no gates or doors, but a narrow staircase where the cave mouth had been in the Light World, and was the only egress. Despite wearing the blue mail, Zoran armor that protected her from freezing, the frigid air was bayoneting to breathe. Assuming her noumenal morphology again of a pale-yellow ermine, the hair on Zelda's neck stood up when she realized there was no way out of this fortress – prison. Not the cold, but the claustrophobia of the courtyard sent her into an inescapable anxiety that froze her. Mesmerized by the flat slate of sky, decontextualized and framed by the enclosure, the princess let the warp of that topos take her. *Why did I come back here? What if I'm stuck?* she worried, fulfilling the abstract anxiety the more she fretted. The unexpected motion of a zirro flying obliquely above caused the princess to jump out of her stupor. LET GO! AIEE! she yelled as a mean pumpkin-like monster pickpocketed her with its tendril tongue. Distracted by the sky, the princess had overlooked she was not alone there. How did this thing get in here?

Dropped in here by a zirro. said Epheremelda, pulling down on the cork to keep it tight.

A wha–HAY! You can't have that! Zelda shouted at the mendacious pikit pod[135] that had taken her bottle – with Epheremelda in it! *Flurp.* fully enveloping it and retreated to the corner. However chillwitted and slowminded these arctic monsters were, they knew that no one was supposed to be there. The zirro heard her yell and returned, *Vweeer!* it spat explosive loogies that whistled as they fell around the frantic ermine below. *Bcweoh! Bcweoh!* the mines landed everywhere Zelda zigzagged

---

135 A globular terrestrial invertebrate creature that exists in the Dark World. Capable of opening up its body along the rib creases that resemble pumpkin grooves, its barbed tongue can whip up to six feet.

across the small courtyard in her red pegasus boots. AIEEEEEEE! The zirro[136] and pikit were both unable to predict her erratic motions, consistently lagging behind the trapped intruder. After establishing her pace of sustained evasion and in a flash of stillness Zelda noticed that the ice was so unusually strong that not a single crack had formed from the barrage of bombs. This has to end right now! the ermine careened past the pikit that continued to whip its tongue at her – accidentally catching a whistling zirro spitshell, swallowing it whole and fulminating into a mess of monster guts. Epheremelda! Zelda rushed to the frosty carcass while the menacing zirro bombed after her from above, undeterred by the collateral damage. Are you safe? she picked up the magic bottle, inspecting its integrity while juking to-and-fro.

Yes! Couldn't break this glass if you tried. said the blonde faerie, chilling in her globe and evidently unaffected by the anxious warp of the place. *Now take those stairs!* she yelled at Zelda.

You don't have to stay in there. said Zelda, speedwalking down the hatch that was the only entrance. I was just worried that if the bottle had broken, you might get digestive juices on you or... I don't know – what happens if a faerie touches a monster? Do you dissipate as well?

No, it has to be uh... consensual, said Epheremelda, and monsters aren't compatible... They don't conduct a sprite's spirit as there's nothing in them to resonate with. Might be mean, but they aren't metal enough – spineless souls *that moldable* don't really click with me.

Like rubber? They don't absorb your energy? Well, I'm also insulated in this Zoran gear, if you want to let fly your pixie power and accompany me freely. said Zelda standing at the base of the ice stairs and holding the bottled faerie[137] with both hands.

---

136 A flying spotted Lorule mushroom the size of a cabbage that can spit bite-sized bombs.

137 All pixies are young nymphs, girlie wisps who are not yet great faeries. Little faeries are kept in glass because if touched they discharge positively into a mortal body; dissipating her entirely. In high demand, the trafficking of bottled up faeries became a craze during the sessantine, ruining countless relationships. Ogled by men obsessed with the unfading youth of a captive faerie, women have tried to put themselves in glass too in attempt to compete with the glowing sprites, and for the attention of Hylian men, alas real women cannot fit in bottles and so the black market for illicit pixies grows unchecked by the magistrate.

Not a good idea. I can pop the cork if I need to get out though. said Epheremelda, *Just put me back on your hip please, and from here on out I believe you should use your magic cape. I'll stay hidden too, until we find the maiden.* she hid.

I hear you. Zelda listened intently to the quiet guide's advice dampened by the glass, fixing her concealed faerie carry – immediately noticing the familiar plaque on the back wall. *That's one of those telepathy tiles...* she said, stepping between the two statues in the lobby each with a mocking expression. Zelda put her hand on one of the tongue-protruding effigies.

Listen! said Epheremelda, opening the bottle to make herself clear, *Don't go near that. You don't know who else might be listening...*

Wouldn't want Sahasrahla to know we're here. she remembered her projection from a similar tile in the Misery Mire when she then communed with the old man and also the imp.

See those people frozen into the wall? the faerie looked out for her, *They are not friendly.*

Are they stuck? she stared at the two recessed figures, annealed blue to the glacial wall flanking the plaque. *They look pained... that wretched expression on their faces, and red eyes!*

Nobody is meant to come here. They are like the gibdo that will embrace you to death, but these undead freezors[138] *will hug you into an icicle if they reach you.* warned Epheremelda. *Always keep your distance, and don't underestimate their speed, despite their frozen torpor.*

If only we had some fire... Zelda looked to her left, where a bulwark door had been melted by a previous and better prepared intruder. *By the goddess Din, then we'd be safe!*

But we don't, and our only chance is to remain undetected. said the faerie flying up, pulling the hood over the ermine's head. *The way is open there,* she hovered out in the lobby and pointed to the refrozen open passageway. *I'll watch your magic meter, so we don't appear!* Epheremelda darted back into the bottle, somehow knowing exactly

---

138 Unlike the gibdo, not all freezors were formerly mortal Twili but any Hyrulean now turned into undead cryozombies, mummies made of frozen flesh who are found only in the Ice Palace as their soul is bound to their cold master the evil eye whose gaze can turn anyone into ice. Only fire can stop a flailing freezor.

where it was despite the princess standing invisible – and everything on her underneath the concealing magic cape.

What is this magic meter? Zelda didn't believe it was real, but wasn't about to doubt her guardian faerie after all they had been through and this acrobatic feat of supernatural perplexity. How could you find the bottle when I'm invisible? the princess thought to just ask.

Every pixie navigates by perilocation.[139] she divulged enigmatically from within the bottle.

Yeeesh! the ermine slipped on the smooth tiles in the adjacent room.

Hey, keep it down. the faerie bossed the princess, Just because we're invisible doesn't mean you're inaudible!

Understood. Zelda whispered, skidding sideways trying to turn toward the door to her right that descended to the first basement floor. Ironic, isn't it? she paused to confirm something using her map – augmented thanks to Venus' invitation – that should show the palace floor plan.

What? she realized that Zelda never tested out her expanded chart in the grotto.

This all started with me climbing a seven-tiered tower... prefaced the ermine.

So? Epheremelda waited to hear something she didn't already know.

...And now we're risking life and limb to rescue a maiden from the bottom of a palace that has *seven levels!*

Quiet! From seven to seven again, yes I get it. said the faerie. *The irony illustrated full-bleed indeed.*

'Palace' is such a misnomer, this is a bunker dungeon – truly a prison; icebox more like it! Zelda realized.

Hylia has the greatest humor. Sometimes she laughs with us, and sometimes she laughs at us. she giggled.

Hah... There's no way to know which kind of joke we are until the very end I suppose. said the princess, arriving at a reticle room of two intersecting hallways; a crosshairs of cardinal directions with four doors.

Go the right way. said Epheremelda.

Right it is. Zelda turned orthogonally down the hall.

---

139 The locating of objects by resonant spirit, used by pixies and other supernatural beings to navigate what we perceive as three-dimensional space. Everything has a frequency, and faeries can feel it out.

That's not what I meant, but right is fine. the faerie was cool with it, along for the ride.

Are they sleeping? the ermine stalled.

I think they're toast! said Epheremelda. Those are pengators, vicious flightless bird demons!

What happened to them... Zelda inspected one of the alligator penguin creatures, and found they carried various vials of green potion in different sizes.

Oh perfect! Take little sips of that as we go. advised the pixie.

Why? said Zelda.

For your magic meter! she whispered back.

Famous last words. cheered Zelda, throwing back a small single-nip mini-vial, pocketing a few more of the travel-sized bottles and taking a taller carafe she found as well.

Easy, don't get drunk. The ice is hard enough to stay balanced on! said her faerie escort as they took another right from the reticle room and into the next chamber full of more roasted pengators.[140]

Alright, this is weird. They're all cooked? Charred even... said the invisible ermine, dodging a gyrating 'anti-faerie' bubble[141] that flew in straight lines, bouncing off the walls.

Somebody else is here, and they have fire magic at their disposal! she warned, Stay secret my princess...

Agreed. This must explain the melted door in the lobby too. said Zelda, deciding to turn back and check the other doorway from the reticle room behind them. Leaving and turning right again, they dropped down into the second basement floor where they spotted another telepathy tile, this time guarded by a mighty stalfos soldier who didn't seem to notice them. Just as well – Zelda was not about to get near the plaque that if touched might alert Sahasrahla to their presence. So they tiptoed off and into the following hallway, and proceeded through this upside

---

140 Hylian-sized carnivorous alligator penguin monsters that are socially intelligent and thrive in extremely low temperatures. Unable to speak and endemic to the Dark World, they were not once men now warped rather animals affected by the Golden Power. Unclear as to why, they collect and carry vials of green fluid.

141 Not at all related to faeries nor derived from pixies either. A crudely imbued skull, set to guard a room.

down subterranean tower that got colder with each descending floor. Arriving on the third basement, there was an identical reticle room – this time guarded by a giant blade trap[142] whose spikes grated against the hallway walls it was so wide. The living obstacle sensed their presence and slid toward them, stationed there to prevent any passage. But the big yellow phlegmatic thing predictably returned to the room's centerpoint slowly, allowing them to proceed along with its automatic retreat and sneak along. Dropping to the fourth basement, there was another plaque at the end of a long ice rink hallway – this was the third telepathy tile they made sure to avoid, along with the rotating fire bar traps that seemed only recently ignited by someone, as the floor around them was beginning to melt and buckle from their heat. Down the long hall was a room with several freezor guards chilled for all eternity into the wall and watching with their red eyes. Zelda and Epheremelda kept their distance, although there were more freezers on the fifth level, and the ermine accidentally awoke one which flailed about the room, unable to find the intruder, so they carried on quietly but she tripped when looking back to see if the freezor pursued them. The cloaked duo whirled down to the sixth basement, directly into one of two wide braziers that were thankfully unlit, and better yet: a secret passage to an oubliette cell that held three faeries.

Sisters! Epheremelda flew out of her bottle, I thought you were taken to Castle Town!

EPHEREMELDA! the clique of pixies gailey reunited and clasped hands around her.

Take your time. said the ermine, flopping her hood down for a moment and standing off to the side so as to not bump into one of the imprisoned faeries and ruin their reunion forever.

Many of us were taken... sold into bottles. EPHIE! one of the faeries gasped, Are you...

Bottled? It's not what it looks like. said Epheremelda. I'm here to help the Princess.

---

142 A giant sedentary monster that grows as wide as any hallway it is raised in. Without eyes the living trap slides rapidly toward the vibrations made by a visitor. Chimerical, their Lorule phylum is utterly unknown.

The imprisoned pixie trio leaned out in a splayed formation, judging the ermine.

Her?... She doesn't look like a meanie monster. said one faerie.

Definitely not a Kokiri, so why even bother Ephie? said the second.

But wears the Zoran crest, and... OH! a waif pointed when Zelda displayed her cape, *And that's the royal embroidery of King Hyrule too!* squealed the third fanatical faerie sister.

Yes, we're here to save the maiden, crystalized by the wizard and guarded below... Epheremelda explained, to which her three sisters nodded approvingly – albeit in disbelief.

We broke the grate above, you can all fly free. Go back to Venus! said Zelda.

But the anti-faeries and monsters will catch us...

Someone has taken care of almost all the apprehending fiends, said Epheremelda, Now's the time to escape! she flew up to the hole in the ceiling and waved her sisters goodbye.

Be careful, the last faerie hugged Epheremelda, which warmed Zelda's heart to witness as she sometimes worried that the pixies didn't get enough touches of ephemerality due to their discharging energy with corporeal beings such as her Hylian self.

And they're liberated at last... said the sideflit faerie. I take this as good sign.

What a nice detour! said the princess, swigging a small vial of green potion. Ready?

Aye. the sprite returned to her bottle, and Zelda stepped on a teleportation slab[143] that had activated once they broke the ceiling grate. This will take us back up I think... *VrzZz-VrzZz!* Zelda was correct, as they materialized between the two brazier bowls in the sixth basement, and proceeded into the next room where more freezors stood guard. AH! What's that over there! the ermine risked asking out loud, already pursued by one of the freakish azure ghouls who had detached from its alcove in the wall and groaned a hideous raspy noise, *KchRch! RchRkrkrkr...*

---

143 A single occupancy square tile that teleports anyone one-way to a predetermined destination within an ancient temple or between worlds. Not to be confused with the vertical telepathy tiles used only by sages.

There's someone down there… Epheremelda saw it too – fireballs were being thrown around in the slender hallway off to their left, but they couldn't see who the pyrotechnician was. Go straight! her little voice suggested from within the bottle. Zelda concurred, and ran into the penultimate chamber, with the freezor quick behind them. *KchRchRkrkrkr!* it crackled as the stalfos soldier[144] they had evaded earlier caught up, joining its undead colhort and intent on stopping the ermine from reaching the seventh floor below. *FPLOOF!* a gust of fire blew through the doorway and knocked the stalfos apart from behind, melting the freezor entirely, but the air pressure also bowled the cloaked ermine and her faerie down the porthole and into the final chamber.

Flomp. the ermine landed like a netted catch of fish, wrapped in her cloak.

Nothing evades my stare… thrummed a deep disembodied voice.

…

You can't hide… he glowered, while Zelda and Epheremelda said nothing. The ermine didn't dare budge, but silently looked up from the floor, where a giant eyeball was fixed inside a huge prismatic mound of ice in the shape of a mazarin gemstone, polished and perfectly clear. Without the slight tinge of glare upon a facet here and there, the eye's ice would be invisible. **You've come to my lair then, after slaying my brother Vitreous, Lord of the Misery Mire. We see everything, we are the Three Eyes of Rauru, along with Arrghus. What one spies, we all discern in turn. Our gaze penetrates earth, fire, ice… And yet, why can't I see you? I feel your warmth, you are not of this world…**

…

Mortals are nothing but material, blood is the admixture of elements we monitor and surveil in service of our master. It is his wish that we keep the Sacred Realm always within his vision, for the security of all people in Lorule… Surveillance

---

144 A skeletal knight almost certainly in the service of the king while alive, but now at the wizard's behest. Exhumed knights offered a second service through necromancy and by abdicating their past allegiances.

will keep us safe! *Who are you intruder, if mortal yet immaterial?* **Kholdstare must know...** said the demon.

...

There is one law, that cold entropy claims all in the end. The social atomizing of souls for me to survey in a world increasingly isotropic, homogeneous. You are alone in my palace, as all mortals are in a kingdom characterized by anxiety since the pestilence. Countless people now *fear to fear* – but what? They do not know... They cannot ascribe an object to their fear, but fear itself. I am their relief, but also the source of their anxiety! You see, Kholdstare is the icy eye of the administration, of Agahnim's regime, projecting weakness onto men to keep them helpless and frozen by anxiety – and under our sway.

...

No matter, *whoever* you are, I know *why* you came – you seek the maiden crystal. It is my very heart, her delicate soul powers my dependent being. You shall never have it!

...

Arrghus! Do you see what I cannot? Kholdstare communed with his far away brother, **Have you met this mortal? NO? But travelers had passed by your Plains of Ruin before? Then I am alone, not in my oversight but with them here... Which are you?** *The bunny... The boar... Or the uhh–rat?* he wasn't sure what his evil eye kin had shown him from afar.

STOAT! declared the ermine princess, causing Epheremelda to spark in shock.

There you ARE! Kholstare fixed upon her.

Princess what are you doing! Your magic meter must've run out, WE'RE VISIBLE!

Chill, I've been saving this tall bottle of green potion—pilfered from a fried pengator... Oh. No... Zelda stalled to take a sip and then stiffened, dropping the magnum of magic juice which shattered on the ice demon's lustrous floor that was as hard as refrigerated diamonds.

It was empty! EEK! Are you all out? Epheremelda yelled at Zelda. But it was too late… Succumbing to the topology of anxiety, the princess had frozen, and standing out in the open Kholdstare gazed her into a pillar of ice that extended from the ground to the ceiling.

Stoat you say? An ermine, in that winter coat. Anyone who enters is fair game… Princess Zelda I'll savor your lifeforce, as a supplement to the maiden bound inside me. If I'm lucky, that boy will come searching for you too! roared Kholdstare's mouthless voice. **You have doubled my possession for now. But there is a discrepancy… *Are you single?***

SINGULAR! Avert thyself, lecherous eye of Rauru! She's with me! waved the pixie.

Not you fay wisp… he focused in on Zelda. **Two more maidens around her neck! With these I shall become mightier than my master ever imagined. Your Highness, together we will freeze the far reaches of Hyrule and complete… *The Icing!***

So it's decided: The Boiling is off? she doubted it, leaning against her glass.

All life will bend and bow to the cold… The whole world bare to the master's stare, none shall evade my glacial gaze fortified eternal by the new sacrifices you brought me!

No! Oh my goddess this is not good… the faerie couldn't get out of her bottle which protruded from the pillar of ice holding the princess – the cork was subsumed by the column. Epheremelda spent the last seconds of her semiautonomous existence staring off into space. She couldn't help noticing that this square lair of Kholdstare's down here on the seventh level basement of the Ice Palace was the same size as the top boudoir suite she first met Zelda in, way up on the seventh floor of the Dark Tower. This inverted irony will be the end of me. she resolved.

I shall now have you too. Not even your magic glass will deflect my stare…

FPLOOF! fire billowed down from the entrance in the ceiling.

A demon after my own heart! Kholdstare rotated up to scrutinize the raining cinders. *Or are you something else?* **Another maiden for my collection then...**

Fwoosh! a fusillade of fire pelted the stationary demon's prism case.

You're too late, no fire can melt me now. Now conform to the cold! the evil eye stared undeterred at the wild intruder whose feet never touched the ground, if it had any at all.

You will find comfort in succumbing to the freezing anxiety, as my many freezor creeps have already. The ice forms a social bond like none other! Dissolve yourself and become one with this grand crystalline structure that not a single soul can escape!

ZWOOSH! ZWOOSH! ZWOOSH! searing beams accosted Kholdstare.

Gyaaah! Too bright! the eye's protective prism became cloudy.

Crack! the pillar that held the princess fell onto the floor and shattered. *KRS-SHH!* Disconnected from Kholdstare, her soul and crystals no longer leached through the ice that the frozen overlord used to conduct his energy. *SHWOOOSHHH...* An eruption of steam filled the lair as Kholdstare's protective prism sublimated from the megacandela luminosity of the lasers.

TING! Dirbble dirbble... the shatterproof magic bottle fell down, rolling askew in an arc. GWEEE! Epheremelda pushed, *Bloop!* and popped the cork off. Wake up Princess! she flew to Zelda who lay in a partially melted casket. You can't sleep here! the faerie whipped the slush off her cloak, BVVRRR! and tried to drag her out of the fray but was too frail to do so. *Mehhh... Fwoosh! Fwoosh!* spitfire mortars continued to pelt about pell-mell, deflagrating against the walls and blossoming into a brocade pattern of red flak. The faerie laid low by her princess.

Blind me you cannot, fiery insurgent. I am sight incarnate! Kholdstare roved about the lair, unanchored by the prism that had vaporized. Without an armature to give the evil eye structure he unmolded and became a soft spherical pink cloud with a large piercing black pupil. The ceiling began to drop large chunks of ice as the demon boss partitioned himself into three cumulus clones, matching his assailant's tactics. **In equal proportion to the power inside me, I will sacrifice my lidless existence to crystalize you too!** The three clouds converged and engulfed the thief, dissipating without a trace except for two elongated black diamonds that stood vertically on point, impossibly balanced and reflecting their octahedron form on the ice.

Epheremelda swiped the two crystals, one under each arm. Princess Zelda! Wake up… Whoever that pyromaniac was defeated Kholdstare! But they were turned into a crystal too. Does that mean, they were a maiden? the faerie fumbled to try and fix them to the necklace. AHH! she fell onto the cloak as the crystals spun away, scaling up and levitating translucently.

Zelda, Because of you, I can escape from the clutches of the evil monsters. Thank you!

She didn't do much – *it was all her!* Epheremelda told the hovering purple-haired boy, gesturing to the other lifesize octahedron that contained a woman who she then addressed. *Thank you…* You don't look at all like the fluttering fury that bested the lord of the Ice Palace.

Almost all the descendants are accounted for. she told the faerie, Two on Zelda's neck, two with the King of Thieves, and the two of us. Only three remain. The princess must take us–

–Is she… *dead?* interrupted the crystalized boy who had been the battery of Kholdstare.

Don't speak like that! the faerie shook, I can't take a pulse without touching her.

She's rigid. said the second maiden who wore an orange dress. Are you her guardian?

Yes. said Epheremelda, avoiding eye contact as she knew what the question implied.

The princess is not going to wake up… if you don't touch her. she told the pixie.

Wake her, before the palace collapses without Kholdstare to keep it frozen!

This place is not melting anytime soon. she reassured the purple-haired youth.

Someday when you two are freed from these crystal prisons of Agahnim's alchemy, please tell Princess Zelda that it was my pleasure to fly by her side. Epheremelda slapped her hands on the ermine's nose and disappeared with a flash. The two descendants went opaque while the dark diamonds encapsulating them shrunk down – same size as the necklace pair.

Her Gift to Ganon

AIECHUUU! the ermine sat up, shaking off any column shale and battle slush with the force of her sneeze. Snap– she clutched her necklace, thinking for a moment that the two dark maiden diamonds floating in front of her had become detached from their string tie. *Two more?* How are there two? Epheremelda? Yahhh... Zelda rubbed her nose. Where are you? Not a soul was in sight nor earshot and all the princess could hear was the groaning and creaks of the ice reverberating disconcertingly – did not recall hearing on her way down to Kholdstare's deep lair. *Epheremelda?* she called again, taking the two maiden crystals and fixing them to her necklace. Turning around, the entrance in the ceiling had partially melted down from the sixth level above, providing a precarious slump of footholds to climb back up. Epheremelda? Zelda whispered, poking overhead the contorted porthole, unsure if any freezors or stalfos remained; there were none. Double checking Ariosto's bottle she had secured to her hip, alas there was no faerie inside. Sorting it out as she backtracked, Zelda wasn't sure what to look for as there was no way out. The princess ascended anyway – perhaps she'd find her faerie, or another melted oddity in the otherwise impervious glacitecture.[145] Nothing of interest on the sixth or fifth, Zelda returned to the long ice rink hallway in the fourth basement, where the fire bar traps continued to slowly swing their incendiary arms. The uncloaked ermine knelt to inspect a squadraft[146] of deceased pengators that she had snuck by on

---

145 Using the ice rod to form unified architectural structures directly out of frozen water.
146 A group of pengators.

the way down. Taking more of their vials, she combined them to fill up her unoccupied magic bottle – now full of green potion, should she need it later. The eye is gone. Zelda presumed this was a safe given to declare to herself. That accounts for one of the two maiden crystals… But who defeated the beast? Someone was ahead of us, or was here with us. There was fire in the hallway, before we encountered Kholdstare, that glow on the sixth level… But I must've blanched out when he froze me. she spoke to herself in private, but had the feeling her voice was heard – the plaque on the wall was nearby. The same kind of telepathy tile she had touched in the mire. *All I can imagine is whoever defeated the lord of the Ice Lake was also a maiden-powered demon boss… and they must've destroyed each other?* she speculated, half-correctly. Then it dawned on her, Venus must know! How else could this mysterious rescuer have entered the fortress, if not by the great faerie's pond? That's right, she had mentioned a 'woman' but Venus said little about the traveler who offered a necklace of two maiden crystals to enter the forbidden Ice Palace. Zelda tried her mind at cohering the pieces, But if that pilgrim was an evil possessor of a descendant herself, then why would she forfeit a precious necklace of maiden souls? That woman offered two diamonds to enter this dungeon from Hylia Isle, and then saved us from Kholdstare who left a crystal, but not without nullifying the stranger who also left a crystal of her own. *Is my calculus correct?* Yes, that accounts for my four diamonds here. Venus never mentioned anything about this explorer wielding fire however. OH WAIT! She did! A 'fiery mien'. That must be it. I'll have to consult Venus if I ever get out of here and return to the Light World. Maybe if I offer this quartet of crystals, she will tell me who left the aureate amulet pair in the first place. Zelda took a step closer to the plaque on the wall, sensing the familiar fizz in the air from the energy that the tile emanated. Time noticeably stalled the closer she got – the fire arms behind her rotated at a much slower rate. Zelda was still a few paces away, but her hair stood up from the palpable field generated by the white telepathy tile. Only a few inches away from the tile, she stood apart from the languid energy surrounding her but the solitude prompted an epiphany: *Epheremelda is gone!* she realized after inferring a brief death of her own preceded by an ice coma that must've prompted her faerie to sacrifice herself. *Then there's nothing for me here...* Zelda touched the tile, and found herself standing on a blue platform again, back in the same liminal aspect where she first met the imp Midna and the wise old man Sahasrahla, upon initially finding such a tablet and ingress from within the Misery Mire. But they were gone this time. Neither of them stood on the other two blue pedestals as they did previously, but there was someone else now, waiting for her, or perhaps serendipitously however silently called to the Chamber of Sages as she was.

What are you doing here?

Ganon... the ermine contrived a tone of distrust, but was happy to see the familiar boar standing there on a red pedestal across the floating mesa that was his prison for ten millennia.

Where are you?

Here. he grunted.

No, where did you touch a telepathy tile?

Swamp Palace.

You're back in the Swamp of Evil?

No.

Oh, where is this then?

...

Hello?

Plains of Ruin. he clarified, after a rude pause.

Arrghus! she remembered what Link's uncle warned them about. Find a maiden?

Not yet.

What's the wait? The third evil eye must be there.

I need to raise the water... apparently. But from the Light World.

To enter that dungeon? You're out of luck then, because we're both in Lorule.

GANON! PRINCESS! the child Link appeared on a green pedestal equidistantly away from the boar and ermine – each the vertex of a coexisting equilateral triangle.

Found the moon pearl again I see. said Ganon to the boy.

No, I just came back to life this way—when we washed up into Hyrule.

...

We still don't know why he's a child however. said Zelda, eschewing elaboration. Link... Objects exist simultaneously in both worlds with similar shapes. If the form of a thing changes, it will affect the shape of its twin in the other world.

Yes I know. the boy felt matronized.

What's your point? the boar wondered.

Link's in the Light World, and clearly we were all called to each other here at precisely the same time – entering all at once, is that nothing short of destiny? What are the chances!

Sorry, I was a few seconds late.

Hylia ex machina.[147] snorted the boar in response to the boy's convenient arrival.

Venus had me clean up the henge on her island, using this! Link raised the earth rod, causing some pebbles to leap in the center of the chamber's mesa platform. Oh! he lowered it. One of the sunken rocks had a carved console on it, and I could've sworn that I heard you two...

Talking? Just now? she asked.

Mmm... it's hard to explain. Like a silent voice, but familiar, so I had to respond.

Perhaps the telepathy tiles only amplify a faculty for those of us who are sensitive, or already communicating on a different plane of cognition, like this place... she looked up to the pinkish firmament above and took in the pitch-black astral horizon that wrapped around them.

I recognized it because I saw you touch one before, but only for an instant, on our way down to Vitreous beneath the Swamp of Evil. said Link, I had no idea this is where you went! You told me it was 'just a deadend' Princess. he admonished.

---

147 Hylia from the machine. Hylia machinated, or fabricated by the goddess. A saying coined from theater, suggesting an abrupt solution to a story could only come from on high as if from the goddess or by divine intervention because it is so unbelievable and unlikely. An unexpected impossible injunction from beyond that suddenly solves a character's impasse or resolves a plot knot in the narrative. Cheating, lazy writing.

That's what *you* said. the boar reminded Link who was a bunny knight back then.

I never told you that. the ermine swallowed, surprised Link remembered the mire at all despite everything else he had forgotten since the linkalope incident. She also never told Ganon about Midna, and wasn't sure the best way to broach that encounter. Is this not beyond words?

Maybe. the boy looked over his shoulder to the sea of iridescent clouds below them.

But to your point, it would seem that time stops in *that instant*. However long we remain here is of no elapsing whatsoever to a bystander, as from our perspective approaching the tile, time slows, and as far as I can tell completely halts while we are transported here. That is to say, if we are actually here or just 'projected' as the old man told me. she said, superstitiously refraining from mentioning Sahasrahla by his name as to not summon him to their gathering.

Not everyone can use these tablets – time only slows *around* those who can, ever since I got out. said Ganon, but my sentence was served inversely, during cosmic prison time.[148]

If this is a projection, the boy pinched himself, then I hate to think what else might be!

What's the difference? Don't lose your mind over it. the princess grounded him, I think we're here, therefore we are. *Just get over reality…* we can't afford to second guess ourselves. The ermine turned to the boar who was staring at her new outfit, but he said nothing and Zelda didn't mention that she noticed him staring either. With the help of— oh, quite a few allies along the way I've managed to deliver the maiden from the Ice Palace, who was imprisoned and powering the glacial demon who introduced himself as Kholdstare. But wait – that's not all… The princess took off her necklace to explain, Two crystals came to us from the great faerie, after someone deposited them in her wishing

---

148 Because the King of Thieves was not projected into the Chamber of Sages while imprisoned but fully transported, the asymmetric temporal relativity, or time dilation, did not freeze others but rather elapsed ten-thousand years outside while he waited only a few hours inside – not true for telepathy tiles though.

well. And then two more (she couldn't tell which was which) were found in the aftermath of defeating that evil eye.

Kholdstare... reiterated the boy. What was he like? And where's Melda?

Ephie—is, ummm. ~~I think she's gone.~~ *Forever!* she covered her face.

You touched her! Young Link couldn't believe it.

Zelda bowed her head in remorse. *Must've been her choice.* But if she hadn't, I suspect we wouldn't be having this conversation. Kholdstare was... strangely conversant; speaking of! There was no way I could've managed alone, not without that boon of a blaze...

Fire? In the Ice Palace? the boy couldn't fathom it.

What does a demon boss have to say? the boar interjected, soon to find out for himself.

Tell us what you two talked about!

He was in kinship with Vitreous. But there is another—Arrghus...

Oh? Ganon was curious since the vile eye of the mire never spoke to them.

...who guards a maiden, descendant of the Wise Men. *In the Swamp Palace.*

I can handle it. Did he say anything else? asked Ganon.

Kholdstare said they were the 'Three Eyes of Rauru', triangulated by the wizard to surveil the kingdom, each capable of seeing through earth, fire, ice, respectively. 'What one sees, we all see'. He had a very materialist worldview. she shook her head at the notion.

Rauru... was a sage of ancient times – before the cataclysm, am I right? said Link.

Strangely the first time that name came up was here, in this very place. There's too much to prattle about, and while we have all the time in the world we're not the only ones who can enter this place and I'm also... extremely hungry. said Zelda. Can we get on with it?

I'm not prattling! said Link, I get the message, I'll go raise the water for Ganondorf...

Much appreciated. said the boar, tickled by hearing his former name.

...

What. Ganon asked Zelda whose silence suggested she had something to say.

...I'm waiting for your admission. she tinkled the four diamonds.

Yes you were right. he admitted strategically to get what the ermine held.

About?...

More maidens are required to enter. said Ganon as if he had tried his hand at breaking the seal but in truth was unable to get anywhere near the evil structure as it was surrounded by more monsters than any place in the realm. He suspected she was right all along however, but unlike the argument before, acquiescing now would yield him the additional crystals she held.

The?...

–The Pyramid of Power. Link filled in the blank to spare Ganon this silly game.

Tah hah! I'm just teasing. Until I can find a way out of the Ice Palace, you'll need these. OH! Zelda tossed the necklace to Ganon, but they fell short. NO! she slapped her knees.

~~That was a horrible toss.~~ Link pulled his face down in astonishment.

What are we going to do now? We can't step off these platforms!

CLING-NG-NG-NG! Ganon startled everyone by activating his loud hookshot, *FWINK!* deftly grappling the necklace – effortlessly retracting the chain to claim the four crystals.

You have six now. said Link objectively and without desire, jealousy, nor envy.

After you defeat Arrghus, *can you come get me?*

You can't get out? the boar smirked.

Princess, please! One thing at a time! the child Link cocked his head back.

Well he's already in the Dark World, and you're not. she told Link.

Yeah we'll figure something out, just chill!

Zelda nodded pensively, recalling how that was the last thing she told Epheremelda. Link, take this... she tossed her magic bottle full of green potion – a much better second throw. If your 'magic meter' happens to run low helping Ganondorf, you can imbibe to revitalize.

Ah-hah! Link caught her pass and celebrated the bottle above his head with both hands.

And my apologies for ordering you around... The anxious warp of the Ice Lake must have me bent out of shape. I'm not looking forward to waiting down there.

I understand, apology accepted. said the boy, never afraid to forgive.

Having received an admission and given an apology, Zelda felt balanced and bowed out.

Is she going to be alright? the boy asked the boar. *Epheremelda was a good faerie...*

You know better than me. said Ganon. I'll wait for the water to rise. he disappeared.

How did you know how to do that? Link wasn't sure how to disengage the telepathy tile while standing there on the green platform that wouldn't let him step anywhere. Hello? he closed his eyes and imagined himself back in the Henge of Hylia, removing his hand from the intaglio stone console he had unearthed with the rod. And when he opened his eyes, he was no longer touching the tile, but on the island where he had been an instant before. They're waiting on me! Link put his thumb and finger between the western horizon and the low sun, which looked about where he had left it after finishing his quick work for Venus which had only taken about an hour. Westward was also the direction he needed to go. If I leave now, he talked himself into it, then I should be able to get there by dusk. Then it just occurred to him... He could lift the heavy stone with his earth rod – the stone that Venus kept on top of the hidden portal to the Dark World, one of several anomalies in Hyrule that the wizard ensured nobody knew (other than the first portal on the top of Death Mountain that pilgrims preferred; arguably disclosed by the wizard for his wicked agenda). Link imagined taking the princess by surprise, showing up in the Ice Palace. And I could even bring her something to eat! Where am I? he kicked the dirt... Decentered... Venus told us this elevation is the 'topography of selflessness'. *That's the spirit.* But then we'd both be stuck there, although I'm sure there's something I could push with this rod to break us out of that frozen prison. No… he puffed up his chest. Ganon is waiting for me too. In order to save the princess, I have to be a little selfish now. he said, gulping a third of the green potion and waving his wand, commanding a slab on the beach to come hither. Sometimes even the blessed spirits of the Light World need to be wrestled − not just the cursed Dark World warps! Jumping onto the outcrop, Link lunged like a fencer with the rod, expending his magical mojo and made haste across the lake riding the levitating laccolith driven by Farore's scepter.

From a Dark Tower seventh floor queen.
To the Ice Palace seven levels
Down a princess dungeon of cold sheen.

REVIEWS OF
THE HYRULE PARODY

———

"This is not a reboot, nor a fanfic, but a parody unlike any other. Situated entirely within the popular franchise The Legend of Zelda, this trilogy ambitiously coheres all the otherwise empty symbols of that kitsch world and creates a resonant story with underlying narrative tectonics so solid I haven't read a book this architected since Eleanor Catton's The Luminaries. Having grown up with Super Nintendo, I can attest that The Hyrule Parody is both highly respectful of all the 1992 video game details, but also tactfully subversive of what has been left unexamined."

"Proves that philosophy can be lighthearted without sacrificing substance."

"The Legend of Zelda is an incredibly popular postmodern pastiche of Arthurian legends and Peter Pan, along with a whole bunch of other culturally appropriated junk. This book has taken that all back and in a sense reclaimed these myths for a very timely parody of A Link to the Past."

"I never played the Zelda games, but I loved this sprawling saga that is both annoyingly dumb and frustratingly profound all at once – the reader is situated in the epic journey (this book is thick) and will get what they put into it. I recommend diving in wholeheartedly."

"As far as spiciness is concerned, I'd rate this trilogy as PG at worst: minor violence, some romance but nothing inappropriately juicy for young readers. That said, PG is aimed at ages 8-and-over, but unless your kid has a college degree in comparative literature, you might want to read it to them. Lots of lovely wordplay and nuanced turns of phrase in this tome."

"Some books have only one idea. Some books have an idea on every line. This book has a medium density of didactic dispersal: fantastic ideas discussed within any given chapter."

"Nabokov is groaning in his grave – the Literature of Ideas is back with a vengeance!"

"I hope Nintendo sues the author – this parody is worth defending."

If you could make any wish – but not without warping the entire world in your image, mirroring your delusions, would you make such a wish?

Oh? Who are you, mister bunny? This world is like the real world, but evil has twisted it. The Golden Power is what changed your shape to reflect what is in your heart and mind...

Ever wonder what was inside the big green Book of Mudora? Well here it is. Inspired by the 1992 classic game: *A Link to the Past* with several characters from across greater Hyrule, dive into the "Dark World of true forms" where the unlikely trio of Zelda, Ganon, and Link reluctantly come together in order to get themselves out. Trapped in this realm of shadows and warped into animals, the ermine princess promised to return a magic mirror, the boar thief seeks the wish-granting Triforce a second time, and the bunny knight quests for his lost Master Sword.

For anyone who feels that they too have been banished to the Dark World and bent out of shape, this philosophical parody is for you. *May the way of the Hero lead to the Triforce...*

"Alice in Wonderland meets The Wind in the Willows meets Dante's Inferno."

"Like if Eudora Welty grew up in the nineties playing Super Nintendo with Hannah Arendt."

"This takes a shallow consumerist mythos and turns it into deep philosophical logos."

"When something that is dumb by default is then made meaningfully smart it becomes a parody worth reading. It just so happens this trilogy is also our existential guide out of the dark first half of our 2020s decade and into the hopeful light of the second half, and well beyond!"

"It's a landscape tale: concepts are the very ground that the characters explore. The story is indexed by elevation in which topography (and topology) structures this discursive allegorical journey. Most fantasies follow a top-down map, but this book is based on a side-view map."